I

Dragon

By

Cheryl

Matthynssens

ASIN: B0189OSNCU

Dedication

This book is dedicated to all those who have supported me in 2015 through cancer treatment. From those that just would not let me give up, to those that helped with financial support when I couldn't get this book out on time. As I write this, I am in early remission and I can only credit all the support from fans, friends, family and doctors. There is not one in that list more important than any other.

Acknowledgements

I wished to acknowledge Alex Hunt and Robin Chambers for their editorial and general guidance for improving my writing. As many of you that read Outcast know, I have come a long way since my first novel.

I wished to acknowledge my beta readers for all the input and excitement they shared during the editing process. They are truly a wonderful part of my editing team.

Lastly, I wished to acknowledge Russ Matthynssens who has been my caregiver through chemotherapy. He listened patiently as I read and reread chapters to him. Writing with chemo brain, (a real thing I assure you), was a real challenge, and he was a great sounding board and support during this difficult time.

Prologue

Alador fled down the empty city streets: most of the Council members and fifth tier mages were still at Luthian's ball. He slipped in through Henrick's front door and made straight for the library. He found the door open and shut it behind him as he entered. Henrick too had changed his clothing. He was standing next to the fireplace, dressed in simple black trousers and tunic.

Alador tossed his cloak to the side and moved towards his father. "How is this possible? How could a Goddess show up like that in mortal form?" His voice held an edge of panic, reinforced by Renamaum's reaction within him.

"Very easily for one of her power and knowledge. There are spells that allow another to take a certain form. There are also spells that allow one to inhabit the body of another and take over their will." Henrick looked anxious. "A Goddess of Death would probably even have volunteers for such an honor." He slammed his hand onto the mantle. "These spells are spells we have touched on in the past - forbidden by the Council. I suspect that, being a Goddess, she has them at her fingertips." Henrick did not look at his son as he spoke, choosing instead to stare into the fire.

Alador paced back and forth. "If she unites with Luthian we are doomed."

Henrick looked up and smiled coldly. "Not necessarily. If she takes a mortal form, she also accepts the frailties of that form. To fall and die here would diminish her greatly, if not destroy her on the plane of the gods. If nothing else, it would weaken her to the point that she could no longer interfere, at least for some time."

Alador stopped and stared at him, wide-eyed. "Dragon's ***droppings!*** No!! I am NOT taking on a Goddess. What would the other gods do?" Alador puffed up as if speaking as a god. "There is the mortal that brought about the downfall of our sister Goddess." Alador ran a hand through his hair as he let the mimicry go. "No mortal would survive such godly scrutiny.

Henrick shook his head. "I did not say you should. I merely pointed out that she is less powerful if she moves about in our world in mortal form." Henrick moved to the table and instead of pouring wine, his usual drink, he poured them both a stiff drink of smalgut. He held the cup up in offering and Alador did not miss the subtle shaking of his hand.

"Also, she will not have access to a godly eye on all her followers. It might be better for us that she is here. If she favors Luthian, then we will know what mischief she is about."

Alador shook his head. "It would depend on when she got here. What if she knows my plans? What if she tells Luthian what is to come?"

Henrick pressed the drink into his son's hands. "It does not matter. Either we will both find guards on my stoop in the morning, or we move on as you have directed." Henrick downed a good half of his glass. "The goal will be to stay out of her gaze, at least until Renamaum is fully absorbed. Right now, a Goddess will know that there is a dragon within you."

"And after he is absorbed?" Alador pressed. He sipped the drink and wrinkled his nose at the burn.

"Then she will likely be confused." Henrick held one hand palm up then the other. "Here stands a dragon that is not a dragon. Should you ever face her, it might either intrigue her or confuse her enough to give you an edge, an advantage." Henrick considered, then added: "*Maybe.*"

Alador took down a big gulp of the smalgut. The thought of facing any god was terrifying. They were gods because they were powerful. The knowledge that this one just happened to be the Goddess of Death only added fuel to that fire.

"Why would she come to the ball like that? She said she was not invited." He frowned, for he knew that Luthian had been just as shocked as they had been. However, it was clear the two had met before.

"I suspect she was making a declaration to Luthian. It was obvious she had power, and clear that she wanted it acknowledged before his court. No other woman would have dared to treat him like that." Henrick was choosing his words carefully. "Any other woman would have been publicly humiliated or worse. The fact he did not deny her or rebuff her spoke volumes. He was either afraid, or he truly welcomed her - despite his surprise."

Alador replayed the scene in his head carefully. "I am fairly certain he was afraid. He lost color - I hadn't thought that possible - and his eyes…" The young mage had watched the woman glide into the room, as if she were the High Minister, herself. The way her chin had tilted in arrogance, the dismissal of Lady Aldemar and her manner of speech to Luthian all indicated her perceived power and contempt for those beneath her. It had drawn the eyes of everyone in the room. Her pale, unearthly beauty was a sharp contrast to what on any other woman would have been a scandalously cut black dress. Had he not realized she was the woman from Jon's wall, he would have been as captivated as the rest of the court.

Henrick was silent for several seconds. "Then we must consider that he may be under her control, or spell, or if nothing else, her influence. I would not mention her unless Luthian does: best not give away you know who she is, and best we do not speak of her unless we have to. Her ears are everywhere; even the ravens answer her bidding." Henrick glanced to the window and downed his drink. "I think I will find my bed. It has been a long day."

Alador nodded. He finished his glass as well, hoping the burning liquid would help him find sleep. However, with all that had happened since they had awakened in the valley that morning, he doubted sleep would find him for some time.

Chapter One

Sordith watched from his hidden position behind a bookcase. It was a small area that Henrick kept spell-books in, though he could not help noticing the empty spots where there was no dust. Obviously, Henrick had removed some things before he had shown his elder son this small, unseen alcove. The enclosure was left open slightly, allowing only a view of Henrick. With a clear view of the mage reading in the chair, he would be able to read any changes in posture or expression.

Henrick had placed the chair so that he was in Sordith's view and facing a mirror that would let him watch the veranda door. The Trench Lord had warned him that the assassins would most likely strike from there, as it was unlikely they would want to risk a scene or battle with any servants in the hall. Even so, Henrick had given his servants the night off, just in case. The room was as ready for their trap as the two men could make it.

Sordith had hand-picked the men to assault Henrick, based on his lack of trust in them. He had paid close attention to those who had surrounded the mortally injured Guarin. Sympathizers had swiftly made themselves known in the way that they had responded after Guarin returned from trying to help Kester become the next Trench Lord. The chosen men would die here tonight, solving two problems. By allowing them to attack the prepared mage, he would lower dissension in his own ranks, as well as be seen to have attempted to follow Luthian's order to kill his own brother.

Sordith was uneasy, nonetheless. He had placed his father — whom he had only just found — in a possibly fatal situation. It did not help his uneasiness that Henrick seemed so relaxed: just reading his book, as though he did not have a care in the world. At least the man put on a good show.

The first hint that the assassination attempt was underway was not a shouted warning from Henrick, nor even the appearance of assassins; it was the mage's sudden action. His book seemed to disappear from his lap to catch an arrow. Sordith heard the small, dull thud and blinked to see the arrow quivering in the cover mere inches from Henrick's head. He cursed under his breath: the aim had been perfect. Henrick would have died right at that moment had he not been warned. A sharp whistle pierced the air and both the inner door to the hall and the other to the veranda flew open.

Sordith squeezed the hilts of his blades. He had promised not to reveal himself unless things looked dire for the mage. His eye was pressed tightly to his slim line of sight. Henrick had bolted up from his chair, sending it crashing to the floor. His robe flared as he turned so that his back was to the fire. Sordith could not help himself: he pushed the case a bit wider so that he could see more clearly. He doubted any would notice in the commotion.

Henrick sent a wave of fire across the floor, forcing the three that had burst through the hall door to dive out of its path. The mage then pivoted to the two coming in from the veranda, his hands swinging around as fire reformed within them. Sordith shifted uncomfortably. What did Henrick consider dire, if not this? It was already looking grim enough to call for assistance as far as the younger man was concerned.

Sordith watched with his mouth agape. Mundane arrows leapt from the bows of both assassins and simultaneously arrows of fire burst from Henrick's hands. Even as the fire arrows struck home, Henrick took an arrow in the shoulder. The second barely missed as the mage was pivoted by the impact of the first.

'That's it,' Sordith thought, ' …that's dire enough for anyone!' He burst from his hiding spot and leapt towards those who had been forced out of the path of the wall of flame. The carpets were now burning, but fortunately, they were only throw-rugs that took up small portions of the floor.

The nearest assassin looked startled to see a masked man bearing down upon him. He deflected the first blow from his position on the floor and opened his mouth to scoff, but uttered only a startled gasp as Sordith's second sword impaled him. Now that his elder son had distracted these two, Henrick could focus his attention on the two men who had entered from the veranda. The other two men from the hall had already vaulted up when Sordith turned to face them. Having lost the element of surprise, he moved to close the distance between them…

His swords came up to meet the two remaining men as they rushed him. He was able to slip one beneath the first blow. Not wishing to fight two men at the same time, Sordith kicked this man back while attempting to block the second man's blade coming in from the right. He succeeded, but the second assassin also used two blades, and the Trench Lord was unable to parry a second thrust. The sword struck his right side, managing to pierce his armor before he fell back, cursing and pivoting to face the man who had cut him. This made him turn his back on Henrick, as he worked to keep the two men from the hall in front of him. The mage would have to deal with his assailants on his own while his son connected with both blades of the second opponent, deflecting them away.

Sordith spun and brought his blades in from underneath. One was blocked, but his second blow bit deep into his opponent's thigh. Blood welled from the wound, and as the man growled in anger and pain, he glanced to Sordith's left. The Trench Lord caught the first opponent's movement out of the corner of his eye. Thankful for the telling glance, he was able to pivot in time to meet the man's sweeping blow.

He stepped back in an attempt to get both men once more in front of him. The one whose thigh he had cut retreated, trying to stem the bleeding. The smoldering fire made the air thick with smoke, and Sordith's eyes were watering. The only consolation was that their assailants faced the same difficulties.

The assassin with the single blade rushed him again. With the other attacker otherwise occupied, Sordith was able to use both blades to shove the blow down and to his left, then back-swipe the sword in his right hand across the man's throat. Blood sprayed over him as he kicked the dying man back onto the smoldering carpet.

Sordith then turned towards the heavily-bleeding man with the two swords. The man's eyes were filled with fear, but the Trench Lord could not offer mercy: he had selected him because of the threat he posed, and for the plan to work no would-be assassin could leave this room alive. He moved across the short distance, putting this second opponent on the defense.

The sound of colliding blades rang out as the two men circled, exchanging rapid blows, the flashing steel parried first by one and then the other. An explosion to his left almost made Sordith lose his concentration. He was reminded that there was a fire mage behind him and steeled himself. His opponent, less prepared, dropped his guard slightly. Sordith took his chance and slid his sword deep into the man's chest. It was a mortal wound. Eyes widening briefly with pain, the dying man looked down in disbelief, then sagged, sliding off Sordith's sword to the floor.

The wounded victor did not pause to make sure his opponent was truly dead: he needed to see to Henrick. He danced around the smoldering carpet and saw that his father had dispatched one man, who was curled in a blackened ball on the floor. The mage stood facing the leader: a man Sordith was certain had been about to make his move to become the next Trench Lord.

He did not want to take the risk of Henrick sustaining further injury, and seeing that the mage's opponent had his back to him, Sordith dropped his swords. Three knife blades flashed across the room with the same deadly accuracy that he had shown to the previous holder of his title. The poisoned blades sank deep into the man's back, dropping him to his knees. He looked behind him to see Sordith. The Trench Lord lowered his mask, taking pleasure from the widening of the dying man's eyes as the realization he had been betrayed sank in.

"Should've kept your plans closer to your chest, Ameil." Sordith watched with satisfaction as those eyes clouded and the assassin collapsed, face forward, onto the floor. Swiftly he picked up his swords and swept the room with his eyes to ensure no stragglers were left to join in the fray. The only sounds were the strange hissing of the carpets and Henrick's labored breathing.

"You all right?" Sordith asked as he moved across to the mage.

"I have been … better," Henrick muttered, his voice rough and grating. He glanced at the arrow still lodged in his left shoulder and Sordith's gaze followed the mage's. Henrick also had blood oozing from his left side, the trailing, dark stains across the pale grey robes testifying to the fact that he was wounded there as well.

"Can you put these fires out? Then we can see to that." Sordith wiped his blades on Ameil before sliding them into their scabbards, coughing as the smoke continued to thicken. He pulled his knives from the man's back and repeated the action before replacing them in their respective sheaths.

Henrick took a moment with closed eyes, then stared at the carpets. It seemed to take him a long while to put out the flames. Sordith imagined that the pain of his wounds was likely interfering with spell casting. Once it was done, he helped his wounded father into a chair. "This arrow is going to have to come out," he said.

"In my desk, second drawer down, there are a couple of healing potions." Henrick's speech was slow and labored. "It looks to me as if we both might be in need of them. Take one yourself first. I'd prefer you to have a steady hand before you go pulling an arrow out of my raw flesh." Henrick closed his eyes, his face pale.

Sordith moved swiftly to the appointed drawer and pulled out two potions, both clearly labeled for healing. He splashed some into his cut then drank the rest of the first small bottle. The immediate relief from pain was welcome. He grabbed the other and set it on the side table.

"Let me pull this and put some in the wound. If you take it now, it will likely heal around the arrow." Sordith's own breathing was beginning to slow from the exertion of battle.

Henrick just grimaced and nodded. Sordith realized that the mage had probably known that better than he. He shook his head somewhat in awe of the man's composure in the face of such pain, and felt around the back of Henrick's shoulder. He discovered that the arrow had not gone all the way through. Judging by the depth of the shaft, it appeared the shoulder blade had stopped it. Pushing it through was therefore not an option.

"I am going to have to pull this out the hard way," he said, surveying the angle of the arrow.

"Just do it," Henrick spit out. He ripped off his sleeve and wadded it up. Shoving it into his mouth, he set his teeth against it.

Sordith waited until Henrick nodded before pulling the arrow free, hearing the flesh tear as the barbed tip sliced its way back out. Despite his readiness, Henrick screamed, the sound muffled against the cloth in his mouth. Blood boiled from the wound while Sordith snatched up the potion. He poured some into the open wound. Henrick spit out the wad of cloth so that Sordith could pour most of the rest into the mage's mouth. He poured the last bit over the wound in Henrick's side.

He set the bottle down and returned to watch the wounds heal with miraculous speed. They closed up with a creeping growth of new skin over rapidly healing flesh. The sight had always amazed Sordith. Seconds later, the skin appeared to cease its snaking movements, though it still looked fragile.

"You are either going to need to be careful or take another potion. I think these would break open without too much effort," Sordith cautioned.

Henrick cleared his throat then answered with hoarse tones. "It is better that way when I go to see Luthian. A little blood and damage will further the plan we follow."

He paused for a moment. "I will take a potion with me. If it breaks open, I can take it after I leave," Henrick's breathing was still labored.

"What if he takes your challenge?" Sordith asked.

"He won't."

"How can you be sure?" Sordith was not as certain as the mage that the High Minister would back down from a challenge.

"He doesn't like witnesses. Alador will be there. He will not strike down the boy's father in front of him, even if Alador has expressed his dislike of me. Luthian is not stupid." Henrick gave a wry smile. "At least he thinks he is not. However, he will not give the mageling any leverage." Henrick gave a slight shake of his head.

"I wondered why you insisted that Alador was with Luthian. I thought it was to keep him out of harm's way and innocent of these matters." Sordith grinned. He wondered, at times, which of them had the more devious mind; though, in fairness, Henrick had more time on him.

"You had best go." Henrick sat up straight, the movements stilted. "You smell of smoke and battle, as we planned. You have the wounds to show you were here." Henrick paused surveying the room. "I will see to the proper disposal of this garbage with many witnesses." He waved at the bodies as he spoke. "I shall cry foul and declare to all that will listen that someone tried to assassinate me." Henrick returned his gaze to Sordith. "You have that black mage lined up to take the fall?"

Sordith grinned. "Of course. I found the most Dethara-loving mage there was to be had." He ran a hand through his hair. "He has been bragging about moving up soon, too, so it was easy to plant the evidence. He will take the fall, and we will rid ourselves of a death mage."

Henrick nodded his approval. "The more of them we can get out of Silverport, the better."

"You still haven't told me why you have this sudden hatred for death mages," Sordith pointed out.

"Who said it was sudden?" Henrick cracked a smile.

"Well... I... With the appearance at the ball..." Sordith stammered.

"Let's just say I have more motivation since the Priestess of the Black Sphere made her appearance. It never bodes well when Gods meddle in mortal affairs, let alone the affairs of a whole city." Henrick took a deep breath, the potion continuing to ease his pain.

Sordith nodded. He had seen the look of surprise on both of his kin's faces that night. He had seen the fear in Luthian's eyes. There was more to this matter of the priestess than the two men were telling him. 'No matter,' he thought. He had other ways of gaining information.

"Go, before the smoke draws unwanted eyes," Henrick commanded, slowly rising from the chair and indicating the smoke filtering out on to his veranda. "I suggest you take the servants' exit."

Sordith nodded. He made his way out and down the hall, taking the back passage. He had no concern about leaving Henrick to utter whatever explanation he had concocted for his neighbors. He had his own dramatic performance to enact: that of a Trench Lord beaten off by a fifth tier mage.

Chapter Two

"Alador!" The sharp call made him jump. "Pay attention."

His eyes snapped back to his uncle. His mind had been on Henrick and Sordith. What if the ruse had been discovered? What if Sordith had chosen too many men, or ones with too much skill? His gaze refocused on his uncle, and he realized that Luthian was staring at him.

"I am sorry, Uncle; I fear you are right: my mind was not on your lesson." Alador rubbed his eyes. "I do apologize." He sat forward to scrutinize the spell book that his Uncle had been teaching from for the last couple of hours.

Luthian's eyes narrowed as they raked over the younger mage. He shook his head. "What could matter more than learning how to shield from spells? You will need this defense if you are to take a home on the tiers." Luthian snapped the book shut. "Share the weight on your mind, for clearly, until you do, we will get no work done today."

Alador was frantic to find something other than what had really occupied his thoughts and grasped at the first thing that came to his mind. "The lady at the ball. The one that came in when you were dancing with Lady Aldemar. Who is she?" Henrick had advised against questions, but a part of Alador wanted to know her connection to Luthian.

Luthian's gaze left Alador to stare at the spell book before him. The long pause only emphasized the nervous plucking at his sleeve. "Lady Morana," he began quietly, "is the high priestess at the Temple of Death." He reached for the wine he often kept close at hand and drained the cup.

"You have temples to the gods?" This caught Alador's attention; he had not expected such reverence in this city.

"Not all the gods have temples; but the one to Dethara was finished about eight turns ago, and Lady Morana was chosen as its high priestess. It is a magnificent place, set back into the mountains." Luthian toyed absently with his empty wine goblet.

"Who paid for such a place?" Alador figured that such a building had to come at a high cost.

His uncle stiffened, then cleared his throat before answering. "I did," Luthian admitted. "The priests of Dethara approached me with an offer. Despite my being of the fire sphere, they offered blessings on Lerdenia and protection from plagues and rot in exchange for a place to pay homage to the Goddess."

"Yet you did not seem pleased to see her," Alador pointed out. "If this priestess has given such a blessing on our people, then one would think you would be glad to see her." He had a million questions, but for now, he was going to have to step carefully.

"You would think so." Luthian looked up at Alador then back down at his spell book. His words took on a cold, hard edge. "Sometimes, when you lead people, nephew, you have to make difficult choices with little reliable to go on. At the time, such a blessing on the people seemed a boon which I could not reject." He blew out a long stream of air

Alador waited, but after a long period of silence he asked cautiously: "And now?"

"Now, I have discovered that some blessings come with hidden costs. Never forget that." Luthian looked at

Alador, the mask of teacher slipping back on to his features. "People will offer much – and lard their offer with generous praise - to gain what they say they want; but often what they really seek is not apparent: their primary purpose lurks beneath their avowed aim." Luthian got up and moved away to refill his goblet, then walked back to the crackling fire near where they were sitting. He stared into the flickering, golden yellow flames.

"Since the day the temple opened, Lady Morana has continued to grow in power and followers. Black dragons now nest in caves that her priests opened up for them, far above the temple. She is not one I can lightly cast aside."

Luthian's voice softened to a murmur, more as if he were speaking to himself. "First, she has power and influence. Second, what might Dethara cast down upon our people if I were to act against her followers?"

Both men considered the situation in silence for several seconds. "Tell me, nephew," Luthian asked suddenly, "with that quick mind of yours, what would you do?" He stared at the young mage.

Alador blinked a few times in surprise and stared back. This was a side of the man that he had never seen. He had always assumed the High Minister to be fearless, but there was resignation – almost an air of defeat - in the way he spoke about Dethara. In addition, his proud uncle had just asked him for advice. The man confused him at times. Luthian seemed bent on conquest and power, yet here he was showing a concern for his people.

Alador gave the situation some thought. He rose and moved to his uncle's side, scooping up a few sweets as he passed the table on which the wine decanter was also placed. "I would declare that the temple must be self-sustaining, now that it has had time to gain its footing," he offered. "At least then, their claws are not in your coffers." He stared into the flames, thinking hard. "I would try to correct the discrepancy in power by offering land and supplies to other spheres, assuming they have similar levels of power and representation." He popped the sweets into his mouth.

"Fine thoughts," Luthian acknowledged. He pinned his nephew with an intense gaze. "Stay away from the Lady Morana." He put a hand on Alador's arm, clutching it tightly. "If she gets her claws into you, there will be no release: you will have to do whatever she demands."

Alador winced as the word "claws" was pressed into his flesh. "Are you afraid of her, then?" He met his uncle's gaze evenly.

"Listen to me, boy." Luthian searched his nephew's gaze. "There are few things in the world that make me feel fear." Luthian's tone became more of a cold hiss. "Lady Morana is one of them."

The uneasy silence lay between them for a long moment. Alador shifted: the closeness that had manifested between them was discomforting. He pulled away from Luthian, not liking that for a moment he had felt a sense of kinship. "Well," he quipped, "let us hope she stays buried in her mountain temple."

Luthian chuckled slightly. "Somehow, I think she will find her way to wherever she wishes to be." He led the way back to the table.

Alador winked at his uncle when the older man glanced at him. "What woman doesn't?"

Luthian grinned. "Yes, what woman does not," he agreed. He moved back to the table. "Enough of the fair Lady Morana and her ample charms. Let us return to this spell." Luthian's tone had become firm and commanding again.

Alador groaned. "Uncle, you have been drilling me on this spell for hours." He pinched the bridge of his nose. "I swear I will shield myself in my sleep, and end up shoving some fair maiden out of my bed."

"Really…?" Luthian's long-drawn-out question seemed to follow his finger as it traced the symbol on the front of the book. He did not even look up as his hand shot up and fire flew from his fingertips straight at Alador. The stream shot straight for the mageling's chest.

Alador almost did not have time to form a shield. His hands flew up as if to ward off the flames. The line of fire hit a wall of shimmering water and steam hissed into the air as the flames parted and snaked to either side of him.

Luthian cut the line of fire at the first hiss of the shield. "Very good." He grinned coldly and clasped his hands behind him. "But the shield cannot always be made of water, nephew. While that works with me for fire, a wind spell would just push such water into your face. You MUST make the shield out of power and not your element." He circled Alador, eyeing the pattern of water on the floor.

"How am I to reach for power when my element is always around me? I can feel water's call, even from a distance." Alador shivered as if chilled, and patterned his movements to Luthian's, his curiosity piqued.

"So does power, boy. We are not limited to our spheres when we know this. You can use power as a replacement for your element. Some spheres use that source of power more than any element. If you had been listening, you would know this." The older mage shook his head and a heavy sigh escaped. "Apparently, I lost you at least an hour ago."

Alador had the grace to look guilty. Luthian, of late, had been trying hard to teach him, and Alador did not sense much deception. The lessons he was giving were far different from those inside the caverns of the guard, most of which were direct spells concerned with combat. Perhaps his ruse was working; but it was equally possible that Luthian was playing him as well.

"I need to understand something. It plagues me and only you can answer it," Alador said.

Luthian sat down at his chair at the table. "It seems many things plague you, today. It is better you learn to keep your mind on the task in front of you. Distractions can get a man killed." Luthian glanced up at Alador and grinned. "What is your question?"

"Why two forces? You have the Lerdenian army. Many of them have lower magical skills in addition to their military training." Alador paused, struggling to phrase his questions in a way that would give him the answers he needed without revealing his intentions. "I know from tales of the war that your Council keeps them well trained, and that there are standing garrisons around your territory. Why create the BlackGuard separately? Why not make it one force?" Alador sat down beside his uncle.

"It is a matter of attitude to be honest," Luthian mused, taking a long sip of wine. "Many in the Lerdenian army turned to a military life when they could not advance in magic. So to them, it is a home of last resort." Luthian set the glass down and sat back, arms crossed as he considered the question further. "If you train these soldiers in magic they don't know, you would soon find them jostling for position and power. There is nothing more intoxicating to a Lerdenian than an increase in power. The feeling you get when harvesting a bloodstone of any weight is often said to surpass any got from having a fine woman in your bed."

Luthian paused as if lost for a moment; his eyes glazed and he let out a soft sigh of pleasure. "To feel that power racing through you… You would do anything to feel it again." Luthian's words were low, and his eyes closed as if better to experience some inner intensity. "Unfortunately, it is never the same again. There is nothing quite like that first stone.

Collecting himself with a shudder, his eyes snapped back to Alador. "Half-breeds, such as yourself, do not seem to feel this, so there is no constant desire to find more and more. In addition, while there are exceptions, most are grateful to find a place where they are accepted. Few Lerdenians are grateful they are in the military."

"So for the most part you can train them safely without worrying about them being distracted by a craving for power." He gave a small chuckle before his tone took on a cold edge. "But it seems to me the bigger reason for employing 'half-breeds' is the sense of gratitude that you expect them to have; yet Uncle, there are stories of horrible brutality suffered by them at your hands before I joined the guard." Alador looked at him with dark scrutiny, attempting to hide the disgust he felt.

Luthian looked over at him, his face devoid of any emotion. "I was determined that they would respect my authority. At the time, I did not care if it was genuine or out of fear."

Alador was surprised that his uncle had not tried to downplay that more. "And now?" he asked.

Luthian sighed, almost as if the conversation were now boring. He began to flip through the pages as he spoke. "Now the guard is large enough on its own, so that the stories of what *could* happen are enough." Luthian opened the spell book back to the pages on shielding spells.

Alador shook his head, distaste written openly upon his face. He did not try to hide it, as so far he had found truth far more effective with Luthian than deception. Luthian looked over and stopped flipping through the book.

"Your displeasure is evident, nephew," Luthian drawled.

"I was not trying to hide it." Alador looked over and met his uncle's discerning gaze.

Luthian sat back and steepled his fingers. "You learned to fight in the guard. You took on Aorun in his own home over a bed-servant. Yet, you stand in judgment of my harsher hand." He eyed Alador with a bit of amusement. "I find that curious."

"I use violence because I have to in order to defend myself, to protect those I have come to care about, and in your cause…" - Alador paused - "...because I am ordered." He looked from his uncle's fingers to his face. "You use it as a means of manipulation and control. It is *that* which I find distasteful." Alador moved away from his uncle and the recent bond between them slipped away.

"When you are in control of many people, the threat of what you 'could' do is greater than what you 'would' do. But to get that mind-set into people requires the sacrifice of a few for the good of the whole. Much..." Luthian appeared to search for words as he spread his hands to indicate a flat surface. " ... Much like you have to pull seedlings from the row in planting to thin out the weaker stalks and leave room for the healthy to grow. The sacrifice of the few produces a far stronger and healthier yield."

Alador wanted to dispute with his uncle, but he did not dare push back too hard. If he did, the growing openness between them would cease, and all of Alador's plans relied on Luthian extending him some basic trust.

"I will consider that," he hesitantly conceded.

"I advise not too closely." Renamaum snarled, surprising Alador. The dragon had been quiet for some time.

At that moment, the door to the library flew open with such force that Luthian rose, sending his chair skittering backwards. Alador sprang up, a ball of lightning glimmering in his hands, matched by the ball of fire in Luthian's. Henrick stepped into the doorway. He looked far more furious than Alador had ever seen him, and even though he knew this was part of the plan, he took a step backwards.

"You…" Henrick stomped into the room with two armed BlackGuards at his back, both with swords drawn. "...double-crossing, cowardly, conniving bastard!" He was snarling with his hand pressed to his side. Alador could see blood seeping through his fingers. He let the spell fade from his hand and took another step to the left to avoid being so close to Luthian. Henrick had been certain that Luthian would not accept a challenge, but he and Sordith were not so sure.

Luthian let the fire fade from his own hand. "Why brother, it would appear you have been hurt." Luthian laced his voice with concern. "I will send for a healer; but I have no idea why you are calling me names." His face oozed incredulity, and Alador had to give him credit: it was a pretty convincing performance.

Henrick strode forward to the table they had been using to study. "You know exactly why I am calling you names," he hissed. His eyes held a deadly glare. "You sent your dog and his pack of curs to kill me!"

Luthian's eyes narrowed. "Careful Henrick: you are stepping beyond the bounds of what I will permit." Luthian's hands moved a bit out from his sides, and Alador knew he was preparing to defend himself. Alador took another casual step to the left. "I assure you that I sent no one to kill you," Luthian continued.

"Liar!" Henrick snarled, venom dripping as he continued. "Everyone knows that the Trench Lord dances to the tune of the High Minister. You, yourself, told us that Aorun was your hired hand of death."

The guards behind him stood ready, but Luthian motioned them backwards. They obediently took a couple of steps backwards, and Alador's eyes went wide at the realization that Luthian had put them out of the line of his fire. Henrick had been wrong. Luthian would answer with violence.

Alador's mind raced over what to do. He could not let Luthian kill Henrick - he needed him in so many ways. He would gladly have let Henrick kill Luthian, but there were witnesses: Henrick would be executed for assassinating the High Minister. Even if he threw his lot in with his father at that point, with his current lack of knowledge and Henrick's obviously grievous wound, they could not overwhelm a mage of Luthian's skill as well as his two armed guards.

"I assure you. I did not send Sordith to kill you," Luthian's cold tones held an edge of warning.

"Liar." Henrick hissed. "You want me dead…," Henrick spat on the floor, "…then do it yourself." Fire flared in Henrick's hands, the guards' swords rose as they moved, and Alador made his decision.

Before Henrick or Luthian could release a spell, Alador hit Henrick square in the chest with a bolt of lightning. He had used as little power he could, but still

Henrick flew backwards, hitting the ground hard. Alador pulled his blade as he moved forward, and had his sword at Henrick's throat before the man could recover. His father lay gasping upon the floor. Alador knew that Luthian was watching him closely because neither BlackGuard had moved, either to assist or to hinder him.

"Stay down, Father. I don't want to kill you, but I will before I let you harm the High Minister of this city and your own brother." The blade slid slightly along Henrick's neck, drawing a line of blood; Henrick's chin rose in response. "The people need his leadership and as sure as the Gods are real, you are not capable of leading anything." Alador's apparent disgust was met by a flicker of concern in Henrick's gaze. "Even a drunken bed-servant would think twice before taking orders from you."

"I should have known you would turn on me," Henrick snarled up at him. "Damned half-breed - more concerned about currying favor and gaining power than with family."

Alador's cold smile was warmer than the pain in his eyes: the past giving weight to his mocking tone. "Odd accusation, as I have learned everything about currying favor from you." Their gazes met for one long moment as Henrick lay helplessly beneath the edge of his son's sword.

Luthian's amused drawl was right on cue. "It would seem, my dear Henrick, that

your cost to me is now greater than the benefits you bring." Luthian moved up beside Alador and slowly pushed the boy's blade away from Henrick's throat. "I thank you for a true heir: someone who understands that sometimes hard choices must be made, even amongst family. For the sake of your son, I will not order your death. You should prepare to leave Smallport and your manorial home. It seems a fifth tier position has suddenly opened up."

He motioned to the two waiting men. "Guards. Take my brother to his manor house and confine him there until I decide what my fair and just response should be to these false accusations, and to his drawing of power in my presence. They both grabbed an arm and pulled the mage up.

Henrick attempted to rip his arms free. "I'm going! You don't need to haul me off." He glared at the two men and Luthian nodded permission. He headed for the door, then turned to look at the two mages.

"You are welcome to one another," Henrick hissed. "I would rather be confined to the Daezun routes than ever step in your presence again!"

Only when the guardsman had followed Henrick out and the door had clicked shut did Alador sheathe his sword. He glanced up to see that Luthian had turned to look at him. His uncle's tone was casual. "You, my dear nephew, never fail to surprise me." The High Minister moved to stand before him. "I did not expect you to strike your father." He put his hands on Alador's shoulders, and his searching gaze held puzzlement.

Alador met his gaze evenly. "He breaks his word all the time. You have been true to yours." Alador glanced at the door and back to his uncle. "Besides, you have made me a promise that I mean you to keep."

Luthian's cold smile sent goosebumps racing up Alador's spine. "You will have all you asked for ..." - he slowly pulled Alador forward and embraced him - "...and more."

Chapter Three

Sordith laid back against the pillows of Auries' bed. He had made quite the show of his injuries as he returned to the trench, and a couple of men had made sure he arrived at the brothel safely. He watched as Auries padded about her room cleaning up after them. She had checked his wounds and tended to the pain with an additional potion to accelerate healing before they had switched to more personal pleasures. He smiled as he lay with one hand behind his head watching her. "Don't think you can lie in my bed all day. I have a business to attend to." Auries snapped. She tossed his pants at him.

"You don't see clients personally anymore, Auries," he reminded her with a smirk. He moved to pull the pants closer.

"…that you know of." She let that fall between them. Her sniff was haughty, her nose turned up at him.

Sordith was in no hurry to move after the injuries sustained during the fight at Henrick's manor. The wound to the right side of his stomach had crossed the path of the more serious wound that he had suffered before the ball. Despite being the shallower of the wounds it hurt the most, even after the potions. "Baiting me now, are we?" he teased. "I am not a man prone to jealousy, or by now I would have killed a great many of your customers." He crossed his hands behind his head, eyeing her with appreciation.

Auries pulled a soft, blue silken gown over her head, finally hiding her exquisite body. Despite her age, her skin seemed to have retained much of its youthful silkiness. "Men of the trench pay for a quick roll. Mages of the upper tiers want refinement. I still cater for those with a discerning taste or …" - she glanced at him provocatively - " ... a unique request." She moved to the mirror and sat down. Her soft hum and moving, gilded brush set a rhythmic pace in the stillness of the room. "At least they pay for my time

Sordith opened his mouth to protest and closed it again. He was going to bond with Keelee, and to protest about Auries' lovers in the pursuit and practice of her craft would have been highly hypocritical. She did not protest at the path of death that had followed him in his own line of work.

Sordith rose stiffly from the bed and pulled on his breeches. He was considering how to appease her; clearly something bothering her. Once covered, he moved behind her and gently took the brush out of her hand. When she did not protest, he began working out the snarls that he had helped to tangle

"Do you want me to pay for your time, Auries?" he asked with quiet curiosity as he watched her face in the mirror.

Auries had closed her eyes at the tender ministrations of the Trench Lord. She breathed out a long sigh of frustration. "No," she admitted.

He leaned down and whispered in her ear. "Then why did you speak of it?" He gave her earlobe a tender nuzzle before he returned to working the brush. He was being far more gentle with the long blonde tresses than she had been. From this angle, he could see the hints of age hidden in her silken strands.

"You are the most frustrating man." She opened her eyes to glare at him in the mirror.

Sordith flashed her a mischievous smile. "A fact you have mentioned for years," he pointed out.

"So it's true? - you have chosen a bond mate?" she asked. Sordith was sure he saw pain in her eyes as they met in the mirror. He stopped brushing and turned her to look at him, pushing hair out of her face and tucking it behind her ear.

"Auries, we have been friends for many wonderful years. We have both known what we were, and what our paths would be from the time you first spread your legs and I first picked up a blade." He ran a thumb across her bottom lip as he knelt down to look into her eyes. "You are the one person I trust implicitly," he admitted, his husky tone caressing his words.

"Then why another?" she asked, her voice trembling and her eyes glistened with unshed tears.

"You are a whore; I am a thief. Some would say that is a good pairing." Sordith stated bluntly. "You are beautiful, and trust me when I say I have found none to match your skills in bed; but I look upon you as my friend..." He stood up slowly, frowning down at her. "...Not as a mother for my children."

Slowly, she stood up too. "I could be that woman if you gave me a chance." She searched his face, as if hoping to see some change in his position.

Sordith placed his hands on her face and met her gaze. "As much as I care for you, Auries, you and I both know that you would grow bored with only my company; and I assure you that if we bonded, I would kill anyone who touched you." His words held an edge of violence promised.

Auries' gaze wavered then dropped. "That doesn't mean I don't wish it could have been different." She sighed and moved into his arms, nuzzling her face into his bare chest when he wrapped his arms around her.

Sordith gently kissed the top of her head. "I know, my sweet rose. I have always known." He pushed her back to look her directly in the eyes. "You will just have to be content with being my nurse and my best friend."

"You bond with another, and you will pay just like the rest," she threatened with a pronounced pout.

Sordith grinned. "I suspect that you will demand much payment and it won't all be in slips." He was teasing. "As long as I am Trench Lord, Auries, you and yours are under my protection, bonded or not." His words held a solemn vow as he held her gaze. "Now, I had best be back to the hall. I am expecting a visitor and I have already tarried longer than I probably should have."

Auries' arms snaked around his neck. "Not without a proper goodbye kiss," she stated in an excessively husky tone. Her soft chastisement was followed by a slow sensual kiss.

When at last the kiss ended, Sordith whispered against her lips. "I thought you had a business to run. That was more an offer of a longer stay."

"I just don't want you to forget the pleasures to be had here." She grinned at him then stepped back. Her hands slipped to her hips as she eyed the rest of his clothing now all on the bed.

"Go about your business, Trench Lord, before I forget I have one to run as well." Auries returned to her hair, fastening it up carefully.

Sordith chuckled and moved to the bed. He pulled on his clothes as carefully as he could, his skin still tender in places. He grabbed his sword belt and swept it around him. Those blades would need cleaning when he was back at the hall - he'd come straight here after returning to the trench. He headed for the door and turned to wink. "I will be back."

"You'd better be, or I will come marching up those hall steps wearing nothing but what the Gods gave me."

He swung the door open. "I would pay to see my men's faces if you chose to do that, but I fear there'd be an 'uprising', and I'd have to kill half of them." Sordith grinned back at her. "I promise, Auries, this is not the last you will see of me. After all, you know just how to stitch me up."

He turned and had taken only a couple of steps when a bottle of perfume hit the wall behind where he had stood just moments before. "Missed," he called back. Her scream of frustration and his laughter echoed down the hall as he headed out.

****

Sordith arrived at the Trench Hall to find Henrick already there. He was pale from blood-loss, Sordith assumed. Owen had put the mage in Sordith's private parlor. As Henrick moved to rise, Sordith waved him down. "Don't get up. I have had a chance to rest and by the look of you, you have not." Sordith moved to a chair next to Henrick and pulled it closer. "How is the wound?"

"Closed, but it still pains me," Henrick admitted. He rubbed the blood stain gently. "If any ask, I have not been here. I am under house-arrest."

Sordith smirked. "Are you now?" He looked around. "Seems to me you are far from the fifth tier. Just how did you manage that?" He eyed his father with genuine concern, despite the playfulness of his tone.

"Well, they are outside my door, not in my bedroom. You can hardly contain a high level mage by locking him in his room." Henrick snorted in amusement. "We have much to discuss and I have to give Alador credit: if I did not know he was aware of our ruse, I would have thought him truly turned against me. The force of the spell he used nearly knocked me senseless." Henrick gave a nervous chuckle.

Concerned, Sordith glanced through at the far door, as if the High Minister might walk through it at any moment. "Do you think Luthian suspects?" He turned back to look squarely at the mage.

"I am sure he suspects, but he will not act unless he is certain. He needs Alador too much: to further his plans for world domination." Henrick laid his head back wearily and closed his eyes.

"Is his plan such a bad thing? To unite the isle under a single rule?" Sordith asked carefully. He did not want to anger the mage, but at the same time, unification seemed a positive thing for both cultures.

"It is not the idea of unification that I am opposed to, Sordith. It is the motivation behind it." He opened his eyes. "Renamaum wanted much the same thing, but his purpose was purer. Luthian … Well, Luthian wants it as a status symbol: to manifest his power and glory. He does not work for the good of the Daezun, or of the Lerdenians, and definitely not for the good of the dragons."

"Who is Renamaum?" Sordith was puzzled at the casual use of the name.

"Oh, sorry my dear boy. It's the name of the dragon whose stone Alador harvested." Henrick explained.

Sordith nodded. He had discussed the beast only briefly with his brother, and was still concerned about the path that Henrick and this possessed stone had put Alador upon. "If we defeat him, it will be by Alador unifying these very elements. Would you crown the reckless boy a king?" Sordith had put a lot of thought behind that question.

Henrick shrugged. "Who else would you suggest? It cannot be won without mage powers, or the Lerdenians would never kneel." He sighed wearily, as if the weight of the world were upon him.

"What about you?" Sordith asked curiously. "You work so hard behind the scenes, lining everything up, when you could walk in and best Luthian now. You could seize the title of High Minister without a war; then you and Alador could unite the isle."

Henrick opened his lips to say something, then snapped them shut. He slowly closed his eyes again. Sordith could read on his face that his father had considered this: the warring emotions were not hidden. "I cannot assume the mantle of High Minister, now or ever." The mage opened his eyes; and when they met Sordith's, they were determined. "It is not meant to be. My place… my place will be elsewhere, when all is revealed."

"Your place? Do you know something of the future you are not telling us?" Sordith was not one to let a secret slip past him. He did not like the idea that their father might be keeping vital information from them.

"Yes." Henrick's calm confirmation lay between them for a moment. "And when I can reveal it, I will. Do not press me on the matter," he added firmly, "…but it will deny me any place of power within the Lerdenian kingdoms."

"So you mean to see Alador as High Minister or as a King?" Sordith did not know if he wanted to be under his impetuous and highly temperamental half-brother.

Henrick put out one hand with his palm up. "He will rule as the first King of the Grand Isle. He will bring about a new age for the island as a whole." It was nothing less than a prophecy. "Dark times are coming for the isle, and if it is not united before the tides of change flow, then magic as we know it - and dragons as we know them - will cease to exist."

As if to emphasize his point, his hand snapped shut. "I have not told Alador what is to come. He flees at each level of responsibility. Alador still sees himself as that small, outcast village boy. He does not understand the power that flows through his veins as a Guldalian, and the power that is his to wield from the stone that he harvested. Until he can make decisions as a king, I will not bring him to a full realization of his destiny."

"What if he never can realize it, Henrick?" Sordith asked gently. "What if this task you speak of is beyond him?"

"Then the race of dragons will slowly die away, hunted to extinction by fear, superstition, and for their treasures in blood, bone, and cave." Henrick stated softly. "Magic will be lost to the world of men as we know it. A dark time will come upon the world, and when it ends, all... all I have ever known will be lost in the pages of time."

Sordith sat for a long moment, taking this in. He got up and moved to his liquor cabinet, rummaged through it, found what he sought, poured them both a stiff drink and moved back to Henrick. He handing one over solemnly before toasting the mage, and making his pledge. "We don't just rebel against a tyrant." He looked Henrick solemnly in the eyes. "We also train a king."

Chapter Four

The lightning cracked overhead, illuminating the practice yards. The day was dark with clouds creating shadowy figures dancing in the eerie light and falling rain. The crack of swords clashing and the spattering of large drops of rain combined with murmurs and curses between the rolling rumbles of the storm. Water ran down the walls, creating streams that swiftly ran into the scattered drains. It was the job of numerous recruits to keep them clear.

"I said keep at it! Alador, get that guard up! Do you think your enemy will wait to attack till a sunny day? No, he will find you shivering at your post and run you through." Toman's voice called over those in the 'advanced' yard. "Your first warning will be the point out your gut," he shouted with disgust.

Alador circled his opponent: a very muscular man who favored two swords. Alador still found more freedom and flexibility in his use of one. He had mastered the pulling of lightning with one hand as his sword-hand deflected a blow. He did not know the man's real name; people just called him 'Bull'.

Rain dripped into Alador's eyes making vision difficult as it mixed with the sweat of practice. He took a centering breath to relax and watched his opponent closely. He used the next flash of lightning to his advantage and danced in with his sword swinging. Bull met his swing evenly - for a large man he moved quickly - then swiftly delivered a riposte to Alador's left shoulder. The pain of the dulled blow sent him scampering back.

Bull did not seem inclined to give Alador a moment to regain his footing and came in swinging, first left then right. Alador met each blow apparently being worn down as Bull pushed him back around the circle. Alador then 'slipped' in the slick mud of the circle yard and went down. Bull brought both swords up to drive them into the padding on Alador's chest. Alador let him begin the movement before lunging forward with his longer sword to catch Bull square in the center of his chest-protector.

"Enough! Bull, that would have been the end of you at least, and maybe both of you." Toman shouted. "Next two."

Deftly Bull swung his practice blade under his left arm and offered a hand down to Alador. "Good move." His voice was ragged from effort.

"Thanks." Alador let him pull him out of the mud, and they both moved over to the edge to watch the next two. Alador was going to need a bath after class, even before he got dinner: he had mud everywhere. He could use a cleaning spell, but it was not the same. Though maybe, he mused, cleaning spell, dinner, and then a long soak. He smiled at that thought. Yes, that seemed a much better plan.

Distracted from his thoughts, he looked to his right as someone moved up beside him. The cloaked figure leaned against the fence, just as he was doing. He was surprised when he felt something pressed against his hand. He looked down to see a smaller hand slipping something into his. The figure beside him was a woman with dancing, copper eyes. The hair framing her face beneath the hood was the color of a dark cherry. She smiled, nodded and withdrew her hand.

He found he was holding a piece of paper with the smeared mark of Dethara on it. Alador recalled Jon's words about sending others to him and nodded back, his smile grim. He looked about; this was really not a place to talk.

Deciding he could kill two birds with one stone, he leaned over and whispered. "I was thinking of taking a bath after practice. I know a private pool, should you care to join me."

She nodded and looked back out at the fight in the yard. It had ended almost as quickly as it had started. Alador followed her gaze and noted that one of the combatants was bleeding from the nose. "That's enough for today," Toman barked. "It sickens me to think what our enemies could do to us if we had to fight in a bit of bad weather." He strode off snarling. Alador chuckled lightly. If this was a bit of weather, then he would hate to see what Toman thought was a real storm.

The dripping young mage sought shelter like many of the others, though he made a point of going slowly enough for the trailing guardswoman to keep him in her sights. He led the way to the private pool that Flame had shown him, pausing at the small unfinished tunnel to be sure no one was watching.

He waited inside for her, then led the way to the narrow crevice that led to the actual pool. He called light to a couple of stones at the pool's edge, creating a dim glow.

"My, I didn't even know this was here," she breathed, looking around. Like Alador, she was covered in mud. He noted that even here, the cold rain water was trickling in. It ran in small rivulets into the pool.

"Yes, well I would like to keep it from public knowledge if you don't mind. What's your name?" - Alador was pointedly assessing her - "…and how did you come by the knowledge that led you to give me that mark?" Now that he was not being blinded by rain and water dripping from his hair, he was able to make out more of the woman, even in the dim cave light. She was only slightly shorter than he was, and a little more solid.

"I am Nemara." She smiled at him and dropped her sodden cloak onto a rock. She wore a tunic bearing the symbol of the green sphere. Next, she began taking off her weapon belt. "…And I came on it after Jon made me promise not to let you trot off and get yourself killed." She turned to look at him. "How did you get Jon to befriend you?"

"We were both friendless when we met, and I had no idea what a death mage was at the time." Alador admitted. He watched her toss her belt aside and began unbuckling her armor. "What are you doing?"

She paused at the buckle she was on and looked up, first at him and then the pool. "Well, I don't intend to bathe with my armor on." She grinned mischievously as she threw her next question at him. "Do you?"

Alador flushed a little. "I…well... I just offered the bathing space as an excuse to talk privately."

"And talk we shall, but I am not passing up the chance of a semi-private soak." She laughed lightly at the look on his face and put a hand on his shoulder, gazing up at him with big eyes and a little pout. "Be a good water mage and heat it."

Alador was uncertain exactly what to do at this point. He stared at her for a moment, then turned to the pool. It did not take him long to have it steaming. Sensing movement at his side, Alador looked over to see that Nemara was completely naked. He swiftly turned his back to her to afford her some privacy. "S-sorry."

He heard the water movement and the soft sigh of contentment. "Perfect," she purred. "Are you going to join me or stand there dripping mud in tightening leather while we talk?" She splashed him from the pool and the droplets scattered at his feet.

"Perhaps, it would be more proper for me just to stand here." He swallowed hard trying to think of exactly how to handle this situation.

She swam to the edge closest to him, teasing him. "Are all water mages so … proper?"

He looked over quickly and back to the stone wall. What little he had seen had been rather pleasant. "Are all nature mages so… carefree?" he retorted.

"Most," she admitted. "After all, we were created by the Gods and our nakedness is nothing to be ashamed about. Come, get in. I promise not to ravish you... much." She laughed lightly and swam back across the small pool. "After all, we do have much to discuss."

Alador stood for a long moment; he needed the bath and the woman seemed casual about nakedness. He sighed in frustration and moved to a rock to disrobe. He cast a 'clean and dry' cantrip on his armor so that it did not shrink, and slipped swiftly into the warm water without looking at Nemara.

"See, doesn't that feel better?" she purred. With effortless fluency she moved to sit on the ledge beside him. The water was deep enough to ripple against her cleavage, but the pool was crystal clear and did not hide anything. Thankfully, his own response was hidden by the dim light and shadows dancing around the room Alador leaned back against the sloping rocks and cleared his throat. "A warm bath is always welcome after practice," he admitted, keeping his eyes on the far side of the pool.

They were both silent for a long time. On Alador's part, the water was soothing, and he was not sure how to begin the task of converting BlackGuard members to his cause. His mind drifted in the steaming heat and silence.

Nemara broke his sense of peace with a playful splash. "Sooooo, talking usually involves speech in some manner," she teased. She trailed her fingers slowly through the water as he opened his eyes to look at her.

"Yes, well, I'm uncertain where to begin. One misstep in trusting the wrong person, in planning, or even in being overheard could mean the death of many people." He looked over at her, not hiding his concern, or the lack of trust that he had in almost everyone.

"Let me see if I can mitigate at least one of those." She moved off the ledge and swam to where she faced the small opening. She whispered a spell that he could not quite make out. In her upturned palm, a seed appeared. She tossed it into the crevice carefully. It was not till he felt her pull of power that his eyes moved from her shapely behind to the opening in the cave. He watched in wonder as the seed quickly grew, much of it filling in the crevice. Strange yellow, bell-shaped flowers with bright red centers opened as the plant reached its maturity.

"What is that?" he asked. "Surely a plant will not keep eavesdroppers from listening?"

She sank back into the water and turned to smile at him. "It is a yellow bell. They make a strange, light chime when someone gets within about five feet of them." She swam back to the resting ledge.

"That is very useful." He made no attempt to hide his admiration.

She nodded in agreement. "Now, I can't do anything about your lack of trust. I wouldn't trust anyone either if I was planning to make a fool of the High Minister. So let's narrow that down a little bit. You trust me and only me. I will be your go-between with those I pull in to help you." She looked up at him with a warm smile that reached her glimmering copper eyes.

"Why would you do that?" Alador asked.

Nemara pulled her hand from the water and put up one finger. "First, Jon asked it of me and he saved my life when I first got here." She looked across the pool and took a breath. "Secondly, my best friend came with me to join the Black Guard. She failed her archery test." Nemara's voice took a faraway tone, filled with pain. "The High Minister abused her before everyone, then burned her alive as an example of his power, and of what would happen to those who failed him." She stared intently at Alador, her voice bitter. "I will back any plan that causes him misery or brings about his death," she hissed.

Alador did not miss the hatred or pain that simmered in her gaze. He was quiet for a long time, thinking about her words. "How do you know this isn't a trap set by my uncle and your words will reach his ear? Trust goes two ways." He looked away as if considering the truth of her words. More to the point, he had realized his eyes had been locked on her unhidden charms.

"The one thing I learned about Jon since we have both been here is that he has an uncanny knack of being able to read people," Nemara stated. She waited for Alador to glance at her before continuing.

"He vouches for you." Her matter-of-fact tone softened and she began to braid her long locks into a single braid "Besides, I have asked around. Other than being related to the High Minister, I didn't find anyone who spoke poorly of you."

"You have me at a disadvantage in that regard," he admitted.

"It is in our best interest for others to think nothing more of our meetings than that we are lovers." She put a hand on his arm, now that her braid was finished. "It will cover our communications and account for our closeness. So let others volunteer tales about your new lover. It might seem strange if you go asking questions." The mischievous smile returned to her face as she winked at him.

"Wait… lovers?" He swallowed hard as he sank a bit deeper in the water.

"That is why you asked me to this secret pool, is it not?" Her voice held a husky tone with a bit of teasing as well. "I mean a walk would have sufficed."

"I had been thinking of bathing when you approached me." He ran a wet hand over his face. "It was the first place I thought of after you gave me the mark."

"If you say so…" She let that drop between them.

Alador scrambled to change the topic. "You said you would be the go-between. Won't it be obvious who you cover for if we are seen in each other's company?" He was pondering the wisdom of her plan, even as he sought to hide his embarrassment at her forwardness.

"Except no one would believe a Guldalian would side against the ruling class," Nemara lazily pointed out. "I will tell others that I am close to you for information and to avoid suspicion." Her voice held a musical quality despite the matter-of-fact delivery.

He had to admit that her idea had merit. Alador sat there considering it and Nemara let him, lazily lying back to enjoy the steaming heat of the pool. He absently stirred the water, making sure it did not lose its warmth with the incoming rainwater. Alador finally decided it was a risk worth taking. He had to trust someone or do this alone. "Okay," he answered quietly.

She clapped her hands together in approval, the sound echoed around them. "Wonderful. I assure you that I will find only those who have a similar axe to grind against the ruling class or Lerdenia in general." She turned over lazily, her body refracted in the water. Holding the edge to remain still, she looked over at him. "What is the first target?"

"The main bloodmine." He looked over at her to see her reaction, but instead, his eyes came to rest on her bottom curving out of the water.

"That is impossible. It is manned by loyalists and well-fortified." She frowned at him.

"Yes, but I have advantages that will overcome those obstacles." He looked back across the pool. "I have Jon on the inside," he admitted. He hoped it was an advantage, and that Jon would not decide that it was in his own best interest to turn to his sphere and faith.

"Well, there is that." Nemara swam in front of him, resting her hands on his knees to look into his eyes and to support herself. "What is your other advantage?" she huskily whispered.

"I have allied with dragons." He met her wide eyes with a bit of a grin. "No, I'm not crazy," he added quickly. "It took some doing, but the dragons will side with me."

Nemara moved up his body so that her knees were on either side of his legs resting on the same ledge. "You just became a lot more interesting," she whispered into his ear as she pressed herself against him.

Swallowing back the rush of excitement her closeness brought, he managed to whisper, "Nemara, what are you doing?"

She ran a wet finger over his face and his lips as she spoke. "Well, if our cover is to be lovers and anyone were to manage to spy, shouldn't we look like lovers?" Her lips hovered just short of his. He could feel her hot breath against his lips, and her body moving closer as she settled against him. She stopped moving and looked down, then back up to his eyes. "And, you seem to be… interested."

"I… Nemara, my experience with women hasn't been… Well, it hasn't ended all that well," he managed to whisper back. His eyes locked with hers. Her lips were so tantalizing close to his.

"Good thing I am not looking for a mate then, isn't it?" Her hands coiled in his hair, and Alador could feel her hard nipples against his chest. His hands moved slowly down her silken sides to rest on her hips. He stared into her eyes for a long tense moment, her breath still teasing his lips before he closed the distance and kissed her.

Chapter Five

It was two days before Alador was able to get a half day to go and see Henrick. To his knowledge, his father was still confined to his manor house. Alador thought this the most ridiculous of confinements, as higher tier mages all had some form of travel spell. It did mean, though, that he could not wander around the city, so maybe there was some merit to the restriction.

The two men standing outside Henrick's door were not of the Black Guard, but were city guards. Alador nodded politely and offered one of them his tier pass allowing him access to his father. After checking its validity, they stepped aside to give him entry. He was relieved, as he had been a bit concerned that maybe Luthian had decided no visitors were to be allowed. The young mage made his way through the halls, surprised at the noise going on. Usually Henrick's manor was quiet, but today there was a great deal of cursing and banging.

He walked in to find the usual calm warmth of Henrick's library in complete disarray. The scent of burned fabric hung on the air and he looked for the source; the floor still showed signs of recent fire. His father, dressed in casual trousers and tunic, was going through the shelves, tossing selected books into a pile for the servants to pack.

Alador leaned against the wall, watching his father curiously. He had never seen the man actually work before today. But then the wall of dust assailed his nostrils and he sneezed. "Ah, there you are." Henrick hopped down from the ladder, dusting his hands.

Alador stepped carefully over some loosely strewn papers "What are you doing?" he asked, looking around pointedly at the complete disarray.

"Packing. The self-serving bastard can have the house and its contents, but he is not getting my library, which is probably what he wants most." Henrick finished with a 'humph' and crossed his arms in defiance. Compared to his usual playful demeanor, his sour look seemed strange.

"Where will you go?" Alador had not thought about asking him this when they were planning the staged entrance for Luthian.

"I plan to sequester my books in a safe place, and then I think I will take up residence not far from Smallbrook. Seems I have some use there." Henrick grinned at him.

Alador let out a tense sigh. "I'm glad. Maman will be glad to see you and I like the idea of you keeping tabs on my family."

"What is this; are you ill? You did not mention the girl first?" Henrick looked genuinely surprised. A slow smile replaced the sour frown he had held just moments before when he had spoken of Luthian and his library. "I would have never thought to see the day when she was not your first concern?"

"I care about what happens to Mesi, but it is doubtful she will ever have me now, after what I did. I just want her to be happy," Alador conceded. "Maybe some things, no matter how perfect they seem, are just not meant to be." Alador moved to the window to stare at absolutely nothing.

Henrick moved to him and put a hand on his shoulder gently. "Still growing up I see. I am sorry you didn't have more time, son. I know this year has been a hard one for you." Henrick squeezed Alador's shoulder before moving back to the center of his version of packing.

Alador shifted uncomfortably at the familial attention. "Yes, well, it's not as if I ever had a choice in the matter." Alador gave his father a grim smile, then moved to pile of discarded books. "What of these?" He picked one up and leafed through the fragile pages before closing the book - it was a familiar story.

"Common enough tomes." Henrick waved his hands at the pile at Alador's feet. "I will have the servants organize and shelve them, just in case you test high enough to take over the manor. Such places are normally filled quickly, but given hints from *my* brother, I think it will remain open for a time. I am fairly certain that if you can test out at the fifth tier, then Luthian will grant you this residence." He moved to his son's side. "Are you ready for that?" he asked with genuine concern.

Alador tossed the book in his hands back on to the pile. "I don't know. I've never even seen a testing." clasped his hands behind him. "What does it entail?"

Henrick nodded towards the chairs where, as usual, food and drink were laid out. Alador could hardly remember a time when his father did not have food laid out. He smiled at the normalcy of little things in the midst of upheaval.

"All of you, see to other tasks for now." Henrick called over to the servants. Henrick poured them each a drink as the servants scurried out of the room. He offered one to Alador before he sat down. Once the door shut, Henrick swiveled towards his son with a much more serious demeanor.

"The first few tests are easy. First-tier testing is merely your range of common cantrips. Anyone with any magical nature at all usually passes this test. Then for the second tier, it moves on to easy spells such as your ability to change clothes. You must demonstrate three spells – minimum - to gain second-tier status." Henrick paused to take a drink and give Alador a chance to absorb this information.

Alador nodded. That would be simple enough, he thought. He had mostly mastered the simple tasks necessary for a battle mage. He could focus on those spells since as a member of the Black Guard he would not be expected to know much more. It would help not to reveal his hand too soon. "Go on." He had slipped into a chair next to Henrick and was paying rapt attention.

Henrick smiled. "The third tier is the ability to manipulate your sphere spells. In your case, creating ice or fog. A pool of water is present so that you can demonstrate your ability to move and master the nature of your sphere."

Alador smiled. That would make it easier, having water close at hand. He had used fog to help bring down the guards at the stable, and his ability to create and reverse water movement had become quite easy. His first ability to heat water came almost naturally now. Furthermore, he had finally learned to part water so that man or beast could walk through as long as he held the spell.

"These tests seem too easy." Alador looked at Henrick with a bit of concern. There had to be a catch.

"The first three tiers are easy. That is why so many people choose to live in the city within those tiers. They are common spells for common people." Henrick took a sip while staring past Alador. "It is the last two tiers you must worry about. Many mages just choose to stop at the third tier and not press on."

Alador swallowed at the serious tone that his father had taken. "What is the fourth tier test?"

Henrick refocused on Alador. His tone became that of a teacher, firm and focused. "It is defense. You will have ten spells from differing mages cast upon you. If you can remain on your feet and deflect or absorb these spells, you have earned your place on the fourth tier. A good mage must be able to defend himself at all costs or he is useless."

"I would have thought that the last tier test." Alador was surprised to find out that this was only to the fourth tier. "If battle is the fourth-tier test, then what in the name of the Gods is the fifth-tier one?"

"Battle is not the fourth tier, defense is. You are merely expected to keep the spells from hitting you or damaging you so much that you cannot cast." Henrick smiled coldly. "It is a cruel system. I did not say it was a fair one." Henrick leaned forward, holding Alador's gaze. "They do keep a healing mage on hand for those who fail."

"Then what is the last test?" Alador could not imagine anything more than this.

"It actually comes with a choice. You can demonstrate a spell of magnitude - one that most cannot master. For example, you could use your weather spell. It is a hard task and, as you know, very few master it." Henrick tone was tinged with pride as he toasted his son.

Alador knew he had far from mastered the spell. He knew how to cast it, but every time he did, he felt the edges of something wild that threatened to seize control. "You spoke of a choice. What is the other possibility?"

He wasn't sure he wanted to show the Council what he could do.

"You are given a choice to fight one of the ruling mages of any sphere. It is a battle to submission. If you give in before your opponent, well, then you are forever limited to the fourth tier." Henrick reached over and popped a piece of fruit in his mouth.

Alador dwelt on this revelation for a long moment. "So what if neither mage submits?" He asked, trying to discern the best route for his own testing. He was beginning to regret not paying more attention to the men and women at the meetings Luthian had forced him to attend.

Henrick stared into his glass not speaking for a long moment. When he did finally answer, he gave Alador the answer that he had deep-down expected. "Then one of them dies." Henrick did not look up from the amber liquid in his hand.

Alador downed his glass at this revelation. He got up and refilled his glass, taking the decanter over to fill Henrick's. Neither man spoke. Alador was absorbing this news, and Henrick was giving him time to adjust.

"So the choice is to risk death or to expose the level of my power." Alador weighed these options. "I am not sure which is the wiser course," he mused. "Which did you choose?" He refilled his father's cup then returned the decanter.

Henrick sat back in his chair, legs crossed as he stared into his cup. "I find it is never good to let the enemy know everything you can do. The question is debatable: do you show one spell of great power, or defeat an enemy with a barrage of lesser skills? I chose to barrage an opponent with a range of lower spells."

Alador had retaken his seat as he listened. "Did he yield?" Alador asked curiously, leaning forward in his chair.

"No," Henrick stated. "Pride on the fifth tier is often a dangerous thing. To be bested by a testing mage is to cast doubt on one's own skill. Many would rather die than admit a younger mage had better skill." Henrick's gaze took on a faraway gaze. "…Or that they had been mistaken in the pursuit of their own path."

His last words did not quite make sense to Alador. He did not really want to take either path that his father had laid out for the final test. "Would it be better for me to just test out at the fourth tier?" Alador asked curiously. "I could ensure that I fail in my defense." He sat back, running one hand across his face as he considered the weight of that decision.

"You could." Henrick admitted. "It would let you hide the true level of your skill, but it wouldn't place you where you want to be in Luthian's circle." Henrick smiled into his glass and took a slow drink. He looked up at Alador clearly amused. "However," he pointed the glass at him. "You declared at the ball that you were a master of your sphere."

The fifth-tier mage stood and circled the chairs contemplatively until he was to Alador's far side. "Many are going to come to this testing to see if a Daezun can really be a master of his sphere. The future of all half-Daezun who can cast rests on your test."

Alador sat back as the realization hit him. He HAD declared himself Luthian's heir and master of his sphere. For the sake of all future Daezun and for his place as heir, he had to pass the fifth test. "I am not sure which route to take." He looked up at his father. "What do you suggest?"

Henrick smirked. "Has the world gone mad? Did Alador, son of Henrick Guldalian, just ask for someone's opinion before rashly charging into a fray?"

Alador rolled his eyes and took a drink. "Don't be a korpen's ass and rub it in." He leaned across the table and grabbed a sweet cake. His mind was in turmoil, and he set to munching on it, not deigning to answer his father further.

Henrick moved back around and sat down. "I suggest you don't show the weather spell. It will cause concern in Council, and in the mind of any highly tested Lerdenian for that matter, if it is learned that you have mastered such a powerful spell. I would either find another spell of similar weight or fight for your position." Henrick looked over at Alador.

Alador threw up his hands in defeat. "What spell could I possibly cast that would have as much weight as that?" Alador did not even feel he had that spell mastered. The thought of learning something that required anything even close to that level of effort seemed daunting.

"Ah, well there is that. Perhaps I can help by giving you a small gift." Henrick sat his glass down and stood. "Come, I should show you this anyway: in case you gain the manor house."

Henrick led Alador to a section of the wall still filled with books. "See here?" He pointed to an old skull that sat at the end of one shelf. Alador looked on curiously as Henrick stuck his fingers in both eyes and pushed down. There was a click, then Henrick pulled the shelf out. The tall bookcase swung slightly, revealing a small room. There was a table in there, with three large tomes on it. Light stones were strategically placed on the walls

"These are my spell books. I will be taking two with me. This one..." - he picked up a large black book that was at least three inches thick, filled with old parchment and with pieces sticking out here and there - "...is for you."

Alador took the book reverently. "Where did it come from?"

"Well," Henrick grinned mischievously, "you must promise never to reveal it to Luthian."

"Of course," Alador said, caressing the old leather with genuine care.

"It is Rydanth Guldalian's spell book." Henrick eyed it with a hint of disdain.

"You mean ... the betrayer?" Alador dropped the book onto the table in shock, disgust dripping from his tone.

"Yes," Henrick admitted, "…but he was one of the greatest mages in history. He ruled far beyond the normal life-span, and was never once bested in a tier test. Though you may not like the man who held it, Alador, the value of its contents are certain."

"It seems vile to even touch anything of his." Alador whispered coldly.

"If a man killed your brother with a sword, would you not grab that same sword to kill him if you could?" Henrick asked quietly.

"Of course." Alador looked up at his father.

"It is not the sword or the book that is evil my son, but rather the man who wields them." Henrick searched Alador's face for understanding.

Alador nodded slowly. He reached out and touched the book again. "How did you get this without Luthian's knowledge?" Alador looked up at Henrick in amazement. "He would kill you for this book alone."

Henrick reached out and touched the cover. "In the first great war, the dragons were so angry at their betrayal that they attempted to take back all the knowledge they had shared over time." He moved to the next book, bound with a green cover, and his fingers clenched against the top of it. "Many of the magi's spell-books were discovered - torn from alcoves and laboratories. Literally no stone was left unturned once a mage's holding had been found."

The sheer anger emanating from his father caused Alador to take a step to the side. Henrick looked up at Alador, his voice low and cold. "There was a great battle between Rydanth and the leader of the Red Flight. The dragon won," - Henrick took a breath - "…but he was unable to kill Rydanth."

He moved to the book with the red cover. "The aged dragon took Rydanth's spellbook. It has been passed down to each flight leader to hold until the time was right for such knowledge to be revealed." He opened it fondly.

Alador listened in amazement. "That does not explain how you came upon it." He waited with keen anticipation.

Henrick smiled at him. "I talked Keensight out of it after you convinced him you were dragonsworn. He told me to give it to you when you stopped acting like a petulant child." Henrick laughed. "I think now might be that time; though…" - he looked at Alador mischievously - "...one never knows with you."

"All these years it has been held by dragons?" Alador looked at the book in amazement, letting his father's quip slide off him. "Did you open it?" He surveyed his father's face for some hint as to what lay beneath the aged cover.

Henrick smiled. "I am a mage; what do you think?" He eyed the book.

"I think you have read it cover to cover." Alador chuckled as he caressed the strange cover's texture. "Does it really contain things you didn't know?" He looked back up at Henrick.

Slowly Henrick closed his own spell book and his voice took on a serious warning tone. "It contains things you will wish you did not know. There is another class of magic user. They call themselves warlocks. They cast dark spells using blood and spirits of the dead." Henrick looked at the strange symbol etched into the cover. "Necromancy and much more." He looked back up at Alador. "Rydanth was a cruel and cold man."

The fifth-tier mage closed his eyes as if to center himself in the confines of the small room before going on to whisper: "Be careful, Alador. What lies within this book is the power over death; but it comes at a high cost. However, there is magic within that book that may be of use to you as well."

Alador looked at the book with apprehension and pulled his hands off it. He suddenly felt as if something cold and evil had touched him. "If something that dreadful is in it, why would you give it to me?" He looked up at Henrick.

"It is your legacy as the oldest, magic-using Guldalian remaining of your generation," Henrick stated softly, "…and a chance either to prove that blood will win out, or to clear our family name." Henrick moved to him and squeezed his shoulder. "I will leave you alone."

Alador was left alone in the small alcove with the three magic books. Henrick had not hidden the other two away from him. He looked at all three; but the one immediately before him was the reason why Henrick had shown him the hidden alcove. He ran his fingers over the unknown symbol in its center. It seemed to glow as he did so. His hand trembled as – very tentatively - he raised the strange-textured, black leather cover.

Chapter Six

Alador was so lost in his exploration of the pages of the book that he had not noticed the passage of time. There was nothing in his world but the horror that lay within those pages. There were spells to animate the dead and control them for a short time. There were spells to take away the will of another: spells prohibited by the Lerdenian mages.

"I know it is fascinating reading, but dinner is on the table. I thought maybe you should take a break." Henrick's voice broke through the swirling mass of dark information.

Alador spun as power surged within him. He had not heard his father enter and the sudden voice brought forth instinctive power. "Don't do that," he hissed. "How long have you been there?" He was angry and snappish, not liking the fact that he had been so absorbed in the book he'd let another sneak up on him.

"Not terribly long. However, given the depth of your attention, I was hoping to intrude on your consciousness gradually. When it didn't work, I spoke." Henrick had his hands out to either side. "I apologize."

"There are spells in this book," Alador whispered, closing it slowly, "…that should never be cast." His mind swirled with confusion. He felt anger and deep resentment towards his ancestor, but also a sense of fascination. Henrick had been right: there were spells in it he could use. One that stuck out at the moment was a spell that would allow him to spy on Luthian undetected for short periods of time.

Henrick moved to him. "Things that should never have been done," he agreed, "…but that Dethara teaches to many of her high priests. After her appearance at the ball, I thought you should know what we are up against."

The alcove was suddenly overheated and oppressive. Alador licked his dry lips and his voice rasped when he asked: "Why does this knowledge even exist?" He felt a desperate need to purge it somehow, as if just knowing such things existed had stained his soul.

"There is a time and place for many things. Sometimes, the most horrible things are created with the best intentions." Henrick laid a hand on the black book. "Some men are so evil that they twist what is right and good into something dark and foreboding in the hope of gaining more power."

Alador nodded. "Luthian cannot ever get his hands on this book," he added, his tone adamant. "We should burn it."

"There are many spells in there of value. The spell to give Renamaum his last goodbye is within those pages." Henrick tapped the book, his finger still lying upon it.

"Then it should be rewritten with things of use retained and the rest expunged forever." Alador stared at the book.

Henrick's tone was low as he answered Alador, trying to lead him gently through the horrors that had to be faced. "What if you ever need to repel one of these spells? Knowing how they were cast will enable you to counteract what others may attempt." Henrick eyes searched the younger mage's face for some sign that he understood.

Alador rubbed his brow in exasperation. "I see your point. I just fear what could happen if another finds this book. Maybe it should stay with Keensight."

Henrick indicated the doorway. “Let us talk over dinner.” He led the way out of the small, secret room. “Some things are better digested slowly, and without the distraction of hunger pangs.”

“How do you ever get anything done? You are always hungry.” Alador quipped as he slipped from the room. The sense of relief at being away from the book was palpable.

Henrick chuckled at the thought and clapped his hands together in front of him. “Yes, well staying young does take a bit of energy.” He moved the bookcase back into place and once more it was as if the room and its dark secrets did not exist. Even though Alador knew its location, he was hard pressed to find a sliver of indication that a door was there. He studied the shelves.

“Why don’t you just let yourself go gray as others do?” He touched his own streak of vivid white hair at his temple.

“I find this appearance far more influential on those with beds I wish to occupy,” Henrick quipped as he turned to head for the door. “After all, a man has more than one appetite.”

“Yes and your two appetites take up most of your time.” Alador laughed and shook his head.

“Better to live sated, than to die wanting, I figure.” Henrick smirked and led the way to the dining room. After they were served, he dismissed the servants so they could talk, going as far as to bespell the room, much as he had at the alehouse in Smallbrook not so long ago.

Alador was able to recognize the spell this time when Henrick’s ring empowered it. They both ate in silence for a time, lost in their own thoughts. Henrick finally spoke, setting his wine cup down, his eyes on the glass goblet in his fingers. “I know both of us have avoided talking about Dethara since the night of the ball, but I have been doing some investigating."

Alador forcibly swallowed the food in his mouth. He put his fork down slowly, and only then did he look over at his father. "What have you found?"

"Dethara has been amassing forces within her temple walls. Her followers are increasing daily." Henrick fiddled with his fork and some noodles. "It is even said she is accepting mortal sacrifices."

"Why are the other Gods not doing anything?" Alador asked, outraged.

"I don't know," Henrick admitted.

"Do you still think it is really her?" Alador sat back, deeply concerned.

"I do," Henrick stated. He took a thoughtful bite and swallowed before going on. "But if it is not her, then her priestess is possessed with her, or allows her body to be used as the Goddess decides."

Henrick shook his fork at Alador. "Perhaps that is exactly why the Gods have not discovered this. If she is imbuing her High Priestess with her essence, the woman would not be able to act independently, much as your hand can only do what your brain wills. The other Gods would have no concern, as they do not meddle in the affairs of one another's orders." Henrick considered this further. "Now that I think and speak on it, I'm pretty sure that is the case."

Alador thought it over. "I need to go see Sordith. We need eyes in that temple. If anyone can get a spy in there, it will be him."

"Why? I have already told you what is going on." Henrick sounded slightly offended and his glance was little short of a glare.

Alador chewed as he considered. "You are getting news that anyone outside their gates or in the taverns of the guards might pick up. If those sort of happenings can so easily be discovered, what much darker things don't we know about yet?"

Alador wiped his mouth and looked at Henrick. "Sacrifices, whether human or of any other mortal creature, are for a purpose. We need to know that purpose. I don't need a bunch of zealots in my way when I'm taking down the mine, and I really don't want to face them when we remove Luthian from power."

Henrick sat back with his cup, popping a piece of fruit into his mouth before speaking. "So you have accepted the path Renamaum has set for you?" His question switched the topic effectively.

"No!" Alador slammed his hand down on the table. "I don't accept any path any of you have chosen for me. What I do accept is that I might be the one person that can stand between my vile uncle and the destruction of dragons." Alador's fervor took a deadly edge. "I chose that path," He leaned towards his father intently, "…regardless of its alignment with other people's whims."

Henrick smiled. "If that is what you need to feel right with yourself, so be it. It comes to the same thing," he pointed out. The large clock behind Alador chimed, drawing Henrick's attention. "I expect that I will be told to leave soon. What are the things I need to know?" Henrick had not been fazed by his son's burst of anger.

Alador picked up a piece of bread and mindless chewed on it to calm himself as he thought about Henrick's question. "You intend to go to Smallbrook?"

"Yes."

Alador swallowed the bread and took a deep breath. "I plan to take the test when it is offered and do my best to test as master of my sphere. I will meet with Sordith and see to getting some illicit trade routes to sustain the Daezun through a harsh winter. I will be coming to Smallbrook to see Dorien soon after." Alador considered for a moment. "Have him make sure the storeroom with the coal is cleared by the door. I will come by amulet and will set my destination there."

Henrick carefully noted each detail. "You will have to cast the first spell soon; the winter solstice is almost upon us."

"I am aware. I just hope I have the resolve to follow through with it. I wish there was another way, but I am not strong enough, nor am I in any position to depose Luthian without getting my own head cut off." Alador unconsciously put a hand to his throat.

"And the spell book? We have yet to finish our discussion about that." Henrick leaned forward and pulled a prickleberry pie over, cutting a hefty piece for himself.

"I want to burn it." Alador held up a staying hand as Henrick's eyes rose in alarm. "Don't fret: what I want is not what I'll do. I'll take it to Sordith's manor and hide it there. That way I can study it at my leisure." Alador reached for the pie and cut his own piece.

Both men ate silently for several minutes before Henrick spoke. "Are you sure we can trust Sordith?" Henrick asked.

"Yes." Alador took the last bite of his pie and sat back sated. "He is the one person who has called it like it is, whether I wanted to hear it or not. He has never broken his word to me. He could have betrayed you, me and our plans at any moment, but he hasn't."

"I know you are in the habit of trusting family, but…" Henrick began.

"A habit that I don't plan to break," Alador interrupted. "Otherwise, you and I would no longer be on speaking terms. You keep secrets, and you have lied to me by your own admission. It might seem I have more reason to trust him than you." Alador paused and met his father's gaze. "...Yet here I sit."

"Alright, you win." Henrick pulled his pipe from his belt and set about loading it. "You left one thing off your list of things you must do soon."

Alador mentally went over the list quickly. "What did I miss?"

"Renamaum's farewell," Henrick stated simply. He lit his pipe.

Alador paused considering. "You're right; I need to do that before anything else. I have a feeling it may already be too late. There is not much time."

"We'll have to do this tonight," Henrick decided. "I fear I may not have much time either. I would prefer to be nearby. It is a powerful spell you will cast, and not the type you are used to using." Henrick reached into his belt and pulled out a tooth, laying it on the table between them.

"What is this?" Alador stared at the tooth, quickly recognizing it from his mining experience as a dragon's tooth.

"It is from Renamaum's place of death. You need something of his as a component of the spell." Henrick's gaze was forlorn as he gazed upon the tooth. "It felt wrong to take it, but I knew of no other way to gain an item with enough connection for the spell to work."

"You said this spell will be different. Is that because of the diagram and components?" Alador had to admit that other than water he had not used any components in his spell-casting. Well, unless he counted learning to see and move the air stones.

Henrick nodded. "Some incantations require more than a mage's will, and this is a powerful spell. It will only last a short while, perhaps half a day at most, depending on the strength you and Renamaum can give to it."

"Well, I'm done eating. Maybe we should go now and do this." Alador felt a strange sense of urgency: a welling-up along the edge of Renamaum's essence. "I get the feeling that Renamaum agrees." He tossed down his napkin and rose from the table.

"Get the spell book and meet me in the practice room." Henrick rose with his pipe and led the way. Alador made his way to the library, and finding the skull he tentatively put his fingers in the socket. He felt slightly relieved at the audible click of the lock mechanism. He had held his breath, as if something might cut off his fingers or otherwise assail him. He gathered up the black leather book carefully, realigned the bookcase and headed for Henrick's tower.

Henrick was waiting near the table they used for practicing. Alador laid the spell book carefully on the table and turned the fragile pages till he found the relevant spell. He looked up and around at the room. "I don't think we can cast this here. Renamaum's bones indicated he was very large. I don't think this room can encompass him."

Henrick nodded. He handed Alador a quill and empty parchment. "Copy down what you need to know. We will cast it above the cave that Pruatra inhabits. It is a cliff edge I have seen and there's enough room for Renamaum's form."

Alador set about copying from the book while Henrick filled a large vial with powder. The diagram was simple, but would need to be exact. It took Alador some time and Henrick used that time to load a few other items into a backpack. When Alador was done, he checked it and rechecked it before carefully sanding the ink to dry it. He turned to find Henrick waiting, backpack in hand.

"Give me the amulet and I will take us there." Henrick held out his hand expectantly.

Alador swiftly removed the amulet and handed it to his father. "I hope you are right about this," he said. He was apprehensive as he handed the amulet over.

"About the spell or allowing Renamaum a goodbye?" Henrick asked.

"The spell. I want Renamaum and his family to have closure." Alador watched as his father put the amulet around his neck.

"Well son, the one thing I know for sure about magic is that you can never be sure about it." With that, the room shimmered and swirled from view…

Alador still found teleportation disorienting. Another location began to form around him… He felt as if the floor was giving way and his stomach jolted. He realized at the last second that it actually had given way, and he grabbed wildly for the edge…

His fingers connected with cold, wet stone, and their new surroundings solidified. Thunder boomed, and water lashed his face as he fought to hold on to the edge of the stone in front of him. The wind was furious, battering him against the rock face. Lightning lit the cliff side with erratic flashes of jagged light.

Alador scrabbled with his feet to find some place for a foothold, feeling his fingers slowly slipping on the saturated rock. He managed to set his right foot and swiftly moved to get a better hold, the sharp edges cutting into his palms, drawing blood.

"Give me your hand!" Henrick's voice was barely heard over the wind and rain that beat down upon them both. Alador looked up to see that Henrick's hand was only a few inches from his own. He pushed up hard on his foothold and flung a hand to grab wildly at Henrick's.

He barely managed to grasp it before his footing slipped. Both their hands were slick with water, and Alador dug his fingers into Henrick's wrist, nearly pulling the man above him over the edge. He fought quickly to find a purchase with his foot and help by taking some of his weight himself.

It took the utmost effort from both of them - Alador finding footholds and Henrick using a strength that the younger mage had not known his father possessed - to pull him up over the edge of the cliff. They both lay at the top, panting from exertion and excess adrenaline, sweat pouring off them both, despite the soaking rain.

"By the Gods, what happened?" Alador gasped out.

"Seems some of the cliff has given way since I was last here," came the gasping response.

"Shite!" Alador slowly turned over and rose to his knees. "I know you warned me that can happen, but it was too close for comfort."

"Yes, yes it was." Henrick sat up as well. He looked about him assessing their surroundings. "We are in the right place, however." He was having to shout over the storm.

"What do we do first?" Alador stood up, his hair plastered against his head, except for a few loose strands that whipped wildly in the wind.

"You're a storm mage!" Henrick bellowed, putting his hands on his knees to catch his breath. "Get us a few minutes of peace from this storm so you can place the rune on the ground."

Alador nodded and set about finding the air stones to calm the storm. It took longer than he had hoped. It was much easier to start a chaotic mass of weather, he realized, than it was to quiet the temper of one. He finally resorted to creating a shield around them that would hold for a short time and stop the buffeting of wind and rain.

Once this was done, Henrick showed him how to lay a rune on the ground. The powder still drifted slightly in the puffs of remaining wind, but the form held. Alador stepped to the center of the rune and held Renamaum's tooth in his hand. Henrick stepped back.

"Close your eyes and imagine the rune in your mind as you say the spell. Your sphere will power the rune and the rune will power the spell." Henrick's tone was far more serious than usual.

Alador nodded and closed his eyes. He held the base of the tooth so tightly in his hand that it pressed into his flesh. He realized that one could almost use it as a dagger. Refocusing, he imagined the rune on the ground, filling in every detail, watching the water run the course of the rune as he had drawn it.

When the water had filled the shape of the rune in his mind's eye, he intoned the words of the spell so loudly he was almost yelling, his nerves getting the better of him. He heard Henrick yelling back at him in the distance: "Say it again!"

He could barely hear him over the storm, despite the bubble he had created. He repeated the spell, emphasizing each word with feeling; and this time he felt the power around him surge. Lightning struck the rune around him several times. It was all he could do not to flinch as the power rushed through and around him.

The rune on the ground flared up with a life of its own. The world shifted and he struggled to stay upright as his body began to shift and enlarge. He shut his eyes for fear of letting go of the power too soon and being stuck as half a dragon…

When at last, he opened them, the world was different. The colors were brilliant, even in the midst of the thrashing storm. Even in the dim light, he could make out the distinct images of things far from where he teetered.

He panicked and began to flail his arms, but instead, wings caught an updraft coming from the sea. Despite the scrambling of his legs, of which there were now four, he found himself aloft and panicked further.

Henrick shouted up to the floundering dragon. "Give control to Renamaum!" Henrick was forced to duck under the frantic waving of the newly formed dragon's tail.

"RENAMAUM! HELP!"

There was a sudden shift in his perspective, and he found himself with the sensation of floating in warm safety. He could still sense the dragon body around him, and even Renamaum's thoughts. "Relax boy. It is your time to be buried."

Renamaum turned and dove down the cliff face into the sea.

Chapter Seven

Alador felt a sense of elation as he, or rather Renamaum, dove beneath the waves. Pure joy coursed through him as they sliced through the thrashing ocean. Even though he was not in control, he felt everything; it was so… exhilarating! He felt the sheer confidence the dragon felt as Renamaum snapped the wings close to his body just before they hit. The movement of the long tail snaking through the water felt natural and at the same time so strange to the mortal within.

He also had his own sensations that mingled in a maze of confusion. The fear he felt right before they hit the water, and the amazement that the water underneath the surface seemed so calm compared to the crashing waves swirled with the myriad amounts of other information assaulting Alador. The realization that he could see beneath the surface of the waves, and that the world beneath the sea was filled with amazing colors constantly changing provoked in him a kaleidoscope of emotions and sensations that threatened to overwhelm him. Every sense seemed more intense, whether it was sight, touch or sound.

The fear slowly abated as he realized that he was just an observer of whatever was to happen over the next few hours. Slowly, he relaxed and let himself experience what it was like to be such a magical beast. The strength in Renamaum's tail was enough to power them through the sea. The dragon's thrill at being able to stretch out and truly be unrestricted was contagious. Alador had expected

Renamaum to head straight for the cave, but he had headed out to sea instead.

"Where are we going?" he asked the dragon. His voice felt flat and muted as it was an internal conversation. In contrast, the dragon's voice echoed about him with rich tones and booming vibrancy.

"I am not going to my mate without a gift." Alador heard the amusement in his tone. *"She is bound to be… 'cross' with me."*

The dragon suddenly began a strange spiraling pattern down. He stopped at a bed of dark rock and drew in a mouthful of water, blowing it out of his mouth under pressure to reveal a section of rock, most of which looked like steel. Renamaum turned and hit the bed with his tail several times. Alador watched in fascination; wondering what gift such rock could possibly yield. When several pieces had been knocked loose, Renamaum turned and took them into his mouth.

To Alador's astonishment, he ate them. They tasted horrible and even hurt to crunch down upon as the dragon ground them against large flat back teeth. Alador attempted to touch his jaw and realized that he had no sense of personal movement. ***"What are you doing?!"*** The thought that when his body somehow returned it would be full of rock was not lost on him.

"Fire rock. Need it to stay warm." The matter-of-fact answer did not make sense to Alador, and apparently Renamaum felt that this was the only explanation needed. The dragon continued twisting and gliding through spires of crusted rock until he came to a shipwreck. Alador realized that he could see the shadows of these things and not really the details. Everything was outlined in degrees of darkness and he wondered how the dragon could see at all with the storm raging above. Some of the fish

fleeing from their path seemed to glow with a light of their own.

Alador realized the dragon had paused and refocused his attention on what Renamaum was up to now. The great beast nosed around the bottom of the ship and eventually used his large claws to rip open a large hole in the side. From there, he pulled a chest out onto a rock and leaned on it till it cracked beneath his weight. As Renamaum searched through the contents, Alador realized that he could smell the metals and stones. He was not sure 'smell' was exactly the right word, but it was the closest sense he could attribute to the sensations that he could feel coursing through him. He watched as Renamaum finally chose a strange goblet set with dark stones. Clutching it in his talons, the dragon turned and headed back the way that they had come.

As they picked up speed, Alador began to feel a strange comforting heat. It radiated from the center of his being. He realized that whatever it was that Renamaum had eaten was indeed giving him much-needed warmth against the cold confines of the water pressed around them.

"Can I ask you questions until we get to your cave?" Alador shifted, or felt as if he shifted, closer to the mind of Renamaum.

"Only if you promise to be quiet or sleep while I am with my mate." Renamaum's firm tone left no room for argument. Alador could feel the dragon's longing for its mate. It was difficult to not let those feelings become his own.

"Do all dragons eat fire rock?" Alador mentally shuddered at the taste remaining in his mouth.

"No, it depends on the breath-weapon of the dragon. For those of fire and water, it is what powers our breath-weapons and gives us heat when cold waters or weather is upon us. It also produces an air

that lightens our body so that flight is easier to maintain." Renamaum was now swimming rapidly and with purpose in a single direction. *"It fills a second sack, much as air fills your chest."*

"Is the fire rock … when we change back … is it going to be in me?" Alador really hoped that whatever Renamaum did in his dragon form would not damage him in his own.

"I do not know." Renamaum admitted. *"When it is time, I will expel the rock, just to be sure."* The dragon broke the surface of the water, expelled stale breath and took in a couple of huge fresh ones before diving again. The storm still raged on the surface.

Alador considered this carefully before asking his next question. *"Is that why the fledglings held in the mines don't fly? They do not have access to the fire rock."* He felt struck as a powerful wave of anger rose up in the dragon.

"It is part of the reason, combined with the confinement and intentional damage to their wings." Renamaum's anger turned to deep sadness. A memory surfaced of young dragons with their fragile wings slit beyond repair. Alador too felt the loss of such freedom. It was like a man having the tendons at the back of his ankles severed as a child. He decided to deflect the dragon from this line of thought, and tried to focus on something else that was concerning him. It was hard while under the onslaught of senses that he was not used to experiencing.

"Will it hurt when I absorb your final essence?"

Renamaum slowed slightly. *"I do not know. I have never seen or heard of any beings in our situation."*

The admission took Alador aback slightly. *"Haven't there been other pseudo-dragons?"*

Renamaum had come to a cliff face and began swimming down in a spiraling pattern. *"There are stories, but none with a geas. Pseudo-dragons from a Daezun or a Lerdenian, or a combination of the two… I do believe you are the first."*

"The first?" Alador was alarmed at this. It meant no one could tell him what was to come. *"Can you tell me what a pseudo-dragon really is?"*

Renamaum paused, and Alador had a sense of him searching his own vast memories. *"A pseudo-dragon has all the magic of a dragon, and all the ancient memories, once he learns to embrace them. He just does not have the body of a dragon. All that separates him from full dragonhood is the physical form."*

"I will BE a dragon then?" Alador was stunned. He had been given hints, but nothing this full-on.

"As close as you can be, yes." Renamaum confirmed. A dark opening slowly revealed itself in the cliff face. It was large; Renamaum entered it with confidence. *"No more questions; we are here. Sleep now."*

The command seemed to echo around Alador, wrapping him in a strange sense of separation from the presence of Renamaum. It felt like a thick, clear wall had been put up between them. He could still feel his senses: sight, smell and touch were clearly present, but it was as if he were deaf to the dragon's thoughts now. Alador attempted to balance himself and settle into the role of a simple observer.

Renamaum's head broke the surface of the water and quickly looked around. He spotted Pruatra resting on a bed of treasure and seaweed. As the female dragon bristled up and hissed in warning at the sudden intrusion into her lair, Renamaum moved in the water to where she would have a better view of his true form. "Pruatra, it is I, Renamaum. Settle and do not be alarmed."

Every spike and fin on the female dragon was tensed up. Even her face fins were fully forward as she shifted her body, the moment formidable as she moved between the male and her bed of treasure. "How is that possible?" Her eyes raked back and forth over her late mate's form.

"The boy cast a spell to give us a space of time." Renamaum moved out of the water and held out the goblet with a forepaw. "I do hope this small token will make up for the fright I might have given you." His guttural tones held an edge of appeasement.

Pruatra sniffed the air as Renamaum moved out of the water, the fins on her face still tensed out. "Why would he do that?" She demanded with suspicion.

"To let us have a proper farewell before I am lost within him forever." Renamaum did not move, goblet still held outstretched.

Pruatra moved closer and sniffed him. "You smell of mortals and magic," she grumbled. She took the goblet from him and sat back on her hind legs to inspect it, holding it close to one of the lightstones that illuminated the cave with a gentle moonlike glow. "Well at least you did not come without a gift," she conceded. She turned and nestled it with great care into the pile.

Renamaum chuckled and moved forward next to her. Leave it to Pruatra to find reason for complaint rather than joy at his appearance. When she was done placing the goblet, he nuzzled her neck softly. "I have missed you."

The only sign she was relaxing was the laying down of her facial fins. She did not look at him or turn to meet his attempt at affection. "Do not think you can be off dead all this time, leaving me to raise our fledglings on my own, and then just show up as if nothing were amiss." Her tone held hurt and grief.

"Yes, well dying did not leave me much opportunity to prepare you." He chucked her chin with his snout to show his displeasure at her lack of joy at his return.

"There is a great deal that is amiss, Pruatra; of that I am very aware." He nuzzled her again, nibbling at her neck gently before speaking again. "Would you have preferred I did not take the boy's gift?"

The dragoness sighed heavily. "No." She turned and laid her forehead against his muzzle. "But you are here, so now you must stay," she whispered.

"I cannot do that. We have but a few hours," Renamaum answered just as softly.

"You can cast the spell of staying. My mate, you can keep your form and make the boy ride along as you have been doing," she begged. Her head turned so her gaze could fully meet his. "You could be a true father to our young."

"I would have only a mortal lifetime if I did that - a fleeting moment to you and our young." Renamaum pulled his head back. "The geas would never be fulfilled, for I cannot complete it; the boy must do it. Would you really have me be so selfish, mate of my heart?" His eyes dropped with the pain he felt at denying her request.

"Yes!" Pruatra snarled. "Look what your great ideals have wrought: you are dead; and the flights no longer gather in Council." She did not pause, despite the look of shock that he flashed her. "You were killed by the very mortals you seek to change." Her last words were snarled out. "They will never change."

"Pruatra…" Renamaum began to explain. He had to help her understand the larger picture here.

"Don't you start," she hissed, her mouth snapping closed with an audible click. "You left me alone." A strange choking growl rumbled in her as she fought to speak her mind. "You left me alone as you sought to change the world. Mortals are selfish. They think only of their brief existence. They do not care that they are destroying the world they seek to rule."

She drew a breath and snapped her great teeth at him when he started to speak. "They do not care they are destroying the very magic they seek so desperately to possess." Her anger and grief came out in a torrent of words. "I taught your mortal and now he will turn that magic on the very people you are seeking to pr-protect." Her voice broke and her sides heaved with the choked growl.

"Pruatra…" Renamaum began again and when she did not lash out this time, he continued. "There is so much more to this than you know. When Alador returned to the sparkling mountain of magic, the Goddess Dethara was there. She is meddling somehow in this world. It may be her spawn that have been telling the dragon hunters where to find eggs. This is bigger than you… me… our fledglings. This is about every dragon on this world. It is about changing magic from the wondrous power we know to something dark and cold."

He nuzzled the angry dragoness. "I do these things so that our fledglings and theirs have a world to thrive in. It is not for me…" He trailed off, his head drooping with the weight of what he knew.

Their necks entangled and her large sides heaved with emotion. She finally spoke, breaking the heavy silence. "I just… I miss you," she moaned. She moved her head to place her snout flat to his so that their foreheads rested together.

The only sound for a time was the heaving sounds of the dragoness in mourning. Finally, Renamaum picked up his head and nuzzled her snout gently. "My time is short, Pruatra. I do not wish to spend what little time I have fighting with you. Come fly with me one last time," he whispered. He pulled his head back to look at her, his gaze sweeping over the beautiful lines of his mate. Her deep blue scales were lined with edges so light they gleamed like silver. She was as perfect as the memories he held of her.

He forced his eyes up to hers, lost in their silver depths. "Then we will find our fledglings and I will share with them what I can in the time I have," he murmured. He could not finish his thought: it trailed away in longing.

Pruatra sighed - a long wrenching breath - then slowly nodded. "Let us dance in the wind." She turned and waded into the water, diving beneath the surface.

Renamaum smiled and murmured: "That's the mate I remember." He followed her out of the cave and into the water. He watched her surface and climb onto a large flat rock, assaulted by waves and wind in the storm. She shook out her great wings, and then with a powerful thrust, Pruatra took off into the sky.

Renamaum also climbed out on the great rock to shake out his wings. He took a deep breath, and it melded with the warmth in his center, filling his flight sac. When he thrust up, his wings caught the wind flinging him backwards for a moment before his strength forced a turn. He looked about for Pruatra and spotted her tail above him. Grinning, he gave chase, remembering the first time she had sought to elude him.

The two great dragons spiraled up despite the driving rain and wind. They arced in and out of the way of lightning. It was a timeless dance that would have seemed choreographed to a casual observer. At last they broke through the clouds and there above them, the stars shimmered in the cool, brisk air. Pruatra turned to spiral around him. He reveled in her grace in the sky as she dipped and turned. She flicked her tail in his face each time she swooped past him.

Renamaum roared in challenge, his voice deep and thrumming. Pruatra answered by merely flicking her tail at him and dancing out of his reach. They both soared higher and higher until the air was so cold they felt it in their wings. When they came together, they grasped talons and Renamaum swiftly wrapped his wings about his mate.

For a brief moment, the world stood still for the two great beasts. Love surged between them as they conjoined. The two great raptors began to cartwheel, spiraling down to the sea of clouds beneath them. The twisting mass of wing and claw gyrated in a mating ritual that was as old as the dragons themselves. They plunged back into the clouds to be assaulted again by winds and rain, oblivious to the lightning that arced across the sky. When it seemed certain that the two would plunge as a writhing ball into the water, they separated. Wings snapped open and the dancing climb of the long-separated lovers began again.

Chapter Eight

The two dragons danced in the sky until the day began to ebb. Renamaum was determined to leave Pruatra with one more clutch before he had to leave her. It would, gods willing, be some time before she would join him in the afterlife.

He was surprised when Pruatra led him north away from her own deep cavern. "They are old enough to have found their own caves?" He was genuinely surprised. Time in limbo had no dimension and he had had no idea how much time had actually passed on Vesta.

"You have been in the Land of the Dead for quite some time." She beat her wings a couple of times to gain the wind before answering him further. A strange sense of wistfulness emanated from her. "They both have flown to The Pool of the Gods, and both have had their first mating. Though they danced on the wind, neither has found a heartmate yet." Pruatra looked over at Renamaum. "The dragons are dwindling. More and more move to the mainland and remote islands." She heaved a great sigh. "Magic does not flow as it once did. You can no longer find it on the wind. Successful matings are also less, and eggs are fewer. Many lay just one if they are lucky."

Renamaum nodded. He had foreseen this dwindling of magic and dragon when he had first approached the Council of Flight Leaders. He knew that human depredation would continue to contribute to the decline: more and more mortals stole the magic of the dragons. Why couldn't mortals see that if they drove dragons to extinction, there would be no new magic? Inevitably, all magic would fade from the world.

Renamaum could not imagine a world without the wonder of magic. It seemed to him that its absence would bring hardship, disillusionment, and even more fighting amongst the mortals. Why was it that mortals had to have something to measure each other against? Why could they not find wonder in their own individuality?

Renamaum's thoughts shifted to solutions. The great dragon had been saddened to learn that the Council did not meet any longer. He would have to try to speak to Keensight about that. He might not have time, but if nothing else, he could send the boy with a message. Keensight had been a vocal member Why had he fallen silent? Had the red dragon's anger been so great the day they parted for the last time that he had never returned to Council?

He watched the two juvenile dragons slowly flapping their way towards them. It was clear that in many ways they were still fledglings, judging by the way the larger kept dancing in and upsetting the flight path of the smaller. He would have to speak with his son about such things. Renamaum followed his mate as she spiraled down to a clearing below them. He landed so lightly beside Pruatra that it made no sound. He nuzzled her once more before their fledglings joined them.

Renamaum drew himself up as they both landed before their mother and dipped their heads with proper respect. He smiled, remembering their names with affection. Amaum raised his head proudly, face, fins and spines rigid. "Have you taken a new mate, mother?" Much to Renamaum's amusement, Amaum puffed his chest while surveying the older dragon carefully. Renamaum chuckled at the display.

"No," Pruatra answered. "This is your father. He has been able to resume his living form, but only for a very short time." She stepped back a bit to allow the two young dragons to eye the male before them. Renamaum assessed them right back.

"My time is short, so I must pass certain things on to you now." Renamaum did his best to appear fatherly and wise, remembering his own sire's regal manner. He hesitated for a moment, realizing that he actually had no idea how to be a proper father. He had not gotten the chance to adjust in the way most males did. In his mind, they had gone from eggs to fully grown. He shook his head as he realized his own behaviour was mirroring his son's automatic hesitation.

"How do I know you are really my father?" Amaum challenged with a growl.

Pruatra moved to put her son in his place, but Renamaum's tail slipped in front of her. "You do not. You do, however, disrespect your mother with your doubts and therefore cast shame upon her." This time, Renamaum drew on his full size, taking a step forward. He showed his son exactly how large he had been in life. "I expect a son of mine to have more honor than that."

Renamaum took another step forward. Rena wisely sidled away, but Amaum held his ground, his eyes meeting the larger dragon in challenge. "There are spells that might allow an interloper to prey on a mother's grief," Amaum stated bravely, his tail flicked back and forth. It was the only sign that he was at all intimidated by the larger male's presence.

"Yes," Renamaum agreed, "…though there are even better ones for foolish fledglings." He formed the stone spell in his mind; it was not of his sphere, so it took some effort. Renamaum whispered the words in Draconic and suddenly the very ground melded about Amaum's feet, anchoring him before his sire.

Amaum looked down at his feet in surprise. He opened his mouth to respond, but the only sound out of his mouth was the hiss of air.

Rena giggled until her mother caught her eye. She sobered immediately and dropped her head. The larger male moved forward, his voice menacing. "Now that you are silenced and clearly held in place; you will listen." Renamaum stood over his son, glaring down at the concerned younger male.

"First, bravery is a fine thing, but so is fear. Both heroes and cowards feel fear. True bravery is to act with courage in the face of fear. Fear warns us of danger…" - Renamaum pushed his son's muzzle down with his own - "…a warning you need to heed."

He circled his entrapped son. "Sometimes we will feel fear and not see its source; and it is then we must be the most aware. By all means be courageous my son, for courage builds character. Foolish bravado, on the other hand, brings death."

Renamaum spoke directly to Amaum, but he could tell by the tilt of her head that Rena was listening closely. He nodded his head at her with approval before looking back at the arrogant young male. "An older dragon will have mastered many spells and skills you have barely had time to touch."

He came back around to the front of the fledgling and caught his eye before he spoke further. "An older dragon can recharge his breath-weapon far faster than you. He can discharge it for longer as well. If you must take an older dragon on, fledgling, use surprise, not foolish words. You could no sooner have made good your threat than caught your own tail."

He glanced at Rena then back to Amaum. "Seek out older dragons; show respect and learn from them. I don't have time to teach you all I would have done in life. Your mother has done a fine job, but some things a male must learn from a male. Do not believe yourself to know already all that you need to know. The most dangerous thing a dragon faces is his own ignorance; and you cannot seek an answer if you do not even know the question."

He racked his brain for further nuggets from his sire's teachings. He had so little time, and there was a limit to how much his son could absorb in one sitting. He needed to tell him the most important things - things that other males wouldn't share with one not of their line, things that had made his father the leader that he had become.

"There are things worth fighting for, my son, and much not worth your time and skill. Protect your mate and your family. Fight for what is good, and that which nurtures the land and the races that dwell upon it. Do not hold the sins of a few against the whole of any race or species."

Amaum listened, though he looked surly and reluctant. He could not do much more with his feet secured in rock. Rena was watching her sire with large eyes. Pruatra just stood there, proudly watching her mate take their son in claw.

"When a dragon's mind grasps truth, the real truth of this existence, then it can see beyond its own lifetime. You still see with the eyes of a young fledgling. It's obvious in the way that you tease and harass your smaller sibling." Renamaum reached out with a talon and tipped the younger male's chin up to look him in the eye. He was pleased to see a little remorse glimmering in Amaum's eyes. "She is your blood and deserves your protection and your guidance. It is a hatchling that plays tricks. Are you a hatchling, Amaum?"

"No Sire," Amaum answered, finally softening. His fins lay back against his face as the true depth of his father's words and chastisements took root.

"Good, then I shall continue." Renamaum circled the younger male once more. "There are many versions of this so called 'truth' in the world. Do not try to prove one 'truth' more valid than any other. If it be truth, then its purity will shine, like the different facets on a diamond, and nothing will chip or crack." He nosed his daughter gently before turning back to Amaum. "Always remember that the most enticing falsehoods come cunningly disguised as truth."

Renamaum felt his time running out. "The most important thing I will leave you with in words is this. Everything matters. What you say to others matters. How you act matters. How you carry yourself matters." Renamaum drew himself up with true pride as he looked at the two younger magnificent dragons. "Live your life in such a way that when you are old and have many fledglings in your wake, they will mimic you with pride."

Renamaum released the spell that held Amaum, causing the younger male to falter somewhat. He turned to look at his daughter and she shrank back from him in awe. "Come here, Rena," he called softly.

Rena moved towards him slowly. She looked up at the great male with large fearful eyes. "Yes sire?" she murmured.

"Life will throw many serious situations at you that you must become the mistress of." He drew up and chuckled, easing the tension a bit. "But do not forget to play. I have watched you with your brother, and I can tell that you are the more serious of the two. Do not forget to love life and live it to the fullest." Renamaum smiled down at her.

"I plan to have a wonderful life." She drew herself up proudly, encouraged by her father's softer manner. "I have even found one whom I desire as a mate."

The elder dragon looked over his daughter with swift scrutiny. He nuzzled her tenderly to prepare her for the tidings that he had to impart. "This is of paramount importance: the boy cannot be your mate," Renamaum stated firmly.

Rena's face fell. "But he has all the qualities I want in a mate," she insisted. She drew up in a token display of defiance, but her tone held more panic than disobedience.

"Except the body and lifespan of a dragon," Renamaum said quietly. He knew his next words were going to be a harsh blow. "He also has a heartmate already, Rena." He spoke with great tenderness.

"Oh." She lowered her great head, and her eyes showed her distress.

He nuzzled her to console the obvious distress this caused. He looked at his mate hopefully, but Pruatra was pointedly looking elsewhere. "You will find a mate worthy of your soul and heart. Do not settle for second best, dear heart. Find one that fills your soul with fire, as your mother has always filled mine."

Renamaum nuzzled Rena. "Do not blame Alador. It must have been quite alarming to have a large dragon declare affection for him." He put a wing about her. "I am sure he did not wish to hurt you. I know he truly cares for you all."

Seeing that this was not easing her pain, he tried another tactic. Renamaum puffed up his chest with pride as he looked down at his daughter. "I am proud of your skill in magic and in your teaching of such things. Your fledglings will have a fine mother."

Renamaum had one last thing he had to give to his son while he knew he had the time. He could not let the boy, Alador, have his power, and withhold it from the younger dragon. He returned to Amaum. "Hold still, Amaum. I will gift you my knowledge and power as a flight leader."

He took the young dragon's head in his mouth; it was still small enough to fit. His daughter squeaked with fear; Renamaum could hear Pruatra's reassuring tones behind him. He closed his eyes and gifted his son with the powers of the flight, all Renamaum's ancestors' knowledge in magic, some of the power he held, and as many of his memories from his own sire as he could put into the magic.

A circle of blue radiated out from the two males. When Renamaum finally removed his mouth gently from around his son's head, Amaum fell to his knees. His eyes filled with tears when he looked up at his sire. "I am so sorry Sire. I did not know," he whispered.

Renamaum nuzzled the boy. "I know. There is no way to make such a shifting of power less overwhelming. The memories will settle in time."

Renamaum looked at them all. His love for his family threatened to overwhelm him. "Let us settle for a time and speak of more pleasant things. I would know all I can before I must return. I want to hear stories of your time as hatchlings. I want to hear of your travels to The Pool of the Gods. I only wish there could be enough time: that I might know everything."

The four dragons settled down onto the ground. Renamaum passed on every tale and history that he could think of that might be of use. He asked many questions, and as he had requested, the two younger dragons shared their own experiences growing up. It was a true time of family and bonding. They all had a chance to laugh at the tales of the others.

Pruatra remained quiet for the most part, letting the three interact. She would smile at tales of childhood antics and occasionally added her own quip. Renamaum could feel her grief, despite her attempts at levity. He could feel her desperate eyes on him, even when he gazed upon the younger dragons.

Renamaum finally rose, shaking his great form and stretching his wings. "I am out of time. I can feel the edges of the spell pulling and faltering, and I still have to return to the place where this spell was cast."

Pruatra moved to him and laid her forehead against his own. They stood that way for some time. "Please… cast the spell and stay," she begged in a whisper so that only he could hear her words. "I know you have the words and power to hold this form." A tear landed on the ground between them and turned into a strange, light blue crystal.

Renamaum nuzzled her gently. "You know I cannot," he answered. He growled as his own grief flooded him.

"You mean that you will not." She raised her head, and her tail flicked back and forth with her agitation.

"Pruatra…" His tone rich with the torn, ragged emotion of having to choose between the right thing and what his heart desired.

"Go mate! Go save the world! It is what you have always sought. I cannot stand in your way." She stepped back angrily. "How can my love compete with the prophecy of gods?" She turned her back on him so that he could say farewell to his fledglings.

Renamaum dropped his head in misery. He hated hurting her in such a way. He felt a slight nuzzle and opened his eyes to see Rena looking up at him.

"She does not mean it. She always says angry things when she is hurting." Rena's words held the simple honesty that only youth can bring.

The great dragon nuzzled his daughter back gently. "I know little one. She always has." He moved to Amaum and gave him a firm nudge. "You are the male of this family until your dame chooses another mate. Protect your dame and your clutch mate as you know that I would have done." He knew that Amaum now had his memories and would know the great lengths to which Renamaum was willing to go to keep them safe.

He stepped back from them both. "I am proud to call you mine. Go into the world and know there is more to it than just ourselves. Everything is connected: the land, the people, dragons, and nature are all intertwined. If one falls, all will be affected. Never forget this. Pass it on to your own fledglings. Promise me!" he demanded.

Both Rena and Amaum made their pledges softly, then moved in to touch their sire one last time. Renamaum put his wings around both and whispered a prayer to the gods to protect them. Then he stepped back, surveying them both before giving one last longing glance to Pruatra.

"I must go," he suddenly growled out. "As long as the boy lives, I will be with you." He leapt into the sky before he changed his mind. The temptation to betray the boy and cast the spell that would secure this form was too great. He had to leave now, or he never would.

Chapter Nine

Renamaum could feel the power of the spell withering away; edges of it were fading and he was clinging to it. He faltered in the air as he fed it his own power. The only thing that he had left in that well was his own life-force. He did not want to leave Alador stranded anywhere between the two points of flight. It had been so hard to make that leap into the sky. Turning away from one's family for a greater good sounded heroic in his mind, but in his heart there was only a sense of ripping pain. The look of anguish on Pruatra's face would be his last memory of her. Renamaum looked back the way he had come. He could still turn back. He brought his vision back around to check his path and roared in anguish. He could not go back: too much was at stake for the world of magic, and he had fledglings to protect.

The storm was a short distance off when he circled the cliff. The wind still made flying difficult, but the thunder now rolled in the distance. He could see where Henrick had formed a small magical shelter from the elements where he stood staring off at the sea. His hands were clasped behind his back with a fire blazing behind him. As long as Renamaum had known him, Henrick had always disliked being cold.

He chuckled somewhat as he made his way to the ground, attempting to use the humor of the moment to push the grief from his mind. As promised, he expelled the fire rock from his second stomach, in case such things did not also transform when the spell ended. He didn't want Alador to suffer any side-effects.

He could feel the young mage pounding against the mental boundaries he had surrounded him with in his mind. The great dragon slowly began to let down the barriers that he had erected so that Alador would not interfere with his farewell.

Alador's voice erupted in his mind. *"I can't do this Renamaum. You deserve that life. I have no small ones. I have no one to give my death more than a token mourning."*

"It is no longer your choice to make, boy," the dragon inwardly snarled. He had not put Pruatra through that just to have the boy make some heroic sacrifice.

"I won't let you do it," Alador shouted. *"I refuse your gift. I refuse to return to my form."* The mage, despite being without a body, attempted to wrest the spell from Renamaum's control.

The hollow echo in the dragon's head was painful. Renamaum almost botched the landing because of Alador's sudden attempt to force down the rest of the magical shield. The boy was not going to take his power. He growled and reinforced it to prevent losing control of the situation. He had always been accused of caring for mortals too much, and now one was willing to sacrifice himself for the dragon. He realized that from what little Alador had discerned in their switching of forms, the boy intended to let him finish the task in dragon form.

"I seem to remember your skill in flying was better than that, old friend," Henrick called up in amusement. When Renamaum let out a fierce growl, Henrick look up startled. "Something amiss?" he asked tentatively.

Steam, remaining from the heat of the expelled fire rock, boiled from Renamaum's nostrils. "The boy wishes to sacrifice himself and leave me to the task," Renamaum snarled. The large dragon lowered his head to meet Henrick's gaze. "Did you have to teach him the concept of self-sacrifice?" The sarcasm dripped as thickly as the spittle now spraying over the mage.

"Don't look at me," Henrick stated seriously, hands still clasped behind him. "He came that way."

"I thought I had shielded my emotions more effectively, but I am out of practice. The mortal doesn't want this to have been my final goodbye." Renamaum's great tail hung slightly off the cliff face, and the sound of it rubbing rock in agitation grated over the wind. "We will have to cast the absorption spell."

Renamaum's determination faltered slightly. He was not sure he could do it. First, he knew he did not wish to leave the land of the living. Secondly, he did not think he could keep Alador in check and also cast the spell. He had been with the boy long enough to know that on his own, Alador had the power to interrupt the spell.

"Let me correct that," the great dragon hissed. "You will have to cast the spell as I transform, while I keep the boy from interfering."

"I do not know this spell, Old Friend." Henrick walked to the left, and Renamaum watched him closely, his head following the movement. "Dragons do not inhabit mortal forms as a matter of course."

"No, they don't; but we both know that you lie," Renamaum challenged. "You knew where to retrieve the spell to bring me back. You have been dabbling in deception too long. Don't think you can lie to me…. ***old friend!"*** The dragon snarled out the term.

Henrick shook his head. "I guess I tell the lies so many times that sometimes I believe them." He put out both hands as if to concede the dragon's point. "I know of it, and I knew it once; but now I have to admit I do not

remember the absorption spell. It has never been done in my life-time, or at least to my recollection."

Renamaum's great head lowered till his nostril was within inches of Henrick's face. "Yes, well if you spent more time studying, instead of chasing females," the dragon snapped, "…you might know more." Renamaum took in a deep breath and rumbled it out, trying to center his fragile hold on the magic holding Alador at bay. He could feel the boy testing the shield for weaknesses.

"I don't deny it," Henrick smirked, "…but you can give me the words, can't you?" Henrick patted the dragon's jowl affectionately.

"Enough chit-chat," Renamaum muttered through grinding teeth. "I am barely managing to contain your adopted spawn." Had he not needed Henrick's immediate cooperation, Renamaum would have bitten him. "I will refresh your knowledge of the spell," he conceded.

The great blue dragon lowered his head so that the space between his eyes was level with Henrick. He waited till Henrick's hand connected with his brow, then set about feeding him the spell. His urgency and lack of practice met Henrick's willing and open - but lesser - human mind…

Inwardly Renamaum cursed when he heard Henrick gasp: he had practically shoved the spell down the mage's throat. He opened his eyes to see Henrick staggering back. "By the Gods, you could have taken more time," Henrick gasped out.

"I apologize; subtlety takes practice and time, and as you know, I am out of both." Renamaum was not sorry: it served his old friend right for being playful when so much was at stake.

"Are you sure this is the only way?" Henrick asked. "It seems a great sacrifice when the chances are there will be little or no gain."

"It is time I rested with my ancestors and the gods. I am weary, and this torch is no longer mine to bear." Renamaum realized it was true: he was tired and felt strangely empty. "The boy will have a better chance in mortal form than as a dragon." Renamaum managed a toothy grin. "Mortals tend to shoot first and ask questions later."

Henrick frowned and rubbed his throat absently. "So do some dragons," he added.

"Yes, well then they end up with some upstart mortals demanding recompense." Renamaum laughed. "I still find the boy's demand amusing. I think I truly decided he was the one when he stood behind that throne demanding a choice from a dragon that could have roasted him on the bone."

"Yes, a tale worth telling when all is said and done. I will make sure the bards hear of it when it will cause no hindrance to him on his journey," Henrick grumbled.

A silence fell between them, cut only by the whipping winds. "Let us do this, before I change my mind," Renamaum finally sighed out. Henrick nodded and disappeared into his enchanted hut, emerging moments later with the items they needed.

It took him a bit of time to draw a casting circle around so great a beast. Renamaum sat still, eyes closed, not making a sound. In truth, he was working hard to hold Alador within him. The young mage had broken through enough to realize what his father and the magnificent blue dragon were up to, and he was doing all he could to thwart them.

A war raged within the magical beast as their two minds combated for supremacy. Renamaum had never encountered such resilience and determination in a human. It took all his power and centuries of practice to keep the young mage contained.

"Renamaum, do not do this. Keep your form. Raise your fledglings. You can start over where you left off." Alador had managed to thin the shields enough to call through.

"My life has been lived as it should have been. I was given respite by the Gods to help all mortals; but I am tired, boy. It is time I rested in the great fields of the Gods." The mage had leached enough of him away and now he wanted to sleep.

"I don't know how to do this without you. Dethara is involved - a GOD! My friend may have to choose her over the dragons and myself. I have lost Mesiande." The dragon felt Alador's panic raising. *"I would rather live out my life in the sky and water."*

"You will want this more when we are done: becoming a pseudo-dragon will inspire that desire." Renamaum's reassurance was as soothing as he could make it. *"You have my kin, you have Henrick, you have Keensight, and you have a Trench Lord."* He swirled feelings of calm and comfort around the boy. *"You have many allies and soon you will have all my knowledge and experience. Find the other flight leaders. Become the dragonsworn you were meant to be… They will in turn - albeit slowly – share with you all that you need to win the day over Dethara."*

"Renamaum, listen to me. Please!" Alador pushed against the barriers that held him beneath Renamaum's will. *"Let it be the other way. You absorb ME. If I can give you wings, then you can walk in my form, and use the mortal advantages that I have gained."*

Renamaum could sense that Henrick was almost ready and worked hard to keep the boy's attention. He was not sure if the boy had the power to break through during the actual transformation and did not want to give him the time to prepare.

"Please, stay. You said it could be either way. You could stay and advise, or give me all that you have. I have changed my mind," Alador insisted. *"...Stay with me and help me do what must be done."*

"It is too late for that, boy!" Renamaum snarled out. He was getting tired of Alador's whining. *You have taken too much. Do you think you could cast such spells as a half-blooded fledgling if I had not been giving to you?"*

"I am ready," Henrick called out.

Renamaum nodded at him to proceed. He formed the spell in his own mind at the same time as he heard Henrick begin. He would have to let the transformation spell dissipate at exactly the right moment to prevent Alador from stopping his father.

Carefully the dragon rehearsed the timing, and when he heard Henrick hit the word he was waiting for, he let all the shields down. All power faded from the transformation spell he had been holding in place. Renamaum gave it all away.

He felt his form begin to shrink and contort back to mortal form. He knew Alador could do nothing until the transformation completed. If he had timed it right,

Henrick would cast the final words of the absorption spell only a second or so after Alador regained his mortal form.

Slowly he changed places with Alador, giving the boy back control. He formed one final thought before Henrick's spell fired the runes around Alador. *"I am proud to have you bear my geas. If we could have met in my time, I would have called you a friend."*

****

Alador had risen his hands and knees with the intention of tackling Henrick and stopping the spell, but the absorption spell hit him hard, knocking him over on to his side. He curled up in pain, his hands clasped to his head. Swirling clouds manifested over them. It felt as if large hands were pinning him to the ground.

Separate from the thunderstorm, a maelstrom funneled down to a space just above the runes. Henrick chanted the words to the spell again, his eyes still closed. His hair whipped about him wildly as he stood with arms outstretched. Fire rose round the perimeter of the spell, blurring Alador from sight. The smell of ozone and sulfur filled the air, and in the distance, the mourning cry of the dragonsong echoed across the hills.

****

Henrick's last words fell away. Now he could do nothing but watch the boy's faint form through the flames. The fire still surrounded his son, while within its circumference, Alador screamed and rolled, clutching his head. The sound of a dragon's wings drew Henrick's attention and a large form settled beside the worried mortal mage.

"Will he live?" Rena asked worriedly. She moved closer to the runes, her wings fluttering with agitation.

"I don't know, Rena," Henrick admitted. "He is strong, but he was unprepared. I didn't even get the chance to try and tell him what to expect. I don't know if a mortal's mind can take such sudden expansion." Henrick took a deep, centering breath.

"I WANT him to live," Rena demanded. Her tone suggested that she could will it to be so.

Henrick looked over at her. "We all do, Rena," he answered loudly enough for her to hear over the wind and fire. "Your sire would not have suggested this if Alador could not withstand it."

"It will change him." She sounded unhappy, and looked at Henrick accusingly.

"It will," Henrick agreed, "…but Renamaum was noble and kind, so I hardly think it will be for the worse. Maybe he can even learn to control that tongue of his." Henrick forced a smile as the attempt at humor fell flat between them.

"Can it be undone?" she asked worriedly. "You know: so if it is not working out, or he is not the man we thought he was, can you reverse it?" Her angst was clear in her eyes. It is a given in the Universe that pubescent creatures feel emotion in its rawest state. "I don't want to lose who he was - who he is," she whimpered out.

Henrick watched the maelstrom begin to rise back up into the skies. "No," he admitted. "Right now, what is happening is beyond my control. I cannot undo it." He paused. "To be honest, I wouldn't even if I could." He turned to face the agitated female. "Your father gave his life for this peace. Both races as you know them - yours and Alador's - will cease to be, if he fails."

She winced as another piercing scream cut through the air over the sounds of wind and fire. "How can you put your own son through that? It is such a great burden." Angrily she pushed Henrick back with her muzzle.

He smacked her away, forced to give ground because of her size. "I did not give him your father's stone, Rena." He glanced at the circle. The fires were slowly dying down and with them the screaming. "By fate, accident or the will of the Gods, this fell upon him without my intervention." He crossed his arms, seemingly undeterred by the young dragon's ire.

"It is still too much for one," she growled out.

Henrick nodded. "Aye, and that is why we will stand with him. He will not be alone, Rena. All of us are with him in this fight."

The fires were now barely burning. Alador lay on his back in the center of the burned outline. Henrick let out a sigh of relief to see that his son was still breathing. Only when the runes completely died out did he and Rena dare to approach. Alador lay staring into the sky, much as he had when Henrick had found him stricken at Sordith's.

"Alador..." Rena called softly. She nuzzled him worriedly, and gave a snort of relief when he stirred. Alador's hand came up to her muzzle and stroked it in answer, though he still stared up into the clouds. The swirling mass was slowly abating. Rena pressed happily into his hand.

Henrick waited. He knew that Alador had to be experiencing a great deal of internal turmoil, and sorting it all out would be hard for anyone — even another dragon.

"Henrick," Alador called softly, still not moving. His voice held a sense of awe. Henrick knelt beside him and offered the boy a hand to sit up. Alador took it and once sitting, turned his head to look at his father. The wide-eyed wonder in his gaze had not abated. "You truly are a bastard."

Alador stared at Henrick for a long moment, then began to laugh. "Why did I not see it? All the signs were there: every step, and I did not see!" Slowly the laughter turned almost to hysteria before Alador's eyes rolled up and the mage passed out.

Chapter Ten

Henrick caught Alador before he hit his head, then pulled the boy up and over his shoulder. "I fear we must part for now, Rena. I must get Alador home. Go and tell Pruatra that it is done," he commanded. His glance to her was hard, and his voice held the firm coldness of authority.

"How come you cannot go tell her, so I be the one to take him home?" Rena asked with an answering growl. She drew up over the mage slightly.

"Yes, you are just going to fly into Silverport, and by doing so, announce to all that Alador is aligned with dragons. When they are done shooting you," Henrick said, his voice dripping with sarcasm, "…IF he lived, Luthian would turn him into a flaming sigil in his anger." Henrick looked up at the young dragoness with a scowl. "You are being a silly hatchling; now off with you." Henrick shifted Alador onto his shoulder.

Rena's face fins flared forward, their quivering a sign of her anger. "I am **not** a hatchling." Steam boiled from her nostrils as anger filled her eyes. "I could end your mortal existence with a mere breath," she reminded him with a hiss. Her wings came in tight to her body, and her tail swept the ground.

"You … could … try," Henrick answered with a harshness not typical of the easy-going mage. He took a breath to center himself. "Rena, I do not want to have to tell your mother why I had to strike her fledgling." There was a pause as they stared at each other. "Stop this nonsense and let me see to Alador."

Henrick could see she was not relenting, and when he continued it was with desperate exasperation. "Otherwise, as you and I are matched in wits and magic, he might wake up and wander off some cliff." Henrick pulled the travel talisman from his tunic; he was impatient to be gone.

His words brought the dragoness' eyes back to Alador. Her gaze softened as she stared at the now helpless man. With a huff, she turned and leaped into the air. Henrick watched her go, letting out a sigh of tension. A lovestruck dragon was just adding to the list of problems surrounding Alador. He whispered the spell to take them home.

They appeared in Henrick's room. The whispering of magic had reawakened Alador, so Henrick lowered the dazed mageling into a chair. He moved across the room and rang for a servant. He eyed Alador for a moment with slight concern. Had the spell been too much for a mortal man's mind? He sincerely hoped that both Renamaum and he had not overestimated the boy's abilities.

He returned to Alador's side, knelt and took the boy's cold hands into his own, rubbing them to give them warmth. "You know, don't you?" Henrick whispered solemnly. "You can sense what it is I have kept from you."

Alador nodded. His eyes still looked a bit dazed, but at least he had responded. He focused on Henrick, and his stare held both wonder and accusation. Before Henrick could inquire further, the servant appeared. It was the shadow that alerted him, forcing him to snap his mouth shut. Sometimes his servants were just too damn efficient.

"You have a need, Lord Henrick?" The man's formal tones forced Henrick back to his feet.

"Take Lord Alador to his room and help him into bed. He has had rather too much to drink tonight. Pay his words no mind, he has been babbling on about the oddest things." Henrick looked around and realized there was not a drink in sight. He panicked for a brief moment, then fixed the man with his hardest gaze. "Check my stocks once you have seen to the boy… I have no idea where he got such elixirs."

"Yes, Milord." The servant moved to Alador and helped him up. Thankfully, Alador was still silent. The only clue to his stability was the strange gaze that he kept on his father as he was led from the room. His weakness from the spells had Alador swaying, lending credence to the lie.

Henrick moved swiftly, running up the stairs in a state of controlled panic. If the boy knew, what would happen now? He glanced around the casting room before retrieving the spell book, relieved to see it lying as they had left it. He did not believe any would dare to enter once the door was secured, but he did not want it to lie about for very long. The mage returned it to the small secret alcove, then glanced out the window at the front of the manor to reassure himself that Luthian's guards were still stoically standing outside his door.

He hurried to Alador's bedroom, taking the remaining stairs two at a time. So much was at stake, and he did not want his son left alone until he could assess the situation. He barged in, bringing a startled sound from the servant. Alador slowly looked up when Henrick entered, his eyes resuming their accusatory gaze despite their glassy state. At least the servant had managed to get him undressed and into bed.

The man bowed low. "Will there be anything else, Lord Henrick?" he asked respectfully.

"Yes, bring enough food for three men - a variety of dishes," Henrick ordered, his mind on other things. "I don't care if it's a cold meal, as long as it's quick." He again attempted to settle himself - he had kept this secret for so long. Only Renamaum and Pruatra had discerned the truth, and he had worked hard to keep it from Alador. He feared what changes the revelation would bring, and he really needed a drink. "One more thing: a pitcher of hard cider." Father and son's eyes were tightly locked.

The servant glanced between them, swallowing at the tension in the room. "Yes, Milord." He scurried off to comply with this latest request. It was only when the man was gone and the latch clicked into place leaving them alone, that Henrick dropped his gaze.

****

Alador was lost in a sea of memories that felt as if they were his, yet he knew they were not. He remembered standing before the gods. One by one, memories drifted like flotsam through his mind. He knew what each of them had said to the great blue dragon, including Dethara. Her gift had been more of a curse than a beneficial boon. No wonder Renamaum had hated her so much. Her words echoed in his head.

"I gift to you a swift death when your time comes, that you may not suffer." She had leaned in closer and whispered, "By the mortal hand you will seek to save, you will be given death."

Alador was still amazed that, after receiving the knowledge that Lerdenians would kill him, Renamaum had still sought to unite them and find peace. His second realization was that he himself – and not the arrow that had struck Renamaum so many years ago - had sent the great blue dragon to the gods. Either way, Renamaum had died at mortal hands.

There were other things swirling in the currents of his mind as well: things that Renamaum had seen that Alador had not even known existed, dragons so large and ancient that their size was incomprehensible to him, even after seeking out Keensight. He watched as a large memory drifted pass on the crest of a mental wave. A name floated up, almost tangible to the touch: Rheagos. Few spoke of the great golden beast for fear of giving offense. The ancient beast was the oldest of all that lived on the lands of Vesta.

His thoughts ebbed and flowed, and somewhere beyond them he heard the gentle instructions of the servant. He followed the bidding to sit or lift his arms as sodden clothing was removed from him. It did not impinge on his amazement at the tides floating within him.

He knew the moment Henrick entered. He felt him before he looked up to fix his gaze on the older mage. Alador did not know whether to be angry right now, or happy: was this man his best friend and father? – or only a friend of sorts, a pseudo-father: advisor, mentor, **liar**…? Emotions swirled up and he swallowed, fighting them back.

He had many questions, but they could wait till there was an assurance of no interruptions. He clasped his hands before him as emotion dove beneath the stream of memories. Though his gaze was on Henrick, his thoughts were adrift elsewhere. The young mage swiftly sorted through his mind for all the facts that he wanted to clarify. It was like fishing with a net that had a large hole in it. He would find one thought only to have it slip through that hole, yet another he had managed to entangle and grasp completely.

He put a hand to his head. It ached with a strange overall throbbing, as if the contents of his mind were trying to escape the narrow confines of his ever-pounding skull. His eyes felt pushed forward and every sense in his body flooded through him. He was more aware of the smells in the room, even those emanating from Henrick. He could feel the sheets, every thread of them beneath him; and all of this novel, sensory overload swirled with the new knowledge that had been forced upon him.

"Are you in pain, my boy?" Henrick asked with low tones. The man took a wary step closer.

"A bit," Alador admitted. "I am also trying to decide if I am relieved that I did not know your secret or… if I should be angry with you." His eyes met Henrick's with rather more clarity now. He still could not believe that he had not seen the truth. It had been in front of his eyes the entire time.

"I imagine a bit of both." Henrick moved cautiously forward and sat on the end of Alador's bed. Henrick looked down at his own clasped hands with a sigh. "I imagine you are filled with questions. But I suggest that the majority of them wait till the meal is brought to us and the servants depart." Henrick glanced at the door almost as though he were willing the servant to step through it.

The young mage nodded in agreement, squinting as if trying to get his father into focus. He looked him over, amazed at what he saw, and what he could not. "When will this flurry of random memories stop? It's like they are racing by faster than I can grasp or understand them." Alador blinked a few times and strove to fix his attention solely on the fifth tier mage.

Henrick took a moment before answering. "Your mind has been forced open in an unnatural way, and it's a lot to absorb. I cannot tell you how long it will take. I had never cast an absorption spell until tonight," he admitted.

Alador sat up in the bed and ran a hand through his still damp hair. "Why have you not killed Luthian?" The question was curt and demanded an answer. With the knowledge he had gained, Alador knew that Henrick was more than capable of beating his uncle.

"I have no desire to lead this city or the Council. You and I both now know that I have no right to do so." Henrick smacked a fist into his hand. "If a leader with some moral fiber is not found…" Henrick paused as if choosing the right words. "It would be pointless to remove Luthian just so some carbon copy could replace him. Better the demon I know," he offered with a grim smile.

Alador nodded. His next question was as random as his thoughts. "Are dragons part gods?" Alador asked, hoping to better sort through the mass of confusing information. He should know the answer, but he could not seem to concentrate on any one given memory. They went to see the gods, so it was logical that there was a connection.

"Dragons were created by the power of the gods themselves, each imbued with certain characteristics important to the god that created them," Henrick answered as if by rote. He stroked his chin. "But part god? Well, I have never thought about that before," he admitted.

The random questions were interrupted by three servants who brought in trays. An assortment of cheeses, cold meat, rolls, and pie was set on the other side of the bed itself for the two men. Another set a pitcher of hard cider and goblets on the table beside the bed.

Two of the servants left, but the original one stopped at the foot of the bed. "Do you wish me to stay and serve you, Lord Henrick?" he asked.

Henrick shook his head and waved him off. "We can see to ourselves. Find your beds, for I am leaving in the morning and will need everyone to assist me." Henrick passed a hand over his face as he rose. "Loading my carriage will take some time."

"Yes, my lord." The servant bowed and hurried out of the room.

Before the door had even closed, Henrick moved around the bed and put an assortment on the two provided plates. He handed one over to Alador. Alador took it gratefully; he felt as though he had not eaten in days. He fell on it ravenously, forgetting his many questions for the moment. When Henrick handed him a goblet, he took and drank the contents down all at once. Though it had been Renamaum who had maintained the transformation spell, it was his body that seemed to have counted the cost.

Henrick sat back down on the end of the bed. "Easy lad, your stomach is still mortal though your mind hungers like a dragon. It will take a while to sort that out." Henrick held his own stomach, as if in recollection.

"Yes, let us speak of that. What should I call you? Henrick, Father, Friend..." Alador met Henrick's eyes evenly. "...Or Keensight?"

The silence that fell upon the room was palpable. Tension filled the air between them as the truth finally surfaced, its blaring meanings shouting so much between them. Henrick finally waved a hand at Alador in dismissal as he gathered up his own food. The only sign of his discomfort was that he did not look up at the younger mage.

"Let us keep it at Henrick or Father." He took a bite, striving to appear casual: as if the matter were not important, but Alador knew his father was worried: he emanated anxiety.

"How is it possible?" Alador pressed in a hushed tone. "Are you even my father?"

Henrick set his plate aside and drained his goblet before answering. "I suppose it is time for me to tell you the whole story," he said with a sigh. He rose and filled his goblet, then held the pitcher out to Alador.

"With no lies…" Alador insisted as he held out his goblet.

"With no lies," Henrick promised. He filled the goblet then returned the pitcher, moved about the bed and sat down. "Do you remember the story I told you of how I met Keensight?"

"Yes, but you **are** Keensight, so that story was not - at least not entirely - true." Alador frowned at the man before him. How had he not seen the signs that Henrick was so much more than he had seemed?

"It was mostly true." He waved his hands as the word 'mostly' left his lips. "The original Henrick did try to make me spare his life by pointing out that Lerdenians were hardly tasty, and that he would stick in my throat." Henrick did not look at Alador as he spoke. His voice was soft and measured as he stared into the distance, seemingly unfocused.

"Which of you is my father?" Alador asked with concern. Had he been half-dragon before he was even born? He watched as the dragon in human form sat back down on the far end of the bed.

"Henrick Guldalian sired you. However, I believe I have been more of a father than he ever was," Henrick said defensively. The mage's vision snapped back from wherever his mind had taken him, and he picked up his plate.

"Where is he?" Alador was gripping his goblet tightly, his fingers white with the anxiety of the question. "Did you eat him?" The question was more of an accusation.

As if the thought hurt, Henrick swallowed audibly in alarm. "Goodness no, he might truly have stuck in my craw. No, he lived with me for a time - my prisoner I guess." Henrick looked up at Alador. "I killed him once I had what I needed to replace him."

"You ... killed ... my father." Alador's words were grasping at these truths, trying to grasp their meanings. He should have been angry with Keensight, or felt horrified and betrayed that the creature now occupying the body of man he had called father had killed his true sire. Yet, as he searched himself, he was not.

Henrick rushed to justify the deed. "He was truly as awful as Luthian, I assure you. He was everything you have accused me of and more. You would have been led by two men with no capacity for kindness unless it benefited them." Henrick waved his fork madly. "I swear by all the gods that I care for you and your mother more than he was ever capable of and… I do see you as my fledgling."

Alador was quiet for a long time. He let Henrick sit there with his suspended fork as he sorted these revelations. He remembered Renamaum's sorrow at the pain that Keensight had shown when his egg was stolen. Being called his fledgling, well that was no small compliment.

Finally, the younger mage looked up at Henrick. "How, and why, did you replace him? I could only maintain Renamaum's form for a short time."

"I went to the God Kronos and asked for help. I wanted revenge at first, for all that had been taken from me. It was not just my own loss, but I blamed myself for Renamaum's death. He had left the Council so angry." Henrick set the plate aside and stood. "I thought if I could get close enough to Luthian, that killing him would repair everything." Remorse tinged his words. "He gifted me a spell that allows me to hold this form with minimal effort," he added as an afterthought.

"But you didn't kill him… What happened?" Alador was carefully taking in this new version of family history. He was not sure how he felt about all of it.

"I …" Henrick took a deep breath and stood up. "In exchange for the ability to use this form, Kronos demanded I wait a year before taking any action." He turned away from Alador and walked to the window.

Alador had to know. "It has been over a year…"

Henrick interrupted before he could even finish his question. "I met you," Henrick admitted as he turned back to look at Alador. "I met your mother. I met the Daezun. I realized that Luthian would just be replaced by someone as equally ... despicable." He pulled a square of linen from his pocket and wiped his face. "So that is when I started searching for Renamaum's dragonsworn. I never dreamed it would be you."

Both men were quiet for some time before Alador broke the heavy silence. "So now what?"

Henrick moved back to the bed and put a hand on Alador's shoulder. "Now that ... is... is up to you. If you do not want my help because of the secrets that I have kept, I will return to my life as a dragon, and you will not see me again." Henrick paused and cleared his throat. "I do truly see you as my fledgling, Alador and … would like to continue to act in your father's stead."

"You killed my father," Alador repeated, still searching for how he felt about this.

"I did," Henrick confirmed solidly. He sat back down and returned to picking at his plate.

Alador realized that Keensight – Henrick, or whatever name he went by - was not sorry for killing Alador's real father. He thought about his geas. He thought about Luthian and what would have happened if his natural father had discovered his son's geas or power? As he thought back, he realized that he knew when Keensight had come as Henrick.

He had always hoped that the change to a doting father had been because his father had finally accepted Alador as his son. He then realised that Keensight had made a conscious choice to foster his enemy's fledgling. He thought carefully about all the things that Keensight, in dragon or mortal form, had taught him. The changes on his face must have been readable for he heard a soft sigh of relief from the end of the bed.

He did not intend to let the dragon off quite that easily. "You let me make a fool of myself at your cave when you knew all along. And at the lake, Pruatra knew too, didn't she?" Alador's eyes widened. His gaze faltered, his eyes shifting back and forth as the memories flurried in his mind. The kaleidoscope of images was slowing, and individual moments surfaced, enabling him to speak rather than to gabble in a great rush.

"I will admit it was rather fun… your meeting of my other self." Henrick grinned at him. "But I had to do it that way or admit my secret and I … well, you weren't ready to hear it."

Alador considered that Renamaum had known, too, and had not let on. "I suppose learning that the man playing the part of your father is a dragon would have been a bit much when we first left Smallbrook," Alador conceded.

Henrick stood up and placed his plate on the sideboard. "I will let you sleep on all this. Tomorrow, I leave. You will need to decide if it is permanently, or if we continue with our plan." He put a firm hand on Alador's arm. "The choice will be yours. I will understand whatever you decide." As if the moment held too much emotion for him, Henrick turned and strode for the door.

"Keensight," Alador called, looking up at the mage's back.

The man stopped, his posture stiffened at Alador's use of the name. The older man turned to look back at Alador. "Yes?"

"I don't need to sleep on it," Alador said. "I cannot think of a better father for a pseudo-dragon … than another dragon."

Henrick's smile grew from a small grin to a full, tooth-filled smile. "I will still let you rest. We will speak before I leave and you return to the caverns." His father left the room with a much lighter step.

Alador finished a second plate before he laid back against his pillow. There was so much in his head now. One thing he knew for certain: he felt much more confident about his geas than he had the day before. With a wave of his hand, he snuffed the candles.

Chapter Eleven

The High Minister of Silverport stood staring out the window of his office. His gaze was on the glistening city below as he replayed one more possible scenario. Luthian was as prepared as possible to meet with the Council. Today he would ask for Alador to be tested. Only if he passed his test could Luthian have him assigned to the High Minister's personal retinue, as the boy had not completed full training in the Blackguard. He did not need the boy battle-trained. Luthian needed him at hand for his own use to unite the isle.

A feminine hand touched his arm and he frowned. "You realize that you are the only female that could touch me without my express permission." Though his tone was meant to tease, there was an edge of seriousness to it.

Lady Morana moved around him; her rounded curves were accentuated by the belted silken robe. "I am hardly just … any ... female, my lord," she purred as she moved her hands to his chest. Her husky emphasis of the word 'any' held an exaggerated caress. She pressed her body to his as she eyed him through her long lashes. "Where are you off to today that requires such a striking appearance?"

Luthian took her hands and stepped back, putting some distance between them. "Do not presume that because you share my bed that you can be privy to all my designs and plans," he said, the coldness of his tone contrasting greatly with the warmth of hers. Her cloying nature irritated him, and she presumed far too much. Now that he thought about it, she wore too much perfume as well. It was heavy, like the herbs used at funerals.

"You and I both know that at times I am more than mortal, and the power I wield transcends humanity," she said. She met Luthian's eyes proudly, squeezed his hands and attempted to pull her own free.

Luthian let her go, offering no resistance. "Yes, my dear woman, but today you do not play host to the Goddess; you are but her vessel on this plane," he reminded her. He really had no respect for this woman. Her mistress was a whole different matter. After all, how often did a man get to say that he had bedded a Goddess?

"For now…" she drawled. Though her words acceded to his point, her tone held the mild edge of a threat.

Luthian moved swiftly. His hands tangled in her hair as he jerked her close looking down into her amber eyes. Their faces were so close that he could smell his sex on her luscious lips. Her eyes glistened with excitement rather than fear, and her gasp of pleasure only further incensed him.

"Your Goddess and I have an arrangement that is mutually beneficial. You are but the sweet wrapping that does her will. Do not think for a moment that she or I could not find another to do her bidding."

Rather than the fear that he was used to seeing at such rough handling, this intoxicating woman's eyes glimmered with triumph. "We could do much, both of us, if we were further joined in purpose. Imagine what our combined skills and power could accomplish," she purred up at him.

Luthian released her hair with disgust. Despite her offer and her obvious skill as a death mage, he roughly thrust her away from him, watching with satisfaction as she stumbled back and fell onto her knees. "I would rather bond with a Daezun than join in purpose with a whoring priestess," he said, his voice dripping with his loathing. "How many others have shared your bed for the power or wealth that they would gift upon you?" He found her truly worse than a whore, for at least with a whore you knew what you were buying. This woman, unlike most death mages, used sex much as a spider used a web.

He watched coldly as Morana crawled to him, looking up suggestively from her knees. Her well-formed lips were set into a pout as her large luminous eyes gazed up at him unblinking. "I don't remember you complaining much during our many times together," she pointed out, pulling up his robe hem teasingly as her hands slowly slid beneath and trailed up to his thighs.

Luthian looked down with an arrogant twist of lips. He trailed the toe of his boot up between her heavy breasts. "Just because a whore is the best in her craft does not mean a man need have her meddle in his affairs." Luthian scoffed. He put the boot fully to her chest and pushed her off him. "I am expected in Council; off me wench," he snarled as she fell back. He actually liked her splayed before him in such a manner; her raven hair spread about her on the floor. The robe had slid open, hinting at all her charms without revealing them.

Morana finally looked insulted. She glared up at him. "How dare you insult me so!" she exclaimed with genuine disbelief.

Luthian looked down at her for a long moment. "I dare a great many things." He turned and moved towards the door. He stopped and paused as he considered his own words. "Speaking of which, your temple has had my patronage long enough." He gave her a genuine smile in response to the fear that he saw flicker in her eyes. So she feared the loss of his slips as well as his ear, did she? "The reports I have on your comings and goings indicate you are accumulating wealth. You obviously do not need mine any longer." He shook his robe as if she had dirtied it.

Morana's eyes grew wide with alarm. She rose to her feet. No longer the teasing, wanton woman from just moments before, her hands curled into fists. "Dethara will not be pleased to learn of this decision," she growled out.

Luthian eyes roved over the priestess. He sighed as he realized at that moment how truly unattractive a woman she was. "Dethara is welcome to speak to me of these matters when she returns." He headed for the door and opened it, then stopped to look back at her. "Be gone when I return," he ordered and tossed a slip at her feet. He smiled at her indignant gasp as he shut the door behind him.

Luthian strode forward with confidence. He had finally had the wherewithal to put that woman in her place. She was but an avatar; one not deserving any reverence when the Goddess was not with her. Alador's suggestion that he withdraw his patronage had been well made.

****

Before he even reached the door, he could hear the murmuring voices from within; something had stirred up the nest of wasps. He forced a smile on to his face and strode into the Council. The members all rose when he entered, acknowledging his position. He waved for them all to sit and took the chair at the head of the table with an air of bored indifference.

Council business began. Luthian tuned out the mundane items being discussed and instead he marvelled at the room. Created by strong bronze mages, the details were amazing. Dramatic images from the first war were depicted on one wall. Opposite, there was a vast tapestry depicting the day that Rydanth Guldalian had stood in the dragon's blood, the transfer of magic depicted in a flash of outward-spreading power. He loved that tapestry as he felt he looked a great deal like Rydanth. The rest of the room was no less grand. The large table was hewn from a single piece of wood and therefore had no planks to break up its highly polished sheen. The room never failed to amaze him, despite the many times he had been here.

Realizing he had lost track of the proceedings, he forced himself to refocus on the current item under discussion. As usual, there were many complaints about the trench - what could be done about it and the stench that came from it on warm days. It was a common topic, and one that usually ended with a stalemate. One side would advocate roofing it over; but then it would be quickly pointed out that the miners and maintenance workers would be asphyxiated by the concentration of trapped fumes. It was an old argument, and one he cared little about. He found himself again staring at the fine details of the tapestry. Surrounded by flickering torches, the scene seemed to move.

"What are your thoughts, High Minister?" a feminine voice called out.

Startled out of his own musings, he looked up and realized that everyone was looking at him. He panicked for a long moment realizing that he had no idea what the question had been. Luthian looked slowly about the table, searching for some clue to guide his answer. He spotted Sordith leaning against the far doorway, arms crossed.

"I would defer to the Trench Lord on the matter, as he lives within its dark confines and oversees its occupants," he said. He waved a hand towards the man as if the matter had been beneath him. In truth, he was glad not to have been caught out. It would not do for him to lose face when he was about to make a significant move in his plot to unify the isle.

There was a collective intake of breath and all eyes swiveled towards the man in the doorway. Sordith gave a casual wave and approached the table, his boots against the polished marble floor the only sound in the room. He took the end seat opposite Luthian and scooted his chair forward. The scraping sound set several members' teeth on edge.

While a chair was always placed at the far end to represent the second ruling lord of the city, no trench lord had ever actually sat at the Council table. The look of disbelief on the mages' faces brought a smile to Luthian's. A green-robed mage stood indignantly. "I must protest at this man's presence, High Minister." The man sniffed and his face contorted as if he had just placed his nose in a refuse bin. "He has no skill in matters of magic and therefore does not belong here." The mage's hair was dark with streaks of lightened brown, his face more youthful than the High Minister's hawk-like features.

Luthian sat back in his chair, one hand toying with a quill as he smiled with amusement. "Odd you should say that, since you bicker about a matter that has nothing to do with magic." Luthian rose, leaning forward with both hands on the table. He fixed a cold look at the nature mage. "The Trench Lord, Sordith, has more sense than fully half of the members currently seated at this table. I will hear no more dissension regarding his presence, which is at my instigation."

His voice was cold and commanding, clearly intending to end objection. Sordith grinned and toasted the High Minister with the goblet that had been left at his place. In this situation, Luthian was grateful that the man's confident manner and grace lent weight to what he had just said.

The heavy silence was broken by the same mage. His tone was equally uncompromising. "You do not command this Council, Lord Luthian; this is a matter for a general vote, not for the personal whim of the Chair." The indignant mage met Luthian eye to eye, clearly not willing to back down on the matter.

"Is that so, Valmere?" Luthian stated coldly. "I 'suggest' we let the man speak and if his words are not wise, I will have him removed." Luthian looked down the table. "Now, Lord Sordith, what say you to the Council's dilemma concerning the odor emitted by the trench?" Luthian sat down calmly. This was the game he loved, and these little surprises only made it that much more enjoyable.

"I am honestly shocked that such a group of learned men and women have not been able to address this issue." Sordith toyed with the goblet before him as he considered his words. "You do not need to cover the entire trench; just send me some stone mages that are well-skilled. We can close off significant stretches of the actual flow to diminish the stench." Sordith glanced at a gray-robed mage near him. "That would bring relief not only to those with sensitive noses," - Sordith winked at the beautiful woman to his right - "...but also to those actually living within the trench, who would then be less prone to illness and death." He let his eyes travel to the upper end of the table where mages closer to Luthian sat. "A workforce too ill to work benefits no one."

A murmur went around the table: his words made sense. "What if there is a blockage within a closed-off stretch?" asked a woman dressed in golden robes. "Such a back-up would be bad for all those in the lower tiers."

"I am pleased to see a healer has such concerns." Sordith smiled at her charmingly, bringing a faint flush to her cheeks. "We install access hatches every few feet, so that any blockage can be swiftly located and dislodged with a long pole."

Many of the mages nodded and Valmere slowly sat down. "Does this Council still wish me to remove the Trench Lord from our numbers?" Luthian asked, his words cold. His condescending glance was for Valmere alone. There were many who now murmured their support for Sordith's presence.

Luthian stood to make sure that he could see everyone as he completed the procedure. "It has been rare hitherto that one with such schooling and sense has risen to the position of Trench Lord. Given the current circumstances, I say we take advantage of his knowledge and experience by ratifying his presence at Council meetings while he lives to hold that position." He looked around the table. "How many still wish the man removed?"

Valmere and three others slowly raised their hands. Luthian was quick to note that two of them were stone mages. He smiled warmly at those that had not raised their hands. "It is settled then; he stays." He nodded at Sordith with approval.

He glanced down the table at the two stone mages siding with Valmere. "Lady Caterine and Lord Paelio, you two will work with the Trench Lord to see this matter resolved. I am sure you are capable of finding him appropriately skilled stone mages." He was pleased to see both take offense at his instruction. Luthian shrugged. "If not, you can do the work yourselves. After all, this is within your sphere."

Both answered appropriately, "Yes, High Minister." The sheer displeasure on their faces amused him greatly.

"Now that this matter is settled," Luthian slowly sat down, drawing all eyes back to him, "…I have a matter I wish to propose to the Council." He drawled out the words, knowing he had their attention - it was rare for him to initiate a proposal. "I propose we open the testing of tiers to mages of Daezun blood."

The Council burst into an uproar. Several members rose from their seat in outrage or horror. Valmere, however, was one of those sitting quietly. Luthian took note of the nature mage's muted response. He had been prepared for this range of reactions. He knew it was going to be a battle.

Luthian stood once more putting his hands out to beseech them. "Silence and let me explain!"

It took several seconds for the mages to regain their seats. He did not continue nor lower his hands till the room was silent again. "I heard whisperings that a hard winter was coming, so I consulted a seer at the Temple of Dethara," he began in a consoling tone. "The seer has confirmed that he sees much starvation in the Isle's near future."

There were concerned whispers, and Luthian smiled reassuringly. "Our cities have sufficient stockpiles in the trench mines for one such winter, but the outlying Lerdenian populace does not." He paused, letting this sink in. Many of the ruling mages had come from pastoral regions.

"In addition, the Daezun people do not have cities with large surpluses to tide them through such an emergency. I expect that they will seek help, especially if there were to be more than one such winter." He let a sympathetic sigh escape for emphasis.

Seeing the looks flash between them, he continued. "I know, what does that have to do with Daezun testing?" He waited as many nodded in agreement with the question. "Water mages are rare amongst the Lerdenian people, but not as rare amongst the half-breeds. To learn to turn such a storm aside takes a great deal of specialized training. If such half-breeds were eligible for this additional training, they could be released from the Blackguard and instead train solely to protect us from such natural catastrophes."

Many eyes drifted to the one blue-robed mage at the table, who nodded in agreement with Luthian's point.

"Why can't we just train such Daezun and send them out to help calm and divert the storms as best they can?" asked another mage curiously. Many around the table nodded in agreement.

"There are two reasons. First, these young mages are treated poorly by both the Daezun and Lerdenian people. They may therefore not be highly motivated to protect us, especially if they were to find little value in it for themselves."

He looked about the table. "Be honest, how many of you want to leave the comforts of our fair city to go out into the winter cold and try to turn aside storms of driving snow and ice?" Many of the mages shifted uncomfortably around the table. Luthian inwardly smiled. One thing he knew about high level mages: most did not like to be uncomfortable or dirty their own hands.

"In addition," he continued, "there aren't enough of them to forestall what the seer predicts." Luthian sounded very worried. "But… I have found a mage who, if he tested worthy of access to the fourth tier libraries, would be able to force the storm away from our own people completely." He sighed. "However, in consequence the Daezun would suffer even more. Why, they might in those circumstances be forced to seek our aid."

"Could we not deny them that aid and let them die?" asked one bitter mage.

Luthian moved around the table as he spoke. "Yes, that is an option. We would then have the whole island in our hands. Or... we could annex them into our realm and still have the whole island," he mused.

"I vote for letting them die out," snarled Lady Caterine.

"Yes, I imagine you would." Luthian smiled at her, but there was no warmth in his gaze. "Yet, Lady Caterine, I notice you wear an exquisite necklace. Did you buy it from our local merchants?"

Lady Caterine's hand moved to cover the necklace as she flushed with color. "Well...N-no..." she stammered.

"Interesting." He tipped his head as he took a hold of a council member's chair back, knowing he was making the man uncomfortable. "Wherever did you find such a treasure?" His eyes were still on her hand which covered the necklace.

"I…I bought it from a Daezun trader," she murmured.

Luthian went for the throat though his voice remained curious. "And why did you buy from the people that you would consign to a frozen death and not from our local artisans?" he pressed.

"They do better work…" she murmured, barely audible.

"I am sorry, I did not catch that; what did you say?" Luthian turned his head as if he did not hear her. He knew that she would not relish making such an admission.

"They have better artisans for jewelry," she admitted.

Luthian nodded. "I would agree." He moved to the end of the table and looked down at Sordith. "Lord Sordith, of what race are your best miners?"

"Daezun or half-Daezun of course. They are hardier, have better vision below ground, and seem to know stone as if it were part of their being." Sordith answered factually.

Luthian nodded. "I see." He looked at the Council from the foot of the table. "We could kill them off, but we lose what they provide. They alone can handle bloodstones without draining them. They excel in blacksmithing, stone work and mining." He smacked his hand down on the table causing the lady next to him to jump and let out a small squeak of surprise.

Luthian put the other hand on her arm as if to reassure her. "Listen my dear friends, they are simple people with simple needs. I would prefer to have a measure of what they create in taxes than to kill them off so viciously." He sighed sadly. "Can we not let an ancient war rest?" He bowed his head, hiding his slight smirk at the murmurs of agreement. A sound of disgust brought Luthian's head up as Valmere finally rose.

"You're like a cat manoeuvring a mouse into its preferred position to pounce." Valmere looked around the table arms crossed with a look of disdain. Provocatively, he moved to Luthian's place near the head of the table. "He does not tell you that this mage he has found to divert the storm is none other than his own nephew." Valmere gestured at the High Minister's empty seat. "His motives are personal and not for the good of the city."

Luthian shook his head sadly. "Valmere... Valmere...Valmere ... always seeing plots where there are none." He looked back to the curious faces now turned to him. "I do not deny this powerful half-Daezun is my nephew. I could have gone against the whim of this Council by training him personally, as is my right as his uncle."

He moved slowly up the table, drawing the eyes of those across from him and noting the squirms of those he moved behind. "However, I wanted to proceed with Council discretion. It is not the boy's fault or mine that the gods have seen fit to give him this power, or that he is my brother's son." He put up his hands in defeat. "We can deny this testing and consign our own farmers to the miseries to come," - he looked at Valmere - "...or we can discontinue touting the banner of tradition and old ways till we are eventually so weak that one day the Daezun can overrun us because of our lack of foresight and wisdom." He moved back to the other side of his seat. He and Valmere now both stood at the head of the table.

The High Minister turned to Sordith and asked loudly to overpower the murmurs of dissension at the table. "How long could this city survive on our reserves if the farmers cannot replenish them this next growing season, **Lord** Sordith?" Luthian did not miss the disdain on many faces at his use of the man's title.

Sordith quietly calculated on his hands, his eyes closed. The mages fell silent as they waited for his answer. "Three turns maybe, with rationing." He considered additionally. "There is already dissension in the lower tiers at the privileges accorded the tiers above them. Such rationing would probably lead to civil strife in less than one." His eyes took on a hawk-like manner as he surveyed those staring at him. "I doubt I could get food past the second tier after two." His admission brought gasps of concern from the high level mages.

Luthian turned back to the Council. "Or we can train the Daezun who can pass at least a third tier test to help in this matter. I doubt whether more than a few will ask to test." Luthian laughed at the thought, his voice dripped with arrogance. "Even fewer will make a rank above the third tier. My nephew's exceptional bloodlines are not his fault." Luthian's chin lifted, unconsciously adding a touch of Guldalian pride.

Valmere leaned forward as he placed his hands on the table and looked into the eyes of the attentive council members. "Do you not see how this man plays with your emotions and your minds? He is a snake in our midst," his words held a hiss, emphasizing his disdain. "He might as well wear the robes of the priestess that he takes to his bed." Valmere rose up. "I challenge for the seat of High Minister before this vote is taken." He indicated the empty chair that sat between them.

Luthian purposefully looked crestfallen. "Are you so hungry for my seat that you would use a matter as crucial as the survival of our two races for your cause?" He put his hands out to his sides in a placating manner. "Valmere, you are hardly capable of removing me from office under the old laws." His edge of mockery was thick so that it would not be lost on anyone.

Luthian could not have hoped for a better outcome. Valmere was casting him the villain, but by demanding office, he had just made Luthian the victim. The High Minister glanced about the room as the heavy silence settled. Some would not look at him. Others looked at the two men in turn with wide, alarmed eyes. He took pleasure at the visible sweat on the brow of a few. Valmere finally found his voice.

"I have no doubt that I am quite capable of matching your skills. You have not fought in the testing ring in turns and, to be honest, I think you are a manipulative, power-seeking liar." Valmere spat to the side of the chair to emphasize his vehemence.

"See, now you have gone too far and challenged my personal honor." Luthian sighed with mock distress. "Will the Council allow this man to challenge for my seat and let the gods decide our fate?" He looked around as one by one the hands went up, every hand at the table except Sordith's.

"You disagree, Lord Sordith?" he asked casually.

"I'd rather not vote a man off to his death," Sordith drawled out as his eyes drifted to Valmere. "This one seems quite capable of ending his own life without any assistance from me." Sordith eyed the younger mage.

Luthian smiled. "Then we will adjourn this meeting of Council and reconvene in the testing ring. Let us say, two hours. I need to change, and well, I want to give Valmere time to put his affairs in order." He nodded to Valmere as if he had just afforded him the greatest respect. He inwardly found amusement at the flash of anger in the other mage's eyes.

Valmere snorted then turned and strode from the room. The council members rose with an excited clamor. It was not often that there was a power struggle of this magnitude on the council; many were excited at the prospect of seeing such deadly magic in action.

Once they were alone, Sordith rose and approached Luthian, goblet in hand. "That was really unfair you know," Sordith said, his voice subdued enough to prevent someone just outside the door from listening in on his words.

Luthian looked surprised, but more at the fact that Sordith had noticed than in doubt about what he was saying. "Why, whatever do you mean?" he asked innocently, his hand coming to his chest. "I was hardly the aggressor there," he pointed out, though his eyes twinkled with mischief.

Sordith grinned and shook his head. "No… you are right; that was much more like a spider twitching his web just right. That poor fly didn't have a chance." Sordith drained his goblet and set it on the table.

"Well then, I do hope you will join us to see me feast upon my hapless fly." Luthian countered.

"Oh, I wouldn't miss this for a long roll in bed with a beauty." Sordith grinned then turned for the door. "I just hope for your sake your fly is as inept as you seem to think he is." Sordith strode from the room.

Luthian slowly sat down and picked up his goblet. He answered the man though there was no one to hear. "So do I… Lord Sordith… So do I."

Chapter Twelve

Sordith stepped through the arches which defined the testing arena. He had never had the authority or rank to enter through the decorative arches before today. It was the centerpiece of the third tier. The seats and walls were all engraved with magical symbols, battles with dragons and other grand images. It had a strange metallic smell that reminded Sordith of a combination of blood and the odor of sizzling lightning in the sky. The dirt below him on the arena floor was dark. Rain had recently smoothed its surface.

The Trench Lord scanned the contents of the grounds. It was an interesting arrangement. The shape was an oval, and around the edges were various items representing the elements: a crackling wood fire, a pool of water, a tall gnarled tree, a pile of stones…

As a youth, he had been fascinated by the testing arena. Any child who failed in their initial testing mostly heard tales and whispers. Occasionally if one were quick and well-liked by city guardsman, you could sneak up to the fourth tier to get a view down into the arena.

Jostled by the growing crowd, he had to step to one side. He looked up as he remembered sitting on nearby rooftops just to get a glimpse of the higher mages taking their tier tests. It was not easy to get a view from the fourth tier. During such events the guards often let the children through, knowing what they were up to and not wishing to deny the urchins a glimpse of excitement. He smiled, remembering one old guard who used to wave anyone who looked to be under ten his way.

It was rare that mages dueled in the open. Most challenges for title were secretive matters held in manor houses or outside the city. It was a bold move for Valmere to take this challenge to a public forum. At the same time, it would force Luthian to fight honorably within his sphere regardless of what skills he may have learned from bloodstones.

The High Minister had appeared confident when the challenge was issued. Did he have any knowledge that Sordith had missed? He had read the information that Aorun had gathered on the current Council. Valmere was a skilled mage in the sphere of nature if rumors that he could command plant life at his whim were true. While Sordith had no love for Luthian, he did understand the man. Valmere was not one he hoped to see rise to the position of High Minister. The man was prone to noble and moral stands, and for a Trench Lord, a noble High Minister was not always an ideal situation. Sordith knew that such a man was not likely to look the other way when it might be in his best interests to do so.

Sordith found a seat in the back of the Council box, taking advantage of the slightly higher elevation. Much of the Council had already arrived and was seated. He took note as he looked them over one by one. Some seemed excited, anticipating what would most likely be an epic battle. A few seemed nervous, including the two stone mages assigned to help the Trench Lord reduce the open waste in the trench. However, the ones that garnered Sordith's deepest attention were the ones that seemed to be anticipating an end to Luthian.

Valmere entered first, his stride confident as he made his way to one end of the arena. A table was set at each end for the combating mages. He seemed to have no care for the crowds or anyone milling close by. His green robes were decorated in contrasting trim of gold and purple. Sordith noted the calm and centered manner that Valmere presented. He had learned this was quite typical of a mage aligned with nature.

Sordith returned his attention to the growing crowd. Word must have spread quickly throughout Silverport as the seating for the public denizens was swiftly filling. He smiled as his eyes scanned the rooftops from the tier above. Much as he had done as a child, the agile youth were starting to line the edges of the tiers above.

He heard a murmur and followed the gazes of the crowd. Luthian had entered the far end of the arena. Luthian was just as striking a figure as he removed his robes. He was dressed in black except for a red belt thick with pouches. His white hair had been pulled back to the base of his neck. The High Minister also seemed unfazed by the crowd. He laid his robe across the provided table and turned as the arena master entered.

The elderly gentleman could have passed for any grandparent sitting on his veranda, pipe in hand. His long graying hair wasn't bleached like that of many of the upper tier judges. Despite his apparent age, he moved with a confidence and grace that spoke of powers hidden beneath that gentle elderly facade.

Sordith had to admire the man who was willing to play the part of judge between these two powerful men. The judge motioned both men forward. Valmere's robe just seemed to slip off his shoulders as he complied. He wore nothing now except a black pair of pants and a dark green belt.

Valmere was much more striking in physical appearance, a fact confirmed by the soft feminine sighs in the crowd when his robe fell away. He was muscled and clearly spent a great deal of time in physical exercise as his chest and abdomen were well defined. This was in direct contrast to the slim lithe build of his opponent. Luthian was translucently pale and really needed to spend more time out in his gardens than with his books.

"Who do you think will win, Lord Sordith?" a female voice inquired softly.

Sordith stiffened slightly: he had clearly been paying very close attention if someone had been able get so close without him noticing. He glanced over swiftly. "I am unsure my Lady." He smiled at Lady Aldemar. "I was unaware you were on the Council?" He took in the sleeveless silver robes over a soft purple linen shirt. Her ribbons and jewelry matched the contrasting shirt with a pale flush of a similar hue. He looked about the box and noted her presence was accepted.

"I was once." Her voice held an edge of wistfulness. She smiled at Sordith. "I stepped down when Luthian rose to High Minister. I am still accorded some privileges, and this is one of them." Her air of authority and confidence was confirmation enough that she belonged in any space reserved for fifth tier mages.

She looked at the two men who now stood on either side of the arena master. "I can only pray that Valmere has not overestimated his abilities." She nodded towards the bare-chested mage. Whereas Luthian stood before the arena master with hands clasped behind him, Valmere stood with arms crossed, his defiance clearly written in his stance.

"I find many do not like our current High Minister. May I ask what your objection to him is?" Sordith asked softly. The tension of the quieting crowd was now palpable. He heard bets being placed on both men.

The lady gave Sordith a knowing glance and he had to admire the spark of confidence in her eyes as her face and body posture signaled her distrust of the new Trench Lord. "I think I shall keep that information to myself, for my own safety."

Lady Aldemar switched her attention to the proceedings below. "What is your opinion?" She hooked her hand through his arm as if they were casually standing at a ball and not witnessing the possible death of two of the ruling class of mages. Sordith had often imagined what it would be like to have such a woman on his arm.

"I prefer the evil I know to the one I do not," Sordith admitted. It was the safest response in the circumstances. Lady Aldemar may not be part of the Council, but she still held major sway over the city. She had helped Alador when he had been out of his wits, and had demanded no answers or favors. He preferred to remain in the woman's good graces. "However, my preference really has no bearing as I will be forced to work with whoever holds the office."

"A fair point sir." The lady smiled and nodded thoughtfully. Their conversation was interrupted as the arena master began to speak, his voice magically amplified. The crowd fell silent.

"The rules are as follows. The combatants may not leave the arena until one or other has yielded or been killed. The arena mages will maintain a shield keeping all spells within to protect spectators. Should either man yield, the other must stay his hand: for yielding brings shame enough."

Luthian's rising tone was as hard and cold as his gaze. "This affair goes far beyond place: it is a matter of honor. Permission to fight to the death and remove this traitorous dog once and for all." Luthian made sure everyone heard. "He has continued to speak falsely behind my back and to cast my family name into the mud. Now he seeks to usurp my position of authority. Let our battle end here once and for all."

All eyes were pinned on the three men in the center. Sordith could hear the flies buzzing in the cool afternoon sun as the crowd held its collective breath. The arena master looked inquiringly at Valmere, for both men had to agree to such terms.

Sordith noted that Valmere's returned look toward Luthian masked his shock. "I challenge you for the High Council seat, and you have the audacity to want to kill me for it? I was here for honor and better leadership, but it seems that you are here for blood and power." His loud answer dripped with his disdain. He spat into the dirt. "I accept the terms."

The uproar was immediate. People began booing, cheering and over it all, the sound of bets being raised filled the air. Sordith's smile was grim as the lady at his side let out of gasp of concern. He tapped her hand reassuringly with his own. "I am sure Lord Valmere would not have accepted if he did not have the confidence to win the day, m'lady." Though she flashed him a thankful look, Sordith did not see confidence in her brief smile or nod.

The crowd surged with excitement at the realization that the odds had been upped. The noise swept around the marble enclosure. This would be something told in taverns for years to come, Sordith thought. He did not have any doubt why Luthian had raised the stakes of this fight: taking the opportunity to remove an obvious enemy was a smart move. The question was… Sordith mused ... did Luthian have the means to kill this man?

The arena master held up his hands for silence. He did not continue until the noise had dropped to an acceptable level. "This duel will be to the death." He glanced from left to right, receiving a final nod of agreement from both men. "The shield will not fall until one or the other leaves this life."

The murmurs of the crowd swelled louder for a moment, and the man was forced to hold his hands up again to silence them. "Take your marks."

There were two circles set equidistant from the middle. Luthian turned his back boldly on the other mage and made his way to his end of the arena. His hands were still clasped behind him as if taking a leisurely stroll. Sordith shook his head and hoped that Luthian's appearance of unconcerned arrogance was feigned for his opponent's sake.

Valmere was more aggressive. Sordith could tell by the man's stance that he knew how to fight. The nature mage was already pulling things from his pouches though Sordith could not see what. He was not going to be able to help Luthian in this matter. The High Minister was on his own.

The Trench Lord's attention was distracted by four additional mages taking up positions on the edges of the arena. The Arena master took up a spot in the middle, and they raised their arms high and began to chant words that sounded like Owen singing after one too many brews for the night. Unlike when Owen was singing, however, a sizzle of power filled the air. It began as a point of light starting at the top, so strong that even Sordith with no magic at all could feel the pull.

A blue dome began to form, the spider-web-like tendrils of dark power arcing outward then down to the edges of the arena wall. They were filled in by the strange blue glow, creating a cage-like effect over the combatants. When it touched the wall in front of the four casting mages, it became translucent so that all could see the battle to be waged before them. Sordith watched the arena master toss a large ball of lightning on to it and nod his approval as the spell fizzled out.

"Begin!" The arena master's call to battle echoed ominously, as if the Lady of Death herself had bid them fight. The arena crowd stilled, a collective holding of breath. Sordith watched in amazement as Valmere's hands became covered with writhing and pulsing gauntlets of thorny vines. The right hand grew out an additional length of vine that grew into a pool of rope at his feet. Sordith realized it was a whip of sorts.

He glanced quickly at Luthian; the man seemed too casual for comfort. He was striding towards the center of the arena staring at his knife. The fire mage pulled something off it and flicked it to the right of Valmere, clearly disgusted that his knife had not been clean. Showing displeasure at a shoddy job should surely have been secondary in this situation. Sordith shook his head. At this rate, he would be breaking in a new High Minister before the day was done.

Luthian was apparently paying more attention than Sordith had given him credit for. The crowd gasped as Valmere sent the vine whip lashing out. Luthian flipped the dagger to the ground and a violet wall rose up just a foot in front of him before turning to orange, fiery flames. For a split second it seemed that the fire mage had reacted a moment too late: the vine snapped past the wall, barely missing him before the flames cut off the end.

Luthian moved to his left as the vine writhed and withered on the ground where he had just been standing. Sordith glanced over to where the pointless dagger lay flat upon the earth. The man had not even had the skill to bury the blade so that the handle was readily accessible to him. Sordith shook his head in genuine concern.

Valmere wasted no time. He snapped the damaged whip again, a trail of green ooze flickering about as it sprayed into the hungry flames. The flames turned from orange to a sickly pale green. Luthian fell back, coughing violently, his face covered by his arm. The ooze must have held some form of poison.

A flash of light caught Sordith's eye and he realized that whatever Luthian had thrown down off the dagger, was now glowing. He and the crowd gasped as it exploded loudly despite the magical buffer between audience and combatants. A circle of fire radiated out from where it had been, racing towards anything in its deadly path. The crowd cheered as both men had now struck blows.

The force of the explosion had pushed Valmere off-balance. He stumbled to the ground, rolling until he found his footing. Vines began to wrap around his chest in a protective shield. Sordith wondered how effective such a shield really was against fire. The explosion - or perhaps time - had dismantled Luthian's protective shield and Valmere rushed towards him, gauntlet swinging back for a deadly blow. Luthian pivoted to his right; gone now was the seeming casual indifference. Fire shot from his fingertips aimed at Valmere's deadly gauntlet.

Many were now on the edge of their seats. Sordith realized he had been holding his breath and noiselessly took in air. He darted a quick glance at the lady at his side; she seemed just as riveted as the rest of the crowd.

Luthian's aim had been true, forcing Valmere to toss the now flaming gauntlet off his hand. The nature mage moved around the ring, his back now to Sordith. Luthian was keeping pace with him, trying to keep him in front. Valmere had his free hand in his pouch while Luthian sprinkled a strange, sparkling powder from his.

Their manoeuvring put Luthian directly across from Sordith with Valmere between them. Sordith did not know about Valmere, but Luthian had eyes for no one but the man before him. The look of cold hatred in his eyes made Sordith's stomach turn.

Again, the whip snapped out. It lashed around the High Minister, and by the arching of Luthian's back, Sordith realized that it had hit home. He suspected that such a weapon was poisoned, for it would hardly have been of use in a fight to the death otherwise.

Despite the pain of the whip, Luthian did not hesitate. Four balls of fire streaked from his hand, one after the other. Valmere was agile enough to dodge the first three, but Luthian anticipated his final move, and the final sphere hit the nature mage full on the chest. The force was so strong that the man flew back and hit the ground. Truly a man of battle, he rolled and regained his feet, albeit more slowly this time. Small rivulets of blood oozed through the vines around his chest, which had not managed to absorb and withstand all the force. Either that, or the thorns had been driven into his own body.

Valmere struck out with the whip again, drawing Sordith's eyes back to Luthian, who looked to be attempting to take a potion. The High Minister managed to dodge the blow, but hit the ground hard. The vial went skittering just out of reach on the arena floor. Luthian was attempting to scramble for it when Valmere threw something at him. It seemed to be small pebbles or maybe seeds — it was too far to tell. Vines quickly emerged and one grabbed hold of Luthian's foot, stopping him just short of the vial.

It was then that a small swirling vortex of sparkling dust caught Sordith's eye. He quickly glanced back at the fight. More vines were forming around Luthian and Sordith's hands slipped reflexively to his swords.

"Easy Lord Sordith. To interfere is to be condemned to death yourself." The soft feminine hand on his arm squeezed gently as Lady Aldemar spoke.

Sordith nodded to her and found the vortex again before glancing back at the two men just in time to see Luthian erupt into flames. A gasp of alarm and some cheers sounded throughout the arena. Surely no man could withstand such burning flames upon his own body? Had Valmere used Luthian's own sphere against him?

Luthian's back was exposed, but for the moment … if he were alive… Valmere could not approach him. Sordith's eyes found the vortex as they settled over Luthian's discarded dagger. He watched wide-eyed as the dagger transformed into a lithe snake of fire. It was maybe two feet in length. It began to move towards the two men.

Looking back at the battle, he was just in time to see Luthian's body crawl towards the vial as the flames slowly flickered out. The fire mage took the stopper out with his teeth and downed the potion. He was willing to let the vines reform around him to get this potion, either because it gave him a distinct advantage, or because he needed it to be able to stay in the fight.

Luthian had been able to shift enough within the growing vines to send fire out again towards Valmere. Valmere had been rushing in with dagger in hand and the mage was too close to avoid the flames. Valmere's arm burst into flame and he staggered backwards.

As Valmere was pulling out a vial and dousing his arm, Sordith checked on the snake. It had made up three-quarters of the distance to the two men. What was its purpose? Luthian had come into the arena with it, so Sordith knew it had to be deadly.

"This is it!" Lady Aldemar said with excitement.

Sordith glanced back to see Valmere approaching the now helpless High Minister. It was unlikely that there was to be any escape from Luthian's rooted prison if the earlier body of fire had not totally freed the mage. The crowd held its breath as Valmere knelt close to slit Luthian's throat, his dagger poised…

Luthian, however, had not resigned himself to this fate so easily. A small flaming dragon seemed to erupt from his body, narrowly missing Valmere who dove to the side in surprise, his dagger skittering out of reach. He and the crowd watched wide-eyed as the dragon circled back around.

Sordith's eyes were riveted on the serpent. It was as if everything slowed down at that moment. Valmere grabbed hold of one of the vines, which began immediately to thicken and to pulse with a strange green light. The nature mage lunged at Luthian and pressed the vine across his throat, ignoring the small dragon diving towards him with flaming talons outstretched. Sordith watched the small flaming snake coil up and strike its fangs deep into Valmere's calf before swiftly coiling about his leg.

Valmere let go of the vine as his pants leg burst into flames. Swiftly he pulled a vial from his pouch and shook it over the flaming snake. The dragon disappeared, bursting into a shower of flaming stars; but the fire mage had managed to work one hand free, and he brought that hand up towards Valmere's back.

Even as the crowd yelled their warnings, fire shot from the High Minister's hand, catching Valmere in the rear. His pants went up in flames and Luthian did not stop, caressing the fire upward even as he fought against the choking vines.

Valmere fell forward as his whole body burst in flames. It appeared to Sordith as if the fire had spontaneously combusted within the nature mage rather than from the hand of flame Luthian held before him. He uttered one long, drawn-out scream of torment, the torturous moments etched into his face before fire finally filled his eyes and mouth. Valmere fell slowly forward into the dirt.

The crowd erupted into a cheer as Luthian just fell back against the ground, the vines slowly withering about him. The dome turned blue once more and regressed in the manner that it had formed: rising up, then snuffing out as it returned to the top.

Luthian was slow to haul himself to his feet. He glanced at what was left of the nature mage. The remnants of Valmere's clothes still burned and crackled while his corpse blackened, its flesh melting in the unnaturally intense heat.

Luthian moved to the man's body and waved his hand over the small snake. It dropped to the ground and disappeared, and Luthian picked up a dagger from the spot where the snake had been. He slipped it back into its sheath, the only sign of his own distress a small quivering of his hand that Sordith did not miss.

Sordith looked over at his companion. Lady Aldemar had both her hands over her mouth. Her eyes were filled with tears as she stared at the fallen corpse. Sordith took a gentle hand and guided her from the Councilors' Stand.

"I suggest you are not seen here, my lady. I suspect that things for many of you have just gone from bad to worse," Sordith warned. "If he can rid himself so publicly of its leader, how long before he turns on the group that stands against him?" Lady Aldemar just nodded and once clear of the booth, hurried off into the growing crowd now leaving.

Sordith made his way up the stream of exiting Lerdenians and found the ramp down to the arena. The guards held him up for a moment till he flashed his medallion of office. He slipped through the door and joined Luthian as he was leaning against the table where his robe still lay. Sordith took note of the three guards standing between the arena walls and Luthian.

"You know, if I am going to work with you, I would really appreciate if you didn't cut things that close in the future." Sordith crossed his arms and leaned against the arena wall. It was just tall enough to prevent him from sitting on it comfortably.

Luthian looked up wearily. His eyes were encircled with dark, haunting bruises, and his pupils were dull and flat, giving away how fully drained he was feeling. Despite his appearance, his talent for sarcasm had not deserted him. "I assure you, Trench Lord, I did not build that level of suspense merely for your amusement."

Sordith uncrossed his arms and scooped up the robe. His mannerisms were confident and flamboyant, but his words held hissed caution. "Best not to show any weakness at this point," he warned. He helped Luthian put the robe back on. It crossed his mind that he could rid Alador of their uncle right here and now; but by the time Luthian had buttoned up the red robe, Sordith had already discounted the idea.

Instead he pulled a small flask from his belt. "It burns going down, but it should give you enough of a boost to get you back to your manor." Sordith words were so low that even the guards nearby could not have caught what he said.

Luthian glanced at him appreciatively and took the vial. Downing its contents, he set it on the table, leaning on the surface with both hands. His eyes closed as he muttered. "Thank you, Sordith. If you would be so kind as to watch my back, my guards can see to my immediate surroundings."

This was as much an admission of weakness as any had probably ever heard from Luthian Guldalian. Sordith nodded. "Of course. We both know many that might wish to take advantage of a moment of weakness."

As he followed Luthian from the arena, the Trench Lord could not help but admire his uncle. The man had fought to the end where many would have resigned themselves to their fate. Sordith was torn. He suspected that he and his uncle were far more alike than he wished to admit.

Surely there was a way of mending things here where he would not be forced to choose between his newly found brother and his uncle. He kept his hands on his swords as they made their way out of the arena, his face set in a formidable expression. It was not for the benefit of any that might attempt to kill Luthian in that moment. No, it was at the familial predicament he found himself in.

Sordith could not help wondering if he had been better off as an orphan.

Chapter Thirteen

Alador slept deeply, his body and mind exhausted from the trials of the day before. What with his body being transformed into a dragon, the exertions that Renamaum had put it through, and the shock that his mind had withstood from the spell, he had very little left in reserve. His muscles complained at the exertion and his head pounded with thoughts that had been shoved into its depths

The tantalizing scent of food was what had drawn him from the depths of healing sleep. He sniffed and realized that his sense of smell had increased. Without opening his eyes, he knew that there was fresh bread, fruit, and sizzling meat. The meat was what had teased his senses, the smell of cooked flesh bringing him up from the last vestiges of sleep. He opened his eyes and shielded them from the light, the intensity only reminding him that his head was aching. He sat up and groaned as every muscle protested.

He looked around the room and smiled. Every detail was vivid, not just the color but the edges and angles seemed sharper. It was much as it had been when he had been in dragon form. His eyes were drawn to the table where the food had been spread out. A bath awaited him by the fire as well. He sensed the servant before he spotted him on the other side of his bed.

"Lord Henrick requested that you join him in his library as soon as you are bathed and well fed. He said a letter has come that needs your immediate attention." The servant looked about. "Can I get you anything else,

Lord Alador?" He moved forward to check the food table as he spoke.

Alador was frowning at the news of a letter. Who could have known he was here that would have sent written word? Did his uncle still have men noting his every move? He forced his legs over the side of the bed, grimacing as he answered the servant. "No, thank you. That will be all." The servant bowed and left quietly. Despite his body's screaming protest, he forced himself up and over to sit at the prepared table.

He started in on the meats first. Only after the sausages had been devoured did he turn his attention to the rest of the food. He moved to the bath and sank into the hot water before the small flickering fire, heaving a sigh at the soothing heat. The water eased some of the aches and quieted the distraction of his body's complaints.

Alador could have stayed there till the water cooled, but word of a letter was too distracting for him to remain long.. He swiftly dressed, donning a pair of leather breeches and a green tunic. He would don his guard's uniform after he had spoken to Henrick.

He considered for a moment. Did he want to call him Keensight or Henrick? Probably better to call him Henrick so that he did not give away the secret that the mage had guarded so closely. He chuckled as he pulled on his boots. The signs had all been there, but it was so far-fetched that it had never occurred to him. He secured his lengthening hair at the base of his neck and left the room.

He entered the library with a confident step. Henrick looked up from his sorting of books and nodded to his desk. "It is a letter from the Council. I do believe your test has been approved for I can think of no other reason for it to come with such formality." He went back to his sorting of what he would take with him and what was to be left behind.

Alador's heart began to race as he picked up the letter and saw the Council's seal. He was not sure if he were excited or fearful. Had Luthian been true to his word and arranged for him to test as any other Lerdenian mage? He tore open the envelope and as he read, a smile spread across his face. He was glad that his back was to Henrick as he worked to settle his excitement.

"You are right. I will be allowed to test." Alador exhaled the tight breath he had been holding. He did not need the training in the Blackguard now except in matters of the sword. Renamaum's knowledge of spellcasting was pulsing through him. He knew that he still needed to gain in magical strength, but knowing spells was no longer an issue. His mind raced over five or six spells that he had never considered. He put a hand to his head at the accompanied pulse of pain that resonated with the realization.

He turned, holding the letter out. "I have two weeks to prepare," he stated.

Henrick turned from his books and moved to Alador to take the letter. "Two weeks? Why, whatever will you do with the extra time?" The sarcasm was more prevalent than usual. Henrick's eyes held an edge of pride.

Alador grinned and his chin came up slightly. "I do have to regain strength and there are other matters to attend to." He plucked at his sleeve as if they were small unimportant things, then looked up at Henrick who was setting the letter on the desk. "I have a request," his voice was low and warm, but there was a firmness to it.

"Oh, I recognize that tone." Henrick chuckled and turned to face Alador. "My old friend is not completely gone, I fear." Henrick grinned at the surprise on Alador's face. "What is it that you wish?"

Alador paused for a moment wondering which of his words were not his own. "Take up residence outside Smallbrook." Henrick went to protest, but Alador had no intentions of giving him the opportunity. He continued forcefully, "My mother is at her happiest when you are around. Just, I don't want any half-dragon siblings." Alador looked at Henrick with hope flickering in his eyes. "She deserves to be happy. She has never taken a housemate, and I know Dorien is hoping to establish a home of his own if he hasn't already."

Henrick wrinkled his nose in distaste. "I am very fond of your mother and truly care for her." He crossed his arms defiantly. "However, I am not the type to set down roots."

"You were once," he reminded him. Alador took a deep breath. "You both deserve a little comfort, and I need Henrick more than I need Keensight right now."

"You do realize that I am the same being?" Henrick looked amused.

"Are you?" Alador challenged. "I think you have been playing a Lerdenian for so long you have become one." There was a haughty tone to his voice that surprised him. Alador continued rather more gently. "I don't really see Keensight prancing about a ball." He pressed on before Henrick could answer. "Your words and insights might be similar, but just as I hold Renamaum, you hold a piece of my father."

When Henrick turned and puffed up his chest, for a moment even Alador could not deny the similarity between man and dragon. "I will have you know that these mortal balls are no different from prancing around the skies and dancing in and out of clouds to impress one another: It is just a prelude to cart wheeling," Henrick claimed defensively. "Call it what you like, but such things are just another form of mating dance. I would point out that it is no different from the mating ritual your own people hold at the summer solstice," Henrick reminded him.

"When is the last time you mated as a dragon, my friend?" Alador asked, moving to look the man in the eyes.

"That is none of your damned business!" Henrick blustered.

"Perhaps not, but if I am right then you have not in some time. Yet if all the rumors are to be believed, you are quite prolific as Henrick." Alador casually picked up the letter and tucked into his tunic. "I suggest you think about that." His voice held a sharp edge of sarcasm.

"Damnation boy, I think I liked you better as a whining fledgling," Henrick puffed out.

"Too late. You and Renamaum took that choice from me." Alador did not sound angry, more amused at the older mage's expression. "Now you will have to sleep in the bed you both so painstakingly created." Alador put both hands out palm up and bowed to the man.

"Yes, well he is not here to put up with the end result," muttered Henrick clearly unhappy with that thought.

"As to similarities, you avoided the question. Will you go to Smallbrook?" Alador asked again. He moved to stand before his father.

"Yes," he growled out. He suddenly shook his finger in Alador's face. "But not to bond with your mother." Henrick was truly flustered now.

"I think a little courtship and companionship would now be the most I am asking." Alador grinned. "Like you usually do." He paused and stroked his chin. "You will just be there more often."

"I was thinking to still move about as an enchanter." Henrick frowned at Alador's words.

"Yes, well that won't work for long without giving away your use of travel spells as soon the roads become impassable for wagons." Alador poured himself a drink then turned back to look at Henrick. "Besides, I need you to ensure that there is nothing out of place in the coal room. I will be coming to see Dorien in a week. Oh, and also, I will need the amulet." He put out his hand for it.

Henrick rolled his eyes as reluctantly he pulled the talisman out of his tunic. "When did you suddenly become the one making all the decisions?" Henrick griped.

"About a day ago now, I would think." Alador grinned and took a sip. "Does it really hurt that much to give up one small treasure?"

Henrick pulled it up and off his neck. "It is hardly a small treasure." He gazed at it longingly. "I am sure Renamaum had similar feelings when he flew the skies and had his own hoard."

Searching his memory swiftly, Alador shook his head. "Renamaum's treasure is hidden away, and he only visited it when he had something new he wished to add."

Henrick' eyes glistened as they riveted to Alador. "Well now that he is gone, surely you can tell me where THAT is." He held out the talisman as if holding it hostage for the information.

Laughing, Alador swiftly snagged the amulet from where it dangled from Henrick's hands as he shook his head no. "I might have need of that treasure to secure our plans," he pointed out.

"I assure you that a dragon never has enough treasure in his pile." The man looked genuinely put out. He stomped around his desk, putting distance from the younger mage who had clearly gotten under his skin. "So lay out for me what is next," Henrick said, sitting down at his desk.

"Well, I need to arrange with Sordith to send supplies subversively to the Daezun. I need to warn my brother of what is to happen." Alador sighed. "I do not plan to tell him it is I that will be bringing the winter." Alador took a sip of the strong wine. "He would not understand."

"Good to know. I might have let that tidbit slip." Henrick nodded. "What of Mesiande?" There was a softening of Henrick's tone as he mentioned the middlin.

Despite being pleased he had not depreciated Mesiande for a change, Alador still frowned. "I fear I have erred beyond repair there," he admitted.

Henrick rolled his eyes. "Never think a cause hopeless till it is truly lost," Henrick pointed out. "Until she chooses a house mate other than yourself, the battle is not over." The mage tapped his fingers on the desk. "Actually, it is not lost till you are dead. After all, you could always just kill off such a rival." He folded his hands together across his chest and leaned back in the chair.

"I would not do that to her." Alador shook his head. "For such noble and wise beasts, you dragons can be rather animalistic."

"Well, the key was in the word." Henrick chuckled. "It might come with the word 'beast'." He shook his head as his fingers stilled. "I fear that I find mortals more bestial than the most ferocious other creature in all of Vesta."

Alador sat down in the chair to the side of Henrick's desk. He was truly curious as to how Henrick could think such a thing. "How so?"

Henrick leaned back in his chair folding his arms behind his head as he kicked his feet up onto the desk. "Well let me see... Despite the level of intelligence gifted them by the gods, mortals across the world kill for control. In the world of beasts, one might kill for a mate, territory, or food. There are many places in this world you have yet to see, but there you may find mortals fighting to the death about which God is best."

"Other races kill each other because someone in control told them that they had to. They leave their lands, their mates and everything that they would truly kill for… to kill for someone who takes no risk at all." Henrick shook his head in disbelief. "They kill to prove that a God or a view is supreme, yet they themselves may not even believe it." He tapped the arm of his chair to make his point.

Henrick closed his eyes and continued. "The Lerdenian war was about power and control. While the Daezun fought to protect the dragons and the old ways, the Lerdenians fought to control the isle, as well as to gain in power and glory. Mortals are pack animals. They may be righteous on their own, but they will bow to an alpha and commit atrocious acts that they would not do on their own." Henrick looked at him.

Alador considered Henrick's words. "Then why try to save them?" he asked curiously. He knew long ago that Keensight had sworn to see all Lerdenians burn for the crimes of the egg hunters.

"Because … while this is a pattern of behaviour for mortals overall," Henrick stared at his hand on the desk, "…I have learned that there are so many who are not known, who do not rise in power, and who are so much more than beasts. There are many who would be happy to remain on their lands, and with their families. They create wondrous things without the use of magic." Henrick's eyes held a faraway look. "Such beings deserve to exist. It is those who lead them into folly and cruelty that must pay the price." An angry edge filled Henrick's words. "Men like Luthian," he snarled.

"Luthian has good intentions from his point of view," Alador began.

Henrick rose angrily to his feet interrupting the younger mage. "Do not ever say so in my presence again." His eyes were cold and hard. "As you know Renamaum, I know Henrick. As you pointed out, I hold many of his memories. I know what that man did to his family, his brother, and I know of many terrible orders he has given that were carried out by others. Do not forget his use of people like Keelee who is not one of ill intent in and of herself." Henrick leaned across the desk. "I did not come this far… WE did not come this far" the older man continued. "To see you go soft on that vile snake now."

Alador froze in the chair at the vehemence in Henrick's tone and voice. "I did not mean he deserves to rule," he offered, trying to appease the man before him. "He sees himself as being able to heal the isle, even if he goes about it the wrong way." Alador felt some need to see the good in his uncle. His words were partially a surprise to his own ears.

"Trust me, Luthian sees only to himself, and what he desires. If he seeks to unite the isle, it is not for the good of anything but his plans," Henrick spat out. "Good done with evil intentions … is still a form of evil." Henrick's nails raked the varnish of the desk.

"And evil done in the name of good… people who die to see your cause come to fruition? What of them?" Alador rose up to make his point, setting his glass aside. He leaned equally across the desk so that the two men were eye to eye and his words were lowly spoken. "The reverse is not true. Evil done in the name of good is also still evil."

He rose up and crossed his arms. "Yet I will kill for this… greater good. In my mind, that makes me just as evil as Luthian." He glared at Henrick, waved a hand at himself and gestured toward the upper tiers. "The only difference between Luthian and me is that if I don't follow this path, I will die because of the geas placed upon me."

Henrick rose and moved about the desk. "That is not true. What you do… you do to save three races and an even greater number of lives." His voice dropped to one of genuine concern. He put a hand on Alador's arm. "What Luthian does is to save one and absorb the rest while he basks in glory."

"It does not lessen the blood on my hands, Father." Alador turned to face Henrick fully, brushing off the concerned hand. "It does not lessen the stain on my soul. I will soon cast a spell that may kill innocent beasts and children, and plunge half the isle into a period of darkness."

"It is a hard path. I never said it was not," Henrick said, and his eyes took on a haunted look.

"Yes, yes it is." Alador's eyes met Henrick's evenly. "Yet you and Renamaum miscalculated one small matter."

Henrick looked shocked for a moment as if that was not possible. He frowned and raised an eyebrow as he considered Alador's words. "I fail to see any miscalculations?"

"You gave a dragon's mind and power to a man who you just admitted was from a race that is one of the bloodiest on the isle." Alador's soft words held a hint of threat within them. He stepped close to Henrick.

"We gave it to a young man that we both believed had a sense of duty, love for his people, and in the long run, will always do the right thing even if it is not how we would do it." Henrick did not give ground; his eyes met Alador's with concern.

"You don't really know me. None of you really does. I have the power to disappear, and never look back at any of you." Alador let out a small growl as he stepped forward. "I could choose to do what is best for me." Alador could feel that strength pulsing through him as he spoke.

Henrick put a restraining hand on Alador's arm. "Boy, do not play with me. I know you better than you think."

"Do you? Has it ever occurred to you that maybe I want power? Or that, maybe I just want done with all of this?" Alador shrugged him off. "I feel like a piece on a King's board. Except, both sides want control of the piece. I am tired of being pushed about at everyone's whim."

"Of course you think those things. It would be stranger if you did not." Henrick replied firmly. He tapped Alador in the chest. "But it is your soul that is pure and good, Alador. It is the heart of the man or dragon that matters, not the fleeting thoughts of greed or selfishness."

"I hope you are right, Father. For if you are not... I assure you, you have given me the means to be far more of a tyrant than Luthian could hope to be." Alador turned and strode from the room, leaving his father and friend to think about the true seriousness of the situation. They were so busy trying to maneuver him, they had forgotten to consider what he might truly want.

Henrick watched him go and muttered softly. "I hope so too."

Alador smiled as he strode away. He had heard those words. It had been fun to give Henrick a bit of payback for making him climb the cliff to his cave. Maybe the conversation would make Henrick be a little more forthcoming in the future, and maybe he would quit trying to use him.

Alador intended to see the isle freed of Lerdenian cruelty, but not for Renamaum or Keensight. He would do it for the people that Henrick had spoken about earlier. The farmers, the poor, and those who were helpless to defend themselves deserved a life free of such tyranny.

Chapter Fourteen

Alador startled when Nemara's moist tongue teased his earlobe, interrupting his thoughts. He barely stilled his pull of power at her first words in his ear. "So did you and your father get to watch the duel?" She plopped down beside him in the dining hall after sliding her tray next to his.

Alador looked over and smiled. "Duel? What duel?"

"Do you two ever take your nose out of books? The whole city is talking about it, and you don't know anything?" Nemara rolled her eyes as she flipped her red hair back over her shoulder. "Your uncle was challenged for the seat of High Minister." She leaned over to continue in a breathy whisper. "I heard he almost lost too. But... he burned his challenger to a toasty piece of flesh. At least, that is what is being passed about." She began to dig into her food, not waiting for his response.

Alador was staring at her as he tried to digest what she had just cascaded over him in a torrent of words. Luthian had been challenged and nearly lost? "That would have been a fight to see for certain," he muttered more to himself than Nemara. He had missed a chance to see Luthian's skill in the use of magic.

He looked Nemara over and realized that her hair was a lighter red than he had first thought. This was the first time that he had seen it dry. Today it reminded him of fire bricks reflecting the dancing flames of a fireplace. He smiled at his own thoughts and realized she was speaking.

"...said he used some fiery dragon to win the duel." She glared at him. "Are you even listening to me?" Her copper eyes narrowed in irritation.

"I most certainly am." He gave her a winning smile hoping to distract her. "Luthian won the day with a flaming dragon," he repeated solemnly.

"Why don't they teach us spells like that?" grumbled Nemara as she continued to ladle food into her mouth.

"Honestly? I suspect that they are afraid we will use them to rebel," Alador mused, picking at his own meal. Her words had driven the desire to eat away.

Nemara looked about them and leaned over to continue in a whisper. "Speaking of which, I have seven so far. How many are we going to need?" She looked about to make sure no one was too close to them.

"Maybe ten. There is the matter of transportation," Alador replied. Even as the words left his lips, he realized that he could take them all. He would just have to figure out where so as to be certain the area was clear and large enough. Not only that, the memory of Renamaum's observations of the bloodmine were clear. Did dragons ever forget anything? He mused to himself as he realized that so many things had just gotten a lot simpler. Maybe he could complete the geas after all.

"Well, so far those I trust have been excited to see this through. It is like a chance to strike back for being abandoned for some, for the war for others; each has their own reasons." Nemara's voice trailed off.

Alador did not miss the shift in her demeanor. He waited for guard carrying a meal to pass them by before asking: "Are you sure revenge is what you really need?"

She did not hesitate. "Yes! Anything that makes your uncle bleed will make me happy. Nemara looked down at her tray, her hair obscuring her face. She was quiet for a long moment then looked over at him "I want my revenge." Her words came out a whispered hiss.

She pushed her tray back although it was still nearly full. "Meet after class today?" She smiled at him though it did not reach her eyes. Her body and tone shifted to cheerful as quickly as it had shifted to reflection and hate.

Alador frowned. "I am afraid I can't. I was given extra duties for being back late. I have to clean the ovens and help in the kitchens until midnight for the next week. All my half-days were canceled as well." He actually felt he had gotten off lightly. He had been late by almost a full day.

"Well shite," she said. Her tone held her surprise. She flashed him a sly look through her lashes. "I hope she was worth it."

Alador grinned. "First, I have hardly enough time for you. I doubt I will be fitting in any other female companions." He pushed his own tray back. "Secondly, I was with my father and yes…" He grew more serious. "…It was worth it."

"I suspect there is a tale that comes with that look." She turned to face him fully.

Alador shook his head. "Not much of one and what there is, I am afraid I will not tell you."

She leaned in next to his ear, her breath warm against his cheek. "Even if I am in your bed when you get out of the kitchens?"

He felt her fingers trail up his thigh suggestively. "I am afraid, Nemara, you have nothing you could offer that would make me part with this particular tale," he whispered back, despite his stirring interest.

Nemara squeezed his leg as she answered him. "That sounds like a challenge." She swung up and grabbed both their trays leaving him chuckling at the table.

He had no doubt that she would make good on her promise. She was rather an aggressive woman, and he was certain she could hold her own in any arena she chose, not least a bedroom. He sat for a moment watching the room as others milled about, ate or made their way to class. It was fuller now than when he had first arrived. It was time he got to class though. As he left the noisy room, his thoughts focused on the red-haired spitfire who had hinted she would be waiting in his bed.

****

His next class was on strategy, and it was the one that held the most interest for him lately. Renamaum's strategies that he could recall all involved assaults from above. While he might have the spells of the dragon, he did not have wings. He was going to have to learn to approach battle from a different angle than his benefactor.

Master Levielle was not a member of the Blackguard or the magi ruling class. The weathered man was a general in the standing army of Lerdenia. Despite his rank, he would not let them address him as anything other than Master. Though he was Lerdenian in nature, Alador could sense a high level of honor in the man. He had come to admire his straightforward approach to problems as well as his dry wit. Alador managed to slip into the classroom just as the bell sounded.

Master Levielle did not look up from his desk where he was writing. "Alador, it would seem you think this class an inconvenience." He looked up to skewer Alador with his intense gaze, the dark purple eyes narrowed. "You are the only one who continually slips in my room as the last chimes ring."

Alador sat back in his chair as he took in the man's words and the snickering of his classmates. He always found the man firm but fair. He did not have the usual look of most of their instructors. His dark brown hair was short enough to quickly fit within a helm. "I assure you, Master Levielle that is not the case. Why, my tardiness is but a reflection of the time I spend studying." He flashed a winning smile as the man's brow raised.

Master Levielle did not look amused in the slightest. "Then let us put that to the test." He rose and began to pace slowly through the room as he spoke. "Everyone pull out your slates. You may thank Alador for a sudden test of your studies."

Alador squirmed under the nasty looks he received from many of his classmates. He had pushed Master Levielle a bit too far apparently. He suspected that he was in for a tongue-lashing after class. He should not be late for the next few days, he thought.

Master Levielle stood formally before them all. He did not teach in his uniform, but rather adopted a simple pair of breeches and tunic, though they appeared fine in quality. He stood erect with his hands clasped behind. The instructor fired off questions, barely giving time for each student to write down their answers. The scratching of chalk on slate ticked out the hurried answers.

When he was done, Master Levielle strode forward and removed Alador's slate. He quickly read over the answers then glanced at Alador, his face unreadable. He turned and took the slate to the front of the room. Alador felt the triumphant gazes of those around him but he was not worried; he was fairly certain of his answers.

"Let us approach the first question. What are the most important considerations when drawing up an order of battle?" Levielle set Alador's slate on his desk then turned back to the rest of the class.

A woman near the front stood and gave the first answer. "The position of the sun, the amount of dust, and the direction of the wind."

"Very good." Levielle nodded then looked at Alador. "Why Alador?"

Alador stood and took a deep breath. "The position of the sun is necessary as it needs to be in the enemy's eyes and not our own. The same with dust. An army's eyes burning with dust cannot see and fight with distinction. The wind also applies to dust but in the cases of our own army, it is important to the mages. Poisons cast into the wind must not have a chance of blowing back into our own troops' faces." He looked at the man hopefully.

Master Levielle nodded and moved on to the next question. Each time, their instructor had Alador answer the reason behind the answer. It was not until the last question that Alador realized that the instructor had asked them out of order. "What is the most important element on the battlefield?" Though he asked the question generally, he was looking at Alador.

The man next to him stood and gave the answer that had been drilled into them over and over. "The order of mages is the most important element." He sat down with a smile. Levielle gave a nod of approval along with a tight smile.

He picked up Alador's slate and held it aloft. "That is the answer I have told you time and time again: the answer I have been instructed to give you." He looked at Alador's slate as if to reread it. "Yet, Alador, you wrote infantry. I am interested in your reasoning," his tone held no censor, just an edge of curiosity.

Alador slowly stood as he realized that he had indeed written infantry instead of the magi. He swiftly searched for a reason for his answer. It occurred to him that it had not been mages that had beaten back the dragons in the Great War. "I am sorry if my answer is disrespectful, Master Levielle." He put both hands out to his side. "But I feel strongly that my answer is the more correct one."

Much to his surprise, Master Levielle smiled. "Go on," he encouraged, waving the slate at Alador.

"Not all armies will have the number of mages that Lerdenia can supply in a time of war. In many ways, this does indeed give us an advantage. But, if the opposing army can field a large infantry then they merely need to wait until our mages are spent before they deploy their own advantages." Alador gained more confidence when he saw no disapproval in the General's face.

"An infantry is easier to raise, swifter to train and costs the coffers less slips to employ. They can be used on any terrain, and even in defense of dragons. Lerdenian mages did not deflect the dragons that sided with the Daezun; it was the infantry and their ballistae that cleared the air of their assaults." He stood waiting to see if he would be chastised for his answer.

"A fair argument to the mandated lessons on elements of an armed force." Levielle looked around at his students. He motioned Alador to sit down as he turned to make his way back to the front of the class. "A true strategist learns what has been taught, but has the mind and skills to take what he knows and expand on it. If every general fought exactly and only as they were taught, many battles would be strictly a case of who had more men. It is with such an analysis that a general can win the day with a smaller force." He nodded at Alador. This look of approval did not win Alador any favor from his classmates, if the wide-eyed disbelief and frowns about him were anything to go by.

Levielle set Alador's slate on his large desk again, then turned to address the whole class. "I am pleased that you have all been paying attention. Study your stratagem on battlefield formations for tomorrow." His eyes met Alador's. "All of you are dismissed … except for Alador. I wish to speak with you about your continued absences and tardiness." He turned and moved around his desk.

Collective murmurs of pleasure at his being held after assaulted Alador's ears as he made his way to the front of the class. He stood silently as the room cleared.

Master Levielle did not speak nor look up at Alador from where he now sat at his desk until the rest of the room had emptied. "Let me make this clear to you, guardsman. I don't give one slip as to who your family is or what your skill is." He looked up at Alador sternly as he put down his quill. "I don't care what designs your uncle has, or what party your father wants you to attend. You will not miss another of my classes."

Alador shifted uncomfortably. That would be nearly impossible to do as his uncle's request for a hard Daezun winter would definitely overlap with Master Levielle's classes. In addition, the assessment of his two relatives was uncomfortably accurate. "I apologize…"

The instructor raised a hand to silence the young mage before he continued. "I am also aware you are a pawn in a game you did not design." Master Levielle shook his head sadly. "You are a smart lad. I suspect you will play a huge part in the future. I would rather you knew how to win on every field and not just in Lerdenian politics."

He leaned back forward and handed Alador the paper he had been writing on. "Therefore, every time you miss a class, you will seek me out for private instruction at my home." He nodded to the missive. "That will give you leave to attend me in the evenings."

Alador looked at the note in his hand with disbelief. This was his uncle's general. What game was the man playing? He noted the man's fourth tier address. It was a high place for one not with magic. He met Levielle's even gaze and could not discern any deception. "Thank you, Master Levielle. I will be sure to attend you."

"Very good, then you are dismissed." His instructor nodded towards the door.

Alador turned to leave in a bit of a daze, having prepared himself for a full lecture on timeliness. Levielle's voice called him back.

"Guardsman..."

The mage turned to look at the general who was now standing. "Yes, Master Levielle?"

"Don't forget your slate."

Chapter Fifteen

Luthian was making his way through a pile of correspondence: one mind-numbing letter after another. He had put off much of this work while he recovered his strength from the duel. Now, it lay in an oppressive heap of mundane boredom.

Keeping the city ministers around the country of Lerdenia in line and productive took a lot of political maneuvering. It was the one aspect of his position that he did not like. While he technically ruled over all of Lerdenia, the system allowed for so much debate that often issues stalled without resolution. There were mages that seemed to take excessive pleasure in hearing their own voice as they rambled on about issues they did not want to pass.

Luthian had overall responsibility for Silverport, the capital of the Lerdenia, as well as liaising on the full and new moon with the other cities' high ministers. He was currently reading through a letter requesting that additional supplies be sent north to High Plains Spire. It was a city with four tiers that provided trade in many gems and metals. It seemed that word of the impending difficult winter had already made its way to that Council's ears.

A knock sounded at his door. He did not look up, merely motioning for his guard to let the person in. Alador should be here this evening so he was expecting such an interruption. He did not look up till he heard the footsteps of his guest. He raised his eyes when there was a throaty cough. He noticed the tight clothing before he saw the face. It was not Alador standing before him, but Severent, his Master of Knowledge.

Severent had been sent to Smallbrook to discern more about Alador's early life and those that might be of use in controlling his nephew. Slowly he laid the letter that he had been reading upon his desk.

"You were gone for some time." Luthian sat back in his chair, glaring at the man. His eyes roved over the thin figure clothed in drab grays that stood before him. The man's hair was a dull color of red, almost an orange. He was pock-faced and his magical skills were limited, but what he did have seemed to allow him to move unnoticed through busy halls. This ability had drawn Luthian's attention long before he was made minister. Severent had worked for him since he was a fourth tier mage.

The man bowed low before answering. "Daezun are a suspicious people." His rough voice grated on the High Minister's sensibilities. "It took a great deal of time and effort to get the information that you were seeking." He pulled a rolled piece of parchment from his vest. "I believe this report contains everything you were looking for from the village of Smallbrook." Severent handed the scroll across the desk.

"First things first, did my nephew really kill a man?" Luthian curiously asked as he leaned forward to take the scroll. He did not trust anything that Henrick had told him at this point.

"Indeed, knifed an older middlin over a girl." Severent clasped his hands behind him after he handed over the scroll. He stood before Luthian, his body posture stiff. Luthian noted the dust of flight was still on the man's clothing.

"A girl, you say?" Luthian smiled. Men only killed over women when there was an emotional attachment;

for some men it was a matter of pride or possession while others spoke of love. Alador did not seem the type to fight for pride. He waved the scroll as he asked, "Any words as to her connection to my nephew?"

"They were to be housemates when she became eligible for their barbaric circle." Severent's disgust was evident even before he spat out the word 'barbaric'. "Of all the things in your report, I think that will be the most useful."

Luthian tapped the scroll against his lips. "Pretty girl?"

"By Daezun standards," the lithe man answered. "Too stocky and willful for my tastes." He wrinkled his nose in obvious distaste.

"Perhaps I should send her an invitation to come for a visit?" The sly look faded as he unrolled the scroll. The edges of Luthian's mouth twitched upwards at this thought. The report was thorough, but then he had expected nothing less. There was a sketch of the village and the houses with occupants of interest were marked. In addition, there was a brief paragraph on all of Alador's family and friends. The boy had a large family, which would be of use as well. He tossed the scroll down for a more in-depth reading later.

Luthian reached into a drawer and pulled out a small bag of slips. "Well done. You deserve a break." He tossed it to Severent who caught it deftly. "Return to me in three days as I will have another task for you."

Severent bowed low. "As my Lord commands." When he rose, he turned on his heel and left the room. His boots made hardly any sound as he crossed the floor.

Luthian watched him till he was out the door before returning his attention to the report. Alador had negotiated to spare this small village from the brunt of

Luthian's plans. While the family aspect had been obvious, the girl was the key. Alador could be maneuvered through his affections for those in this village. It had been well worth the wait. He paid special attention to the words describing this Mesiande and what information his man had been able to dig up.

Luthian unrolled the last of the scroll and was surprised to see a detailed sketch of the girl. Severent had captured her daydreaming with a faraway expression in her eyes. There was a strange sadness in them as well. Luthian stared at the Daezun female's likeness. He could see what Alador found appealing in the girl's face. Her braided hair only accentuated her cheekbones. It was too bad that she was from such simple pagan blood. Though Alador was a half-breed, Luthian had plans for his nephew's bonding that didn't involve some village tart. He rolled up the scroll and slid it into a drawer of his desk.

Speaking of his nephew, the boy should have been here by now. He rose up and moved to the bell pull. Dinner was most likely on the table, and Luthian was not one to be kept waiting.

A servant slipped through the door, eyeing the two stoic guards with concern. "Y-yes Lord Guldalian?"

"Send a runner to the caverns and find out what is keeping my nephew," commanded the High Minister. "Have him report to the dining room."

"The runner or your nephew?" asked the young man.

Luthian's eyes narrowed. "Whichever one gets here first," he stated coldly.

The servant nodded and hurried from the room. Luthian returned to the wine table and poured himself a glass before proceeding to the dining room. The two guards fell in behind him. Luthian took no note of their watchful presence. He had come to expect such positioning since becoming High Minister of Lerdenia.

He was halfway through his dinner when the young boy who had been sent to the caverns returned. The servant laid a small piece of parchment on the table beside Luthian then moved back keeping his head down in a manner that suggested that Luthian would not be pleased. Luthian raised a brow as he reached over for the note. Surely the boy had not refused to attend him on his half day as was their custom? He noted the High Master's seal and broke it carefully, unfolding the short note.

Luthian did not notice the stilling of the serving women around him as he hissed and crumpled up the note. He rose so suddenly from his chair that one of the women squeaked as the chair went over and slid a short distance across the floor. "Boy, fetch me my cloak." His words were so low in deadly tone that only the stillness of the room allowed him to be heard.

The young servant turned and ran. Luthian turned to one of the two men by the door. "Fetch four others, we are going calling upon the High Master of the Blackguard," he sneered.

He turned and headed for the front of the hall. How dare the High Master deny him his nephew? What was worse was that the reason given had been that Alador had not returned to his duties and classes from his last half day. That would have been the day that Henrick left the city. The boy had expressed hatred and contempt for his father, and yet had not returned from his appointed half-day with the man. Luthian's temper was so apparent that as he moved, others stepped far out of his way and became immobile, as if remaining unnoticed might save them from the ire that was written on his face.

He swept his cloak from the servant's trembling hands as he passed through the door. Guards fell into step with him as he headed for the stairs down to the fifth tier. Today, he thought, today it would be made clear who was in charge.

As Luthian moved swiftly through the city, a silence descended in front of him and a murmur grew behind him. He had no eyes for the populace as he was deep in his own thoughts and anger. He was not sure what he was going to do yet, but he planned to make it very evident that such matters were not to occur again.

The High Minister swept into the caverns much as the tides enter the caves below the city: a torrent of movement and force. He slammed open the door of the High Master's office and the young man attending him jumped to his feet from his desk. Two more men were guarding the High Master's inner door. Men who he knew had seen him when he used to come visit the caverns regularly.

"Leave us," he commanded of the two men who guarded the High Master. They looked at each other with uncertainty then fled. Two of Luthian's guards took their place.

Luthian turned to the boy behind the desk of this outer office. "Fetch the High Master's second. He will be needed shortly." His cold tones only created a wider look of fear in the young guard who then fled to do as he was told.

Luthian turned and eyed the door that stood between him and his prey. He hit it with a blast of commanded air so that it hit the wall behind it so hard that the wood split.

The High Master jumped to his feet. He swallowed hard before speaking; his eyes were wide with surprise. "M-my Lord. We were not expecting you."

Luthian turned and beckoned the door to close and it again slammed shut against the frame, dust fell from the nearby support timbers. He turned slowly to face the High Master again. "You dare to keep my nephew from me and do not have the nerve to deliver those words yourself!" The tone of accusation lay like frigid ice between them as their eyes locked.

Neither man moved for a long moment, then the High Master drew himself up and spoke. "You instructed he was to be treated like any other man of the Blackguard." The man's voice held an edge of frustration.

Luthian moved to the desk and leaned on it so that he was closer to the man. "Do you remember anywhere in those instructions that I was to be denied his presence?" His hissed words darted between them.

"Well no, but it was what would be done to any other man who was absent without permission," the man crossed his arms with his own anger.

"He is not just any other man, now is he?" Luthian rose picking up a pen knife to twirl it lightly in his fingers. He recognized the handle as dragon's bone. It was a finely made tool. "I find your incompetence has finally reached a point I can no longer tolerate." He flipped the wood knife in his hand as if admiring the handle.

The High Master's tone took on a dangerous edge of his own. "Lord Guldalian, please allow me to explain the larger picture." The High Master's hand wandered down towards his sword.

It was the move Luthian had been waiting for; he smiled as his hand moved subtly over the pen knife. He whispered the spell: "wiap ekess wer sauriv." The High Master's sword was pulled, the sword clearing the sheath as the spell ended. The pen knife jerked and flew from

Luthian's hand. It embedded deeply into the High Master's eye.

The man had swung back to take a swing at Luthian, but the sword dropped from his hand as he fell to his knees howling. Luthian did not hesitate. Fire flew from his hands and he burned the man alive where he knelt. When he stopped, the burned corpse fell over slowly, the hands still clutched its face.

"Pity," Luthian began, staring down at the body for a long moment and taking in the penknife protruding between the man's fingers, "…I rather liked that knife." He turned on his heel and strode back to the door. He opened it calmly and stepped through, being careful to shut the door behind him.

The boy from the desk was all but cowering over in the corner and at the same time, trying to stand at attention. There was a proud, older man now standing with one of Luthian's guards. Luthian strode to him, expecting it to be the High Master's second.

"You are the high master's second?" Luthian asked. The edge of venom was missed by no one in the room.

"Yes, Lord Guldalian." The man dipped his head in acknowledgment.

"Your name?" Luthian's eyes were hard as he met the new High Master's gaze.

"Reynel Bariton, High Minister." The man bowed low. He had the poise of a man who had seen battle before and knew how to fight. His hand remained on his sword despite the presence of the guards attending Luthian.

"Master Bariton, you are High Master now." Luthian stepped very close to the new High Master. "Let me make this very clear. My nephew is to be treated as any other guard in these halls except in one particular." Luthian held up one finger. "He is never to be kept from me, again." Luthian leaned in to speak into the man's ear. "Are we clear?"

Master Bariton did not turn his head to meet Luthian's gaze. There was a hardness in his words though his tone remained respectful. "Very clear," he answered back just as quietly.

Luthian stepped back and smiled. "Well, that takes care of that small matter." He brushed his hands as if removing dirt from them. "I will borrow your young attendant for a short time as I would like to see my nephew. It has been some time since I have been in the halls." He glanced at the terrified lad and back to Bariton. "That will not be a problem, will it?" he asked, as if he had not just killed a man just minutes before. His face seemed congenial.

"The halls were opened by your will, and are therefore yours to wander through, my lord." Bariton pointed to the lad. "It is after dinner. Take the High Minister to the blue halls. If he isn't there, then someone there should know where he is this evening."

"Y-yes High Master." The young man hurried to the door and looked back. "Right this way your Lordship."

Luthian moved to follow but then hesitated and turned back to Bariton. "I fear I have made a mess of your new office. You may need to air it out for a day or two. I do apologize." There was no sincerity in his words. Luthian turned to follow the nervous young guard through the maze of the Blackguard caverns.

Chapter Sixteen

Alador and Nemara had carved some time out and met up in his cell. They were sitting on the bed and Alador was laying out the terrain around the bloodmine. Nemara had been fairly successful during her classes on mapping and between the two of them, with his descriptions and her skill, they had managed a fair sketch of the area.

"If you have never been there, how did you get such detail?" she asked. She made a correction on one side where he had pointed out a conflict between map and memory.

"I flew over that mine many times." Alador inwardly cursed as he realized his error even before her anticipated question.

At first, Nemara just nodded but then the truth of his words sunk in. Her eyes narrowed as she searched his face. "How did you get a lexital to fly that close to dragons?" There was a hint of suspicion in her tone. "Don't tell me one of your dragon friends flew you there because, well, no one has ever managed to ride a dragon in all of history."

Alador took a deep breath as he rubbed the bridge of his nose. Sometimes Renamaum's memories were so much his own that he did not even think about his words before they escaped his lips. "I won't lie to you, but I can't tell you how I managed to get this information."

Silence descended between them as she lightly sketched in the last detail that they had discussed. Alador could sense her suspicion and regretted that he could not tell her how he knew so well the outlay of the compound.

Her hand paused in her sketching. "Can't or won't?" she asked, not looking up at him.

Alador reached over and took her free hand. "A bit of both, Nemara. Besides, it is doubtful you would believe me anyway." Alador offered her a small smile when she finally looked at him. Alador was beginning to understand how Keensight had felt keeping his secret for so many years.

Her mouth opened as if she had been about to press the matter when a strong knock startled them both. Nemara looked at the door and whispered quickly. "Were you expecting anyone?"

Alador shook his head no. Nemara swiftly messed up her hair and was unlacing the top of her vest as Alador got up to answer the door. She swiftly laid down, shoving the map and supplies between the wall and the bed.

Seeing her quick thinking, he swiftly did the same to his tunic shirt. Alador opened the door as the knock rapped loudly again. He stood in utter surprise as he realized that it was Luthian that stood there. "U-uncle," he stammered. He stood shocked to see his uncle in the caverns. He swiftly hoped that Nemara could hide her hatred of the High Minister.

Luthian strode by Alador and into the small room. As he turned to face Alador, he caught sight of Nemara stretched out on his bed.

Nemara sat up wide-eyed from where she had stretched out. "Milord" Nemara acknowledged. She began tying the swiftly pulled laces.

Luthian's eyes were hard as his gaze returned to Alador. "So this is what you would rather do than attend your lessons with me?" The anger and disappointment were evident on the older mage's face and in his tone.

Alador's eyes flew to Nemara then snapped back to Luthian. "I assure you, Uncle, had I been allowed to leave the caverns then you would have had my full attentions." Alador began tucking in his tunic as if embarrassed.

Luthian turned to Nemara. "If you will excuse us, guardswoman, I would have words with my nephew." His tone was firm and left no argument. His face was hard, and his mouth was in a straight line of displeasure.

Nemara gracefully slid off the bed. "Of course, High Minister, I would not want to interfere in matters of family." Her tone was husky and her movements subtle with a hint of sexuality as she got off the bed and moved to where Alador was still standing by the open door. Alador had to give her credit; she was convincing.

She reached up and snaked one arm around Alador's neck, pulling his head down for a long and intensely intoxicating kiss. She placed her mouth next to his ear as she nibbled on his earlobe before whispering, "I will come back later." She made her promise just loud enough for Luthian to hear. As her eyes met Alador's, he could see the warning in them.

"I am sure this matter with my Uncle will not take long. I will see you soon," he promised with a worried smile. He shut the door behind her then turned to face Luthian. He did not glance at the bed for fear of giving away that there was more to Nemara than a mere tryst.

Before Alador could react or even prepare, he found himself pinned to the door, Luthian's hand on his throat. Alador's hands grasped his uncle's in reflexive surprise. "What were you doing to earn yourself this loss of privileges, Nephew?" Luthian's voice was cold and his eyes hard as they met Alador's.

The young mage's first reaction had been a pull of magic and he could feel the thrill of power dancing between his fingertips. He swallowed hard, not in fear but to force that urge down. He did his best to look contrite, but fear was pulsing through him.

"I drank far too much the night before; I cannot even tell you all that occurred. I woke late in the day," he explained, stumbling through his explanation.

"Given your firmly-stated distaste for your father's company, I find it hard to believe that you would choose to spend the evening drinking with him," Luthian pressed. His eyes sought Alador's and the bitterness and rage seemed to pulse through his fingers to Alador's neck.

Alador felt the pressure on his ability to breathe. Anger boiled deep within him, and he blinked a few times to try to contain it. He could not keep the first snaps of power from filling his hands. He was still trying to free himself and the power danced up Luthian's arm a short distance. "He is still my father," he stated. "I might never see him again."

At the first surge of power, Luthian let go of him, and Alador sagged a bit against the door in relief. He coughed and rubbed his neck; half bent with a wave of dizziness. He watched as his uncle turned away looking about his small room.

"I fail to understand this sentiment you have towards blood. Either a man is with you…" Luthian turned around to look at Alador. "...Or he is against you. I wonder sometimes which is the case with you." Luthian clasped his hands behind his back.

"I assure you, Uncle, some of the wine was to dull the senses as my father went on and on at how he was being wronged." Alador rubbed his throat as he stood straight once more. "That man can talk the fleas off a prang."

"Yes, yes he can." Luthian twitched with a hint of a smile. As quick as the smile had come, it left in the next shift in conversation. "You did get the missive on your testing before you drank yourself into a stupor?"

"I did," Alador confirmed. "And I thank you for the opportunity." He managed to force himself upright. He needed to pander to his uncle as best he could right now, or Luthian might start digging.

"As soon as you pass your test, you will move into the manor your father held. That is… if you can pass the test." Luthian stroked his chin as he thought. "As soon as both of those tasks are complete, you will start the winter we spoke of so that this plan can begin to move."

"Of course, Uncle. I had intended to go the next half day I would have spent with Henrick, but if you wish me to wait…" He let the words fall away. He let the question hang between them in awkward silence.

"Right now, you need to be studying to pass your tier test. This must be your first priority." Luthian insisted. "Get your things, we are returning to the top tier." He moved to Alador's desk, picking up a book to examine it. His manner now settled with a decision made.

"But the evening is nearly over," Alador said. "By the time we get there, won't it be time to seek our pillows?"

"Oh, you will not be sleeping tonight," Luthian calmly stated. "You lost that right two times over." He put one finger up. "First, drinking to the point of no memory is dangerous for any mage." He added a second finger. "Secondly, instead of contritely studying, I find you in the arms of a woman." Luthian folded his arms as firmly as any father. "Now get your things before I roast your arse right here." His tone brooked no argument from the younger mage.

Alador inwardly smiled, knowing that Luthian might have a bit harder time with that now. However, he also wasn't ready to reveal the extent of his power now that Renamaum was a part of him. "Yes Uncle." He swiftly gathered up a few things.

He suddenly remembered his penance from the High Master. "What of my duty in the kitchens?" He glanced over as he packed.

"I am sure that those have been...reassigned." Luthian moved to the door to wait for Alador to finish gathering his things. "Also, change your clothes," Luthian insisted with disgust. "I am not traveling through the city with my supposed heir without him properly attired."

Alador nodded and formed a picture of simple but well-made robes and let the spell snake around him. Satisfied he had what he needed, he followed his uncle out of the halls. He did not miss the snickering of some of his peers or the widened expression of others. He did not see Nemara as they left, but he was fairly certain that she would learn of the scene.

Alador knew he was going to hear about this for weeks. He smiled at his uncle's back. Too bad he could not thank his uncle for cementing his image as a whipped dog following in his uncle's shadow. They were joined by Luthian's guards as they moved out of the caverns.

The trip to the top of the tiers transpired in silence. The streets were quieter on the upper tiers. As the sun went down, the third tier always grew louder while the fourth and fifth became more settled. Their boots snapped out a cadence that echoed on the upper tiers, drawing more eyes. Alador sighed and kept his head down as if properly defeated. He would be glad of the day when he would not have to be quite so subservient.

When they reached the top, Alador was surprised that Luthian headed for the gardens rather than into the manor house. The broad flat top of the tiers made for a perfect garden in the spring and fall. Now, it was wind-swept and barren with the start of the winter winds. Luthian stopped at the entrance to the expansive garden and whispered to one of the guards who merely nodded and hurried off.

"Uncle, what is it we are doing tonight?" he asked, his confusion evident.

"Practicing the deflection of spells." Luthian stated as he strode into the gardens. He led the way to a wide clearing near the gates.

Alador sighed softly. He did not really want his uncle to know how quickly he was excelling, and at the same time, he could no longer pretend to be inadequate as he would be casting such a strong weather spell for his uncle. This was going to be a hard balance to keep. Alador had thought lying was the hardest thing when he had first met his uncle; now, it was knowing when to lie and when to be truthful.

"Place your things on the side and disrobe." Luthian instructed as he pointed over to a sheltered bench on the edge.

"Disrobe?" Alador looked at his uncle with genuine concern.

"You must learn to fight no matter the distraction." Luthian stated. "A man feels vulnerable in a state of undress. As you seem to have taken after your father in regards to his interactions with females." The sarcasm from his uncle dropped along every word. Luthian folded his arms confidently.

"It is likely a smart fourth tier mage would just assassinate you when you are distracted in a state of undress." Luthian's displeasure with Alador was clear.

"Uncle, I fail to see why you are upset." Alador set his rucksack down on the bench. "When we first met you gave me a bed slave. I know you have women in your bed." He pulled off the robe and laid it across the rucksack. The wind was cold against his bare chest.

"Yes, I do take my pleasure as any man. But never," Luthian drawled out slowly," ... never when I have other matters of priority to address." Luthian's final words were growled out.

"So you plan to punish me because I took a woman to my bed?" Alador's face reddened with a combination of surprise, embarrassment and anger.

"I prefer thinking of it as…" - he smiled before continuing - "...educating you." Luthian dropped his own cloak onto the bench and pulled off his robe. As usual, he was dressed in black pants and a black tunic beneath his robes.

Alador breath caught as he realized that Luthian was going to take part in this practice. Working with his uncle when he was calm and focused was hard enough, he had no doubt that working on deflection with his uncle in an angered state was going to be harder. He stood in just a pair of breeches, the wind already reddening his exposed skin. He was thankful that it was not blowing harder. He looked at his uncle and hoped it would be enough.

"Pants and shoes as well," Luthian commanded waving his hands up and down the line of Alador's body. He strode away and moved around the clearing. Torches lit around the circle as he brought fire to the first one.

Alador realized that Luthian had used this clearing before tonight by the way it was lit and the comfort

Luthian showed in his movements. It just did not have tables of food and wine, music or women. He sat down and pulled off his boots then removed his pants. Standing in nothing but his under garment, he hoped his uncle would let him keep that.

Luthian returned to him once the last torch had flared to life. "Good, take the opposite end," The man was all business tonight.

Alador took the first step and cursed. He picked up his foot to find three spiked thorns attached to his feet. He had not wandered barefoot since leaving Smallbrook so long ago. The younger mage pulled them out and stood up, shaking the foot to ease the sting. He took in his surroundings. Luthian was putting him downwind. The cold wind was cutting in the high, cold air of the top tier. There were no leaves on the trees to blunt the knifing effect and he shivered. Before absorbing the bloodstone, he would never have been able to consider fighting at such a disadvantage. Fortunately, while he was aware of the cold, it was not debilitating. The thorns interspersed into the grass were another matter.

"Uncle, surely I can keep my boots?" He looked back at Luthian.

Luthian shook his head as if saddened at the lack of wisdom of his pupil. "A man in war may find himself awakened in his tent. His attacker is not going to sit calmly by while his prey puts on his boots." Luthian looked evenly at Alador. "You must be able to protect yourself regardless of the distractions or discomfort."

Alador wanted to argue that point, but there was some wisdom in his uncle's words. He picked his way to the other end of the clearing muttering curses and turned to face his uncle. He had barely turned when a ball of fire hit his chest knocking him backwards. It had felt like a heavy metal fist and burned with a sharp intensity. He lay on the ground gasping for air.

Luthian was moving to his right. "Do not expect me to play fair, boy. Your enemies will not."

Alador pulled water to cool the obvious round burn on his chest. His uncle was tense and his eyes darted over Alador with assessing precision. The younger mage's eyes narrowed as he realized that his uncle no longer cared if he were injured. He moved to his right as well, attempting to keep his uncle in front of him. He did not dare stop to pull out the piercing thorns that dug into his tender feet. This time when the fireball flew from his uncle's hand, he was able to form a wedge of power, letting the fire slide by him. The shield flashed when the fire first hit it, letting his uncle see what deflection he had used. The ball of fire exploded on the ground behind him.

His eyes narrowed as he eyed his uncle. There was not a part of him that did not want to unleash all his anger on the man. Now was not the time; he was going to have to wait, but that did not mean he could not defend himself. He watched as Luthian nodded and prepared another spell.

This time several arrows of fire formed over Luthian's head and went speeding towards Alador. He swiftly raised a wall of water, effectively putting out each of the arrows. He let the power go when the last arrow sizzled and fell at his feet. The wall of water splashed onto the ground, dousing him with welcomed relief as well.

Alador was hit in the chest by a fireball that he had never seen coming. He had let the wall down too soon. He flew backwards again, and hit the ground hard. The thorns dug into his back as he slid along the grass. The burning pain drew a feral growl from his throat as he forced himself to roll up before Luthian could fire another spell.

Luthian shook his head with disappointment. "A smart mage knows what his opponent will do and waits for him to drop his defenses." Luthian counseled. "Do not be predictable." He spoke as one would when teaching a small one.

Alador realized that though he had the knowledge to defend himself, he did not have the skill. As the evening turned into night, Luthian literally burned the lesson into him repeatedly. Every time he would think he had it figured out, Luthian would change his attack, and Alador found he could not predict his uncle's next move. By the time Luthian chose to end the lesson, only Alador's face was free from some level of burn. There was little left of his leggings, and he was exhausted. At this point, he was ready to let his uncle kill him just to be able to stop moving. A false dawn was beginning to filter up over the ocean.

As he tried to stand up the last time, he found he did not have the strength. Luthian still stood without a hair out of place. He stared at his uncle in confusion. Alador had a dragon's knowledge and as much power as his mortal frame could handle. Yet a memory of a skill was not the same as competently using it. While Luthian was attempting to teach him to defend himself no matter the situation, he had shown Alador that he was not ready to take on his uncle, at least, not yet. He had to wonder where Luthian pulled his strength. Alador had the ocean at hand, what did his uncle have? He was vaguely aware of Luthian calling for his guards.

Luthian nodded to the two Blackguards as they jerked Alador to his feet while another grabbed his belongings.

Alador could not help the cry of pain the sudden movement created.

"Take him to his room. He has time to get a couple of hours of sleep before he must return to the caverns."

Alador blinked wearily. "I need healing," he managed to hoarsely call out.

Luthian moved to Alador. "Healing, my dear nephew," - he tapped Alador's tender face gently - " ... is reserved for competent mages." With that said, his uncle turned and walked away, leaving Alador in the gentle but firm hands of his guards.

Chapter Seventeen

The next morning, Alador had been unable to put on any of his armor due to the burns covering his body. The night before had dragged on endlessly. The servants had filled a cool bath for him, but it had done little to ease the pain. The way back to the caverns was agonizing as the cloth of his robes seemed to rub some burn with every step. Alador reported straight to the healer's quarters upon entering the caverns. Alador was thankful that someone was always in the healing quarter regardless of the hour.

He limped into the room slowly and called for help. A man that he knew as Jasper came from behind the curtains that separated patients from the entry chamber. He took one look at Alador and led him to a bed where he eased Alador down carefully.

"What happened, Alador?" came the simple question. "You look as if you fell into a fire pit."

"Seems I earned my uncle's anger and retribution." Alador groaned out.

Jasper left his side for a moment and came back with scissors. Alador put up a staying hand. "No need." He dispelled his robe and the soft leather boots. He had formed them around his body as donning anything had been nearly impossible.

The healer's gasp of breath only confirmed his own suspicions. "It is that bad?" Alador tried to look down at his chest, but every movement seemed to hurt.

"Was the High Minister attempting to kill you, or did you just stand still and let him roast you like prang on the pit?" Jasper's sarcasm was edged with distaste. He shouted towards the curtains. "Dina, fetch two bottles of numbing water."

He looked back at Alador. "It would be bad for the common folk on the farmlands, but for us it is less so," the healer stated calmly. "I have not seen burns this bad in a long time." Jasper smiled at Alador, his eyes holding a calm reassurance.

"Yes, well my uncle seemed quite intent on making sure you saw them now," Alador murmured. He winced as the older man began to clean his burns. Despite his attempt to be stoic, a moan of pain escaped.

"I am surprised you are conscious to be honest." The healer was as gentle as he could be. Dina came in with two flasks. Jasper wet a new rag with this numbing water and continued to clean the wounds. Alador could see the concern on her face as she took her own rag and set to cleaning burns on the other side of him.

"Can't you just cast a spell and heal it?" Alador grimaced despite the tenderness of the man.

"I could." Jasper stated solemnly. "However, healing skin that has such filth ground into it is likely to cause an infection." He paused to look Alador grimly in the eye. "Not everything should be solved with magic."

Alador nodded. He remembered Sordith saying something similar. He was now thankful for the numbing water. He had not felt the burning as much as the force of the blows. Alador wondered if that had been because of its similarities with heated water; that hadn't bothered him either. However, the boiling bathing pool in Smallbrook had not left open lesions like those that the fire arrows had left in their wake. These left a residual burning and trail of pain across his body. The numbing water was justifying its name as Jasper and Dina cleaned.

After the front of him had been bathed, they helped ease him onto his stomach, then began to minister to his back. He must have passed out or fallen asleep because he awakened to find himself tucked into a healer's cot. Alador realized that he felt no pain. He looked about and seeing no one close by, he peeked under the cover and was relieved to see that while his skin was still pink and tender, the open wounds and blisters were all gone.

"I am sure everything is as you left it," Nemara teased from near his head.

Alador swiftly put the cover down. Where had she come from? "That was not what I was checking." He blushed lightly which only made her laugh.

"Sure it wasn't." She moved to sit down beside him on the bed. "He went at you hard, I heard. You okay?" She glanced at his face with genuine concern. She took his hand carefully as if touching him might hurt.

He moved to sit up and realized everything was still somewhat tender. "Yes. I have never seen him that angry; but I have heard stories." He watched as Nemara tensed.

"Yes. There are stories." She shook off the strange look on her face. "So, a few were worried this changes things - with the High Minister coming here and all." She pushed a loose hair back into her tightly woven hair.

"It changes nothing. My uncle will have me test for tier placement and, if I pass, then our plans can move forward." He reached and took her hand. "Here, I thought you were worried about me."

Rolling her eyes, she got up. She threw him a robe. "Healer says to quit taking up space." She did not bother to turn away as he threw the covers back and pulled on the robe. "Rest of your things are already in your room."

He motioned for her to turn around which brought a look of amusement. "Seriously? I have seen you naked."

She crossed her arm and grinned at him with a look of pure mischief.

Alador sighed and pulled the robe over his head, pulling it down carefully before removing the covers to stand. He managed to make it to his feet. "Nemara, do you have any passes?"

She grinned. "I do, but I don't know if I like you enough to give you one of them," she teased.

"I don't dare leave the caverns right now." He let her hook her arm in his as she guided him out of the healer's hall. "I was thinking you could get a message out for me?"

"Oooh, secret stuff. I haven't taken a day out in a while." She drew herself up. "Maybe some nice man will take me for a drink." Her teasing glance was coy and suggestive. "Should I wear a dress?" She smoothed a hand over her curves.

Alador's long tolerant sigh brought out a giggle from Nemara. He checked behind them and seeing the hall empty of others, he murmured softly. "I need a message taken to the Trench Lord." He about fell over when Nemara stopped.

"You are kidding, right? No one just wanders into Trench Hall." She was staring at him wide-eyed. "You hit your head too, didn't you?" She grabbed his face, turning his head left then right.

Alador pulled her hands loose and they continued walking. "I have a…" - he searched for the right word - "…pact with the man," he admitted in a hoarse whisper.

"How, by the gods, did you manage that one?" she whispered as they passed a couple of others headed for their own rooms.

"I have my own ways of doing things, just as you do." Alador smiled at her. "And they don't involve tight vests and low slung tunics."

They walked a few steps when suddenly pain shot through his arm. "Ow!" he exclaimed, realizing that Nemara had punched him in the arm. "What was that for?"

"I hardly ever do that." She glared at him.

"Oh? So that first evening we met and went to talk at the hidden pool, that was all just an exception to your rule?" He grinned and laughed lightly at the pout that formed in response to his words. "I would hate to think I made you suffer too greatly."

She leaned up as a couple of guards passed them by and whispered into his ear. "Keep it up and you will suffer in ways you cannot imagine. I am very good at well-placed thorns."

He winced not only at the idea of where she might put such thorns, but also because at that moment she reminded him of Mesiande. He put up both hands as if to pacify her. "All right, all right… you win." He laughed as she pulled him down the hallway.

Neither one spoke till they slipped into his room. He was intent on checking to make sure his weapons had been placed securely. Finally, Nemara that broke the silence. "Were you serious?"

"About a message to the Trench Lord?" He turned to look at her. "Yes."

"It will be safe for me to go alone?"

Alador moved to Nemara and put a hand on both of her arms. He gazed into her wide eyes hoping to reassure her. "You would be in more danger in the trench itself than from the Trench Lord." He pushed a lock of hair out of her eyes and tucked it behind her ear. "Just wear your armor; no one is going to tussle with a member of the Blackguard." He gave her a gentle kiss. "Everyone knows that they are not only fighter-trained, but mage-born as well." He let go of her and moved to his desk.

Nemara jumped backwards onto his bed, much like an excited child, considering what he said as Alador picked up a quill to scratch out a quick note to Sordith. "So, it is true then: those half-Daezun with casting abilities can test out of the Blackguard and into the tiers?"

Alador dipped the quill into the ink and carefully blotted it before beginning to write his note. "I suspect only those that can reach fourth or fifth tier will be allowed out of the Blackguard," he said. His voice held a tone of absent musing.

"Mmmm, I see." She was quiet for a moment then asked. "When you take this test, are you leaving the guard?" Nemara's voice held a strangled sound to it. So much so that Alador stopped his scratching on the piece of parchment to look at her.

He thought about this for a moment. "Yes," he said, watching her closely.

"How will we coordinate?" She was toying with a loose string on his quilt.

"Well, you do get half-days. If I succeed, I will give you a pass to come see me on your half-days," he offered as he signed his name to the note with a flourish. He put the quill back in its stand and turned to look at her rather than sanding the note. "It seems the easiest solution, especially since everyone already believes we're seeing one another." His answer was matter-of-fact.

"Aren't we?" She looked up from the thread.

Alador moved to her in confusion. "Aren't we what?"

She searched his eyes. "Seeing one another?" Her soft reply held a slight edge of hurt.

Alador took a deep breath and sat down beside her. He took her hand to comfort her. He enjoyed Nemara's company, and she was a skilled lover and genuinely joyful person. "I suppose on some level we are, but not in the way that others think." Realizing how heartless that sounded, he attempted to rationalize his answer. "We both have a lot on our hands right now."

Nemara bit her lip as she eyed him. "Is that because of this poor history you have had with women?" Her usual confident and sensual manner had fled in the face of her pain at his answer.

Alador had hoped this conversation would not happen. He did not want to damage the planning that was going into taking down the bloodmine. They just stared at each other for a long moment before Alador sat on the bed beside her and took her hand. He had kept things between them either light and playful or business. He had let her know little of his past other than the things that were necessary or to confirm or deny rumors she would ask him about. "I guess it is time I told you some things about me."

Alador began to talk, just looking at Nemara's hand. His thumb traced the vein that stood out on the back of her hand as he spoke. He told her everything about Smallbrook, Mesiande, and the bloodstone. He ended his tale with Mesiande's visit to Silverport. The only things he did not reveal was Sordith's relationship to him, the fact that Henrick was really a dragon, or the fact he had absorbed a dragon within his own form.

Silence filled the space between them, the kind that you could almost cut with a knife. Seconds turned to minutes as she sat absorbing all he had shared. Alador did not look at her as he was not sure what to expect. The truth had become his best weapon against his uncle, but with Nemara, he had everything to lose.

Nemara spoke and Alador was startled out of his quiet musing. “It was quite stupid, you know.” There was a distance in her eyes and voice that had not been there before.

Alador sighed. “Which part?” *At least she has not pulled her hand away and gone stomping off*, he thought to himself. “

“Telling Mesiande that she could stay but only as a bed slave,” she pointed out. “I think of all the things you have told me and I have seen you do, that is the dumbest.” Her voice had lost some of the pain that had been present before he had opened up to her.

Alador winced when she pointed out the error that he still regarded with great remorse. “So I have been told.” He unconsciously ran his hand over his jaw where Sordith had hit him. “I still love her. I … I just don’t know how to fix it now.”

She groaned at his answer. “Why are men so dumb?” She tossed his hand aside.

“What?” He looked up and glared at her.

“Seriously,” she interrupted before he could say more. She turned to face him, sitting cross-legged on the bed, pulling her hand away. “You go apologize for being such an arrogant shite!”

“I hardly think an apology is going to be enough,” he sighed, running his hand through his unbound hair.

“Maybe it won’t be, but it is sort of where you need to start.” She reached over and tugged his hand from his hair to hold it. “If she can’t forgive you, well then you know you can move on. If she does forgive you, it is a start to rebuilding her trust. If she is as wonderful as you describe, well, she is probably going to make you work for it.”

"What makes you say that?" Alador eyed her with curious concern.

Nemara shrugged. "It is what I would do if you were that stupid with me." She grinned. "Though I have an advantage," she quipped playfully.

"Oh," he grinned back. "What is that?"

"I can kick your arse in the ring anytime I want to." Nemara's eyes danced with merriment. "So if you are stupid, I can just beat sense into you with the flat of my blade."

"I hardly think so," Alador rolled his eyes and coughed a couple times to hide his laughter.

Nemara hopped off the bed with a grin. "I have seen you fight. You are predictable and you broadcast your next move. The only time I have seen you fight in a way that would give me the least concern is when you tried to kill Toman." She moved over to his note, sanded the ink then rolled it up. She slipped it into her vest.

He glowered at her, but did not comment. His uncle had also called him predictable so it was something he was going to have to look at. "You're leaving now?" he asked.

"Healer said you should rest. No fighting today. As all your other classes are done for the day," she paused as she turned to face him. "You should get some sleep."

"You are not staying?" A slight tone of disappointment danced amongst his words as he realized he was becoming used to her presence in his personal quarters.

Nemara moved to him where he sat on the bed and took both of his hands. "You gave me a lot to think about with your story of lost love and murder." Her lips twitched into the merest of grins. He noted that her eyes did not hold the same amused glimmer. "Besides, this note of yours must be important if you are asking the Trench Lord to find you."

"You read quickly," he pointed out. He squeezed her hands. "You are right, I am tired. I will see if I can get some rest." He let her hands go. "Thank you for taking the message."

"Yes, well it is what partners do, right?" Her voice was strained and even Alador could tell that her smile was forced. "And if nothing else, we are partners in the big scheme of things." She turned to head for the door. "Oh, one other thing…" She looked back at him with her hand on the door knob.

"Yes?" Alador yawned as he realized he was still exhausted despite sleeping in the healer's quarter, and now that he thought about it he was hungry as well.

"You missed Master Levielle's class again." The look and groan that this jab brought from Alador must have delighted her because he could hear her laughing even after the door shut.

Alador flopped back onto the bed, grimacing as the tender skin screamed a reminder of his injuries. He was going to have to go to General Levielle's home after dinner tonight or tomorrow. He decided to wait till tomorrow night. He had faced enough conflict for the day.

Chapter Eighteen

Alador slept most of the rest of the evening, even through dinner despite his hunger. The battle between sleep and hunger waged in moments of waking, then sleep would win. The next morning brought a little more relief from his lesson with his uncle. He was feeling more his usual self although he was still stiff from the work out both in magic and in his muscles. His uncle still far outpaced him in skill, and had made it clear he had much to learn.

In his morning classes, rumors were still flying about the cavern as to what had really happened to the High Master. Everything from that he had simply retired to the possibility that Luthian had killed him. Alador was sure that it was the latter, but he had not specifically asked. Given the temper his uncle had demonstrated, it seemed like something Luthian would do. Regardless of what had happened to the High Master, everyone was giving Alador a wide berth today.

Normally, this would have upset him as it reminded him of a lifetime of being set apart as different. It seemed so long ago, but it had only been several months. However, today he was relieved to be given the space. He was also coming to terms with the fact that he was different, and that there was nothing wrong with that.

It was not until the midday meal that Nemara made her presence known. She slipped in beside Alador with her usual smile, leaning over to give him a brief kiss on the cheek. "Lord Sordith is quite charming. You would have been better off to warn me about that." She grinned at the immediate reaction that Alador's face revealed.

Alador rolled his eyes. "He has a woman in his life," he pointed out with a hint of acidic tone.

"Yes, well unlike you, that does not stop some of us from enjoying ourselves." Her voice held an edge of teasing as she innocently picked up her fork and began stabbing at the meat on her tray.

Alador had not thought about the fact that Sordith was much like his father with women, or that he was sending him a rather attractive one. Not only that, but he had told her he was in love with another woman just minutes before she left. "Did you?" he asked softly.

"Did I what, Alador?" she quipped. She looked over at him, her eyes were sparkling with mischief.

He stabbed a tuber on his plate much harder than he had intended. "Did you ... enjoy yourself?" he was not sure he wanted to know. He stared at the tuber as if it had offended him.

She smiled with genuine glee. "Oh yes, I had a marvelous time." There was a hint of pleasured breathlessness as she spoke.

"I see." He grumpily shoved his tray away.

"Why, Lord Guldalian, one would think you were jealous by the look on your face." She let her words hang between them for a long moment. "Come, others are watching … Let us kiss and makeup." She scooted closer to him and with those big eyes, looked up at him with adoration. As if to emphasize her role, she batted her eyelashes at him.

Alador glanced up and noticed they were indeed being watched. He pulled her roughly to him and claimed her lips in a quick kiss. While they were close, he whispered.

"Don't play games Nemara, you might not like how they end." His whisper held a firm warning.

She came right back at him in a swiftly whispered answer. "I am not playing; you just don't ask the right questions. Lord Sordith was a perfect gentleman and took me and his betrothed, Keelee, to dinner." Deciding she had tortured him long enough, her voice was more matter of fact. She reached up and tapped his lip. "Wasn't she your bed servant?" she curiously asked.

Alador could not contain the instant flush of anger that the mention of Keelee brought to mind. His hand swiftly grasped her wrist while it was near his mouth. He was forced to squelch the instinctual urge to pull power into himself. Nemara's eyes widened in both shock and pain. Alador did not miss the glimmer of fear in her eyes. He forced his hand open and she jerked it away. "Don't ever …" he hissed, "…use Keelee to tease me or play games with me again."

Nemara bit her lip and her eyes glistened as she stared at him. The tables around them had gone quiet, even though they could not hear what Alador and Nemara were speaking about. Nemara was still holding her wrist when Alador pointedly turned from her and picked up his fork. It was taking everything he had at that moment not to lash out at everyone around them. Without Renamaum to help him calm, he was struggling to push the anger back down.

Nemara finally raised enough courage to speak. "I am sorry. I - I didn't know," she stammered out, clearly uncomfortable with the looks that everyone was giving them.

Alador changed the subject though he did not look at Nemara. "Did Sordith say when he would find the time?" Though he spoke evenly, he could not hide the anger he still felt. He forced himself to casually take a bite acting as if nothing had just happened. Slowly the diners went back to their own conversations and meals.

Nemara followed suit, but she just pushed the food around a bit with her fork before answering. “He said he would stop by your room after supper was cleared.” Her voice trembled.

Alador nodded and forced another bite into his mouth before speaking. “I am sorry I lost my temper.” He managed to put a little feeling into the words.

“I am sorry I was teasing you," she answered. “I...” Her words fell away.

He looked over and sat down his fork watching her as she pushed food about the tray. “You were hoping to make me jealous,” he pointed out.

“Yes, I guess.” Nemara’s admission only brought a sigh to Alador.

“Nemara, for now, let us just focus on the objective. Later, once I have talked to Mesiande as you suggested, maybe I can focus on that part of my life.” He continued in a consoling whisper. “Right now, I am trying to outstep a highly skilled mage and politician, make a group of dragons happy, and hopefully stay alive as I dance through that dangerous maze.” He put a hand on Nemara’s hand, the one that was pushing food around. “I just can’t think about anything else right now. All right?”

Nemara met his gaze and nodded. “Does this mean I can’t come to your room in the night anymore?” She watched him warily and as he slowly grinned, she returned it with one of her own.

“I think I can find room in my dancing schedule for a little midnight dalliance,” he conceded. “Though I will admit, after that display, I am surprised you would want to."

Nemara shrugged indifferently and gave a soft sigh, appearing to center herself again. "Have to keep up appearances." She glanced over to him before taking a drink from her mug.

Alador picked up his own and held it up in toast. "To appearances." Nemara giggled and toasted him back. He could tell she was attempting to pretend that nothing had just occurred, but he knew it was not a light matter. He did not believe in hurting women, yet he had almost struck her. Though he had managed to recover from his near loss of control, he knew that neither of them were soon going to forget that moment.

For his part, Alador had been surprised at the extent of power which he had felt at his command. It had felt like he had stood on the very shores of the ocean itself. In a lesson earlier today, he had learned that many lesser skilled water mages made their living on the sea by protecting shipments from the weather, sea creatures and pirates. It put them in their element with more power at their command: for the ocean was a force unto itself, and gave off far more power than a mere pool or stream.

Alador had realized at that moment that not only did he have access to the ocean's unlimited depths, but for a moment the very currents of it had flowed in his veins. It left him with a longing to slip beneath the waves as Renamaum had done and just move through its murky, cold depths. He shivered as he set the mug carefully down upon the table. A frost had built up on the mug, and it stuck to his hand for a second.

He was so lost in the allure of that power that he could smell the salt and hear the ocean waves. The sounds of the others dining faded as the full power of the ocean washed over him. He closed his eyes and completely opened up to embrace it. The caress of the cold water through his hair did not bother him, and he watched in awe as fish swirled around him. He could feel his pounding heart and the containment of his weak lungs. He whispered words he did not even remember learning, then opened his mouth. Breath came easily as he opened his eyes and looked around.

Alador had expected to see Nemara or others staring at him. He was not prepared for what mysteriously appeared instead. He must be dreaming. The mage thrashed a bit, but the feel of the silky water on his skin and the floating of his cloak drove home that he had somehow ended up in the sea. Not only was he under water, but he was able to breathe. Had he turned the caverns into ocean depths? Was this merely the act of imagination or had he transported himself into the ocean's deep arms? He swirled about in the watery depths, but saw only fish and the sandy bottom. He cast a spell to form simple leggings as his cloak and armor were weighing him down.

Alador found that he could see using the dim light from the surface. His initial panic began to settle as his mind rationalized that he must have touched his amulet. That was how he came to be here, it must have brought him. Fortunately, he knew how to swim and he had a fairly well trained sense of direction. He swam along the ocean's silted bottom towards what should be the shore.

As the bottom slowly rose, the light grew brighter around him. He was still amazed at the beauty of it all. There was a world all its own beneath the surface of the ocean. It was unmarked or spoiled by mortal hand, and he hoped that this would never change. The water was cold, and as he moved forward rock formations began to rise up out of the silt below him.

He swam through a forest of orange kelp dancing forward and back with the motion of the waves above him. An eel swam up to him, and Alador reached out slowly. He was surprised to see that the creature was so friendly. Even more so, the eel allowed him to pet it and soon after was swirling around his body. Other types of fish soon surrounded him, and he gurgled with delight as more and more of them gathered. He noted them all; from the dark spotted fish that kept to the bottom below him to one of a brilliant blue that nibbled at his ear curiously. He brushed it away before it decided to take a more serious bite. As he was enjoying this silent symphony of color, the fish came to a fluttering stop. As if one body, they turned to his left then turned to opposite way and fled.

Warily, Alador turned to face whatever predator had brought such fear from the marine creatures. Instead, all he saw was a murky ink blot of blackness that light did not pass through. He realized after a moment that it was making its way slowly to him. It drove fear into him as he stared at it. Deciding to follow the wisdom of the marine life that surrounded him, he turned to flee for the shore.

He was not as fluid in the water as whatever came for him. Alador would frantically check behind him and around him only to find it in front of him again. Feeling trapped he headed straight for the surface, breaking the top of the water and looking about frantically. He still had a fair distance to the beach, but there was a rock nearby. Alador swam for it hoping that getting out of the water would be safer than being enveloped in whatever it was that the fish had feared.

He scrambled up onto the rock and watched breathing heavily from the exertion as the black water slowly surrounded the rock. Water pooled around him as he stood dripping on the safety of the stone.

"Do not fear; it will not harm you unless I bid it." A melodious voice spoke from behind him.

As he whipped around, he nearly fell back into its clutches. There stretched out on the other side of the rock where it was somewhat flat was a mermaid. He had heard stories of mermaids: sirens that could sing a man to his death beneath the watery waves. This one looked oddly familiar to him. Her skin was pale and her hair, long and flowing ebony was threaded with red strands of seaweed which did nothing to hide her upper body's naked form.

"Who are you?" he asked. He shuddered, suddenly feeling chilled despite the sun's rays.

"You know who I am. Search yourself, pseudo-dragon." Her voice caressed the word pseudo-dragon as if she called a lover's name. She stretched lazily, and he found he could not look away from her. She was so perfect, a combination of fish and woman who melded into seamless beauty. Her tail flipped making the scales dance with a myriad of colors in the sunlight. It was her flawless red lips and deep set emerald eyes that gave away who she truly was.

His breath caught in his throat as the realization of who she was sunk in. "Dethara?" He moved cautiously now. He was fairly certain that it was her as the similarities of the face, eyes and hair to Lady Morana were too great.

"Very good, little one. Very good." She beckoned him closer, and Alador found his feet compelled to comply. "I chose this form because you seemed so enthralled with the fish of your domain." One hand slid suggestively down her side and onto the hip that was scaled in a cascading melody of blues and greens. "Do you like it?"

What words could he possibly say right now? He found himself totally enthralled. "You are very beautiful," Alador admitted, looking down at the Goddess clothed as a mermaid.

"Tell me Alador, have you ever lain with a fish?" She teased as her hand reached out to draw him closer and down to his knees. "Would you want to?" Her husky tone caressed him as he sank into the depths of her gaze.

Alador found himself kneeling before the alabaster beauty, attempting to keep his eyes locked on her face. Fear shot through him as he realized that not only did she know his name, but she had called him pseudo-dragon. "I believe that such a feat would end in my drowning or worse," he answered truthfully. He did not dare lose himself here.

She laughed lightly, the delicate peal was pleasing to his ear. "Yes, I suppose you are right." She put a cold hand to his heated face, running the back of her fingernails over his cheekbone.

"Why are you here, Dethara?" he managed to ask. Alador watched as color swirled around her, and she stood as fully a woman before him. She looked down at him with a gentle smile as she ran her fingers through his wet hair. "Death is often feared by mortal men. It is the end that all must face, and those that serve me are assured smooth passing to what is beyond." She did not answer his question.

She knelt slowly down to look him in the eyes. "Do you fear death, Alador?"

Alador realized that in many ways he did not. "I think I fear the manner and lingering of my death rather than the actual passing from this world." He attempted to rise, but found that he could not. A moment of panic swept through him as he fully realized that he was on his knees against his own will.

He licked his dry lips trying not to pay attention to her fully naked form. "What is beyond?" he asked curiously. Maybe if he could intrigue her enough, he would not die here. He was sure that this was why he was here, so that she could end his interference into whatever plan she had.

"That, we are not allowed to reveal." She put a finger under his chin and pulled him slowly up with her until they were looking eye to eye. "What are you?" she asked, more of herself rather than him. She turned his head left and right.

"You named me as have others, a pseudo-dragon." His voice was the merest of whispers. Her presence was as intoxicating as it was terrifying. He could see why Luthian had succumbed to her wiles.

"Yes, but none has ever existed, not truly one with the dragon that claimed them." She moved around him, her fingers lingering behind her slightly drawing over his shoulder, neck, and to the other side of his chest.

Alador eyes were shut as he attempted to ignore her allure. He could smell the strange mixture of musk and sea salt on her. It was pleasing to the senses, and he shivered as her fingers caressed slowly around. A fact he was sure she had not missed.

"We could make a wondrous team, you and I." She pointed out as she came to stand before him again. She put a hand to his chin, leaning in close so that her lips were but inches from his own.

Alador was so tempted to reach out and try to claim those luxurious lips. He felt his body stir in response to her teasing. It took every measure of his will to resist that pull. He shook his head, opened his eyes, and drew in a deep breath. "My mother taught me never to bargain with death." He closed his eyes again to stop staring into hers. "Such bargains never end well for the mortal and always favor Dethara. I have things to accomplish and I fear that my early ending in your tempting arms would cost more than I could bear."

"Handsome, powerful, and smart," she quietly answered. She crossed one arm beneath her breasts, lifting them as the other hand touched her lips reflecting on his words. "You are indeed an enigma."

She reached out and trailed a finger from his chest towards his groin. He caught it smoothly in his own before she could truly touch him. His body would betray his words. He was not sure that he could deny her if she pressed him any further. He opened his eyes to meet hers bravely. "I do not desire to lie with you, Goddess." He swallowed hard as the words had sounded hollow even to his own ears.

She leaned forward, allowing him to keep her captured wrist. "Liar," she whispered in his ear. He tensed as her other hand came up to the side of his face. "Let me make your position very clear, young pseudo-dragon. You will join me here in life," she pulled back slightly to look into his eyes. "Or you will join me in death. Either way, I will have you." She laid her lips gently upon his. Her body pressed to his, grinding suggestively against him.

Alador moaned in response as the taste of her lips was salted heaven. Her body pressed tighter against his as she deepened the kiss. He closed his eyes in sweet surrender. Suddenly, he could not break free, nor could he breathe. He released her wrist and grabbed both of her upper arms in an attempt to push her off him. He struggled against the tug within him. It felt as if she sought to rip the very magic from his soul. He panicked as the realization that she was suffocating him became clear. He shoved hard and felt her fall back as she released his mouth. He drew a deep ragged breath. His head swam as he fought for continued air.

When he opened his eyes again, he was lying in his room on his bed. In a sudden gasp, he sat up still feeling the need for air. He rubbed his eyes with a momentary sense of relief. It had all been a nightmare, just a dream. He took a few deep ragged breaths and lay back down. It was only then that he realized that he was soaked, as was his bed. There, lying on his pillow beneath his hand, was a strand of red seaweed.

Chapter Nineteen

Alador quickly shot out of bed and barred the door. After forming back into his armor, he cleaned his bed with the use of cantrips. He reached out and took up the piece of seaweed gingerly. Seeing it was nothing dangerous, he slid it through his fingers. It was proof that he had faced no dream. He sank onto the edge of the bed, his thumb caressing the red strand against the palm of his hand.

Slowly the realization washed over him that everything had happened; he had really found himself in the confines of the ocean depths. He touched his lips: that kiss had also been real. Dethara's warning echoed in his ears.

She knew who he was. Cold dread began to take hold of him. He could feel the fear feeding his rapidly beating heart. Questions flooded his mind. If she knew his name, did she know of his connection to Luthian? How long before she betrayed his new-found power to his uncle?

He sat mulling these thoughts repeatedly. How had she discovered him? Had Jon truly decided to serve the Goddess of his sphere? He was lost in the myriad of repeating questions to which he had no answer. When a knock sounded at the door, he jumped up in true, fearful surprise. He instinctively grabbed for his sword, and his other hand filled with power protectively.

The door was tried, then there was silence for the moment. He could hear feet move away, and with that retreating sound, he let the power fall from his hands and took a centering breath. He imagined people were looking for him. Mages did not normally just disappear from their lunch table. He had no idea what time it was or even how long he had truly been gone. He also knew that if he had actually been in the sea, then he had just disappeared in front of Nemara. That in itself was going to bring up questions that he did not quite know how to answer.

Toman had taught them breathing exercises before one went into battle. He used these to calm and settle himself before he began planning. He would need to go to the library and research everything that he could find on Dethara. In addition, it was time to start asking questions of the priest of Death, who resided in the caverns.

He could pose as someone curious. While most placed in highest honor the God of their sphere, this was not always the case. It would not seem too far out of place for him to be seeking spiritual answers. It was a part of the caverns that he had avoided, having no desire to add gods to dragons in his current plight. Now, however, it would not be a lie: He was curious.

Alador paced back and forth, trying to figure out what moves he could still safely make. What was now too much of a risk? The only thing he knew for certain was that Dethara knew he had more power than Luthian had been counting on. He also knew there was a good chance that she would share this with the High Minister. He could see little benefit to the Goddess in withholding the information. His mind spun in a thousand directions, all trying to grasp possible outcomes. Again, he was so deep in his thoughts that he was startled from their grasp by a loud knock on the door.

"Alador, I know you are in there." There was a heavy masculine voice. "The only way the door can be barred is from the inside." It took him a moment to realize it was

Sordith's voice. Sordith was not supposed to come for a few hours. How much time had passed?

Going from fearful to relieved, he hurriedly moved to the door and threw the bar up. He opened it ready to welcome Sordith when he saw the new High Master at his brother's side. His open mouth shut slowly. He saluted across his chest and dropped his eyes. "High Master," he acknowledged.

"Might we come in and speak?" The new High Master asked with an unusually polite manner.

Alador was confused why man was asking and not just striding in, but he nodded yes and moved aside to let the two men enter. He looked up and down the hall to see it was full of curious eyes. Sighing, he shut it again, latched the door and slowly turned to face the two men. The High Master was looking about curiously by his bed; Sordith was across the room. The space suddenly seemed too small with the other two men standing there.

"I am fairly sure, Alador, that we had discussed you keeping your head down and not making a scene." Sordith crossed his arms and leaned back against the wardrobe on the far wall. "I have heard you have been doing everything but." When Alador glanced with alarm at the High Master and back to Sordith, the Trench Lord grinned. "Ah, may I introduce a trusted friend," He waved his hand and gave a slight flourish, "…and now one of my highest placed men: Reynel Bariton, now High Master Bariton."

Noting Alador's tense posture and confused facial expressions, the High Master spoke. His rich baritone voice was low to stop those surely pressed with their ear to the door from hearing clearly. "Before we speak further, may I suggest you shield your room, mage?" He gave Alador a wink, sat down on the bed and picked up the strand of red kelp. He looked at it curiously before setting it back down.

Alador nodded. It had never occurred to him to shield his room, but obviously the High Master had reasons for concern. Not wanting to touch that internal sense of the ocean again, Alador reached for the small private pool that was close by. The shield was not made of water, but he pulled the power of water to garble and mute sounds. Using this, he shielded the room, his hands and voice weaving the spell into a tight net. When it was done, he reopened his eyes and took a breath before nodding to the two men.

"Let us start with the most pressing matter." Master Bariton eyed Alador. "It is not normal for mages…" - he looked pointedly at the seaweed and back to Alador - "…to just disappear in the middle of a meal and conversation. It is even less so for those in the Blackguard." His voice was tinged with awe. "No one saw you cast a spell or employ any teleportation device. By the gods, boy, what happened?" Alador saw genuine curiosity in the High Master's face.

Alador flashed Sordith a concerned look. "You're sure?"

"As sure as a man can be in this city," Sordith answered with a shrug. Sordith was leaning back against the wardrobe with his arms crossed. His eyes held the same curiosity that Master Bariton's held.

Alador was slowly learning to trust Sordith in all matters. He began to explain as best he could, starting from the moment that he had toasted Nemara and realized he could touch the seductive power of the ocean. He left only two things out: the kiss of the Goddess and her recognition of his state as a pseudo-dragon.

Neither the High Master nor Sordith interrupted while he relayed his experience. When he had finished, the silence was overbearing and he looked up. Both men were staring at him as if he had lost his mind.

"I assure you both that this is the truth of the matter." Alador added quickly. He moved to the seaweed and held it up as evidence.

Sordith stroked his chin, one arm still crossed and holding the other. "Yes, well we can't exactly offer that to the hundred or so witnesses to your disappearance," Sordith pondered. "Or the young guardswoman who became quite hysterical after you were gone." Alador groaned at the mention of Nemara.

Master Bariton was nodding as he considered. "I may be able to use this to my advantage." He glanced up at the Trench Lord.

Alador shifted uncomfortably. "How?"

"It is an opportunity to cement my position. Very few of the guardsmen know me much more than as one of the High Master's advisers. They have no idea what my level of mage skills is, or how well I handle a sword." Master Bariton looked between the two men, his brow wrinkling somewhat. "I shall say that I summoned him peremptorily because of his consistent failure to be punctual, and of course, follow through with a list of corrective duties assigned to him as punishment."

He looked at Alador with a grin. "You are about to become a rebel, son. This garrison is sadly lacking in morale. It will make you friends amongst those that oppose the tyranny of the tiers," - he nodded to the Trench Lord - "…something Sordith tells me that you could use. So we serve two purposes: increasing fear of and respect for what 'I' can do, and building your reputation as someone with the guts to kick against the status quo." Bariton sounded quite pleased with himself.

Sordith shook a finger at Bariton. "It will be important that you and he have the same tale. Others have seen us enter here, tonight."

"Yes, yes, you're right, of course," Bariton acknowledged with a wave of his hand. "Alador, you must tell them how you suddenly found yourself before me, and how I went through your file and hauled you over the carpet for every little misdeed." He counted off the points on his fingers. "How I threatened you with dismissal or worse, and the only reason you were still here was because you were related to the High Minister." Master Bariton looked at Alador to make sure he understood.

Alador was not sure how much he liked this idea. He had tried to remain unnoticed for the most part. He did not really want to be the center of attention. He thought back to the time -about two turns ago - when he had thought it was all he would ever want and need. He had been so wrong.

If he could turn back the wheel of time, he would warn his younger self. He would have let Mesiande have the find and welcomed his status of outcast. It was far more distasteful to be different with hundreds of eyes watching your every move than it was to be discounted and overlooked for those differences.

"Yes, High Master," he responded politely. He did not really know what else to say.

Master Bariton moved to him and clapped him on the shoulder with what turned out to be a large heavy hand. Alador winced slightly. "I shall put the boy on lock-down except for his half-days with Luthian." Master Bariton was now speaking directly with Sordith who was still leaning against the wardrobe with a look of amusement. "That will allow him to do what must be done freely, since we now know he can use a travel spell. Will that suffice?"

Sordith kicked off the wardrobe and moved to Alador. "It will do more than just suffice." Sordith met Alador's worried gaze. "When enough time has passed, come and see me in Trench Hall." Sordith turned to the High Master. "We will have to do something about the girl," he said. There was an edge of steel in his tone, and Bariton gave a solemn nod.

Alador's heart leapt and he rushed forward, grabbing Sordith's arm. "No, I need her free. She is part of the plan." Alador felt a wave of panic. He didn't know what doing something about her meant to most people, but he knew what it meant to Sordith.

"Oh, when were you planning to enlighten me on this… minor change to our plan?" Sordith's voice was full of censure and contained more than a hint of sarcasm. He looked at the young mage sternly, and Alador felt a leap of adrenaline in response. He saw for a brief moment what those who crossed the Trench Lord must experience. It was not pleasant.

"When next I saw you. I need a message given to her and I can further this plan of Master Bariton's." He looked from one man to the other hopefully.

The High Master nodded. "I can call her before me with a stern lecture, overheard by others, on how her behavior was unseemly for an advanced student of the guard." He grinned at Alador, "…and pass your message."

Alador let loose a sigh of tension. "Tell her to meet me where we spent our first evening."

Sordith clapped Alador on the back. "Good to see you not holding Keelee's actions against all women, lad. You will have to tell me of your first evening some time over some ale or whiskey." His tone was filled with amusement. The High Master also chuckled deeply.

"It wasn't like that," Alador snapped. He turned red immediately, acknowledging at least to himself that it had really been just like that.

"Right…" Sordith nodded with a mischievous grin. He let it go and turned to Master Bariton. "Let's get this new gossip rolling about your dark halls." He smiled at Bariton and headed for the door. Sordith's humor seemed to have snapped right back into place after he had shown Alador a glimpse of his harder side. He looked at Alador as he passed him and shook his head. "Try to keep your head down."

Alador nodded and rubbed his jaw absently: he had felt the spontaneous edge of Sordith's personality, and imagined the calculating man was worse than the one who had punched him out of sheer anger. He watched Sordith stroll to the door and fling it open.

"I hardly see why you would want me to foster such an arrogant mageling, High Master Bariton!" Sordith boomed in apparent disgust. He looked back at Alador with a smirk.

Alador watched seemingly innocent men and women suddenly hurry off on some remembered task or dash into a room close by. He shook his head as the two men exited. Bariton hardly missed a step.

"The boy has an arrogance I thought you capable of bringing to heel, Lord Sordith. I would think you would be glad to have the High Minister's nephew in your keeping." The High Master headed down the hall, affecting not to notice the scurrying guards.

"You mean get the High Minister's spy out of your nest and plant him securely into mine? I do not think so, Sir." Their voices trailed down the hall as the two men cemented their rumor. "He is your problem, not mine! I don't need a repeat in my halls of what happened to the last High Master in yours…" Alador shut the door with a long-suffering sigh, cutting off Sordith's contemptuous tone.

Chapter Twenty

Alador slumped into his chair and ran a hand over his face. The cloud of dread caused by Nemara seemed to overwhelm the facts that the High Master was in Sordith's pocket or that he had just been given the freedom to move around as he needed to between now and the test.

Alador considered, he had three things - no four, he amended to himself - which he distinctly needed to take care of before the test. He needed to explain things to Nemara, he needed to talk to Sordith, see his family in Smallbrook, then begin the storms on the northern lands. He ordered them in his mind.

Dethara's words and actions kept diverting his attention from the things that he needed to do. There was no way of knowing where or how – or for that matter even if - she would interfere. His head hurt from the deep thoughts that raced through his mind. He was fairly sure that when Henrick had said that he had the means to complete the geas, no one had counted on a Goddess in the mix.

He moved to his bed and threw himself down. Sleep did not find him, and as the bell tolled in the great caverns for the time, it pulled him from his thoughts. Enough time had passed for Sordith to have returned to his own manor. Alador stood and switched his practice sword for a real blade. He pulled the talisman out from beneath his tunic and concentrated on Sordith's office. As the room manifested, he took a deep breath. It was still a disorienting sensation no matter how many times he had used the talisman.

He looked about as soon as he was able to see that Sordith was not there yet. He found a chair by the wall, placed it in front of Sordith's desk then went around and sat in his half-brother's chair. The man had a way of sneaking up and he did not want to be caught off guard with his back to the door.

He scrutinized the redwood desk and was admiring its craftsmanship when the door opened. Upon seeing Alador in the room, Sordith turned and murmured something before shutting the door behind him. Alador did not see to whom he spoke, but merely sat back and slowly put one foot then the other up on Sordith's desk with a challenging grin.

Sordith crossed the room. "And just what do you think you are doing putting your feet up on my desk?" Sordith took off his gloves as he crossed the room coming to a stop next to Alador. He tossed his gloves onto the great desk.

"I do believe, my dear brother, you called me an arrogant mageling." Alador's voice took on a haughty air. "I was just confirming the opinion." He leaned back, rocking the big chair back onto two legs. He crossed his arms behind his head and grinned up at his brother.

"I fail to see the falsehood in that," Sordith quipped. His foot shot out, catching the chair's bottom crosspiece. He gave it just enough thrust to send it off-balance and toppling over backward. Flailing and failing to catch his balance, Alador found himself landing hard on the floor and tumbling out the chair. The solid thwack to the back of his head brought stinging tears for a moment.

"Damn Sordith, you could kill someone doing that!" he grumbled. He rolled up onto his knees rubbing the back of his head.

Sordith set the chair upright and sat in it, wiping the imagined dust of Alador's boots off his desk. "Doubtful," he stated, ignoring the ignominious position of his brother next to him on the floor. "Your head is far too hard." He didn't even offer Alador a hand up.

"Bastard." Alador hissed. He got up and went around to the chair that he had placed when he first arrived. He was still rubbing the egg growing on his head.

"A fact that is well established." Sordith grinned at Alador. "You need to be faster and more creative with your barbs. That was hardly original."

"Yes, well I have a headache, thanks to you." He dropped into the chair and grimaced when it jarred.

"You're welcome," Sordith quipped. He opened a drawer and pulled out two cups and a small jug. He poured each about half full and handed one to Alador. His face grew serious. "We have a lot to talk about."

Alador sobered as well and nodded. "A lot has happened since last we spoke. Where would you like to start?" Alador sniffed the mug.

"This woman, of course." Sordith grinned playfully and toasted Alador. He took a drink and sat back to listen.

Alador rolled his eyes and took a careful sip. He never knew what Sordith or Henrick were serving. The mage had been right to be cautious: the initial sweet flavor had a hard burning bite after he swallowed. He grimaced at the burn, and Sordith gave a slight chuckle.

"Nemara was the contact that Jon sent to me. She is sorting through the guards to find those with enough hatred of Luthian or with clear disregard for their

Lerdenian blood. She is also the one I sent to you with my last message." Alador added, "Our budding relationship is just a cover."

Sordith shifted in his chair. "Just a cover? Somehow brother, I get the feeling that you have been quite thorough with that cover." Sordith sat back, holding the cup with both hands, and grinned wickedly.

"It was her idea, and I saw no reason to dissuade her," Alador admitted with a rueful grin. "I did try to be a gentleman at first, but she was rather insistent." He shrugged, as that really had been the way things had occurred.

"Yes, I saw the woman." Sordith drew a feminine outline with one hand. "I am sure you suffered greatly while making your cover convincing." Sordith laughed outright at the dark look on his brother's face. "I jest… I jest." He put up one hand as if to hold Alador at bay. "Has she had success?"

"I believe we will have about ten to twenty guards to join me at the bloodmine when the time comes." Alador shared. "It would be helpful if the High Master arranged for those I designate to be in a practice ring or class together."

Sordith nodded and leaned forward, setting his cup down. He pulled a parchment out of a top drawer and made note. "I will see that is arranged for you after your test. No sense in it if you don't live."

"Thanks for the confidence in my abilities." Alador glowered, considering his brother's statement. "I have the right to stop at a lower tier if I feel myself tiring or think I shall be bested." Alador looked up with a moment of realization and confidence. "I don't really see myself not passing," he confessed. He went on to explain about the night with Henrick: how he had spent the night and part of the morning as a dragon and afterwards had received the power of Renamaum.

Alador's got to the end of the tale, and Sordith was quiet for a time. He considered everything his brother had just said with deep scrutiny before looking up at him, his gaze revealing the degree of calculation. "You are going to need it," he finally shared, not looking up from his quill. "I suspect you will need every spell and trick you can recall from the dragon's gift." Sordith's voice was tinged with concern.

"Why is that?" Alador swirled the contents of his mug and considered. "Luthian and I have been practicing, and while I am not yet quick enough, I do have the spells and power at my command." Alador looked at Sordith curiously.

"My informants tell me that there is a group of mages that is against Daezun testing. It is conspiring to ensure that all the final mages assembled for your fifth tier are ready to kill you," he warned. Sordith looked back up. "They will not stop if you falter. They will seize this chance to remove what they see as a stain on the tiers." Sordith shook his quill with concern at Alador. "You are trying to change a practice that has been around for hundreds of years. Change is never welcomed by those who are comfortable with the status quo," he warned.

Alador sighed and shook his head. "I really hate this place." He pinched the bridge of his nose in frustration.

Sordith grinned. "Don't worry, it will grow on you." He gestured about them.

Alador drained his cup and slapped it down on the desk. "I sincerely hope not." He ran a hand across his face and digested this new bit of information.

Sordith refilled both their cups. "So let me recap what I know," he said, "and you tell me if I have missed anything." He set the jug down and held up a hand, ready to tap a finger for each item. "The plan for the bloodmine is on target and there will be enough men to pull it off. You are taking a test where every man and woman in it hopes that you will fail." He continued to count off, emphasizing each point with that tap to the desk.

"You are about to bring a deadly winter down on your own people. The man you hate the most is the one you must please right now. The Goddess of Death knows who you are and what power you hold. She just happens to be Luthian's current mistress or he is a tool she is using." He looked over at Alador. "Did I miss anything?"

Alador did not even pause. "Our father is a dragon." His tone was matter-of-fact and devoid of emotion.

Sordith picked up his cup and took a long slow pull. He licked his lips then simply said: "Interesting." His face was devoid of any response.

Alador watched him closely and noted nothing but a couple of extra blinks of Sordith's eyes. "Well, your reaction was a bit calmer than mine." Alador chuckled and picked back up his cup.

Sordith leaned forward with his mug in both hands. His fingers were a bit pale due to clenching it tightly, further showing that the news was at least concerning to him. "So, how do you know this?" the Trench Lord managed to ask. There was a slightly higher pitch to his voice, and his face had an expression that held more dismay than disbelief.

"When I absorbed Renamaum's power, I absorbed his essence as well. He knew therefore when the maelstrom of memories began to settle that I also knew." Alador was enjoying the clear discomfort on Sordith's face. Usually he was the one squirming and trying to adjust to Sordith's harsh revelations. "Henrick did not deny it when I confronted him on the matter."

"So…" Sordith took a deep swallow before asking his next question. "Are we… half dragon?" Sordith put a hand to his chest patting about.

"Does it matter?" Alador asked casually sipping his drink. He was enjoying the clear look of distress and the slipping mask of control his brother was so adept at maintaining.

"In fact, it does." Sordith gave a nervous chuckle. His voice was still high and tense, further giving away that the news causing him a great deal of distress. "If I am half a dragon then will I live longer? Am I missing power that I could be using?" Sordith frowned. "And if I am a half-dragon, how could I have failed my tier test?"

Alador chuckled. "Be at ease, brother, you are not half-dragon." Alador thought it far more amusing that Sordith now looked both confused and disappointed at that answer.

"I don't understand then. How can Henrick be a dragon and we not be half- dragon unless…" Sordith squeezed the cup in his hand till the knuckles were white, "...unless he's not our father?"

Alador knew that Sordith has spent years looking for his father and so considered carefully how to break this next piece of the news to his brother. "The Henrick that sired both of us - assuming he was truly your sire - is dead." Alador softened. "I am sorry, Sordith." Alador set the cup down and looked at his brother, the teasing gone from his face and eyes. "The Henrick we know, that we both have come to care for, killed him." The admission was soft, an attempt to ease the blow.

Sordith took a deep breath. "Why did he kill him?" There was no anger in Sordith's words, more a sense of loss. He broke his gaze from Alador and sat tensely staring at the cup in his hand.

Alador knew that there was no way for Sordith to know with certainty that the Henrick that they knew was being honest. He also had been able to confront Henrick directly and had not had to learn it second-hand. "I know it's hard to comprehend. I'm still struggling with it as well. You have the luxury of not quite being sure that Henrick was your sire. I know for a fact that he was mine."

Alador considered how to continue. "What Henrick said was that he found the actual man to be as bad as Luthian with little in redeeming qualities. Since taking his place would be to his advantage, he killed the real Henrick Guldalian and did so." He spoke softly and remained quiet as a silence descended between them. Alador knew that Sordith needed time to work this through his own mind.

"So who is the Henrick we know?" Sordith was beginning to regain some internal control as the information began to settle. He drained the cup and immediately refilled it.

"Keensight," Alador answered.

Sordith blinked a couple of times as he looked at Alador trying to piece where that fit in. "Wait, is that not the name of the dragon you went to see?" Sordith's eyes narrowed and his puzzlement wrinkled his brow.

Alador had not found that part quite as amusing. Especially since he was certain that the man, or dragon as it was, had seemingly left out the fact that there were stairs to his own cave. "Yes," he snapped. He shook his head; his displeasure at the fact must have been written on his face because Sordith began to laugh.

"Son of a whore…" He sat back and absorbed this fresh information before draining the cup again. "This type of information should not have been shared until I had consumed a great deal of alcohol." He pointed at the glass in his other hand. He sobered a little and sat back. "So the man who brought your Daezun girl here, the man who I told I thought was my father, the man who graced these halls: That man is a … dragon?" Sordith's questioning words and searching gaze gave a hint that he was trying to make sure Alador was not paying him back for the chair incident.

"Yes," Alador said and waited.

"Well shite, man, why didn't he just kill Luthian too?" Sordith asked in disbelief.

"I asked that very question." He sighed out the frustration that the answer had given him then and still did now. "Dragons don't think quite like we do. They are very long-sighted." Alador paused. "He decided a better replacement was needed before Luthian could be killed or the rituals of dragon-bleeding would just continue."

Sordith nodded: this appeared to make sense. "He and I did speak about that once. He wanted to find and train a man to take … up that mantle."

"You do not need to talk in careful circles. I already know that he means for it to be me." Alador shifted uncomfortably. "He is currently residing as Henrick at my home village of Smallbrook. I will need to tell him of this situation with Dethara to get his counsel as to how to proceed." He looked up at Sordith and hesitated.

Sordith's quick gaze did not miss it. "What?"

"I left out one thing when I shared my tale of meeting Dethara," Alador began.

"Lad, if I am going to trust you then you have got to quit showing up with all these things that I don't know." Sordith tossed the empty cup onto the table and both men watched it spin and slide to a stop. "I can't make good decisions on false information."

"I didn't want anyone else but you and H... Keensight to know." Alador explained. He said in a quiet hesitating manner that made it clear that he was not sure if he wanted to tell Sordith.

"Well out with it. Let us clear the table completely." Sordith was clearly going from shock to irritation.

"While you are not a half dragon, I am a... a pseudo-dragon and Dethara knows it."

Sordith blinked a couple of times. "What, by the gods, is a pseudo-dragon?"

"I didn't just harvest Renamaum's power and memories." Alador explained. "I absorbed him. I am mostly still Alador, but… I am also Renamaum."

Sordith stared at Alador so long and with such disbelief that the mage became worried. "Sordith?"

"Well shite," Sordith replied. He gave up using the cup and tipped up the jug.

Chapter Twenty-One

Sordith had always prided himself on being able to take in the most devastating news with a calm demeanor. In spite of this ability, he could not help feeling that his half-brother had completely rattled him, and he did not like it. If he had not seen Jayson crumble before his eyes, then he would not have believed the words spilling out of Alador. He had seen Alador's power first hand, and he knew that when it came to matters of such enormity, the man told the truth. Well, he mused, either his brother was truthful or he was a horrible liar of the first magnitude.

He sat holding the jug. He was at a crossroads at this moment - one that would determine the rest of his life, whether it was to be short or long. He could side with the High Minister as the Trench Lord should. That had been his long- term plan from the moment he had first stepped into the previous Trench Lords' shoes. Add to that, he would still – technically - be supporting family.

Otherwise, he could throw his lot in with Alador. This was the riskier path, but the possibility of greater power was certainly an incentive. The boy had united a few dragons to his cause. He had just admitted that he was some form of dragon. Alador had also just disclosed that another of the allies that Sordith had been courting was actually a dragon who had taken both the life and the shape of his father.

This thought provoked another pull from the jug. That took some swallowing. Henrick must be a very swift thinker because Sordith prided himself on being able to spot such ruses. The dragon had to be a very old one if he had enough power to effortlessly maintain such a transformation. Though, he mused, it did explain why the man ate so much. This brought an inward smile.

When a polite cough cut the silence, he realized that Alador was quietly waiting for him to speak. Sordith was not sure how to go on. His mind was racing over the facts as if racing over the air course on a lexital - such races were a favorite pastime of some of the younger and bolder occupiers of the upper tiers. Speaking of time, he needed to buy more to sort this all out properly. He did not need to rush his decision concerning who to support, especially as the choice would have enormous consequences for the two possible paths his future might take.

He glanced up to Alador who was sitting patiently. "How did he know so much about my mother?" Sordith asked. He pushed the jug away from himself before he just upended the entire contents into his mouth.

"I don't know. That is something you will have to ask him if you ever cross paths again." Alador stood and picked up the cup that Sordith had tossed. He refilled it and pressed it into Sordith's hand.

Sordith took it absently. "You think he won't return to Silverport?" He sat staring into the cup, turning it around and around.

"I know he won't for a time. Luthian banished him as Henrick and he has made me some promises." Alador sat back down. "Promises ... that I need help from you to fulfil as well."

Sordith's mind grabbed at the offering of a concrete task. He set the untouched cup down and picked up his quill. "What is it that you need?" He looked up at Alador.

"I want to minimize the impact on the Daezun as much as possible." Alador shifted uncomfortably. "How much would it cost for me to send routine secret shipments of basic food needs? Nothing luxurious, but food that people could survive on."

Sordith pulled out a book as well, then dipped his quill and quickly did some calculations, using this book for reference. "Well, there is the leasing of a less reputable ship, the extra fee the captain will charge because he hates Daezun… whether he truly hates them or not." He mused as he worked. "There is the cost of the goods themselves; I can afford to give you those for what they cost me." Sordith quit speaking as he calculated how much a ship could hold. He looked up when he was done. "You are looking at about one hundred seventy-five full medure slips a trip."

"How long would such a trip take to the closer ports and back?" Alador's face was scrunched up as he also calculated.

"Depends on the seas, the winds and the port." Sordith trailed off.

Alador jumped in at the pause. "Let us assume the winds are fierce and the seas rough," he pressed.

"Well if in one direction the wind was favorable, maybe two weeks to the nearest port and back." Sordith was now watching Alador closely. "What are you thinking?" He looked up at Alador with more than a hint of disbelief. Surely the boy was not going to try to feed an entire nation of people.

"What if I could guarantee the cargo? The captain can sell any exchanges the Daezun can give him for his own profits? Bloodstones… ore… gems and such." Alador pursed his lips. "In addition, I can guarantee that ship safety from the storms and pirates? What would my cost be then?"

"I don't truly know lad. I would have to approach the two or three captains I have in mind and see what they say." Sordith laid down the quill. "I can tell you that the one thing I am going to hear is that you can't guarantee safe seas."

"I think I can," Alador's firm tone spoke of confidence. He paused for a moment. "Approach your captains with my offer. I'll pay eighty medure up front for the cost of the supplies and I'll pay another one hundred upon return if the seas prove rough or pirates are encountered, in addition to any goods not damaged or sold."

"What if the seas are calm and pirate-free?" Sordith wanted to have all the facts to take to the captains.

Alador considered and then went on: "It is unlikely that they'll believe such safety is of my doing. They can sell the cargo with a guarantee of the one hundred from me. I will make up the difference if the cargo is light. They can keep any additional profits over one hundred as well."

"You realize that you are encouraging them to lie for the additional profits." Sordith shook his head. "It is to their benefit to tell you the seas were rough or they barely escaped from pirates, or even a step further and hide a portion of the cargo."

"Then I guess you had best make sure they understand that I'll know if they lie." Alador's eyes glistened with mischief.

"And just how will you do that?" Sordith could not imagine any way that any mage could be certain of such a thing for a two-week trip.

"You don't get to know all my secrets." Alador shook his head and firmly stated. "I will, however, give them a flag to fly. It will be required for them to receive the protection of fair weather, and other protections."

Sordith was quite surprised at Alador's change in his carriage and confidence. This was not the same man that he had punched in the gut for being an arrogant bastard to Mesiande. He considered the proposal. The negotiation tactic was a smart one for such a risky venture. Any captain taking the commission would be risking both the wrath of the Lerdenian Council and the predation of pirates. There were few in the water during the winter, but the risk still existed.

"I'll propose it," he agreed with a nod. He picked up the quill and quickly noted Alador's terms. "Are you sure you want to spend your own slips?" He looked up at his brother with concern. "

"The trader who paid me is dead. The stone I sold was worthless. I am going to be the cause of a storm that is rarely seen on the isle. I think…" Alador wiped his hand over his face before he continued. "I think it is my responsibility to ensure no one starves." He sighed with the weight of that responsibility.

"We are talking about a large number of slips. How flush are you?" Sordith was truly curious.

"I still have a great deal left. I will bring some down before I leave the city." Alador left it at that, and he did not look Sordith in the eyes.

Sordith wondered if his brother had found a dragon's hoard with these new skills of his. He decided a change of subject was in order. "You realize that there are so many places that this plan could go wrong, right?" Sordith replaced the quill in his hand with his cup. The spreading warmth of the alcohol he had already consumed was soothing his fractured composure.

"It may have already gone wrong with Dethara's more personal appearance." Alador admitted. "But if I fail, at least I know I'll have tried to make right all the things that I inadvertently made wrong."

"Much of that was not your responsibility," Sordith pointed out.

"No, I am responsible." Alador stared into the cup that sat on the desk. "I have had so many chances to do things differently, but either my pride or my temper won out."

Sordith chuckled, unable to disagree with the mage. "I am glad you finally acknowledge you have a temper, and often jump without looking." He shook his head with a rueful grin. "And there I was thinking about finding a trace of family and a sense of belonging. Instead, I think what I found was a nest of vipers better left alone," he quipped.

"Ah yes, speaking of viper nests." Alador shifted his posture. "I have another need for your unique ... skills."

Sordith raised a brow. "Oh, what is that?" His brother was asking for help, which in itself was a vast improvement. Since he had met the boy, Alador had been rushing off after making knee-jerk decisions. It was a welcome change, he thought, as he waited for Alador to answer.

"I need a spy in the temple of Dethara." Alador said.

Sordith blinked at Alador a few times in genuine surprise. "Can we go back to the discussion of pirates and storms? I think that venture has far more chance of success," he quipped. Sordith frowned. He did not like mages, and mage priests were a whole breed on their own. They had a nasty sense of God-fed morality that seemed to add power to their already seemingly impressive skills.

Alador flopped backwards in his chair in frustration. “I am serious,” he said with a scowl.

Sordith did not even pause. “So am I.” He had already decided that drinking was a prerequisite to meetings with his brother, and grabbed his cup. “You are asking the impossible. Death mages are rare; trustworthy death mages rarer.” He sat back with his cup in both hands. “Shite man. Why do you need a spy in there?”

“I need to know what she is up to,” he said. Alador took a moment and shared what Henrick had discovered. “I figure if he can find such things out just in tavern gossip, then something far more sinister might be afoot.” He tipped his head to survey Sordith. “Am I wrong?”

Sordith shook his head. Alador was learning quickly. Then again, he needed to learn quickly with everything stacked against him or he was a dead man. “Probably not,” he admitted. “I will see what I can do; but seriously, do not hold out much hope of success.”

Both men fell silent. "We need to talk about Luthian," Sordith ventured after a long moment.

Alador tipped his head curiously. "Oh?"

"I was present when Luthian was challenged to a duel.” He paused: telling Alador what he had observed would be tantamount to making his choice between the two possible allies. "He will not be easy to kill, Alador."

Alador smiled. "I assure you that the odds have been evened."

"Yes, I imagine this change to a ‘sort of’ dragon has changed the odds a bit..." Sordith emphasized the words ‘sort of’ with his hands and was about to continue when he was interrupted.

"Pseudo-dragon."

Alador sat back, seeming much more at ease. Sordith waved away the interruption. "Yes, yes. Whatever. Having knowledge and power does not guarantee a win in a fight if your opponent is crafty and practiced. Luthian is both." Sordith tapped the desk with his free hand. "You forget that he is the one training you to take the test."

Alador looked up at Sordith and nodded. "Yes, but by doing so he is also revealing the tactics that he uses in such battles."

Sordith watched Alador with concern. "That may serve you well in a ring for tier placement; but when you two finally come to blows, he will also know what to expect of you. He did not get to High Minister by default. He won his position through politics, scheming and challenge," Sordith firmly reminded him.

Alador leaned forward and set his cup down. "You sound as if you admire our Uncle." His words were terse.

"I do," Sordith admitted. "It takes brains, guts and determination to rise up as he has done. Only a fool would discount the traits he must possess to gain what he has. He could have lost that battle the other day. In fact, he nearly did." Sordith eyed Alador still feeling somewhat divided. "You are asking me to side with you and dragons based solely on the fact that we think we are related. But if we are related, Luthian is my blood too."

He pointed a finger at his brother for emphasis. "You had best take a second look at what you are doing: because, right now, you are an unwilling pawn of dragons against your own kin. Are you sure this is what you want?" He would have preferred a situation where his new found family was not trying to outsmart and kill one another. He shook his head at his own thoughts; what else did he expect in Silverport.

Alador rose to his feet and leaned across the desk. "Don't tell me that you think he should remain in power?" Alador's face was tight and his look was piercing.

Sordith did not miss the look of anger, the dangerous edge to his brother's tone, or that his own hair at the back of his neck had just stood on end. "I do have to wonder if his calm calculations are not safer than your rash temper." Sordith attempted to use humor to defuse his brother's sudden angst. Sordith kept his posture relaxed and his hands visible.

Alador stood up from where he leaned and his hands clenched and unclenched. "The man kills dragons like a miner digs for gems. If he is not stopped, there will be no dragons left." He took a deep breath. "If that happens, magic will fade from our world."

Sordith shook his head. "Is that my brother speaking or a dragon," he asked with gentle tones.

"Both!" Alador snapped. He turned and began to pace behind his chair, his hands clasped tightly behind his back.

"Have you ever considered, little brother, that maybe our world would be a better place without magic?" Sordith had to wonder what Lerdenia would be like if mages did not have the power to lord themselves over the commoners.

"No!" Alador stated with alarm. "Magic is a gift of the gods."

"A gift…" Sordith also stood up, " ... or a curse?"

Sordith moved around the desk to face his brother. "I know you have no choice as you are cursed by this geas of yours. But if the gods were truly enraged by the actions against the dragons, why have they not struck down the house of Guldalian?" He took a hold of his brother's shoulders. "Yet one is in power and another is the hand of the dragons' revenge. Maybe you are both tools for a game neither of you understand?"

Sordith scrutinized his brother's face before reaching out to clasp his him by the arms, stilling his pacing. He squeezed his brother's shoulders. "I am not trying to start a fight between us. I want you to consider that for every move you make, a highly intelligent man counters." Sordith took a deep breath. "It is possible that Luthian moves to the bidding of one god and you to another's." A heavy silence rose up between them, the air tense. Sordith let go.

"What else can I do, Sordith?" Alador looked up in exasperation.

"You can learn to fight without magic," Sordith offered. "You may have to use it in the ring for testing, but you do not have to use it in battle. Also, you listen to what I am trying to share with you. A wise ruler hears all good counsel, and even if he does not choose to act on it, he cannot say he was not well-informed." Sordith did not miss Alador's wince at the word 'ruler.'

Sordith cursed inwardly. He had revealed more than he had intended, but at the same time, Alador was racing towards a cliff as if he could not see the danger.

Alador took a deep breath and let it out. "What would you have me know?" he asked as the anger seemed to leech from him as fast as it had spiralled up between them.

Sordith considered what to share that would allow him some credible deniability. "You need to watch his use of items, particularly a dagger that turns into a fire snake when he tosses it. Its poison burned the opponent from the inside out as far as I could tell. The pain of it allowed him to finish the mage."

"I have never seen him use such a thing, but now I think about it, I have seen a dagger on his belt with a snake head at the end of the handle." His voice just trailed off. Alador's eyes glazed and his face took on a faraway expression.

"Alador?" Sordith called with concern. When he did not respond, Sordith called a little more harshly. "Alador!" He shook the man with a single hand.

His brother jumped at Sordith's touch and blinked a few times. "Sorry! Sorting through Renamaum's knowledge can often be distracting," Alador murmured.

Sordith could imagine that having the knowledge and memories of a dragon must be disconcerting at the very least. "You all right?"

"It gives me a bit of a headache, but as time passes it is getting easier." Alador rubbed his temple. "I do like the fact that as the information becomes my own I am becoming less anxious and more confident," he admitted.

"It is a good thing you already had a big head," Sordith quipped with a mischievous grin. He tapped Alador alongside his head.

"Gee thanks." The sarcasm was not veiled and he rolled his eyes at his brother's goading.

"More seriously, will you be able to control such knowledge and power?" Sordith was growing concerned that the dragons were creating a bigger threat than Luthian supposedly posed. As he saw it, Luthian was good for the city of Silverport. He understood the position of the dragons and Daezun, but did he, the Trench Lord, really care about their concerns?

He mentally reminded himself that this path would improve the lives of those in the trenches: an issue he did feel strongly about. He decided he was going to stick by Alador based on this largest factor. A greater equality for those without magic was never going to happen under Luthian.

Alador shrugged. "I don't honestly know. Renamaum took a calculated risk when he passed his core into me. To his knowledge, it has never been done before." Alador looked up at Sordith and grinned. "Perhaps you are right about that big head."

The troubled Trench Lord surveyed the mage's posture. "Alador, I need to make one thing clear. If…" Sordith paused as Alador met his gaze. "If I ever believe you are more of a threat than Luthian to the people under my care …" He put a finger to Alador's heart. "I will kill you."

Sordith held his brother's gaze until Alador finally answered. "Understood."

****

Sordith sought out Keelee after Alador left. He found her in a warm sitting room with a cheerful fire. She rose, setting aside her embroidery when he entered. He liked seeing these little bits of normalcy as if he ruled a real manor and not a quarter of thieves and vagabonds. He put his arms about her as she reached up to give him a gentle kiss.

"I have missed you today," she whispered.

"I am sorry, my love." Sordith squeezed her tightly then kissed her forehead. "There has been much to address today."

Keelee took his hand and led him to a chair. She pressed him down then slid to the ground at his feet, resting her hands and chin on his knee. "Tell me, you look distressed."

Sordith looked at her long and hard. If he was to bond with her, he needed to trust her. He had never given any woman other than Auries such trust and even then there were things he would not tell her. Could he trust Keelee with what he had just learned? He needed someone to talk to and yet fear of being betrayed coursed through him.

"Keelee, if I share what is in my head then I must be able to trust you with it." Sordith looked down at her, stroking her silken hair. "It can never leave this room."

Keelee met his eyes evenly. "You are my mate. I have given my word to bond with you. There will never be another who could pay for my lips to open." Her soft words meant so much to him yet he still feared to extend that trust.

He licked his lips. "I am faced with a horrendous choice. One that could affect us both if I choose poorly."

"Then should you not share this choice with me? We can decide the course together." She took her hand from her hair and reached up to put it over his.

She was right. The choice would affect her and as such, she needed to know what he was up against. "You know that a Trench Lord rules until his death, and that such deaths do not come from old age."

She nodded. She kissed his knuckles tenderly. "I know I may be widowed without notice." She looked from his hand to his eyes. "It is a frightening thought but one that I have accepted."

"Two possible paths now lie before me," Sordith began, staring absently above her head. "I can support Luthian as I am supposed to do. It would mean plenty of coin, a long lasting relationship, and would move us in higher circles." He glanced down at Keelee. "I know you have no love for the man, but he may very well be my uncle."

Keelee frowned. "I do not; but I also am very aware of the politics of the tiers. You cannot be successful without the Council's approval. The work being done to cover the trenches is a good example of this."

"Yes, but there is a horrid catch." Sordith sighed and squeezed her hand. "I would have to betray Alador. He is my half-brother. "

"I don't understand. Why would you have to betray Alador?" She eyed him with concern. "Though he is angry at me, I had cared for him. I would hate to see him hurt. It is why I am absent when he visits: to ease his pain."

Sordith looked down at her with concern. "Do you love him?" His eyes narrowed with a feeling of unaccustomed jealously.

She smiled at his words and manner. "No. I care about him, but I do not love him." Her expression sobered. "I do not want to see him hurt after what he went through to try to rescue me from your predecessor."

"Nor I," admitted Sordith, "…but to stay the course with Luthian I would have to let him know that Alador moves against him."

Keelee's eyes widened. "He still means to remove him?"

"He does." Sordith pulled her up to sit in his lap. He needed her close at the moment.

She nestled into his chest. "What is your other option?" she whispered.

"I work with Alador to see it done," Sordith answered kissing the top of her head. "But if we fail, we will both be killed or later executed." He mused for a moment. "My brother does have an advantage."

"What advantage?" She asked. He could almost hear her analyzing the choices, just as he was.

"He has aligned with the dragons." Sordith shared in an awed whisper. "They plot and plan with him."

"The dragons have not worked with mortals since the great wars." She glanced up at him with her eyes wide, her amazement and disbelief written on her open face.

"I am aware." Sordith hugged her tight. "It is a difficult position."

"Can you play both sides for a time, until a more obvious path is clear?" She touched his cheek tenderly.

"Aye, I can for a time." He had been already doing this.

"Then as your mate in this course, I would not choose until you have to do so." She kissed his lips tenderly. "But, keep in mind. To go against Luthian will be a grave matter. But even so, to go against a man aligned with dragons could lead to a fiery end."

Sordith smiled. "I have chosen my mate well." He squeezed her against his body, loving the soft feel of her. He swept her up as he rose from the chair. "I will wait until I must choose, keeping my options open. But you are right, I will not act against dragons unless I can see they will clearly lose."

Keelee smiled. "Where are we going?" she asked.

"To bed. If a man must choose a path in a coming war, he had best enjoy the moments of peace he has right now." He strode out of the parlor and down the hall towards their room. "And… you my dear, are well worth enjoying."

Her giggle was cut off when he firmly shut the door behind them.

Chapter Twenty-Two

Alador was moving to the next step of his plans. He had to talk to his brother in Smallport. Having his brother understand the situation and help him to alleviate the damage that the winter would bring was critical. There was no value in sending goods to the port cities if the critical nature of the coming situation was unknown. It was possible that the Daezun would not trade at the start, not realizing how urgently they needed to stock up.

Alador focused on home and narrowed his memory to the coal room where his chest was secured. If Henrick had spoken to his family, the room should be as he had left it, or at least close enough for him to materialize safely. He clutched the talisman and murmured the words. The room he stood in turned into a whirling blur.

The world snapped back into focus, and the coal room of his mother's home was exactly as he remembered it. He had taken a huge chance that either nothing had been moved or that Henrick had not forgotten to tell everyone to make sure everything was where he remembered it being.

He smiled to see the chest buried behind the pickled stores. He knew his brother would not have accessed more than was absolutely necessary of the remaining slips. Before he left, he would have to gather some more to pay for the supplies he would be sending to coastal cities. He straightened his clothing so that his mother would not scold him. He was dressed in a simple pair of brown breeches and a longer green tunic. He hoped his Daezun clothing would help his family forget what he had become.

His hand went to the door, and he stood holding the handle. His heart raced in his chest and he could feel the cold sweat between his palm and the metal handle. He was counting on Dorien more than was probably fair. He was also hoping that they would not expose him to the village. By the village law, they should turn him over to the Counsel. While he could escape easily enough, he didn't want to lose his family completely. He took a deep breath to try to settle his nerves and carefully opened the door.

He could hear laughter and the mage's voice. Henrick had been here a couple of weeks now, so he hoped that the older mage had managed prepare his family. He wasn't sure how they would feel about his excelling as a mage. He was not the same middlin that had left them a turn ago.

He stepped out of the hall and made his way to the main room. Everyone was sitting about the table eating dinner. It was a typical fall evening with merry laughs and a crackling fire over in the sitting room. The house had not changed since he left it. It was one long room with only a slight division of beams between the dining table and the sitting room. To his right was the kitchen. It served two purposes: cooking was done in the oven and the clay benches to either side were hollow, allowing heat to radiate across a larger surface.

Dorien saw him first, his laughter abruptly cutting off. His spoon half to his mouth, he paused leaving his mouth hanging open. Either he was not expected, or Alador's sudden appearance had still been surprising.

Dorien set the spoon down carefully. Henrick followed his gaze and set his mug down. One by one, the room went silent as eyes turned to see him. Sophie was the last to stop her laughter and turn to see what everyone was looking at. Alador stood there uncertain, unsure of what to say. It was his maman who broke the tense silence.

"My boy!" she screamed. The chair tumbled back, barely missing Alador as she heaved from the chair. She crossed the short distance to wrap her arms about him, bursting into relieved tears.

Everyone else but Henrick followed her and gathered around. One by one his brothers and sister hugged them both, as their mother was not letting go for the moment. Tentret and Dorien had large smiles on their faces and Sophie was crying like their mother. The relief Alador felt at this welcome nearly caused him to lose his footing beneath the onslaught. His legs trembled with the flood of emotion. His eyes met Henrick's and mouthed a silent 'thank you'; the mage merely toasted him in return with his mug.

There so many questions being fired at him that finally Dorien intervened. "Quiet!" Everyone looked at him with slight shock. "Tentret, close the curtains tight. Maman, stop that caterwauling before a neighbor comes knocking. Let Alador have a seat and we will take turns with our questions."

Alador flashed Dorien a grateful look as Sofie led him to the table. His mother was busy dabbing her eyes with her apron. Alador knowing his mother well, looked over and smiled.

"Maman, suppose I could get a bowl of that stew? It smells amazing." As he predicted, his mother's face split into a huge smile and she hurried over to ladle him a bowl.

Alador slipped into a chair and everyone sat back down. His mother put a bowl and spoon before him, and Sofie slid over the loaf of steaming bread. Alador looked about as everyone stared at him, waiting expectantly. Alador took the expected taste of the stew and nodded to his mother.

"I have missed your cooking so much, Maman." He was again rewarded with her happy grin as she joined the others at the table.

"Now there, my dear boy, you know very well I fed you quite often." Henrick frowned at Alador. The others laughed, breaking the tension of the unanswered questions on the tip of everyone's tongue.

"Father, no offense but there is nothing better than maman's cooking. Why, I think that is half the reason you visit so often," Alador teased.

"That and other delights." Henrick conceded with a grin.

"Henrick!" Alanis squeaked.

Chuckles went about the table at the look on Sofie's face and his mother's girlish blush. Alador found that the thought did not bother him as it first had. He had accepted that Henrick, the Henrick whom he knew, was not responsible for the spell placed upon his mother the night he had been conceived. That his mother was cavorting with a dragon was a bit more than he wanted to consider.

The next couple of hours were spent answering his family's questions. What was his day like? What was it like to live in a mine? How long could he stay? What did he think of Silverport? What kind of spells could he cast? Alador was careful to keep his answers very general when it came to matters of his magic. Dorien caught his eyes with a questioning look at one point, and Alador had given him a slight shake of his head. He knew his brother would have surmised that this was not just a family reunion. After that, Dorien left the questions to everyone else.

"What did you do to Mesiande?" Sofie asked. The room became silent, and Alador did not miss the withering look that his mother gave his sister.

"What do you mean, what did I do to her?" Alador frowned uncertain how answer that question and buying time.

"One day, she was just a little sad and missing you. The next, she was all angry and quit talking to everybody." Sofie explained. "She spends most of her time in a mine or at home. She hardly ever is about the village anymore."

"I don't live here. How could I have been responsible?" He glanced at Henrick who just shrugged and ladled stew into his mouth.

Sofie rolled her eyes. "Oh please! Like any of us believe for a moment that you two don't communicate somehow."

Tentret uncharacteristically came to Alador's rescue. "Sofie, your mouth and gossiping ways are going to be the end of you one day. You make assumptions without facts to base them on."

"I have facts." She pouted in that childlike manner that she had perfected. "I just believe that you can love someone. Love has a way of crossing barriers. Tentret, everything isn't a matter of logic and cold-hearted korpen dung."

"Sofie!" Alanis' face clouded with a look that every one of her children had come to fear. "You will leave now, and you will keep your mouth shut about Alador's presence here tonight. Am I clear?" Alanis enunciated every word.

Sofie looked as if she were going to argue for a brief moment. Alador realized that it would not be long before Sofie found a housemate to establish her own household. It would not have ended well for his sister if she had tried to stand up at that moment. However, he suspected that the day she would try was not too far off. It was usually how a woman came to find a housemate and a house of her own: mother and daughter would finally reach a point where the authority of one was challenged by the other. Usually, the daughter did not win.

Sofie stood up angrily and pushed her chair in. "I just asked a question. You all act like she is the one who 'died'." Her glance at Alador was haughty and condemning. With this last gibe, his sister turned and flounced from the room. The force of the door slamming rattled the pans hanging on their pegs in the kitchen.

Tentret put a hand on Alador's arm. "Don't pay her no mind. You know how she is."

Alador nodded. Despite knowing Sofie, her parting comment had still stung. It wasn't that she had hurt his feelings, but more that her gibe had been the truth. Technically, Alador was supposed to be dead to them.

Dorien looked around the table, leaned over to the older man and murmured. "Henrick, I would like to speak to my brother alone if I may. Would you take maman down for a drink or two?"

Henrick nodded. "I would be happy to." The older mage rose up and offered his hand to Alanis. "Shall we, my dear?"

"But he just got here and … I want to stay." She crossed her arms in that way that Alador had come to dread. His mother could be rather stubborn. Despite her age, he was fairly sure his mother was pouting.

"I promise you that you will get to speak to him before he disappears again, Alanis." Henrick caressed her cheek as he gave her a gentle smile. "However, I know that Alador has something that he must speak with Dorien about as well, and well, the less you and I know, the better it will be." He put a concerned hand on her arm. "You wouldn't want to endanger our dear boy, now would you?"

Alanis looked at Alador with uncertainty. "Well no…" she admitted, allowing Henrick to pull her from the chair by her arm. "It's just…" She swallowed the rest of her words.

Alador tried to give her a reassuring smile. "I promise, Maman, I will not run off and leave you without a proper conversation. It'll be just the two of us."

"Swear it!" Alanis said, glancing at him with genuine fear he would disappear.

"I so swear."

Tentret stood up. "I think I will go double-check the fire at the forge, make sure it is banked properly." The two brothers always banked it properly so Alador knew it was just an excuse to give his two brothers privacy.

Alador waited till Henrick and his mother had left before saying anything further. When the door latched, he looked at Dorien to find his brother deeply scrutinizing him. "I suppose you want to know why I am really here," the mage said.

"If it were so easy for you to come and go without consequence, then tonight would not have been the first night you came home." Dorien leaned back, teetering his chair on its back legs. The big man was clearly waiting for Alador to explain for he said nothing more and crossed his arms.

"I have.... There's this..." Alador ran a hand through his hair. "I am not sure how to explain this," he admitted.

"I find starting at the beginning is a very good way to start a complicated explanation." Dorien advised solemnly. He winked at him.

"The beginning?" Alador wondered where that even was after everything he had learned from Renamaum.

"The beginning seems a right smart way to start," Dorien restated.

Alador rubbed his face and sat back, considering how to start. "There are so many strands, and each strand has its own beginning." He took a breath and eyed his brother, wondering if he were making the right choice.

He decided to begin by setting the stage. "Silverport has a High Minister, like most cities. However, it's the capital: it leads all the rest." Alador stared at the wall behind Dorien. "It turns out that this man, Luthian, is my uncle."

Dorien whistled. "Well, that is news that had best not get out. We will have people lying in wait to see if you ever appear and will each want to be the one to claim your or Henrick's head." Dorien still sat cross-armed and relaxed.

Seeing his brother had not reacted in anger emboldened Alador to go further. "These things are going to seem unrelated for a moment, but I will tie them all together when I am done." He waited for Dorien's nod then continued.

Alador pulled the mug over and stared into it. "The bloodstone I harvested was clear because my mage powers had just reached a point where I would have passed the test. When I pulled the stone out of the ground, somehow I harvested the powers in the stone itself." He looked up but Dorien just nodded at him to continue.

"This stone was a bit different. It is a geas stone. When a powerful dragon is dying, it can press its dying wish into the stone. The mage that finds that stone must complete the dragon's last request, but gains the power of the dragon to help him do so." Alador turned the cup absently in his hands, watching the liquid within slosh back and forth.

"The dragon of this stone was very powerful. So much so that an echo of him was retained within the stone and transferred to me when I harvested it. It is rather complicated to explain it all, but the short version is that he is now a part of me." Alador took a deep breath and did not look up to see how his brother was taking it.

"You have asked me to accept your word a great deal, brother." Dorien stated quietly. "But now you tell me that you hold within you one of the beasts that we revere. It is… a little much to accept." Dorien sat his chair back down on four legs and leaned forward. He looked Alador up and down. "I have never heard of such a thing happening."

Alador looked up at his brother. "Imagine how I feel, knowing that my powers came because of the death of a dragon. Or that I took his powers and his memories." Alador swallowed hard. "That leads me to the next part. I have made a pact with his family and another dragon."

Dorien's sat staring at Alador for a very long time. When he finally spoke, it was as if he feared being overheard. "You have spoken with dragons?" His question was slow and Dorien's eyes were very large.

"I have." Alador met Dorien's gaze evenly. "The last request of the dying dragon needed to involve them." Alador's face lit with excitement. "It was more than I ever dreamed, Dorien. They talk, act and play just like Daezun or Lerdenians, except, well, they are dragons."

"What is this dragon's last request?" Dorien pressed.

"Oh, yes sorry. I got off track." Alador spun the mug between his hands spilling liquid onto the table. "Well, it is rather broad and hard to interpret, but it basically is to save the dragons' young from Lerdenia."

"How is one man to do that?" Dorien asked incredulously.

"If you knew how many times I have asked that question." Alador laughed at the thought. "However, one man does not. He reaches out to those he trusts for help."

"And this is why you are here?" Dorien asked.

"Yes, this is why I am here." Alador admitted. "I could think of no one I trust more."

Dorien ran a hand over his face and took a deep breath. "I suspect by your posture and tone there is more. Let us have the rest of this incredible news."

Alador planned to be a bit more careful in the next revelations. His brother did not need to know quite everything. He had already trusted him with a great deal that could lead to many trying to end his existence. He nodded and pushed the mug aside.

"Luthian, my uncle, wishes to unify the island under one rule..." Before Alador could continue Dorien rose up, his chair falling backwards.

Dorien spit on the floor. "It will be a foul day when any Daezun bends their knee to a mage ruler."

Alador remained calm. He looked up at his brother and stated firmly. "A foul day is coming." He held Dorien's angry gaze and remained still.

Dorien finally broke the stare between them and picked up the chair, setting it upright angrily. "What do you know?" he spat out.

"Luthian has a weather mage. One that is capable of casting and controlling great blizzards and storms." Alador hated not telling his brother the whole truth, but he was fairly certain that the man would not understand the delicate game that he played. "The plan is to bring a hard winter down on the Daezun, then a late spring frost, and between weather and failing crops, force them to draw in." Alador could not continue to look at Dorien and speak, so he rose clasping his hands behind him as he walked to the crackling fire.

"He will force starvation upon the land, then come in offering the people salvation. The condition for food, aid and help with the weather will be to bend that knee you so adamantly claim will never bend." Alador picked up a small grass pot that his sister had woven for his mother when she was young, eyeing it fondly. When Dorien did not speak, the mage turned around to look at him.

"I do not understand." Dorien look flustered as he dropped back into the chair.

"It will be a war of attrition. Not a single man will be lost in Lerdenian holdings. The longer the Daezun stubbornly refuse to ask for help, the more of them will die. In Luthian's mind, either way, he will win." Alador moved to stand before Dorien, his apprehension gone as he spoke with confidence.

"And your part?" Dorien asked with suspicion. "What part are you to play?"

Alador cleared his throat and shifted nervously. "I have abjectly refused to assist him in the destruction of my own family." Alador raised his chin a little. At least that part was true and allowed him to meet Dorien's harsh appraising look calmly. "He has agreed to save Smallbrook from the worst in exchange for my loyalty and silence."

Dorien's eyes narrowed. "But you are telling me?"

Alador nodded. "Yes, so it is best he not find out," he answered. Alador moved closer to Dorien. "But to remain close to him, I may have to do things I don't like." He took a hold of Dorien's shoulder. "When I am powerful enough though, I am going to remove him from power and kill him."

Dorien rose back up, surveying Alador as he did and his movement forced Alador's hand to fall away. They stood quietly assessing one another. "You have changed," he stated.

"More than I can ever explain, brother." Alador nodded in agreement. He grinned at his brother's recognition of the fact.

"We will not leave our home, Alador. We will not run and leave the others to this fate." Dorien's tone was deadly and cold.

"I was counting on the fact that you would not." Alador admitted. He glanced up at the beast of a man.

Dorien ran a hand through his unkempt hair. "You have a plan?"

Alador pulled out the chair by his brother and sat down. He reached across the table to retrieve his mug. Only then did Alador look at Dorien and smile as he beckoned his brother to sit. "I have the plan."

Chapter Twenty-Three

Alador had stayed almost the entire night talking to his family. He had not dared to leave their house for fear that someone other than his kin saw him in the village. He had spent time with each of them alone, even Sophie, who had settled down in the wee hours of the morning. It had been important to show them that despite his skills in magic, he was still the same Alador who had been forced to leave them.

He rubbed the ache from his eyes caused by the lack of sleep and staring into the fire for far too long. He had one last person to see; it was a visit he dreaded and hoped for all at the same time. Alador focused his talisman on the small clearing by the swimming hole. Dawn was breaking, so no one would be about. Sophie was on her way to see if Mesiande would meet him there.

As he manifested in the small clearing, he was relieved to find that it was unchanged. He had half-feared appearing with a twig in his leg. Alador built a small fire to provide heat for her. Once he was satisfied with the small blaze, he looked about. He had built the fire to filter up through the trees and had used the driest wood he could find. He did not want anyone to come investigating.

Alador paced for some time before he heard the first steps of anyone approaching. The sun was fully visible over the far ridge when Mesiande stepped into the small copse of trees that sheltered the pool. Alador smiled at her despite the state that he had left things. She had that pert upturn of her chin, and it was clear that even though she was angry with him that she had still groomed to meet him. Not a hair was out of place, and she wore a skirt rather than her usual breeches. Alador was uncertain if the dress was a good sign or a bad one.

Mesiande did not answer his smile. Her arms were crossed, and her words were clipped when she finally spoke. "Well, I'm here. What do you want?"

The smile on Alador's face slowly slid down. It was clear that she was still more than a little vexed with him. He could not blame her. He had acted the perfect ass, and while he had gotten the results he had wanted at the time, the cost had been harsh.

"I came to apologize and to tell you that you were right." He would have to step carefully. Mesiande had one of those tempers that was hard to rile, but once fired up she took her time forgetting one's offense. Alador put both hands out, beseeching her forgiveness.

"Of course I was right." Her hands moved to her hips. "You can't just show up and say I am sorry," she pointed out angrily. "It won't just make things magically better, no matter how good a mage you have become."

Alador's tone was soft as he answered her. "I realize that, Mesiande. However, it seemed a good place to start."

She took her hands off her hips and stepped forward. It was a good sign. "And what was it that I was right about?"

"That I was being a korpen's ass. That what I said and did was beyond simple forgiveness. That I was becoming a man that you would not wish to be with." Alador indicated the ground to offer her a place to sit with him by the fire. When she shook her head no, he continued. "Mesi, I just wanted you to go home. I thought if you were mad enough at me that you wouldn't want to stay."

He took a step towards her. "I would never want you to be a bed servant. I... care for you too much to use you so callously."

"Well, it worked," she pointed out. "I'm home." Mesiande gave a flippant toss of her braid as she turned away from him to walk to the edge of the water.

"Mesi, please forgive me. I didn't mean a word of it," he begged in a soft whisper, stepping as close to her as he dared.

Mesiande's answering growl was also a low murmur though he could hear her sheer displeasure at the man behind her. "And why should I?"

"First, you are my best friend." Alador began. "Second, there is no one I would rather bond..." He cleared his throat having slipped into Lerdenian ways of speaking. "…housemate with than you." He touched her shoulder and though she stiffened, she did not pull away. He slowly turned her towards him. "Lastly, if not for me, our people need your help, and you and Dorien are the only ones I can trust to aid me." Her eyes came up to meet his at the last.

"What do you mean?" Mesiande's eyes narrowed, and she tipped her head a bit to the right to look up at him.

He let out held tension with a sigh. Her question indicated the thawing of her displeasure. "The matter is worse than I first told you. Luthian means to starve the Daezun into submission. I came with a plan which Dorien helped me refine, but he is going to need your help to convince the elders. With you, Henrick, and Dorien, I believe you can do it." He would take the third route closer to her if it were all she would give to him. He knew Mesiande. Once she started talking to him, the rest would be put behind her over time.

"A plan?" She looked at him curiously. "What plan could stand against the magic that you spoke of in Silverport?" She wandered over to the fire and plopped down. She straightened her skirts, casting him a frosty glance.

Alador grinned. "That is where the convincing is going to come into play." He slipped to the ground beside her, being careful to respect her space before he continued.

"After you left, I went to speak with a red dragon. Actually, the one that burned our village." Mesiande began to speak, but he held a hand up indicating it was a long story. "First of all, he will be providing as much meat to the villages as he can to make up for the damage he caused. However, he can also arrange for a bronze dragon to come and open a cavern at each village: a place away from the freezing cold where food can be stored and in the extremes of cold and snow that Luthian will bring, the villages can take refuge." He paused seeing her eyes widen.

"Spoke? You spoke with a dragon?" Her clear disbelief made him smile.

"Yes, I find them rather arrogant and pompous, but as intelligent and resourceful as any in the old tales. It took some convincing, but..." Alador frowned when it came to him that Keensight had already decided to help - Henrick had arranged their meeting, and since Henrick was Keensight, the exercise had been nothing but showmanship. He would have to speak to the man about that later. Realizing that he had not finished his sentence by the way she was watching him, he continued: "…but the dragons are going to help."

Mesiande was now enthralled, her anger nowhere evident as she leaned forward. "And ... Dragons are said to do no favor without an exchange of favor returned." She paused for a moment. "Are you still going to take out the mine as you spoke of before. Is that the price you will pay?"

Alador nodded. "If I don't take out the bloodmine, it's doubtful that we will get any help from any dragon other than Keensight. I have to complete that before I can turn my attention to saving our people from Luthian's need to control all of the Great Isle." Their eyes locked and Alador could not help staring into those big brown eyes. He missed her so much.

"What is it that you need me to do with Dorien?" She picked up a stick and spun it in her fingers, before absently stripping the leaves from it one at a time. Alador was still blankly staring at her. When he did not answer, she glanced up and blushed. She punched him in the arm lightly. "You didn't answer me."

Alador started and grinned. "Sorry, I had almost forgotten how beautiful you were." He liked that he could make her blush. Despite the distractions of being next to her, he continued. "The elders will need convincing that this storm is coming. They need to start conserving now. Luthian does not intend to let the next crops grow. My thought is to plant an early false crop - not too much effort but enough to make it seem a valid planting. Once that crop has mildewed and faltered, plant a second crop. It will have a lower yield, but if we plant the first early enough at every village, the second should have time to gain ground before he discovers the ruse." Alador stared off at the water. "Also, the crops can't be visible from the trade routes. He uses the traders as spies - with or without their knowledge."

"So by creating these caves, we have storage and shelter." Mesiande began to calculate as she followed his train of thought. "With us storing away everything we can, the traders will be reporting that less is coming out of the villages which will make it appear that the man's plan is working. Right?" She paused and looked over at him.

Alador gave an answering grin. Mesiande had such a quick mind, it was one of the things he valued about her. "Yes, but it will have to be an orchestrated effort with almost every village north of here. If they don't all work together, the plan won't work." He glanced over at her. "You and Dorien are going to have to be convincing. The villages have not united since the last war."

Mesiande was quiet for a moment, and Alador let her think. "What is to stop the weather from continuing? If this is the man's desire, he is not going to stop just because we thwarted him a winter or two."

Alador sobered at that thought. He knew that Luthian would not stop until he had everything he desired. Power meant more to him than anything. It was one reason that he could never let the older mage find the black spell book. He shook his head to clear it from the distracting thoughts and answered her in a low murmur. "I am going to kill him." He did not look at Mesiande. He knew her thoughts about such acts. Mesiande was one who preferred peaceful solutions.

"I see." Her words were hollow.

He cringed at her delayed answer. It was everything that he had expected, and yet it still cut to hear the tone she used. He reached over to take her hand; when she did not resist, his thumb caressed her palm gently.

"It is the only way Mesiande. There is no reasoning with him. He kills and hurts those that get in his way. He is quick on his feet and highly intelligent." Alador squeezed her hand, attempting to reassure them both.

"Add to that the power that he wields both in magic and in politics of the city and he will be no easy man to remove." She put her other hand over his and leaned in closer. His heart quickened at the mere scent of her, and the reassurance of her touch.

"How are you going to gain that much power?" She sounded genuinely concerned. "You are so much younger than he is." She searched his face, a soft frown on her own.

"I have the advantage of a dragon willing to educate me without the need to rely on finding an old spell book." He paused. "Though Henrick has provided some access to such tomes as well." He still had not decided the final fate of his ancestor's black spell book. "But, I think the best way to kill him will be without magic at all," Alador admitted. "A well-timed arrow may be far more effective than a spell. He is constantly prepared to defend himself against magic, poisons, and other such methods used by Lerdenians."

"Why does this all have to be you?" She squeezed his hand between her own. "Can't someone else take up this cause?" She frowned as she slowly let go of his hand. "Shouldn't the elders decide how to put a stop to this terrible mage?"

"Mesi, the last war lasted far too long with no clear winner. Our people will not be able to fight a prolonged war against mages. Especially since the Lerdenians have learned from the last war, and have created a unique set of soldiers that can wield both sword and spell." He ought to know as he was one of them, he thought before he continued. "Many of those in his elite unit have an axe to grind against our people because of the way they were treated as half-breeds." He ran a hand over where hers had been moments before. "I can get close to him because we are kin. He still hopes to use me to help him against our people."

"Use you how?" She asked, her look had a cautious edge. She pushed a twig into the fire before looking back at him expectantly.

He met her eyes with a solemn expression. "It is best you do not know," he quietly answered. He held her gaze, hoping she would leave it at that. He did not dare tell any Daezun his part in Luthian's plan. He did not know if he would be able to forgive himself, let alone gain the forgiveness of his people.

Alador was surprised when Mesiande did not press the issue. Usually her curiosity was an unrelenting force of persuasion. Instead she just nodded and they both sat quietly for a few moments. Alador did not want to break the uneasy silence. He was certain that whatever forgiveness he had gained here it was fragile at best.

"I wish it wasn't you," she offered sadly. "I wish you had never found that blasted stone." She angrily tossed another twig into the small blaze.

"I wish that as well." Alador watched her toss twigs moodily into the fire. He could not find fault with her frustration because he shared it. "My Lerdenian kin did this. It was my kin that broke the pact. Somehow, I feel like I was destined to be the one to fix it."

"What if you are caught playing both sides? What if your uncle figures it out?" She pressed. "What will you do then?" She glanced up at him, genuine fear for him written on her face.

He did not have much of an answer for her. He took a deep breath before answering. "I hope when that happens, I will be strong enough to defend myself," he offered.

"I don't want you to die," she said sadly. Her voice and eyes flashed with a sudden surge of passion. "You have to promise me not to get yourself killed."

He chuckled before looking at his boots. "You know I can't promise that." He glanced back at her as he put a hand on her leg. "I can promise that living is very important to me." He gave her a teasing grin. "I still want to come to your circle."

He noted the immediate rise of her chin and the scrunching of her nose. "Don't think I am not still mad at you." She stated with indignation.

"It doesn't change what I want, Mesi." Alador slid his hand over to take her hand. "Maybe in time you will change your mind," he breathed out, an edge of hope in his words. "I seem to remember you liked my kisses." He kissed her hand and glanced over her knuckles.

She tossed her head; her braid nearly hit him. "Maybe, but not today." She did not pull her hand loose, and he noted a flush of color to her cheeks. "However, I will help Dorien because, though I am mad at you..." Her chin came up with slight emphasis on the word mad. "I know you would not lie about such things."

It was more than he had dared to hope. He nodded and rose to his feet, pulling her with him. "I need to return before I am missed." He smoothed a hair from her face. "Dorien is expecting you to visit if you agree. He said that the less I knew of your plans the better - in case I somehow fall under Luthian's sway."

Mesiande shuddered. "I don't want to see you leave. It is ... unsettling." She turned to head out of the small cove, and his eyes followed her as she moved. She turned back to look at him. "I mean it." She wagged her finger at him. "Don't you go dying on me." With that, she stomped into the brush and out of sight.

Alador smiled. By that mere statement, he knew that eventually she would relent. Mesiande could be stubborn, but once she gave in a little, she always softened the rest of the way over time. It was not the first time that he had made her spitting-mad at him. His smile faltered. However, his harsh words on that dock in the trenches had been the worst thing he had ever done. It was still possible that he had gone too far to earn her favor enough to be chosen in her circle.

He smothered the fire, his thoughts replaying the last half of an hour. Only time would tell, and unftunately there was not enough of that to go around. He activated the amulet to return to the caverns. He had been given leeway, but he still needed to be careful. If he was gone too long, someone would eventually check his cell; and an empty room and bed would be extremely difficult to explain.

Chapter Twenty-Four

Alador had returned to the caverns after leaving Mesiande. Before he left he had to put in an appearance for his guards outside his door. He manifested in his room and looked around swiftly. Everything was as he left it. He let out a deeply held breath to release the tension and headed for the door.

He nodded to the guard and headed out of the room to be escorted to the food hall to fetch a tray. It was the only time that he was allowed out. A silence preceded him people eyed him and moved aside. He moved down the halls and into the mostly empty food hall. He knew that his disappearance had been spoken about a great deal. He could hear audible whispers of the new High Master's power, Alador's own, and even a summons from the High Minister. He kept his eyes downcast and his manner solemn to appear appropriately contrite.

He returned to his room with his tray without acknowledging anyone. Alador thanked the guards, and they nodded politely as they took their places by the door. When he stepped inside, he found Master Levielle waiting at his desk, a small smirk upon his face as their eyes met. Alador found meeting the man's eyes a bit more uncomfortable. Levielle had those eyes that seemed to miss little.

"You have missed my classes again." The weathered soldier clasped his hands behind him as he stood. "And here I find you feasting in private luxury?" He indicated the tray in Alador’s hands with a nod.

The High Master had said he would be locked down, and Alador had assumed that this meant that he would have no visitors. He had been lucky that Levielle had not been in the room when he had magically appeared.

Alador set his tray down on the desk as the door shut and turned to face his teacher. "I apologize Master Levielle. I got myself in a bit of trouble I fear, and as you can see, I am not allowed to attend classes." As he spoke, the older mage was glancing about his small room as if seeking something.

"Yes, yes." Levielle looked about. "I have come to see how you are progressing in your studies."

Much to Alador's surprise, Levielle shielded the room from those that would listen. He had thought the teacher, as a general in the standing army, would have had no skill in spell casting. He stared at the general, his surprise written on his face.

Levielle moved closer to Alador and cleared his throat. His manner was serious, and his voice held an amused edge. "And how are your Daezun kin, may I ask?" His question was so casual that it caught Alador completely off guard.

"I ... excuse me?" Alador sputtered at the question.

"Your Daezun kin, how do they fare?" At the alarmed look on Alador's face, the man simply shook his head. "You really do not excel well at subterfuge, my dear boy." Levielle chuckled. "If you mean to keep those with a discerning eye from being suspicious, you had best pay better attention. You are wearing Daezun garb, there is a leaf in your hair, and the mud on the edge of your boot holds no match to those in the cavern depths." Levielle moved to the chair at the desk and turned it to sit as he eyed Alador up and down. "Shall I repeat my original question or do you have enough information to decide it would be unwise to lie to me further?"

Alador swallowed down his fear and answered in low tones despite the shield. "My kin are well, Master Levielle.” The look of genuine concern on Alador's face brought a shake of the head from the teacher.

"Do not fear lad,” He held up a hand as if to stop Alador from speaking further. “I do not plan to speak of your antics to any others.” The man indicated that Alador should take a seat on the bed.” I had hoped that you would take me up on my offer to have private lessons, but given the new situation it would seem I need to bring them to you."

Alador slowly lowered himself onto the bed. "Why?" He was suspicious of this man's attention. Had Luthian sent him?

"I would think that is obvious. You cannot move to the next level without having completed my course in a manner of which I approve.” Levielle smiled. Even in the chair, his posture, although somewhat relaxed, seemed at the ready. There was an erect manner about him that one did not miss.

"That is not what I meant and I suspect you are fully aware of that.” Alador put both his hands on his knees; his fingers dug in, betraying his level of concern. "Why do you care enough to give me private lessons?"

"Perhaps the fact that you are astute enough to discern that my interest is unusual, is why I care enough," Levielle offered.

"I am the half-breed by-blow of a Guldalian." Alador's mind was racing with his own assessments. "That leaves me with the following conclusions. Either, you have taken an interest at the request of my uncle, or you want something that you have decided I can provide."

Levielle chuckled as he plucked a hair from his pants and let it fall to the ground. "You missed another possibility."

Alador thought about that for a moment, but could see no other obvious alternative. "And what have I not considered?"

Levielle shook his head with a moment of disappointment. "I am a friend of your father." He paused, letting his words sink in for a moment. "I see something in you worth cultivating. Your father's name would not be enough, I fear, to draw my attention. Although it did not hurt." Levielle looked back up at Alador. "And, on one count you are right. I do want something that I think that you can provide."

"I knew it." Alador breathed out with disappointment. "And what could I possibly afford you that you could not obtain on your own?" Would he ever meet anyone who did not seek something from him?

Levielle shook his head. "A man does not put all his cards on the table. Let me be frank. I do not trust you any more than you trust me. That is how it should be." He rubbed a finger along his nose as if quelling an itch. "A good tactician should give trust sparingly."

"You already know something about me that could cause me harm," Alador pointed out. "It seems fair if you wish to breed trust that you offer me something in return." Alador did not like anyone knowing that he had been home. The anxiety boiling in him made him consider for a moment if he could kill the man. He knew he could pull lightening as fast as the man could pull a sword. Perhaps, if he were casual and brought forth the power quickly, he could send the spell before the man could react.

Levielle's words cut into his thoughts like a knife through butter. "You aren't fast enough to pull it off. Besides, what would you tell the guards?" Levielle placed a hand on each arm of the chair.

Alador frowned. "Fast enough to what?" Damnation, could the man read minds? He eyed the soldier with even more concern.

Levielle shook his head with a grin and laughed lightly. "Never play cards, your face and eyes hide little." Levielle leaned forward a tad. "You were considering if you could kill me before I could protect myself. I assure you that I have been sparring mages far longer than you have been on the planet. It is really not a path you want to take. I applaud your consideration of it, but it will avail you little in the gaining of my trust and end poorly for your own plans."

"I am sure that you know nothing of my plans." Alador indignantly defended. The man was completely unsettling him, and he was struggling to regain his composure.

"Let me see how close I can get?" Levielle put both arms on his legs and leaned forward, clasping his hands together casually. It was the sign of a man who knew he would not have to defend himself. His eyes were trained on Alador. "You have made ground with Lady Aldemar. She is a known dissenter of your uncle's and yet one with a great deal of influence within the city." He smiled at Alador's look of surprise. "You have somehow endeared the Trench Lord to you despite his attack upon your father - a fact little known, as it has remained well hidden."

Levielle looked down at Alador's feet then back up to his eyes. "You have enough power, despite being a half-breed, to cast a travel spell, and you will be the first half-breed allowed to undertake a tier test – a test which, by your own boast at your uncle's ball, you will pass, or at least you believe you will." Levielle sat back clearly relaxed as he spoke. He stroked his beard a bit before speaking again.

Levielle held up one finger as if remembering a small detail. "Oh, and let us not forget your sweetheart here in the caverns. She is also known to me as a dissident regarding your uncle and moves amongst those with like feelings." Levielle sat up clasping his hands across his stomach. "When we add all that up, and with some knowledge of your father's feelings, clearly you plan to move against your uncle in some manner." Levielle looked very pleased with his assessment.

Alador managed to keep his face schooled this time. "A far stretch since you have made it clear that I do not do well at deception," he pointed out. The man's summation had been too damn accurate. He was struggling with how to divert the man's suspicions. Alador ran a hand across his face and returned his eyes to Levielle, knowing that a lack of confidence right now could be deadly.

Levielle nodded, considering Alador's point. "Which means either I am so far from correct that I have put myself at risk, or you are skilled when not caught off-guard. You are an intelligent young man and I am usually right in my observations, so I am going to guess the latter."

"What could I possibly gain by going against my uncle?" Alador was using every ounce of control that he had. This man could see to his undoing with a simple word.

"Now, that is where you gain my interest," Levielle admitted. He stood and went around to the back of the chair, resting his hand upon the top. "It seems to me that you have everything to gain by staying within the man's graces. I can see no personal gain in going against the High Minister. I am a man who likes to make connections and at this moment, you have me completely perplexed."

"Perhaps you should consider that you have made inaccurate connections." Alador stated, looking for that leaf in his hair and fingering it curiously as he removed it. There was a long silence, and Alador looked over at the man to see the teacher staring at him with deep calculation.

Levielle shook his head. "No, I truly do not think I am far off. You have neither denied nor shown any indignation at the charge that you act against your uncle – a course of action that would be treasonous at the worst, and ill-advised at the best." Levielle shook his head. "No, there is mischief afoot. I am sure of it." Levielle grinned broadly.

Alador glanced at the door then back at the discerning man behind his chair. "Let us say for the moment that you are right. What would you do with such information?" If he could kill him, he could use the amulet to remove the body. However, there was the matter of the two guards at the door. Levielle had been accurate in that he would have no way to explain the man's disappearance. Levielle was not known for any use of magic that he was aware of. The shielding spell has been Alador's first knowledge that the man was anything more than a skilled tactician and swordsman.

"Well now, that is the crux of this conversation, is it not?" Levielle grinned, his immaculately groomed image so non-threatening in that mere instance. "Do you trust me enough to confirm if I am correct? Do I trust you enough to tell you why I am interested? One of us is going to have to take that first step."

"I can assure you that my experience in this city has made it very clear I can trust no one. Even my father said it was unwise to do so." Alador rose, moving between Levielle and the door. "In fact, he has never mentioned you as a friend at all." Alador's eyes narrowed as he considered this and turned back to face the man. "It seems to me he would have told me who was a friend if he had dared to trust one."

The soldier followed Alador's movement, an increase of tension evident in the man's posture at having his avenue of escape blocked. "Then I suppose I shall have to be the one to offer a small gift of trust. It is doubtful your father would have thought to mention me as we have little contact. What little we have shared has shown that we both have ... shall we say, disagreements... with the way the Lerdenian ruling class does business. I am often a guest of Lady Aldemar, and have answered many of her questions in regards to your progress."

He put out both hands in a peaceful gesture, being sure to remain behind the chair. "I would not be saddened to see High Minister Luthian Guldalian eat a slice of humble pie. He has moved unchallenged for far too long. To see it come from within his own family, well that is a gift one just cannot ignore." Levielle crossed his arms. "The move is yours."

Alador held Levielle's gaze for a very long time. To the man's credit, he gave Alador time to work through his thoughts and make a decision. "Your connections are far too accurate for my comfort." He finally conceded.

"Ah, now we can have an interesting conversation. Shall we sit back down and discuss this like civil gentlemen, or do you want to go on standing there and staring while still entertaining the possibility of killing me?" Levielle offered congenially.

"I prefer standing for now." Alador crossed his arms across his chest. He felt cornered at the moment, and did not like the position that the soldier had put him in.

"As you wish. I will sit." Levielle lowered himself back into the chair with a slight sigh of frustration. "Now the question I want an answer to is: why?" His demeanor became much more serious, and his voice took an edge of authority.

Alador shook his head. "There is too much at stake for me to tell you my motives."

Levielle frowned. "Let me take another tack. Is it true that Luthian plans to force the Daezun under Lerdenian rule?" At Alador's look of surprise, Levielle waved a dismissive hand. "Not all members of the Council remain tightlipped with a glass or two in their gut."

"Yes," Alador tersely confirmed.

"Mmm, now we are getting somewhere. There is rumor that he has a powerful storm mage at his beck and call. Are you this storm mage?" Levielle continued to press.

"Yes," Alador admitted.

"I see this is going to be a game of a thousand questions." Levielle sighed, considering. "You went home. Unlike most Daezun half-breeds, that means you expected to be welcome. So I am going to guess that you do not wish to act against your Daezun kin."

"You would be right again; which concerns me." Alador finally moved to the bed and sat down heavily. "If you can guess so much, who else is guessing as well?"

"Well, not as many people in the world enjoy puzzles as much as I do." Levielle's tone was reassuring. "Add to that, even fewer have the opportunity to watch you as I have."

"My uncle does." Alador's concern was laced into his words. "He has far more to gain or lose if he evaluates the situation incorrectly."

"Yes, a good point. One you had best keep in mind," Levielle said wagging his finger. He began to speak as the teacher that Alador had come to respect. "However, sometimes men see what they expect to see. Perhaps your uncle has not thought to check your own motives too closely." Levielle tapped the side of his head pointedly. "…Which leads to my next question: why act against your kin? Does he hold something over you?"

"No, he does not," Alador admitted. "My motives I prefer to remain my own. Let us leave it at the fact that I do have a bigger goal in mind, and my uncle's good will at this time is necessary if I am to achieve that end."

"You realize I will continue to puzzle the matter out." Levielle stated with a genuine smile.

Alador shook his head and answered with one of his own. "Of that, I have no doubt."

A heavy silence fell between them as both men were considering the conversation. "Let me help," Levielle offered suddenly.

"Why would you do that? You hold a commission in the High Minister's army. You are a preferred instructor. What could you possibly gain by helping me?" Alador eyed him. "I have not even been willing to tell you my own motives."

"I am a man of action. While matters of schooling and study do interest me, I prefer taking my chances on the battlefield. Whether it involves arms or intrigue..." Levielle leaned forward again, "... my skills are far more useful there than in a classroom of half-breeds, half of which are not even listening."

"For all you know, I could be planning some malicious act of war on behalf of my Daezun kin." Alador pointed out.

Levielle shook his head. "Doubtful."

"For a non-trusting man, you seem to be strangely trusting with me," Alador stated somewhat petulantly.

"It is not a matter of trust. Well, perhaps it is on a deeper level." Levielle admitted. "However, it is a trust of one's self."

"What do you mean?" His words truly confused Alador.

Levielle shrugged. "I have always been a good judge of character. You don't strike me as one who would let himself get tangled up with nefarious plans."

"Yet I am aligned with the Trench Lord," Alador shot back.

"When one observes our current Trench Lord more closely, one detects a genuine concern for the people in his care." Levielle crossed his own arms as his eyes met Alador's. "A man who recently came into power, as you seem recently to be rising in your own. I, for one, do not believe in coincidences."

Again, a pregnant silence rose up between them. Finally, Alador shifted uncomfortably and broke the silence. "I will need to think about it."

Levielle rose to his feet. "We now have something on each other that could do us both great harm. My questioning, if misguided, could lead to my own death." Levielle eyed the younger man evenly. "I think that the revelation of your secrets would mean the death not just of you but of other lives and plans. I have no fear of you breaching my trust. I want to assure you that you need have no fear of me breaching yours." Levielle moved towards the door as Alador rose. He stopped as his hand was on the door handle and looked at Alador.

"Oh, Lady Aldemar wishes to dine with you when you have your confinement lifted. Shall I convey your acceptance of her invitation?"

Alador nodded wordlessly, his mind racing with the new turn of events. He had a million thoughts, but they were falling over one another in his own head to the point that he could not even begin to verbalize them.

"Good, I look forward to speaking to you soon." Levielle pulled the door open. His parting comment was clearly more for the guards than Alador. "Be sure to think upon this lesson; we will speak again of it soon." Levielle's tone was authoritative and confident.

Alador stared at the door long after it had closed behind Levielle. Slowly he moved to the desk and sat down. He began to eat his now congealed and tepid breakfast, but he did not seem to notice. His mind mulled over the last ten minutes, and what they could mean for his plans.

Chapter Twenty-Five

Alador dressed in the warmest clothing that he could conjure. Even with his ability to handle temperatures at the higher and lower extremes, he felt sure that he would need additional protection on the mountain top. In two days, he would go to his uncle's for his half day, and during that time he would attend his tier test. He needed his strength, and he needed to be able to tell his uncle that the first spell had been cast. He had to do the spell today. Fortunately, with the amulet and Renamaum's memories, he had a fairly quick way to get there.

He thought back to this morning. Alador had wanted to wait until he had received his breakfast before leaving - so that someone had seen him that morning. The mage considered the conversation that he had been fortunate enough to hold as he was filling his tray. He had seen Nemara holding back in the line when she saw him, she let others pass her so that she was just in front of him. Alador caressed the amulet as he considered her words.

As they moved down the line filling their trays, she had whispered urgently to him. "We need to talk."

He had not been sure her choice of place had been wise, but his guards also left little opportunity. He had glanced back to find them only casually watching him. "I will be off this restriction of movement soon. Can it wait?"

"No," she had insisted. "There has been a development. I have a letter from Jon."

Even now the fear of the contents of that letter filled him. She told him she hadn't broken the seal on an enclosed note to him. That Jon had sent it to Nemara rather than himself gave him hope that Jon was merely worried his uncle might have intercepted it and discovered what it said; but there could be other reasons as well. Nemara had seemed reluctant to share the contents of her own letter, and had insisted that they talk privately. She had whispered this into his ear, flashing him a coy look for the benefit of his guards.

He had told her to meet him tomorrow night at the secret pool. Alador knew that he had no idea how long it would take him to cast and hold the spell at the level that would be needed. He also did not know how quick of mind or body he would be after such a spell. He expected it to be draining. The mage had decided to wait until tomorrow to meet her to ensure he was not late, and that he had defenses available to him. When it came to Jon and himself, he was not quite sure with whom Nemara would side if a choice had to be made.

Alador took a deep breath and worked to center himself. He could not allow this matter with Jon to distract him right now. He was going to use the amulet to go somewhere that only Renamaum had seen, and he was not sure how accurate his interpretations of dragon-memory were going to be. The mage slipped into meditation for a short time. He was getting better at it. It was something that Nemara had suggested to help with his anger a few weeks ago.

He spent a great deal of time replaying the memory of the mountain top. Dragons seemed to remember a remarkable amount of detail. He chose a spot that was relatively flat. In his mind, he could see the slant of the ledge and the rocks that surrounded it - even the flittering kiss of snow that the dragon had experienced at the time. Working to hold this image in his mind, he whispered the words as he clutched the amulet. The familiar feeling filled him of the world falling away, as did the swirling melding of the colors of his room.

He hit the ground harder than he should have. He immediately realized that the place he had envisaged had been covered with a deeper layer of snow then than now. He must have materialized a foot or two above the actual ground he stood upon. Even now there was hard ice and snow beneath his feet rather than bare rock. He pulled his cloak closed. He looked around to be sure that the ledge was safe. The sun hovered somewhere behind the rock face that he had chosen. It had not yet risen enough to cast its warmth on the shelf.

Alador took a deep breath and realized that the air was different here: thinner - he needed almost to gulp it. Despite the few clouds, the cold knifed into his lungs. The wind howled through the rocks, swirling loose snow about him.

He looked out over the lands below. While the nights had grown colder and some snow had fallen, the land below still held the colors of the season's change. The melding of the gold, red and orange leaves of the trees stood out in contrast to the deep rich brown of harvested fields. A surge of homesickness filled him as he glanced at the familiar landscape below him.

He had seen Daezun villages from above before - one did not mine for bloodstone without accessing opportunities to rise high above the valley floors - bhis was the highest he had ever been, and from here he could see more than one village.

There were many Daezun villages across the land. Unlike the Lerdenian people, the Daezun did not live in cities. Therefore, their villages often lay close to one another. In some places, the outer fields of one would lie within a short walk of the next. From where he now stood it was a beautiful sight. It reminded him of the closeness and helpfulness of the Daezun people. There were always bad seeds, of course, but for the most part, the Daezun were a people as rich in familial connections as the ground they worked.

He eyed the lands about him. He had to weave this spell carefully. If he erred too far to one side, he would create a thunderstorm and rain. If he went too far the other, he would have hail. While hail would work, he wanted to create deep snow: to prevent having to come out here too often. It was cool enough for any snow-melt during the day to freeze over during the night. It would be a deep and early snowfall, disrupting the final harvests and preparations for winter.

His first task was to slow the air-stones at ground level; otherwise, when the sun crested the mountain top, he would have rain. He began to cast and weave, starting north of his position. Slowly Alador worked to slide the slowing air-stones south. He noted with pleasure that as he did so, the faster ones outside his spell were rising up over the mass he was working to create.

He took a breath and began to feed the few clouds rising up over his mass of colder air with moisture. It was a delicate balance of working on the clouds for a time, then working to maintain the colder air at the valley floor. He was slowly managing to enlarge the cold area and increase the cloud cover. Alador had no idea how to keep this up. He could already feel his power beginning to pull at the edges of his center. Even reaching for the power of the sea -something he was reluctant to do after his encounter with Dethara - he found himself at his limits. He cursed slightly to himself as he realized he had counted on this being easier than it was turning out to be.

He began to doubt his ability to actually create a blizzard. There was no doubt he could manipulate weather on a smaller scale, but it felt as if every valley, rock, pond and outcropping were working against his manipulation of the storm. There were so many more factors to consider: small pockets of warm air, a shear to the wind because of the landscape, and even the streams that cut through the land.

A glint of something shimmering up and to his right caught his eye and he lost his hold on the spell for a moment. As it came closer he realised it was Rena and turned his attention back to the work before him. She circled past him a couple of times, dancing playfully on the winds in front of him before he heard her land roughly behind him.

She nuzzled his ear tenderly when she reached him. "You are fighting the natural movement of the air stones, Beloved." She rubbed her muzzle along his arm. "It would be better if you used the topography to your advantage." Her words were tender and guiding as she spoke. "Look for pockets where the land causes the colder air you seek." She settled down on the ledge beside him.

Alador swiftly cast about in the way she had suggested. He realized that she was right: there were places that received less sunlight throughout the winter day, where the air stones moved more slowly. He worked to add and connect them to his growing storm. "Thank you, Rena, I had not considered that."

The clouds above were almost all connected now. He was adding power from the streams, the ponds and the ocean. The clouds mottled colors slowly melded into a thick blanket of soft gray wool. Still there was no snow and he sighed with frustration. He worked to feed the clouds more water. If he fed it too fast, he feared it would just collect into hail and he did not know if he could get it back to the snow he needed.

"Rena I don't think I can do this," he whispered worriedly. He reached for more from the ocean, but his thread to it felt thin and fragile.

"Yes you can." She said. She heaved up behind him. "Here, let me give you my magic." She carefully extended her wings to either side of him. Carefully, she laid her wing talons into the palms of his hands. They were large - he could barely put his fingers fully around them. "Hold these and continue to work the magic. I will add my power to yours."

Alador had not known that was possible, but he could feel the depth of fatigue building. He had no doubt that tomorrow his hair would be lighter if not all white. He could feel, much as a runner reaching the end of his endurance, that he did not have much left.

The mage blinked in surprise when a sudden surge of magic filled him. He latched onto it greedily creating a link that surged with power. It was as if a raging river of magic suddenly filled him. Working with Rena, he began gently to fill the clouds with the rest of the needed moisture. The winds picked up strength as the warm air became trapped between the layer of clouds and the cold air that he had created down along the valley floor.

"You are fighting it." Her soft words melded into his own awareness. The surge of power she fed him was sweet and filled him with a longing for more. "Close your eyes; see what you wish to happen; let your vision flow through your fingers." The dragon spoke in a husky whisper into his ear.

He did as she bid him. He focused on the clouds, imagining the water freezing and the minuscule crystals gathering. Fractal patterns filled his vision as he imagined snow. Beautiful weavings of feathery patterns began to dance in his vision. The power danced along with him. He watched them swirl and collide into one another. Though the snow was far below him, he could feel and taste it.

Their powers twisted from him; he clutched the dragon's talons tightly. He could sense their power spiralling around one another. With greater skill, he moved the air stones, lifted the water to the clouds and formed the small crystals. He was so intent on his task that it took a few moments to sense that something had changed.

Rena had moved to press her chest against him. The underside of her muzzle lay gently on top of his head. He could hear a strange hum emanating from her, the rhythm of its thrumming filling his core. Alador could feel the warmth of her breast behind him. Her wings buffered him from the winds. Her wing talons dug into his palm, and a gentle trickle of his blood slid down his hand.

He realized that his heartbeat had begun to race. His breath came more quickly, and he was suddenly very aware of the dragon. So much so, he began to lose his hold on the gathering storm. He opened his eyes in confusion and looked around him.

By now the wind was howling. It seemed to swirl around them, masking his vision of the valley below. "Rena, what is happening," he shouted above the din.

The dragon moved her muzzle to growl gently into his ear. "Our powers are melding. Do not fight it. It will give you the strength you need. Finish it. You are almost at the point where you can let it go," she firmly urged. Her breath seemed rapid as it pulsed against his back.

Alador gave a nod and began again to weave the spell. It had lost no momentum in the brief exchange. He closed his eyes again, focusing on the snowflakes, willing his vision into reality.

The power seemed to come freely now. He felt no sense of exhaustion. If anything, there was a pleasure and he pulled on the power with greedy determination. He heard a gasp from Rena and eased up a little. He soon had the storm releasing its cold blanket of confinement onto the lands below them.

The feeling of that amount of power flowing freely through him was intoxicating. Alador decided to work a bit longer: expanding the cold air stones along the valley floor. He smiled as the expanding of the spell was now coming easily to him with the amount of power he had at his disposal.

He realized that the power in his possession was beginning to feel and look like one stream, rather than separate spiralling strands. Rena must have been right; the power was merging.

"Alador...," Rena whimpered in his ear. Despite its urgency he could hear the same pleasure in her words.

Alador pushed the moment of concern that filled him aside. "Just a few moments more, Rena." Alador whispered. "I am almost done."

The power swirled within him, centering as if it were his own. The pleasure of its movements filled every sense. He could almost taste the sweet flavor of its caress on his tongue. The thrumming melody of it combined with the strange sound that Rena seemed to be singing. He could feel it in every cell of his body, stroking his nerves with intense pleasure.

Tighter and tight the power swirled in him. He lost his focus on the storm now raging around them. Snow swept over them both. He closed his eyes and leaned back against Rena. She folded her wings tighter. He continued to move the hooked talons in an almost rhythmic dance. His hands conducted the power now, weaving and dancing with the song and the storm.

Tighter and tighter the power welled into his core. The pleasure now exquisite, he did not want it to stop. His head leaned back into the base of Rena's neck. He could feel the dragon shivering behind him. He pulled the power into himself, feeling the intensity of the pleasure surging through him

Time seemed to slow as power swirled no longer in his control. It became so intense that it hurt. He whimpered, unsure of what to do. His body stiffened with a strange combination of pain and pleasure. Alador's breath came in ragged gasps. His hands held onto Rena's talons as if letting go would mean his death.

"Let it go, beloved. You must release the power." The dragon hissed urgently in his ear. Her own breathing seemed labored.

At first, Alador did not know how. It seemed to just keep coiling. He felt as if he would explode with it. Then as if his thoughts guided the magic, it burst from him. His back arched as he cried out. The power seemed to shoot from the center of him out through every pore of his body. He heard a strange screaming roar. The air filled with the smell of ozone as light blazed outward from the pair.

The pain-laced pleasure slowly ebbed, and as it did so Alador realized that the sound had come from their blended voices. He slid down her body, weak and trembling. Rena folded her wings tight across him and her breast and helped him to the ground. Her own nose nestled across his shoulder. He could feel the dragon trembling just as much as he was.

Neither of them spoke for many minutes, the sensations coursing through Alador. It was all he could do to ensure he kept breathing. He felt as if he had exhausted every muscle in his body to the point that pain was slowly replacing the pleasurable rush. His mind was fogged and he could not seem to form a thought and hold it.

The storm raged before them, and only Rena's wings protected him from the icy onslaught that he had created. He stared out at the swirling mass of feather light wonders of ice. It was as if he could see each snowflake in its full majesty. The individual fractals formed in the same way, each unique in their swirling dance and glistening patterns.

Finally, he found his voice. Moving his mouth to Rena's ear, he asked. "Rena, what in the names of the gods just happened?"

"We danced on the wind and power was with our wings," she answered back.

Where had he heard that before: Dance on the winds? He searched his memory and realized that was what the dragons called the strange falling act they did as they mated in the sky. His eyes widened. "Rena, isn't that what you call mating?"

"Yes my heartmate," she answered. "Dragons can rarely dance on the wind using power. It takes two melded in purpose and skill."

Alador sat stunned. He took in her words then cursed softly beneath his breath before asking his next question. "Rena, why didn't you tell me we would mate?" He pulled away from her in confusion. He felt his anger rising.

Rena pulled her head up, her eyes revealing her confusion and hurt at his words. "I did not know. I swear it," she answered defensively over the wind. She loosened her wings slightly after he pulled away from her. "As I said, dragons can rarely dance with power."

The mage closed his eyes. How did you yell at someone for giving you an experience that words could never fully describe? How could you hold on to anger when it had been so wondrous? He tried to catch his breath, but as he did he realized that exhaustion was close to claiming him.

Rena seemed to sense it in him and nuzzled him gently. "Go back to your cave, my heartmate. I will keep your storm in play until the sun sets. Then I will seek my own." She loosened her wings so that he could stand. "We can speak of this when we both have had time to consider what happened."

Alador nodded. He was not sure what he would or could say. He stood in numbed disbelief. The mage realized he was still clutching both of Rena's wing talons and swiftly let them go. The blood flowed more swiftly from his palms, but at that moment it was the least of his worries. He swayed on his feet as he stumbled away from her. She nuzzled him slightly with concern.

He turned to fully look at her. The confusion must have been evident on his face as she leaned forward and gently nuzzled her nose to his.

"I will take care of your storm," she promised. She slowly laid her forehead to his, and he found his hand caressing the side of her head.

Alador stepped back, the snow crunching beneath his feet. He stared at the dragon still sitting before him. He nodded and closed his eyes. The howling wind and weakness made it difficult, but he managed to envision his cell back in the Blackguard caverns. When the room materialized before him, Alador moved woodenly to the bed. He fell into it, not bothering to remove his cloak, snow-frozen boots, or stop the bleeding from his hands.

Chapter Twenty-Six

Alador woke to a stern pounding on his door. He opened it groggily to see the High Master standing there. The man looked over Alador's sodden and somewhat bloody attire with a raised eyebrow. "I suggest you clean yourself up." He handed Alador a letter then pulled the door shut, careful to obscur Alador from curious eyes.

Alador looked himself over and realized he looked a fright. He cast a clean spell, then broke Sordith's seal and quickly read the letter. He stared at it with a frown. Trust Sordith to drop such news so casually. He had no idea what it meant to stand as a man's oath-keeper in a bonding ceremony. Alador started to tell himself that he also did not want to stand for Keelee's bonding after her betrayal, but a heartbeat later he realized he just did not care. He no longer held the deep hatred that he had felt when first learning of her deception.

His mind raced over what he needed to do. He tossed the letter thoughtlessly aside. He had not yet been able to speak to Amaum about the task he was hoping the dragon would agree to perform. He should have asked Rena last night how to find him. The only family cave he knew of was Pruatra's, and he was not sure that the dragoness would receive him well if he just happened to pop in.

However, he didn't seem to have much choice, given that dragons did not exactly have a message system. If they wanted to tell one another anything, they either passed it to dragons that were flying that way, or if it were more personal, they simply flew and delivered it themselves.

Alador realized that knowledge of the dragons' way of life was becoming his own. He was rarely able to distinguish what he had known from what he had learned recently, unless he specifically made the effort to distinguish between the two. The information presented itself as it was needed. There was no librarian ordering and retrieving his thoughts, so he was still fumbling about in some areas.

He swore aloud and only realized he had when the High Master said: "Bad news then; sorry to hear it." The man was watching, and when Alador looked up, he felt the eyes of a predator on him. Davin might think this ally of Sordith's was more amenable, but there was no doubt he was a hunter. He had not hidden it away before Alador had caught it in his gaze. One raptor knew another, he thought. He knew this was something he would not have picked up on before. The dragon had given him more than just spells.

"Sorry High Master. I had not meant to let that slip out," he admitted. "I fear that it is a matter that will send me out of my cell again." Alador picked up the letter and tucked it into his jerkin.

"Do you wish me to see to that letter's destruction, lad?" The High Master's voice held genuine warmth, but Alador could not get that momentary glimpse behind the man's smile out of his mind.

"No, no. I will need it for my next task, I fear. I will destroy it when the matter is dealt with properly. Is there anything else, Sir?" Alador casually picked up an apple from his desk and bit into it. He realized he was starving.

"Are you ready to have your confinement lifted?" The big man crossed his arms. He looked disappointed when his gaze met Alador's.

"Actually, I could really do with a good meal. Following that, I could use an evening without eyes for a very long bath." Alador considered. "Yes, I think if you could lift it with an order to return to my duties following my half-day with Luthian, I would appreciate it greatly."

The High Master held up a hand. "You mean... IF...you return."

Alador swallowed at the reminder he might not live through the test. "Yes, well I do hope to live."

The big man chuckled. "I was thinking more that you would pass, and they would then give you that mansion of your father's."

"Oh," Alador answered as he colored with slight embarrassment. "I don't think they are going to give a half-breed a place on any tier above the fourth. I will be happy just to open up testing to half-Lerdenians: so that if they are gifted in magic, the military is not their only option."

"You're an idealist, lad." The High Master shook his head. "I am sure that as soon as Minister Guldalian finishes whatever manipulation he is about, the Council will rescind this new decree."

"Perhaps, but it is a risk that I am willing to take to get the chance to create a place for those like me who are not necessarily fit for duty on a battlefield." Alador stared across the desk, the vision of bodies lying below him on a great plain filling his eyes. Small streams of red stained the dusty ground around them. The stench of death filled the air; vultures circled the sky, and many were already feasting on corpses strewn about like Sofie's dolls.

"Alador!"

The sharp call startled him. The apple dropped from his hand and rolled toward the High Master who stopped it with the toe of his boot. Despite his vision clearing and seeing the man before him again, he could still smell the decay of the dead that had been before him. Realizing the bodies had been below him quickly made it clear that he had seen the carnage from a dragon's viewpoint.

"You all right?" The man leaned over and picked up the apple, tossing it into a waste box behind him.

"Yes, I just haven't been getting enough food. He did not want to tell the man that he now saw visions of the past ... or at least ... he hoped it was the past.

The High Master turned and strode to the door. He threw it open. "Davin, get your pure little arse in here."

Davin hurried in looking pale and worried. "Yes Master Bariton?"

"Get Alador here to the food hall and make sure he eats at least two helpings," he commanded firmly. I don't want him to return to his rooms till he is sure he's about to burst."

Alador grinned at Davin's expulsion of breath. "Yes sir! What about the guards for this guardsman?"

"There's been enough of that business. Alador here will return to his duties following his half-day ... assuming he returns from his half-day." The high master presented jovially enough for Davin to smile as Alador moved to the door.

"Off with both of you," The High Master commanded. "Some of us do real work around here."

Alador did not need to be told twice. He was starving. Add to that, the smell of death still filled his nose and he could not seem to shake it no matter how many deep breaths he took.

Once they were out of earshot and around a corner, Davin asked: "So what did the High Master mean when he said *'assuming he returns?'*"

Alador considered briefly and decided they would all know soon anyway, so he could see no harm in letting the secret out now. "I am going to be allowed to take the tier test. If I am successful, the Council will allow other half-breeds to take the tests as well if they choose. They will have to ask to test as it is not our normal path."

Davin let out a long low whistle. “Shite, why is that not already known?”

Alador scratched his shoulder as he walked. “I suppose they are waiting to see if I can really do it.” He looked over at Davin. “I don’t suppose there will be any need to make the decree public if I fail.”

“Can you do it?” Davin asked, they moved down the hall.

“I don't honestly know.” Alador admitted. “I would like to think so, but I have been told the odds have been slanted against me.” He did not like the idea of so many hoping he would fail. However, one did not always have a choice when facing situations in the real world.

“What a day it would be if half-breeds like us were given full status in Lerdenia. It is something that Daezun would never consider.” The hurt sound in Davin’s voice resonated in Alador. It seemed a lifetime ago that he had held the same pain.

“I've learned that ‘never’ is a highly deceptive word,” Alador mused, more to himself than to Davin. “One never knows what life will bring.”

“I can't wait to tell everyone,” said Davin. He rubbed his hands in anticipation.

“I had hoped you would be a bit more discreet.” Alador had no doubt in a few hours the news would have travelled throughout the caverns.

It was no surprise as they rounded the corner to the meal hall that Davin was in a hurry to be off. “I'll leave you here and go tell the shift commanders that you are off seclusion. Eat well!" he said, and scurried off.

Alador just shook his head. He took his time and truly enjoyed a vast meal. He did not push back from the table till he had eaten his fill of a second tray. The warm food and watered cider had improved his mood a great deal. He decided the next order of business was that bath.

He very much wanted a long soak and some time alone before Nemara joined him. He thought over her words about a note from Jon. He had every hope that the death mage would remain a good friend and join him in the defeating of the mines. However, a man's beliefs were difficult to change, and if the two paths came into direct conflict, Alador did not have much hope that his path would win out.

It did not take him long to make his way to the cavern where the hidden pool was a welcoming sight. After heating the water, he slid into the steaming pool. His long sigh of contentment echoed off the dark cavern walls: finally, he had a moment to mull over his thoughts.

He knew something significant had happened on that mountain top. He rubbed the hairs on his arms; they seemed to stand with a static electricity creating a tingling across his body. His eyes fluttered shut with the remembered ecstasy. His body hardened in response as he recalled the building power. It had built to the point of pain. If he had not let that power go at Rena's insistence, would it have killed him?

"Well, I am glad to see you missed...."

The teasing tone came out of nowhere, startling Alador out of his thoughts. Nemara's words cut off with a screech as Alador swiveled before the second word was out of her mouth. Lightning flared into his hands and arced towards her. The only thing that saved her was that he hadn't turned completely to face her. Nemara hit the ground rolling on reflex, her training coming into play.

Alador turned and hopped onto the pool's edge the moment he realized what he had done. "Nemara, by the gods, are you okay?" He hurried to her side, regardless of his nakedness.

"What the shite is wrong with you?" She rolled to her feet, still crouched low. Her eyes were wide with shock. She glanced at the scorched wall behind the spot where she'd been standing just moments before.

"You surprised me." He pushed his damp hair out of his face then offered a hand up. It was no surprise when she batted it away.

"You knew I was coming," she said. Her accusing glance spoke volumes.

"I know. I am so sorry." He put his hands out in a placating manner. He had nearly killed his friend, and he had no idea why that had been his first response. "I was deep in thought. You should warn someone you are there before you sneak up on them." His own accusation held an edge of defensiveness.

"I was hardly sneaking." She pushed to her feet. "You nearly killed me."

"I said I was sorry," Alador snapped. His irritation was rising. He knew it was not fair; she was hardly to blame at the moment.

"Sorry hardly covers… turning me into a lightning rod," she snarled. She reached into her jerkin and pulled out a crinkled note. She shoved it out at him, hissing angrily, "Here. I am taking a bath." Once he took the note, she turned on her heel and angrily stalked over to a large rock.

Alador took the note over to a lightstone. It was not bright enough to read. Without even thinking, he brought a ball of light into his hand. Simple cantrips seemed so effortless now. He smiled, remembering Henrick's first lesson - the simple task of making dirt wet. He forced his attention to the letter in his other hand.

Greetings Alador,

I hope this letter finds you in one piece and with breath in your lungs. I doubt this is so, given that I am not there to save you from your impetuous nature. I have thought a lot on our last conversation.

Despite my desire to one day stand as High Priest in the Temple of Death, I find I cannot reconcile myself to the atrocities being committed here. I have positioned myself so that when you decide to visit, if you live long enough, I will not be caught in the fighting. I will not assist you, but I will not stand in your way.

May death delay its visit until we may speak in person.

Jon

Alador read it a second time then he shook his head. Leave it to Jon to decide not to make a real decision. He was relieved to find that his friend would not fight those who would accompany him to the mine. He was not quite sure how he could have possibly positioned himself so that he would not have to fight, but Alador was certain that if there were a way that the death mage had found it.

He smiled as he refolded the note. At least he would not be forced to fight - or maybe even kill - the first friend he had made in the mines; well, the first honest friend. Flame had pretended to be his friend, but the whole time he had been working for the last Trench Lord. He frowned and took the note to his belongings before turning back to the pool.

Nemara was lounging with her eyes closed. Her now naked body reflected the gentle glimmer of the lightstones, and parts of it were magnified by the water that she was slowly moving with her hands. She was really a fine sight to behold, even if she were angry with him. He could not blame her.

Alador moved to the pool and slipped into the water. He found the slight ledge he had been resting against then gently reached out to stir and warm the water further. He did not cease until he heard a satisfied sigh escape Nemara's full lips. The pool was now steaming, the heated water collided with the cool air of the cave. The airstones flitted into his view, and he smiled then he let that focus go. It was getting easier.

"Nemara, I am sincerely sorry. I'd never hurt you consciously," he said. Even though his voice was low and measured, it seemed to echo about them in the silence of the cave.

"It's not the first time you've come close to hurting me," she reminded him. "I'm beginning to wonder about my choice of a suitor." Though her words were meant to tease, Alador could sense an edge of seriousness. Her words hung between them for a long moment.

Alador was confused. He could not remember having lashed out at her before. Their moments of passion had been mutual, but never beyond what was natural. "I beg your pardon," he stammered. "When did I almost hurt you before?" He moved through the water until he was in front of her and waited for an answer.

Nemara opened her eyes and her eyes roved over his face. "I would have thought you'd remember." Her tone of accusation held hurt.

"I'm sorry, Nemara." He frowned. "I'd never purposely hurt you. When do you feel I've done so before?" He reached up and pushed sodden hair from her forehead. She sat up more and put an arm on each of his shoulders. He was forced to grab her ledge to keep from going under. There was not a lot of leverage in the deep pool.

"I'd asked about Keelee at the table right before you disappeared. It made you angry, and you grabbed hold of me." She found his gaze and held it. "You were so angry at that moment."

He pulled himself closer so that he could get a toehold against the rock which she was sitting on, her legs wrapped about him steadying him. "I had forgotten that with the whole disappearing part." He touched her face tenderly. "I'm very sorry Nemara." He was careful to balance himself in the water with a toe and hand so that he did not touch her further. They stared at each other for a long uncomfortable moment. When she did not speak, he changed the topic.

"Your note from Jon, may I know what it was about?" His question was gentle and genuine. He was not sure totally where things stood.

"It was just some fun details about living in the bloodmine. Some of his observations are so serious that they make me laugh." She smiled as she remembered the letter. "He did say one thing I thought was a little strange."

Alador tipped his head. "Oh, what was that?" Most things Jon said were always a little off and he knew what she meant about serious.

"He told me that I might not want to join the others when you assault the bloodmine." The confusion on her face mirrored what Alador felt must have been on his own.

"Did he say why?" Jon had connected the two of them. She was right. It was definitely strange that he should now caution her not to move forward.

Nemara nodded. "That was the odd part." Her fingers traveled down his shoulder then his arm as she finished speaking. "He said that I would gain more than I wanted and lose everything I desired. I have no idea what that means, and to be honest, it seems like one part contradicts the other."

Alador repeated that to himself a couple of times. "I will admit, it is strange. Jon seems to have a way of knowing things at times. For such an articulate guardsman, he can be so cryptic."

He frowned at Nemara's fingers, watching them travel lightly back up his arm. Usually such light touches provoked the response she was seeking. At the moment, he found her touch irritating and - even more concerning - unwanted.

Knowing she was seeking comfort from his sudden assault a short time before, he took both her hands in his. He moved back a bit. "Well, we both know that Jon definitely sees the darker side of things. I am not sure if that is his sphere, or just his own unique way." Alador leaned in and caressed her lips gently with his own. Her eyes were closed and she let out a soft, unintelligible murmur. Inwardly, Alador felt a bit concerned. He had felt nothing. It had felt more as if he were kissing Sofie on the cheek than his lover's lips.

Alador let go of Nemara's hand and met her eyes. "I will leave you to soak in the pool, Nemara. Thank you for bringing me the note."

She grabbed his hand as he started to turn and move away. "Wait," she said. "If rumor is to be believed, tonight may be your last night here." She bit her lip as her eyes roved over his face. "I thought we could spend it together."

Alador felt a moment of panic. He was not sure why, but he knew he did not want her in his bed tonight. He pushed away and sank down into the water to buy himself a moment then came up shaking his head, spraying Nemara with water. She laughed and splashed him back.

"Nemara, I cast the storm spell last night. Since then, I have been feeling slightly off." He colored a bit. "I don't think I can give you a fair go of it tonight."

Her hand slipped down his body to cup him gently. "Odd, you seemed quite responsive when I first walked in." Despite his slight rise to her touch, his face held no interest. "You have found another?"

Alador looked at her in surprise. "Gods no. When would I have had the time?" He frowned. He was not sure why he was feeling off, but knew that she had been right; when he had been thinking of the power exchange with Rena, he had been quite capable of connecting with the part of his body under discussion.

"I am just really tired," he finally offered. "Tell you what. If you really wish to stay, I can certainly… attend to your needs. If that doesn't work, well then there is no hope for me tonight; but at least we can hold one another through the night." He had to admit that even he did not know if he would live through his test.

Her soft smile was all the acknowledgment that he needed before he leaned in to kiss her. He pressed her to him momentarily pulling her off the ledge and dunking them both. After the passionate kiss had ended, he realized he still had felt no inkling of desire. What in the names of all the gods was wrong with him?

Chapter Twenty-Seven

Alador stood at the edge of the testing arena. The stands rose above him in carved cold beauty. He could not see how full they were from where he stood. The floor of the arena was sand, and there were places clearly scorched by fire. There were echoes of magic pulsing through the space. He could feel it pulling and teasing at the edges of that unseen well within him. It surprised him slightly that such a taint remained on such a large area.

It all seemed surreal at the moment. The day was cold, and there was a light dusting of snow flittering about in the air, too dry to even fall properly to the ground. The wind snapped the flags on the top of the tall columns as if beating out a slow death cadence. He shivered and pulled his cloak closed about him. He was not cold, but it reminded him of his time on the mountaintop.

"It will not be cold once the barrier goes up, my dear nephew." Luthian put a consoling hand on Alador's shoulder. "Unless that is anxiety I see shivering through your bones." Luthian smiled at Alador, and the smile seemed strange on the mage's face. His uncle had many attributes but the genuine capacity to care was not one of them.

"No, I am cold," Alador smoothly lied, attempting to hide the fact he was anxious. "Since I was on top of that mountain top, I feel as if I shall never be warm again." He did not intend to let his uncle know the level of his doubts right now.

Luthian noted the appearance of the ring master. "Well, I must leave you here. You will be called forward. Just cast the spells as you and I practiced them." Luthian dropped his hand as if touching Alador was uncomfortable for him. "I will be in the stands."

Alador did not look back at his uncle; he merely nodded. So much depended on his ability to pass this test. Not only the furthering of his own plans, but also the aspirations of many half-breeds in years to come.

If he had his way, there would be less class distinction between full mages, talent mages, and non-mages. He did not see people as Daezun, off-islanders or Lerdenian. They were all mortals, and classed in his mind based on their skills. Sordith had also helped him to see that some problems needed to be addressed without the use of magic.

He took a deep, centering breath as a man walked to the center of the arena. This was it: his defining moment as a mage and the moment of truth: would he ever be able to complete Renamaum's geas? He straightened his blue overcoat. He had opted for a sleeveless coat over a tunic of white. He knew it looked good against his skin and lightened hair. As he had predicted, his hair was only a light brown now. He had braided the growing white streak of hair to symbolize that he knew how it had gotten there. No mage had asked yet, but even if they did he had no intentions of revealing how it had happened.

"Alador of House Guldalian! Fathered by Henrick Guldalian, Mother…" - the announcer wrinkled his nose in distaste - "Alanis of Smallbrook. The first of mixed blood to be tested. Let all know that this man seeks to place himself upon the tiers."

Despite the wind and snow, Alador had heard him clearly. He smiled at how the use of magic so casually affected small things here in the capital city. He strode out, expecting to see mostly empty stands. This was not the case for a roar of approval came from the right.

On this side of the arena, a mass of black armor bathed the contrasting light gray stone. He quickly found the eyes of the High Master who dipped his head at him. The guardsmen stood as one and cheered when he was in full view. He had not expected the High Master to release the Blackguard for the test.

In contrast, the other side of the arena was filled with aristocracy. Many were bundled in thick robes or had small braziers burning for warmth. There was a brief murmur of both derision and support that swept through at a much quieter level. Alador swallowed hard as the true vision of Lerdenian life was painted before him. On one side there was a class that was tolerated and used for the benefits of the elite. On the other side of the arena facing the guard was that elite, staring down at him in cold judgment.

The looks of hatred, disdain and disgust were written on many faces. Alador had gotten better at reading them since that first dinner when he had come to Silverport. He swept his gaze across the elite rows and realized that all they were doing was strengthening his resolve to wipe their smug, condescending looks off their noble faces.

Turning again to the side where he had true support, he swept a deep bow bringing an even louder cheer. Rising with a grin, he turned to face the arena master who would guide the test.

"I shall join the judges and the arena will be closed for the safety of observers. You will have five minutes to attempt each level of the test." The man glanced toward a table. "The judges and I will let you know when you have shown enough to move on."

Alador followed his gaze and for a long moment he felt as if he had been punched in the stomach. Lady Morana sat at the table. He could not tell if she had been truly empowered from where he was standing, but she was one of the four judges. Her beauty was hidden somewhat by a fur-lined cloak, but there was no doubt whom she was when their eyes met. She smiled warmly when she realized that Alador was staring at her. His heart began to thud so loudly that he heard it thrumming through his ears. He startled, realizing that the master had spoken to him.

"Wait, what?" Alador focused back to the task at hand, though his heart thundered in his chest.

"I said do you have any questions?"

Blowing out tension, he shook his head. "I am ready." He decided to turn his back to the judges and specifically Morana, focusing on the guardsmen instead. At least on that side of the arena there was no contingency rooting for him to fail. Well, he did not believe so anyway.

He watched as mages climbed onto four square posts outside the arena wall. As they began to cast the draconic words of protection, Alador felt the magic pull against his skin; his hair rose on his body. He glanced upward and watched in amazement as four types of sphere magic wove together to make a net of protective spells. He stood in awe watching as the arena master fed it a strange unfamiliar magic that filled in between the weavings. It was blue at first, then turned translucent as the weave touched the edges of the arena wall. If that had been the magic that they could use just to protect the crowd, how could he ever impress them enough to pass this test?

"You shall begin with simple spells: ones that any mage should know. Show us an array of such spells. We hope this will prove easy for you, being one of the guard." The arena master's voice held a strange echo now. The voice seemed to emanate from everywhere.

Alador glanced over his shoulder, looking for his uncle and spotted him in the Council box. He was standing, leaning against the wall. His dark red robes stood out amongst the other mages near him; or maybe, it was just that Luthian stood out, no matter where he was. Alador dismissed such thoughts as Luthian nodded for him to proceed.

Luthian had explained that winning the crowd's favor played a large part in the tests. It was not supposed to play a part in the decision-making, but it was widely known that those liked by the crowd were more likely to do well in the judging of higher levels. So, the two of them had prepared a bit of a theatrical performance for those that had braved the elements.

Alador realized that Luthian had been right. It was largely quiet in the arena now; outside sounds had been muffled and it was warm. He took off his coat and laid it aside. He was dressed in simple black breeches, a white linen shirt and polished black boots.

The young mage had to barely touch the well of magic to create the effects he wanted. Flower petals formed into his hands. He turned slowly to show them to all then tossed them into the air. A shift in power turned them into sparks that began to flutter to the ground. Alador smiled at the display, and swiftly formed a light breeze to send them spiraling around the arena. Applause from the guardsman was minimal as most used such spells to practice. Easy prestidigitation was a way to keep in touch with one's ability to touch the inner well of magic. To round up the display of simple cantrips, he let the wind close around him, sending the sparks in a wind funnel like display around his body. He let them fall away to show his clothing reversed. His pants and boots now white, while his shirt was now black.

Alador slowly turned to the judges and bowed low. His eyes moved of their own accord to Lady Morana who dipped her head in acknowledgment with a slight smile. He still did not know if it were a good or bad thing that she sat with the judges. Right now, if Dethara was against the plan of Renamaum, her priestess sat in a chair of power. He was truly at a crossroads, and not all of it was going to be determined by his own choices and skill.

"Alador Guldalian has mastered the first tier. Do you wish to continue?" The Arena master motioned for him to move on.

"Yes, I do." Alador confidently stated. He took a deep breath. For this, there were many spells that one could use. It really came down to useful spells that were not sphere-specific. He and Luthian had picked a few out in hopes of keeping his true mastery of his sphere hidden until he was forced to defend for the fourth tier. While those against him would have a basic understanding of fighting his sphere, each mage within a sphere had their own set of spells they excelled at.

The easiest one was a simple spell of movement. For many it appeared that Alador had disappeared only to appear at the other end of the arena, in truth he had just ran very fast. It was a spell that not all mastered, and so it brought some acknowledgment from the crowd and a burst of applause from those below the second tier. He moved on to call lightning into his hand. It was not technically a sphere spell though it was tightly connected. He sent two balls hurtling from his hands. It had been the first offensive spell he had learned. He did not wait for approval. He wanted the test over, and he had a long way to go to get all the way to the fifth tier.

Next he snapped his hands out; six silver darts formed and flew away as he did so. When they landed against a nearby wooden construct, they shivered in the light. The six darts had each one penetrated within an inch of the other.

Alador had one more spell that he wished to perform. It was one that he had found in the black book of his great ancestor, and one that seemed harmless enough. He put out his hand and formed four arrows. He took a deep breath of relief as they appeared.

Using the strange change in vision he had acquired when he had absorbed Renamaum's stone, the wooden construct with the darts jumped forward. He sent the arrows flying in simultaneously, each landing solidly between two darts. His support in the Blackguards jumped up with screaming applause. Alador just turned simply to the table of judges who held his fate in their hands and bowed.

"Let it be known that Alador Guldalian has mastered the second tier. Do you wish to continue?" The man's monotone question seemed out of place in the furore created by the cheering men. Despite the noise from the stands, the man's voice was nevertheless clear, having been magically enhanced.

Alador nodded. "I am ready, Sir."

This test would be a little more fun, and he was ready for it. The men who had been cheering silenced one another as Alador began, sitting down almost as one. First, he brought a rolling ball out of the nearby pool of water. When the water was most of the way to him, he formed it into a whip. He cracked the whip as he strolled towards the pool, water spraying from every audible snap.

Once at the pool, Alador dropped the whip, letting it turn back into a spray of water as it hit the ground. He parted the water with a smile, remembering his first lesson in his sphere. He had not been allowed to take part in this practice due to his novice status with his power. Now, this spell seemed almost effortless to him. To bring an added flare, he froze the two walls of water then walked through the pool. Once clear, he let the spell go and watched as the walls of water collapsed back down.

He raised the temperature of it till it was boiling. It felt good to just let the power weave through him. It had taken so much effort that first practice, and now it was like putting on his own pants. He did not have to think too hard about what was taking place to make it happen.

He smiled as he pulled on his last spell. This one took a few words of casting, a small amount of sulfur and some motions, but he knew it would be worth the effect. Lightning struck where he stood, but Alador was not there. It struck a second time just inside the arena wall before the judges, and as the light cleared, he stood in its place.

He had not discussed this spell with Luthian. He did not want to be pressed as to where he had learned it when he had no rank to hide behind. He realized that there had been no applause as he had expected. Confused, he flashed a glance at his uncle who just met his gaze evenly; the only sign of his thoughts was the tapping of his bent finger against his lips.

Alador's gaze flew to the judges as a slow-growing round of cheering and applause began to swell from behind him then around the arena. The judges were whispering together, and one would occasionally glance at him before returning to the whispered conversation.

He glanced at the seating around the arena. He could see that everyone was on their feet and stomping. The sound echoed even into the barrier between him and the crowd. Finally, the arena master stood up on a platform and raised his hands for quiet. Slowly, the crowd began to return to their seats and the sound diminished. What had he done wrong?

Finally, the arena grew quieter. All eyes were on the arena master. Alador's nails dug into his hands and his heart throbbed so strongly in his chest that he could hear it echoing in his ears.

"Let it be known that Alador Guldalian has mastered the third tier. Do you wish to continue?" The man turned to look at Alador.

From the raging sounds of approval just moments before, it was so quiet that for Alador the only sound was his racing heart. Did he? Did he really want to move on? He stood there pinned down by the man's gaze while he thought of declining; but her knew that he could not. He had declared amongst this magic-holding, elitist gathering that he was a master of his sphere. He would not let the Daezun down by failing now. He steadied himself and smiled slowly at the arena master.

"Why sir, I have yet to be challenged," he called loudly, letting the natural Guldalian arrogance flow through him, enhanced with a little dragon pride. "I have no intentions of stopping now."

Chapter Twenty-Eight

It took a moment for the crowd to simmer down, and the arena master waited for a short while before answering Alador. His words were a bit surprising as he shouted out, "Let it be known that Alador Guldalian moves to the fourth tier test of his own will. Call forth those that have volunteered to join him in the arena." The man stepped off the edge of the arena and returned to the judges' table.

Alador turned and glanced at either end of the arena as there were openings at both. He had thought that the Council or the judges would choose the mages. He was not sure he liked the idea of 'volunteers.'

Three mages - one man and two women - stepped out of the far end, whereas one woman and two men came from where he had entered: six of them. Henrick had said ten spells, so four were going to cast at least twice. He would have no idea where the spells were coming from. He moved to the center of the arena. He whispered a soft prayer to the gods for protection and took a centering breath. If they were wearing the colors of their sphere, there were two fire mages, one nature mage, one stone mage, a death mage, and last but not least, a silver mage.

Alador cursed softly as he was unsure what kind of spells a silver mage might have for offense. They were mostly known for a level of healing, not quite as strong as the gold sphere. They also excelled at spells of purification. He had never considered having to fight one before; he had not considered them fighting mages.

The other mage that concerned him above the others - not that all were not a challenge - was the death mage. This man could wield poisons and death like fire mages wielded fire. He was deadly in every aspect of his sphere. What was more concerning was that they had all volunteered. That meant that each had their own reasons for wanting him to fail. The only reassurance he felt at that moment was that Luthian had forced him to practice deflection with magic itself and not just the power of his sphere.

The six mages moved around him, building the suspense for the spectators. Alador quickly saw that no matter how he stood, he had someone at his back. He had thought - for some reason - that he would face them. This circling was something that he had not planned for, nor had Luthian mentioned it. He dared not glance to his uncle for guidance.

The first spell movement came from the woman in red robes. A ball of fire hurtled towards him and Alador simply dove out of the way, rolling up and sweeping around to try to discern who would be next. He had not forgotten Sordith's Council that not all problems had to be solved by magic. He realized as the ball hurtled harmlessly away that the magi's spacing ensured that they did not hit one another. He could feel the collective tension of the entire crowd who sat watching wide-eyed on the edges of their seats.

He barely saw the man wearing brown robes move before a huge rock flew from a pile of stones near them. Alador formed the V of energy to deflect it harmlessly away. In doing so, he left his back exposed to the second fire mage who took that opportunity to set his shirt ablaze. The fire flared; he could smell his hair as the flames licked upward, and he could do nothing but clench his teeth until the boulder deflected past him. He immediately called on water, which pooled over him as if from an invisible bucket, drenching him and putting the fire out.

Alador took a couple of centering breaths. He dare not let his guard down, even with the smell of burning flesh in his nostrils. The pain of the burn had not ebbed in the slightest after the drenching. If anything, it felt as if the exposed skin now burned hotter. He was already slightly injured, and only three spells had been cast. He took another deep breath, grateful for the seconds they seemed to be giving him.

The next spell came from the man in silver robes. Alador had seen the movements and turned to face him. Yet as he waited, he saw nothing of offense moving his way. He went to swirl to check the others and found he could not move. His body was frozen where he stood.

A moment of panic swelled through him as he saw the death mage move to the side of the silver mage. The man's cold smile filled his eyes with equal hardness as a green, fog-like ichor began to snake its way towards Alador. Alador knew he could give in. He would fail the fourth test, but he could walk away right now. Anger filled him at the feeling of helplessness, and his eyes narrowed.

He focused on the airstones with as much effort as he could manage, frozen in place as he was. The green snake of poison was two-thirds of the way to him when he was finally able to focus enough to see them. He had always used his hands before, but he recalled one early lesson with Henrick. Henrick had said that movement of the hands was more for the comfort of the casting mage to help them focus. He had cast a spell before without his hands, so he could do it again.

The fog was nearly to him when he managed to shift the air in the arena to create a wind. It began slowly at first, bending the snaking poison from Alador. The death mage frowned, and attempted to turn the spell back towards his target. Alador snarled. He lashed out forcing a sudden shift in the airstones. The sudden movement created a wall of wind and the poison flew into the faces of the two mages to his left. He broke free of the holding spell in time to see that the second fire mage and the stone mage had left the fight. Both were headed coughing and gagging to the healer that awaited at the far end of the arena.

Alador spun about. It was all that he could do to contain the anger that he felt. They were not trying to just test him; they were trying to kill him. He was sure of it. He did not dare strike out, however, as he was limited to defensive spells. Small sparks of lightning flashed up and down his arms as he attempted to contain himself.

There was no one now but himself and these four mages. Alador did not notice the crowd who had silently come to their feet to see better. He did not notice that Luthian had moved to the front of the Council box. He only knew that there were four people around him that wanted him dead. They still had five spells to see the matter finished.

He turned slowly in the opposite direction that the four were slowly moving. They had spaced out enough that he could only keep three in his line of vision at any given time. He knew that the attack would come from behind him. It was just a smart way for the four of them to make sure he failed the test.

He changed strategy and began to pace himself so that he kept the man in silver robes in front of him. That sphere was more used for beauty, healing and other such positive things. Killing would be a matter of defense for most of them as it would go against the nature of such a mage to kill for pleasure. If any of them were going to give away what the fourth mage was doing, it would be him. This put the nature mage behind him with the death mage to his right and fire mage to his left.

As luck would have it, he had been correct. The man's eyes flickered with concern, and Alador chose that moment to flash in the blink of an eye to a position right behind the nature mage. Where he had stood a second before there were now thorny vines blindly striking one another. He would have been in the middle of that. Alador swiftly pulled his boot knife and put it to the man's throat before the mage had even realized he was there.

"Yield," Alador coldly demanded.

The smirk left the mage's face as his hands came up in a sign of peace. The man swallowed hard and whispered, "I yield."

Alador stepped back, and the man moved off towards the healers. An uproar began in the stands, but Alador did not have the time or the energy to be worrying about who was cheering or objecting. He tossed his knife into the stand, eyeing the three remaining mages as he took a much-needed breath.

He repositioned himself as did the three remaining mages. It was a bit easier to keep track of them now, and there was a little more spread. He was glad that they could not just send a barrage of spells. The point was to test his skills, and though he suspected that they meant to see him dead, they had to do so within the parameters of the test.

He took a breath. He was suspecting two at once, so quickly tried to figure out which two would work together the best. He was not given much time as the death mage and the fire mage both moved at once. Alador felt his throat begin to close off, air unable to sustain him. Knowing that the death mage cast this, he ignored it, knowing he had some time to deal with the threat. He spun about just in time to see six arrows of fire lancing straight for him. He pulled up the deflection shield, and to those who watched the arrows seemed to bend around him. Before he could focus on the growing burning in his lungs, the silver mage moved.

A silver mass seemed to spring from the mage, swiftly crawling across the ground. The mage did not know what to do with it; he had never seen such magic. It swiftly wrapped about him. Alador realized that it was like the strands of a spider web, but much larger. He managed to keep his feet with some difficulty.

The fire mage stepped forward and with flaming hands set the web ablaze. The man's malice oozed from him as he spoke over the sound of the flames igniting the web. "Give Dethara my best wishes."

A moment of panic swept through Alador. Focus was beginning to falter as lack of air became an increasing problem. His vision wavered as he fought to remain standing. He called forth water again, but this time it was uncontrolled and the water from the entire pool flew over the four of them. Immediately, he cooled the deluge, his lungs felt about to burst. The fire went out and ice sprang over the web that confined him.

Again because of his lack of control, the water about him froze, including that which had drenched the mages. The death mage had gotten the worst of it and dropped his death grip on Alador as his feet began to solidify in the ice. He backed up swiftly to ensure he did not become captured, his movements jerky and apparently uncoordinated in his frozen cocoon.

Alador took a ragged breath of much needed air, gasping as he fought to break free of the frozen web. The intense cold had turned its strands into fragile glass, and by twisting his body he was able to shatter the frozen tendrils. He stepped out, and the two mages in front of him stepped backwards warily. That he had taken their onslaught and survived was obviously concerning.

The crowd went wild. The Blackguard began stamping their feet in rhythm as they chanted out his name. Alador only felt the thrumming through the ground: his vision and hearing were still pulsing from oxygen deprivation. Realizing the mages had cast the last of their allowed spells, he bent over, putting his hands against his knees just trying to get his breath. His vision swam and his back hurt.

He finally pushed up and made his way back to the center of the ring. A woman in gold robes hurried to him and offered him a healing potion. He nodded to her and drank it down, feeling its effects begin to course through him almost immediately.

It was as he handed the elixir bottle back to her that the Arena master began to speak. Despite the magical amplification, he could not quite overpower the cheering crowd. It took him a couple of tries and it was not till the high master of the Blackguard barked out an order that the arena grew quiet enough for him to do so.

"This testing is under censure. The use of a dagger is an offensive move and considered an attack." The crowd came to its feet again. There were those who approved and those who felt such a censure unfair in the circumstances. Alador grew concerned as the mood of the crowd grew ugly. The division in the stands was becoming increasingly clear.

Alador had not thought about the dagger. His use of it had been instinctive after hours of practice in the weapons arena. He never went anywhere without at least one. That had been the case even when he had lived amongst the Daezun. It was a tool with many uses, including defense, and - he had to admit - offense.

He looked about the crowd. The dissension was mostly from the fourth and fifth tier mages. They were outnumbered in the roaring stands. The Blackguard and lower mages faced off with them, making the division clear. He noticed the number of guards at the upper entrances had increased and he looked to find his uncle.

Luthian was staring at him with an incredulous look. Alador met his gaze, then he glanced pointedly at the crowds that the arena master was failing to contain. The pain in his back was easing and he drew himself up straighter before the judging table. He slowly, as he had seen his father do so many times, clasped his hands behind his back and stood waiting.

Luthian seemed to have caught his eye-movement as he was now approaching the judges' table. Alador watched as Luthian cast some simple spell then began to speak so all could hear.

"May I ask the honored table if there is anything written anywhere in the rules of testing that specifically prohibits a mage from using a weapon to defend himself?" Luthian's slow drawl was loud enough that the crowd was hushing each other to clearly hear what was being said.

The arena master straightened his robes with a hint of indignation as he answered. "Well no; but it has never been done before and..."

Luthian cut him off. "As you can see, most honored of judges…" Luthian's lack of respect was only evident in the slight edge of sarcasm that slid along his words. "... we are testing a half-blood and one trained to attend to our needs." His voice caressed the words with an edge of hint to the man. "Blackguard men and women are trained to use weapons on instinct."

The man had the decency to clamp his mouth shut, he glanced at the opposite side of the arena. The Blackguard were all on their feet.

Luthian moved to stand before the table. His back was to Alador when he leaned down, placing his hands upon it. "However," he continued. "I do know that it is specifically in the rules that no more than two spells can be cast simultaneously in a fourth tier test. It would seem the mages chosen to test the young man have erred in a far more grievous manner then Alador in using a knife."

Though Alador could not see his uncle's face, the cloying nature of his words made Alador smile. "May I suggest that we consider the matter of 'rule-transgression' evened out? - since one alleged misdemeanour is not in the rules and merely a matter of tradition, while the second **clearly** amounts to a life-threatening flouting of the rules that I am sure the panel will make sure never happens again."

Alador could only guess the look that Luthian had given the judges by the alarmed expressions on their faces. Luthian stood and stepped out of the way. He flashed Alador a grin with a slight roll of his eyes towards the judging table. The judges whispered together for a moment then nodded to the arena master.

The loud voice shouted for all to hear again. "Let it be known that Alador Guldalian has mastered the fourth tier. Do you wish to continue?"

Alador let out the breath he had been unconsciously holding as the Blackguard behind him filled the arena with their roars of approval. His hands had been gripped so tightly that he flexed them to allow more blood into them. He knew if he chose to fight that there would be no quarter given. They had tried to kill him in the fourth tier; they would certainly have kept back the best mage to battle him in the fifth. He now understood why there were so few manors on the fifth tier. Not many lived to make it to that level of distinction.

Alador knew he was tired, and would be given no more than five minutes' rest to begin his fifth tier test. His mind fought for which way was most likely to see him seated on the tier. The arena master raised his hands to quieten the crowd so that he could hear Alador's answer.

Alador's mind raced. Could he really kill a man in a test? Yet, he thought, so much was riding on his obtaining the fifth tier. When at last, the young mage was sure he would be heard, he called out. "I wish to continue."

"Which manner of testing do you desire? Battle or skill?" The stands grew quiet, waiting for Alador to answer.

Alador could tell by the man's eyes that he was expecting a choice of battle. He had glanced twice towards the end of the arena where Alador had entered. Alador glanced at Lady Morana or Dethara- he was unsure which. She was watching him impassively. Her beautiful face was not hidden from this angle and he smiled, momentarily remembering her as a mermaid.

There was something in her eyes that made him realize that the Goddess was here, and he doubted that it was a coincidence. He slowly smiled at her. "I will take a test of skill," he called loudly, never breaking eye-contact with the woman. There were gasps of surprise amongst the ruling elite before the noise of the guardsmen overwhelmed them. Again, the High Master was forced to quieten them.

The arena master waited till it was quiet again, which was just fine with Alador as it bought him more time to rest. He planned to make a simple snowstorm and maybe some ice sculptures: something of beauty to fill the arena with white. He found it fitting somehow to place such a vision before the Goddess.

He moved back out into the center of the ring as the arena master gave his final words. "Alador Guldalian will perform a feat of skill to demonstrate his mastery of his sphere. Please remain silent, as such spells are often dangerous."

Alador did not pay attention to the stands. He had practiced this so much that creating it in such a small space should be relatively easy compared to the storm that he and Rena had recently unleashed. He shivered as his mind touched on Rena and he had to force himself to refocus on the spell he would cast.

The spell drew quickly under his masterful hand. The airstones contained within the dome were easily manipulated. A soft gentle snow began to fall and he began to sculpt the ice into creatures of the sea, a reference the Goddess would not forget. He had just finished the rock that he had planned to place the mermaid on when he realized something was wrong. It was as if something were filtering his pulling of magic. His stomach turned as if he were going to vomit. As he moved the water to form the mermaid, his head began to swim. The more power he pulled, the sicker he felt.

Alador slowly turned, scanning the edges of the arena as he worked to keep the spell together. It was pulling at the edges. It felt wild and barely contained as he fought to force the water into the positions he needed to create the mermaid. He briefly scanned the crowd, drawing a breath to steady himself.

Luthian looked disappointed. Alador knew that he had not wanted Alador to reveal he was a true storm mage. His eyes moved to Dethara, and there he paused. She was looking amused, but he realized that her lips were moving as she watched him.

Dethara was attempting to stop him from creating the storm successfully. Why would she let him get this far to discredit him now? An unseen battle began to wage between the two of them. The crowd obliviously watched the snow fall amongst the ice sculptures.

However, Alador was fighting a growing sickness. He felt his legs begin to tremble, and more than once his focus faltered. He struggled to find what was making him ill. Meanwhile, they both fought for control of the storm. Alador grew weaker and weaker, the spell began to slip his control. Flashes of lightning began to snap around him on the ground. Alador's eyes flashed with anger as Dethara simply dipped her head in acknowledgment. He was now sure it was Dethara and not Morana. The priestess did not have the power on her own to compromise the protective shield that stood between Alador and the spectators. His anger grew as he dropped down to his knees, his hands still moving in his attempt to regain control.

He realized suddenly that she would have had to weaken the dome somewhere to access the clouds. Alador sent out a sliver of power to detect other magic. He spotted where a tendril of green was filtering into his own cloud. She was filling his storm with poison, and based upon how he felt, it was a strong one. He realized with horror that if he did not dissipate the cloud before the shield was lifted that many in the stands could grow sick or maybe even die. He was fairly sure she meant them to die: after all, she was the Goddess of Death.

The realization must have been written on his face for she smiled. It was a smile that one could only imagine upon the face of death itself. It shot horror to his very core, for at that moment he realized that the Lady of Death was about to kill a good portion of the city and he, a half-Daezun, would be blamed for it.

This would not bring about Luthian's plan for unification. It would bring a devastating war to the isle again - a war placed squarely on a half-breed who had dared to rise above his station.

A rage he had not felt since Renamaum had seen Dethara filled him to the core. Alador forced himself back to his feet. With trembling legs, he sought the ocean. If she had breached the shield to feed her poison into his clouds, then he should be able to tap the power of the greatest body of water. The ocean was the greatest source of all natural powers. Its depth and breadth exceeded everything in creation, except for the fields amongst the stars.

This time when he found that well of power, it did not frighten him. He grabbed hold of it and straightened with the strength of its nourishment. Alador smiled back at Dethara as her eyes widened in surprise. He used that strength to begin to fold the clouds in on themselves. They grew into a tighter and tighter mass.

When Dethara attempted to pull back the string of poison she had been feeding into it, he grabbed hold of it and, thereby in some degree, her. Their eyes met in a duel that no one else was witnessing. He could feel her tugging to be free, surprise and confusion written on her face.

All he could focus on was that she had been about to kill hundreds of people just to start a war. He let that anger filter into the cloud that was growing blacker as it shrank. Soon it became a dark black ball with a strange tint of green along its outside edges. The crowd watched in utter silence, clearly trying to discern the purpose of Alador's spell weaving. His hands moved in a rhythmic dance as he focused on the small pinpoint breach in the shield.

With all the power that he could feel in the center of his being, that which he could feel from Dethara, and that of the ocean itself, Alador shoved the compressed cloud into the small breach. His intent was to send it far up into the air where hopefully the poisons would distribute harmlessly.

What he had intended was very different from what actually happened. The tiny ball of lightning, cloud and poison shimmered as it shot upward. The power it took to shove that compressed cloud into the hole met with the power holding the cracked shield in place. It began to fracture visibly as power arced out from the breach and down the sides.

An explosion of light shot up into the air, shattering the shield that stood between the crowd and the mage. The resulting torrent of power was so strong that for a long moment, every flag was torn in a direction away from the center. Many standing denizens were caught off guard and knocked off their feet.

Alador did not care. He had one focus and that was the poisonous cloud. There was dead silence after the unprecedented shattering of the dome. Everyone sat or stood wide-eyed in disbelief. Some were holding their ears, and others struggled to find their feet. Alador watched the cloud, it seemed to shatter far up in the air before drifting off over the ocean.

He fell to his knees from sheer exhaustion, his dragon-rage dissipating as he did so. The depth of the poison in him raged up, making his head swim with pain and nausea. If it had been his last act, so be it. The Daezun would not be blamed for the mass killing that Dethara had devised.

His last thought as the poison overtook him and he collapsed onto the sand was that he was fairly sure he would die a fifth tier mage.

Chapter Twenty-Nine

Alador stirred in the big bed he found himself lying in. He didn't want to move. He moved his hand across the sheet and stilled. There were sheets; why were there sheets? He could hear a strange tune at a distance, but he realized after a moment that it was more felt than heard. He slowly opened his eyes and looked around in confusion for a moment. It was his room in Henrick's mansion.

He smiled slowly. He realized that to be here meant that he had passed, and more importantly, he had lived. He groaned as he looked to his left, sensing something was not quite as it should be. Alador saw Sordith sound asleep in a chair, his feet up on a stool. Alador cleared his throat. He did not think it wise to surprise the Trench Lord by contact.

As he had predicted, Sordith looked up and quickly around, one hand came to the dagger at his waist and the other behind him to where his swords must be propped. When he saw Alador looking at him, he too smiled slowly.

"You know, brother, I am getting tired of sitting by your sick bed. Do you think you might manage to stay on your feet for a while?"

Sordith's humor kept the smile on Alador's face. He wiped the sleep from his eyes as he managed to sit up. "It would be easier if someone wasn't always trying to kill me," he said. Throwing back the covers, he found that he was naked and swiftly formed a pair of linen leggings. He was surprised at a momentary stutter in his magic; it too felt overused. He tried to stand and the room swam. He sat back down swiftly with a pained groan.

"Ah yes, the healer said it might be a day or so before you felt quite the same." Sordith rose and moved to the servant bell. He pulled it and turned back to Alador. "Something about poison and exhaustion of power."

The memory of Dethara washed over him, and he fell back against the pillows with a wave of nausea. "Yes… that was not planned." He put a hand to his head: the simple movement had set it pounding.

"I figured as much. When the shield exploded it injured a few who had been on their feet. Odd that it hit the stands of the elite … and not those of the guard." Sordith moved to the bed and tucked his brother back in. He stuck pillows behind him so that Alador could sit fully upright.

"Thanks." He nestled in, deciding some rest was not a bad idea. "Wait, I don't remember seeing you there." He looked at Sordith in surprise.

"I didn't wish to be seen," Sordith admitted with a shrug.

"May I ask why not?" Alador had not even thought about it at the time, but he definitely hadn't seen Sordith. He was also saddened to hear that people had been hurt. He had been trying to prevent that.

"I wasn't sure who I would have to kill." Sordith's bland answer brought Alador's eyes up. By the look on Sordith's face, he decided he would save asking the meaning of that for another time.

"So I am guessing - since we are here - I passed the tier test. What did I miss after the spell went off?" He was trying to remember, but his last memory had been relief that the cloud was far into the sky and dissipating.

"Well, there was massive confusion at first. There was anger at you and cries for your execution till people realized you were not merely exhausted, but ill. Then it was determined that the spell must have gone amiss because you were poisoned."

Sordith grinned, a sly look up on his face. "Luthian sent you here, then turned to the judges to make it very clear he had seen this as an attempt to kill his heir. There was a great deal of argument as people were fleeing the arena."

Sordith paused for a moment, sobering a bit. "Your uncle can be very persuasive. By the time he was done, the judges were apologizing all over the place. They passed you, and had the healer that gave you the healing potion before the fifth tier test arrested."

Alador shook his head. "I will have to go see my uncle. I hope they haven't killed that poor healer. It wasn't the healing potion that was to blame." Alador looked up to see the door open.

"Yes, Lord Guldalian?" the servant asked, bowing after he spoke.

"Food and wine." Sordith ordered before Alador could speak.

Alador had hesitated, looking around for his father for a half second. "Umm, my favorites if you will. What is your name?" Alador realized he had never really inquired about his father's staff.

"Radney, my Lord. I will bring that right away." The servant gently closed the door behind him.

"Well, this will take some getting used to." Alador murmured.

"Nah, maybe a day or two, then you come to just expect it." Sordith pointed out. "Comes with the power and all the problems that come with power." Sordith, not one to let things go, returned them to the conversation before the servant had entered. "So, how do you know it was not the healer?"

Alador returned his gaze to his brother. "I traced the spell back to Lady Morana." He sighed. "If I had not forced the cloud through the breech she created, many of the crowd would have died, my uncle among them, since he was closer to the arena itself."

"I thought they were sleeping together." Sordith frowned.

"As did I. However, he must have angered her, or his usefulness has run out for her." Alador did not mention Dethara, or that the Goddess had made her own move.

"Isn't that shield unbreachable?" Sordith asked. "I mean, if it is not, I will make it a point to sit farther back in the future, or not attend at all."

"I think that it wasn't designed for an attack on the shield itself. I think it is more a wall of containment for the magic that might bounce around, or more likely the items created." Alador considered further. "Either that or Lady Morana is a very powerful mage, and I will do my best to stay out of her way. I truly don't think I was the target. I think I was more a convenient means to an end."

Sordith nodded, considering this latest development. Finally, he reached over and patted Alador's leg as if remembering something at the last moment. "When your head has righted itself, your uncle wishes to see you. I think that had better be soon. He was quite furious and I don't envy that healer her fate."

Alador sighed. "I doubt she is even alive as we speak. My uncle is not one to let his anger simmer. I should know. I have pushed him to the point of frustration many times in the course of our short history." He stretched, testing his muscles. Every one of them protested as if they had been fully worked out. "I will go after I have eaten. What else do I need to know?" He asked, his head slowly clearing.

"Well, after you fell there was a near-riot in the Blackguard. The High Master was hard pressed to get them out of the stands and back to the caverns." Sordith stroked his chin. "You have become very popular while you were sleeping. There are all manner of cards from callers we have turned away, and invitations to be answered on your desk." Sordith stood up and straightened his leathers. They were uncomfortably out of alignment after several hours of fitful sleep in the chair.

Alador groaned. He would have to see if one of the staff could be pressed into acting as his secretary in social matters. He had no desire to spend hours presenting his excuses in writing to numerous invitations. Something about Sordith's words gave him pause. "Wait," he asked, "…how long have I been out?"

"About twenty-four hours, I reckon." Sordith glanced at the door. "I wish that man would hurry up," he muttered absently. "My throat is quite parched,"

Alador swore softly. He had things to do, and lying in bed was not on his list. He cast the covers back, intent on getting up. He had two hands pressing him back before his leg had cleared the side.

"Oh no, you will remain right there till you have had a proper meal. I know you mages need to eat, and facing your uncle might bring its own challenges," Sordith scolded.

Alador sighed. "There are things to be done," he said. However, he did not physically resist his brother tucking him back into the bed.

"Yes, there are, but eating is first on that list." His brother grinned. "Rather fun to boss a fifth level mage about."

"Careful, or I will turn you into a toad," Alador grumbled.

Sordith looked a bit alarmed for a moment. "Could you actually do that?"

Alador laughed at the look on his brother's face. "Don't worry, it's rather a lengthy spell, and I don't have the energy." He could tell that Sordith had noted that he had not denied he could turn his brother into a toad. He let that hang between them with naught but a chuckle at the look on Sordith's face.

"You have a lot of power, don't you?" Sordith's question was hesitant as he looked his brother over. Alador could see slight envy in his eyes

"I guess," he said. "I don't really know its true depth, though I suspect I tested its limits when I pushed that cloud out of the dome."

Sordith nodded. "I was watching Luthian as you took the test. You surprised him a couple of times, and definitely when you blew up the shield."

Alador winced. "To be honest, that was not my intention. I didn't have much time, and I didn't consider what forcing that much magic through the breach would do. Lady Morana has much to answer for, and she keeps adding to my list." He looked at Sordith. "Have you been able to get anyone in yet?"

Sordith shook his head. "To be honest, they are a paranoid lot. I haven't any men or women with enough devout dedication to Dethara who would still remain loyal to me. They seem to take in only those with a certain level of zeal."

Alador sighed. "I am certain there is more going on behind those walls than Henrick was able to discover. I will see if I can find another means; but in the meantime, will you keep trying?"

"Of course," Sordith answered. "To be honest, you've got me curious. I've decided to try another tack and offer trade to the temple. It would be lucrative, and at least then I might be able to get a trader in now and then."

The door opened and Radney wheeled a serving cart into the room. It held an array of Alador's favorites, and a healthy sized decanter of wine. "Shall I serve you, Lord Guldalian?"

"Yes please. I am afraid my brother has insisted I stay in bed until I have eaten." Alador smiled. He fell silent for a moment, watching the servant pile a plate with delicacies that Alador had been known to like when he visited his father. "Radney, do I have a person to see to letters and such, or did Henrick?"

"Yes, my Lord. There is a woman, Seria, who saw to his letters, filing, appointments and such. Shall I send her to you?"

Sordith reached for the wine. Alador smiled and shook his head before turning his attention back to the servant. "Yes, if you would. I have a lot to attend to over the next few days, so I could use her assistance." Radney handed him a plate and the smells of sausage, sweetmeats and warm bread brought a healthy growl from Alador's stomach.

"Yes my Lord. I will send her at once." Radney frowned as Sordith set a glass of wine down for Alador beside his bed. "Will there be anything else, Lord Guldalian?"

"Don't call me 'Lord Guldalian'. That is my father or the High Minister." He grinned up at Radney.

Radney's answering grin complemented the understanding in his eyes. "Of course, Lord Alador. I will spread the word amongst the staff." He bowed and hurried out.

Sordith leaned close to Alador as he finished a deep pull from his cup. "I would go through your staff as soon as you have time." he stated in a low tone.

Alador swallowed a mouthful of sausage before answering. "Why is that?"

Sordith popped some cheese into his mouth. Alador glanced up at him. He answered without emptying his mouth first. "Make sure you aren't harboring one of your uncle's spies."

"Oooh, very good point." He did not like the idea of Luthian keeping an eye on his every move in this house. "I will get a list of staff that Henrick trusted when I see him next, then replace the others."

"I can get you a list of people with relevant skills seeking work from the lower tiers. Good people, not involved in politics." Sordith offered.

Alador nodded. "That would be helpful, thank you."

They ate in silence for a few minutes, then the door opened and an elderly matron stepped in. She curtsied low then stood to eye Alador. He studied her posture and her gaze, looking for any sign of vehemence.

"You must be Seria." he was fairly sure no one else would just have entered without knocking.

"You sent for me, Lord Alador," she answered curtly.

"Yes, yes. Please, come a little closer. I don't want to have to shout." He watched her hesitate. It was clear she did not know what to think of this change of ownership.

"I hear you used to see to letters and such for my father?" He kept his tone warm and open.

"Yes Lord Alador." Her simple words were polite, but they held no answering warmth.

"I would see you hold the same position." This news was rewarded by a slight upturning of her mouth, so he pressed on. "Of course, only if you desire it. I force no one to perform tasks they don't wish to do. I can hire someone else if you would rather."

"Oh no, Lord. It is what I do best. I would be happy to continue in that role for you," the plump matron hurriedly assured him. She smoothed down her skirt a little nervously, though as she did so he noted a slight thaw in her manner.

"Right then. Here is what I wish. Sort through the cards and letters and pass to me any communication from a member of Council." He pointed at her with a warm bread roll. "You can present a polite apology on my behalf to any other invitations for me. I will let you know when I might be ready to attend other social events; but for now, I fear I have neither the health nor the time."

She nodded. "Of course, my Lord." She looked about, uncomfortably fidgeting as she did so. It took him a moment to realize she did not like being in his bedchamber.

"Yes, I am sorry to receive you here, but it was a matter of some urgency," he apologized. "If you could also set aside any missives from Lady Aldemar or a General Levielle," he added. "That is all for now."

"I will see it done at the first opportunity, my Lord." She pulled a package out of her apron and moved to him. "I believe these are your new tier passes, Lord Alador. I thought you might need these first."

Alador smiled at her as he took them. "I can see we will get along fine, Seria. Thank you." He finally got a real smile from her, she curtsied and hurried out the door.

"Yup, apple doesn't fall far from the tree." Sordith grinned and popped a sweetmeat into his mouth.

"We can hardly compare ourselves to Henrick. I mean we don't know our actual father. That tree rather got uprooted," he admonished.

Sordith chuckled. "Death and damnation to Henrick." He motioned to himself. "I meant me." He winked and poured them both another glass.

Chapter Thirty

Alador straightened the deep blue robe one last time. He had found his closet filled with robes appropriate to his tier and sphere. Radney had said it was the last thing that Henrick had ordered before he had left them all. They would have been sent to Alador in the caverns if the manor had been given to another, in spite of his having passed his test.

He looked around in wonder. It was his to live in for as long as he wished. He had always wanted his own home, but this was far beyond what he had imagined for Mesiande and himself. Finally assured that he looked the part of a fifth tier mage and lord of the manor, he left his room.

Radney waited for him in the hall. He had indicated a few minutes ago that there were a couple of matters that needed Alador's direct attention.

"Now Radney, what is this all about?" he asked, shutting his door behind him.

"Some small matters that require decisions from you, Lord Alador; they will not take long." Radney led him down the hall to his father's room.

Alador realized that he had never been in Henrick's personal chambers. When they stopped at the door, he paused. "What are we doing with my father's room?"

"It is no longer your father's," Radney reminded him. He opened the door and stepped inside. "As such, I thought that maybe you would like to…" - Radney cleared his throat with obvious amusement - "... change a few things before we moved your possessions into the master room."

Immediately Alador could see why the man was concerned, but it brought a grin to his face. In many ways, his father's room was decorated much as Keensight's cave had been. There were dark gray walls reminiscent of a cave. The black carpet was in direct contrast to the bed. Alador had to put a hand over his mouth to contain his laughter.

The bed was so large that there were steps to get up into it. It would easily have slept four grown men. He was unsure what the bed was made of, but it was studded with jewels of all sizes, colours and shapes. It must have been worth a fortune. The coverlet was golden with silver blocks filled with blue flecks that reminded him of medure. There were heavy brocade curtains of deep red, held to each bedpost by golden cords.

Alador managed to cough rather than laugh outright. "I can see why you're concerned. What are the differences between this room and my own?" He was considering just leaving it for when Henrick snuck in to visit. At the same time, there were many slips to be had for that bed if it were broken down and sold off piecemeal. He could imagine Keensight's dismay and chuckled, despite his attempt to contain his humor.

"This is a full suite, Lord Alador. In addition to the privy closet, there is a small private study, and a full bath." Radney opened the doors to each room. Alador loved the small study immediately. It was walled in deep, rich wood panels. There was little frivolity: it held a desk, a fireplace and comfortable settee for lounging.

"Why did Henrick not use this?" He could tell that - despite being clean and readily available -the room hadn't been used in quite a while. It had the smell of being shut up and disregarded. The book shelves were largely empty and the serving table to the side was not stocked.

"He said it was too small for his tastes." Radney said and led the way to the next door. The bath turned out to be something quite spectacular. There was a large inset pool that would easily allow a family to bathe at the same time. A smaller pool steamed nearby, and Alador was curious how it was kept warm. He looked around and noted that there were no windows. The air was moist here, indicating very little escape.

"Is this room inset in the rock of the tiers?" He moved around the luxury that seemed far removed from his simple life as a Daezun or a Blackguard.

"I believe so. I don't believe it sits above a lower room." Radney adjusted some towels that sat near the heated pool.

"I do believe I will move into these rooms." Alador stated, placing his hands behind him. He turned to face the servant.

"Do you want to make any changes first, Lord Alador?" Radney's question was tinged with hope.

"Only to the bedroom. I want every jewel in that bed removed, valued and accounted for. Once that is done and the assortment safely in my hands, see to it that the walls are painted at least five shades lighter: cream would be good. The carpet is fine as it is. I want the study made ready for my immediate use."

"And the bed?" Radney glanced at the garish thing and back to his new lord.

"Once I have supervised the removal and valuation of the stones encrusted in it, I will have Lord Sordith commission someone to come take it apart and fence its pieces." Alador considered the thing carefully as he spoke. "Have a bed half this size constructed, and purchase bedding in blue and silver." It would fit the room and be far more to his tastes.

He looked down at the carpet. He should really sell it off as well. That depth of black was hard to achieve, and a carpet woven as large and thick as this one had been must be worth thousands of slips - something to keep in mind if he ran short. He had a feeling, however, given the jewels in the bed, that he would not run short for a very long time.

"I will see to it at once, Lord Alador." Radney smiled with relief, and carefully closed each door. Alador indicated one he had not opened. "What is this?"

"The closet," the servant answered, not turning to look at him.

Alador opened it himself and blinked in surprise. Not only was it the size of the average lower floor of a Daezun home, it was still filled with clothing and accessories. Lightstones lined the tops of it to make sure that all could be seen clearly. "My father did not take his things?"

"He took quite a few." Radney stepped beside him. "Lord Henrick had a love for robes and accessories."

Alador shook his head. However, here was a source of more funds that he could use to further his cause. "Sell off all that are not blue, black with blue, or black with silver." He walked into the vast array of excess. "Keep only the items designed to accompany them that will fit me." He fingered the many assorted jeweled belts. He did not really need them, but there was a sense of panic at letting it all go. Had he also gained the dragon's nature for acquisition? "I can trust you with this matter?" He turned to assess Radney closely.

"A servant of the fifth tier has worked their way up because they excel in two major respects: they are good at what they do, and they can be trusted." Radney looked a little affronted. "Not a slip will be miscounted."

"See it done quickly and you may see a bonus from the slips it brings in," Alador offered, both as a salve to the man's pride and from a desire to see the matter over and done with.

"Of course." Radney licked his lips and nodded.

There was a moment of silence as Alador continued to survey the items in the closet. He did not look at Radney when he spoke. "Radney, how many have joined the service of this house since Lord Henrick left?" His casual question was laced with some concern.

"Only two have been taken on, sent by the High Minister himself," Radney stated: "a man to help in the kitchens and one to see to the fires."

Alador pulled out six medure slips from his belt pouch. "See that each man receives three of these and dismiss them."

"Do you want them replaced?" Radney took the medure carefully.

"Do we need them?" Alador was quick to ask. He did not trust anyone who had not been with the household when Henrick had had mastery over it.

Radney shook his head. "Not really," he said.

"Then no." He led the way out of the room and down the hall. "Is there anything else that needs my attention before I go to see my uncle?"

Radney was following a half step behind him. "Just the matter of wages, my Lord." Radney led the way to the office that Henrick had made use of. "Seria has the accounts ready for you to sign. Of course, if there are any other changes to the house that you want to make, you have but to command."

Alador nodded. When it was clear that his new master could think of nothing else, Radney left him at the door of the library. Alador opened it and smiled at the familiar warmth of the room. This was one room that he had no intentions of changing. Seria stood immediately from behind his desk, smoothing her skirts. It was apparently something she did when slightly nervous.

"I understand I have debts to pay?" Alador stated, he moved to her.

Seria scooted to the side. "Yes, Lord Alador."

"When my father ran the manor, how did he come by the slips he used to pay such debts?" He hoped he was not going to have to further deplete his dwindling wealth.

"I couldn't say, Milord." She murmured.

Alador nodded and sat down. He pulled himself up and looked at the totals in horror. It took a great deal of medure to keep the manor running. He was definitely selling off Henrick's finery. "How often do these come due?" He asked, looking over the numbers to see where he could cut back. He was glad now that he was not keeping those two men.

"Every fortnight," she said quietly.

He looked up at her in shock, then back down to the numbers. He would have to find a way to lower costs as he had no income, only the anticipated slips from the sale of Henrick's excesses. "This amount for keeping the rooms warm. Why so high?" He noted that this was the only number that in the circumstances seemed inflated.

"Lord Henrick commanded that every room be kept warm at all times: in case it might be needed suddenly by a guest or by himself." Seria looked nervously down at the neat numbers she had inscribed, then back to the new lord of the manor.

"Well, that stops now. Heat only the rooms in use: this room, the office in the master suite and those that the servants need. When I am alone, I will take my meals in here." He remembered the Henrick had often insisted they eat in the grand dining room which he thought quite unnecessary for a single man.

"Will you be entertaining a great deal, Lord Alador?" Seria moved to his side, eyeing the numbers with him.

"Not for a time; why do you ask?" He looked up at her, willing to hear her thoughts.

"Then we can cut the food budget considerably. Much of the food is wasted. If you are willing to wait a short while, we can cut this number by two thirds." She offered, picking up on his desire to economize. "Then we can simply order additional supplies when you do wish to entertain."

"That will do me just fine, Seria." Alador looked up at her and smiled. "And while you're making those adjustments, see to it that the staff gets a full five medure increase in their weekly wages."

She stared at him in wonder. Her voice was filled with awe as she clarified. "A full five medure? Are you certain?" She eyed him hopefully.

"Yes, I am certain. I know loyalty can be bought and I prefer to buy it first." He handed her the accounts. "Make the adjustments while I am gone and any others that you believe can lead to a reduction in overall expenditure. I will settle this when I return."

"As you wish." She took the papers from him and was busily scribbling away before he had left the room. If his willingness to still let her handle her previous duties had not won her to his cause, he was fairly certain that the five medure just had.

****

He arrived at his uncle's with an air of confidence that he had never quite possessed before. He knew he appeared striking by the assessing looks that other mages gave him as he passed on his way to the upper tier staircase. His matching cloak was fur-lined against the increasing cold of winter and its incessant rain. He hadn't known it could rain anywhere as much as it had done in Silverport since winter had settled in.

He was shown to the library that was his uncle's primary receiving area. The vastness of it suited Alador just fine: there was something large about Luthian that made small spaces with the man oppressive. He bowed deeply as he was announced then strode to his uncle's side.

Luthian was standing staring into the fire and seemed to still be in a great deal of ill temper. Alador doubted the news that he had for his uncle was going to make the matter better. He pulled off his cloak, and was surprised when a servant appeared to take it from him. He handed it over with momentary confusion. That had never happened before. He looked back as the servant disappeared and a Blackguard pulled the door closed.

"I am glad to see you whole and well nephew." Luthian indicated that Alador should sit in a chair by the fire and moved towards an opposite chair. "I have seen the healer fully punished and executed. I assure you that her death was long and painful as she refused to confess until the very end."

Alador shook his head sadly; he had feared as much. "Did you ever consider that she was being truthful?" He sat down, smoothing the robes as a matter of habit.

"No." Luthian stated as he sat down. "She was the last one to have contact with you. There was no one else."

"Perhaps you should have considered the improbable then?" Alador was disgusted to learn the woman was dead. "She was innocent, High Minister. You should have waited to question me." Alador sat back, flashing his uncle a look of anger.

"I refuse to believe you somehow poisoned yourself." Luthian frowned though he did not seem excessively concerned over the fate of the woman.

"I did not," Alador snarled. "The shield to protect the crowd was breached." Alador decided that he would not reveal his full hand, given Luthian's execution of the healer. He had known this was likely, but he had held a slim hope his uncle would have waited to speak with him. He crossed his arms across his chest, his anger not hidden.

"What?" Luthian looked surprised. "I assure you that is nigh impossible! Are you certain? Do you know who?" Alador waited until the man took a breath.

"It was breached: I saw where myself." He shook his head. "I do not know by whom, but I can tell you it was a highly accomplished mage with the ability to cast a spell of poison." His mind's eye filled with the cloud as poison filled it. He shook his head free of the memory. "It was that which afflicted me."

Luthian grew quiet and Alador gave him the time to come to his own conclusions. He doubted it would take Luthian long to connect the dots to Lady Morana. The fire crackled and snapped in the silence, drawing his eye for a moment. He looked back to see his uncle's unusually passive face reddened slightly. "I know one or two who might have enough skill to have done so," he said finally.

"I figured that you might. I can tell you this. Whoever it was, did not mean to kill me. I suspect they meant to kill the Council specifically, or it is possible they just wanted to kill a great many people." Alador coughed into his hand discreetly as the look on his uncle's face nearly made him laugh. Luthian was not looking at him, but the sheer indignation on his face was priceless.

"What makes you say this?" Luthian managed to ask between clenched teeth.

"The poison was not sent to me directly but into the cloud I was creating. Against your advice, I had decided to let it snow within the dome. I realized as I was growing ill that if I fell and the shield was lowered, the poison in the cloud would kill many people."

He folded his hands across his stomach. "I assure you that I had not intended to blow the dome. It took all the strength I had to push the poisoned cloud through that small hole and up into the sky. The effort is what blew the dome," he explained honestly. Really the only thing he was leaving out was that Lady Morana was the one to blame. He could tell by his uncle's face that the man was already certain who the culprit was.

Alador decided a little more salt in the wound would provide the final push. "I don't know who the Council has angered to that extent, but I would be very wary of them if ever you figure it out." Alador tsked softly. "Whoever it is has phenomenal skill and power, and well, no concern about the numbers they would kill in the process," Alador casually drawled.

Luthian jumped angrily to his feet. "Show yourself out, Alador." His voice was hard and clipped as he spoke. "I have urgent matters to see to. I will speak with you later." He turned and strode from the office.

Alador rose slowly to his feet. The door slammed behind his uncle. "I am sure you do, Uncle," he murmured with a sly smile to himself. "I am sure you do."

Chapter Thirty-One

Alador decided that the rest of his day would be best spent checking on how winter was affecting Daezun land. He needed to talk to Rena, and suspected she would make an appearance. The mage could sense her now that their magic was intertwined. There was a sense of music when he thought of her; it seemed to match the thrumming in his heart.

Because of this strange tune - there was just no other way to describe it - he had known that she had been close by when he had first awakened. He had not mentioned it to anyone because he had not been sure what he was sensing. Now, he was certain that they were somehow connected.

At the moment, that melody was soft and barely felt. She was far off. He was so lost in his thoughts walking to his manor that he blinked in surprise when he reached his own door. He stood outside the door for a long moment. It was hard to believe that as long as he lived, and was in good grace with the Council, this enormous building was his. He caressed the wooden door frame; it made him feel guilty when he thought of the rustic home he had been building in Smallbrook. He shook his head and stepped in the door. A servant appeared immediately to take his cloak, even as he was removing his gloves.

Truly startled, Alador looked the man over. "How did you know I was here?" Alador asked. He handed the garment over to the man.

"My magic is small and only of the first tier, but I have a spell that tells me when the door is opened. It makes certain that my service is as prompt as a mage lord requires." The servant hung the cloak in the room off the hall.

Alador scolded himself. Was he already gaining a tiered mage's arrogance? Of course other people had magic. He shook his head and continued to his room. Outside his door stood the ever-vigilant Radney. His eyes held an expectant look as he opened the door to Alador's current bedchamber.

"What is it, Radney?" Alador paused in the doorway.

"I have dealt with the new servants as you requested. The staff is aflutter at your generosity. I thought you should know that you have been well received as the new lord of the house." Radney pulled his tunic down sharply, brushing off unseen dust. "I wished personally to thank you, my Lord and to swear my loyalty." He slapped his right hand across his heart and gave a stiff bow to emphasize his point.

Alador placed his hand on the man's shoulder. "It was the right thing to do. So, while I deeply appreciate and value the loyalty, I hope it doesn't come with increased formality. My name is Alador, remember?" He smiled at the man who gave an answering grin.

"As his Lordship requests." There was a definite hint of humor in that response.

Alador just rolled his eyes and headed into his room. "Radney, I am not to be disturbed for any reason unless I ring for assistance or you see me emerge from this room."

"Yes, Lord Alador." The man's mannerisms became more serious. "I will post here if you wish?"

"That will not be necessary. If anyone comes to the house, I am not at home. Be sure that all staff are aware of my wishes," Alador commanded. The words of command rolled easily off his lips, and they surprised him. When had he become so authoritative?

"Yes Lord Alador." Radney pulled the door closed.

Not wishing to expend any magic unnecessarily, he changed his clothes normally. He put on an extra layer this time. While he was more resistant to cold since he had mined the stone, he had still felt the cut of it when he was on the mountaintop. He did not feel as replenished as he wanted to be, even after all that he had eaten. Between his last foray to the mountaintop and the test, he felt meagre, like a piece of bread spread with too little butter. It was as if his very soul had thinned somehow.

Once he had layered enough clothing, he pulled the amulet free from his robes. Having a clearer idea of the ledge he intended to use, he activated the amulet. The crackling fire in his room was immediately replaced with the sharp cut of howling wind. The cutting wind and blustering snow were so strong that he could not see. Either Rena had kept the spell going, or winter had brought its own storm without magical help.

He cast a bubble of protection about himself to force the wind and ice from his eyes. He was unable to see beyond the storm, even with his vision cleared. Without the wind in his face, he realized that the ground beneath his feet was slick. He moved back from the edge carefully.

Alador had to speak to Rena, and he knew of no other way to find her. He sat down against the rock face to decrease his risk of slipping, and to be out of the direct cut of the wind. He did not want to have to maintain the bubble of protection with the limited power he felt within himself. He could not build a fire here so opted to warm the boulder at his back. There was enough moisture for him to create a steaming heat.

It was over an hour before he felt her drawing closer, the melody increasing with each stroke of her wings. This new connection would be useful, he decided. He smiled, tracking her progress though he could not see her approach.

"Hello my heartmate." Rena purred as she landed. Her talons dug into the snow and ice to keep from sliding backwards.

"Rena, we are not mated," he said with a hint of irritation. He got carefully back to his feet.

Rena coughed her heaving laugh. "Search your heart, you know that this is not true." She laid her head against his, their foreheads touching gently.

Alador put a hand to either side of her long muzzle and as he did so, a shock rocketed through his body. It was slowly replaced by a gentle warmth and he realized that he felt whole. He closed his eyes and knew that they were now linked by a powerful bond.

"Rena, I love another." His words were gentle, but held a new edge of doubt. This feeling between him and the dragon was strong and a bit frightening.

Rena growled. It was an alarming sound considering that her great fangs were inches from his wrists. Despite her response, she did not pull away from him. "Do mortals think they can love only one in their lifetime?"

Alador did not pull his forehead from Rena when he answered her. "I have not really thought about that," he admitted.

"When a mortal's mate dies, can she love another?" Rena pulled away a bit and nuzzled his cheek. Alador let his hands fall away as she did so.

"Of course they can." Alador did not see her point.

Rena's words were gentle and guiding. "Then why must her mate die first? If she can love again, she can love more than one now."

Alador fell silent, reaching up to stroke her muzzle. The scales here were smooth. He hardly knew Rena, so was it possible that he had come to love her when the spell connected them? Is that why he had not desired Nemara in his bed? His thoughts raced; he continued the connection between them.

"Rena, I don't know what to say or think about this. You should have warned me that we might mate on the winds of power." He dropped his hands, feeling momentarily hoodwinked.

"I did not know that such a thing could occur between mortal and dragon," she repeated. "I think it is only because you are now a pseudo-dragon." Rena shook the ice and snow off her wings. "Do you not want me as your heart mate?" She sounded hurt. She glanced back down at him.

"It is not that, Rena." He pulled his cloak about him. "I just… I always expected to mate with another."

Rena frowned. "I will not stop you if you a mortal mate is really what you want." Despite her generous words, her tone held a great deal of displeasure. "But if she makes you unhappy, I will eat her."

Alador shook his head. "That is exactly what concerns me." He decided that he needed to change the subject as they were both becoming upset, and he found he really did not like upsetting her. *'Have I really come to love her?'* he asked himself again. "I need to speak to Amaum."

"I do not think he will be happy about our mating." Rena warned. "He is not the one to ask for advice about this pairing."

"I need to speak to him about helping with the plan, Rena. I don't think I will be asking your brother for advice on mating." Alador laughed softly. He rubbed his hands together as if to warm them even though he wore gloves.

"Oh, he could tell you a great deal about mating dances. He loves to dance on the wind." She paused and looked at him coyly. "We both do,"she added, nuzzling him playfully.

Alador gave her a disgruntled glance. "Have you mated on the wind often?" Alador found himself not liking that at all. His hands balled up, he realized he was feeling jealous anger.

"I am not going to tell you," she answered with a rumble.

"Fine!" Alador sighed, not quite sure if dragons teased. Remembering he had to find her brother, he brought her back to the point. "How can I find Amaum?"

"I can take you to his cave. There is no guarantee he will be there." Rena pointed out. "It is very far from here."

Alador sighed. "I need his help." He considered for a long moment. "Can you fetch him and meet me at Keensight's cave?"

"You will be in the flight leader's cave?" She eyed him, a look that held both wonder and concern.

Alador realized that Rena honestly did not know that Henrick was Keensight. They had spent time at the lake with Henrick, so he had thought all the dragons had kept Henrick's secret from him. "Yes, I have a pact with him. You may land on his ledge and call for me. Do not fret," Alador reassured the young dragon female, "he is not at home." He reached out to reassure her and stroked her muzzle softly.

The dragon's eyes closed happily for a moment before a thought struck her. "How do you know he is not in his cave?" Rena asked with renewed concern.

"As I said, he and I have a pact. I happen to know where he will be for a while yet." Alador stroked his hand back and forth on her muzzle, evoking a purring sound. "I promise you, it will be fine."

"You are certain?" she asked again. She turned her head to stare at him with one large silver eye.

"I am certain," he reassured her again. He laid his forehead against her muzzle. It felt right to be in contact with her, despite her scales. It helped that those on the muzzle where smooth. He remembered the cut of the breast scales when she had held him close. Alador smiled inwardly at the thought of everyone being so scared of Keensight. He remembered the fear that the dragon had inspired in him. It was hard to correlate that with his feelings for Henrick.

After a long moment of contact, she pulled back. "I will meet you there. It will take some time to reach Amaum's cave. If he is not in, I will need a bit longer to find him. I might need my dame to help me if he is out frolicking." The dragon snorted, and a light steam boiled over Alador, frosting his hair and eyebrows as it met the cold wind. "He is always frolicking."

"I am sure if I had wings and freedom, I would be too." Alador chuckled as he shook his head.

"No, you wouldn't." Rena said emphatically.

"Oh? What makes you say that?" He wiped the ice particles off his face.

"Because you are MINE!" she insisted. She leapt into the air, barely missing him with her sweeping tail as she dove off the cliff face.

He had been about to argue, but he knew that for Rena it was the truth. Alador was certain that was how she now saw him. He was not quite sure about his own feelings on the matter. He pulled the amulet out and let its cold surface settle in his hand. He focused his thoughts on the top of the stairs in Keensight's cave and the swirling tunnel of ice melded into rushing colors.

It took him a moment to realize that he had arrived. The cave was so dark that he could not see his hand. It was warmer without the wind, but not by much. He summoned light to the palm of his hand and found a torch on the wall. It took him sometime to light it. Even normally-produced fire seemed to hesitate before manifesting when it was his hand calling for it. He continued to struggle with anything to do with fire.

Once that was done, he moved around lighting each one. It took some doing, as many were just barely within his reach. At last a flickering light illuminated the cave. Rena had said it would take some time. He hoped that a dragon's sense of time was not too far off from his own. Their lifespan was so much longer that he had not considered if this would affect how long it really took.

Lost in his thoughts, he wandered over to Keensight's hoard. When the sound of metal struck his boot, he looked up at the towering mound. Now that he had the time to inspect it without the dragon, he wondered what the old dragon found valuable. He hesitated a moment, looking about for the absent dragon before his curiosity overtook his common sense.

He smiled at the throne that now was back against the wall. Alador remembered when Keensight had pulled out the throne. He had been so terrified. He knew that the situation had to have been amusing to Henrick. He ran a finger along the arm of the chair, he wondered if he would have handled the news back then. He suspected it would have made more sense to him than some of the other things he had encountered.

Calling light to his hand again, he held it up over the pile. There were numerous items of treasure of the kind one would expect a dragon to have amassed, but there were odd things as well. Many of the books Henrick had taken from the library were now stacked at the back wall behind the pile that made up the dragon's bed.

He carefully began to climb onto the pile. It was difficult as every step seemed to send slips and precious stones tumbling down. At last he made it to the top, the place where the indentation of the great dragon created a flat area on which to stand. He figured the most precious items would be kept close at hand. He knelt down and began to sort.

The first thing that struck him was how uncomfortable it was to kneel in the indentation. Keensight had seemed to be quite comfortable on his pile of slips and rock. The second thing he noticed was a treasure chest. It was quite large and only the top of it was visible in the pile. It lay in between the indentations of the dragon's coiled tail.

Alador carefully slid his way over to it. He pulled at the top, but it was locked. Alador dug around the pile near the chest. He was certain that a key had to be here somewhere. What would be so important that a dragon would feel the need to lock it? With all the treasure here, it piqued his curiosity. He did not want to pry it open and risk damaging the beautiful chest.

It was made of an old wood, nearly black in color, and gilded with medure and gold. To mold medure into filigree and gilding for a box must have taken a great deal of skill; and even then, some level of magic would be needed. It was a hard metal, difficult to work and harder to find. The lock puzzled him. It seemed to have a keyhole, but it was completely round. He began to look for any item that might have the same circumference.

Spotting something that might fit the bill, he pulled an oblong object from its sheath of treasure, only to discover it was bone and that it had belonged to a mortal man. Frowning, he cast it down quickly. How many Lerdenians and Daezun had the dragon killed in his time? He suspected he did not wish to know the answer to that. He closed his eyes as visions filled his mind of Renamaum flying next to Keensight, the two dragons swooping down upon the silver standards of the Lerdenian army.

He continued his search, laying aside pieces of amazing armor, weapons in shapes that he had never seen, and even stranger gemstones. How many turns had the dragon been collecting this treasure, and how far from the Great Isle had Keensight wandered to find such wonders?

His first warning of trouble was the tremor of the cave as something loud hit the ground outside. It was too soon and too large to be Rena or Amaum. Had Pruatra come to give him word? A bellow of rage dispelled that question as quick as it had come.

Alador looked about at the mess he had made. He had a good relationship with the dragon, so he was fairly certain that as soon as Keensight saw it was him, all would be well. His concern was more that it was not Keensight, but rather a rival dragon.

It was with relief when he saw the red muzzle. Before he could call out his welcome, fire roared from the dragon's mouth. Alador barely got a magical shield up in time, all around him items wilted in the heat, some even catching fire. Alador struggled to hold the shield as the dragon's breath raged on, it seemed unending.

When at last the dragon exhaled its last glowing breath, Alador slipped to his knees with relief. "Keensight! It is me, Alador!" he called out hastily, trying to catch his breath at the same time.

The dragon thundered into the chamber. His wing talons clawing the ground angrily as he moved forward. "You had best explain yourself quickly! - before you follow your father into my gullet!" the enraged dragon snarled.

Chapter Thirty-Two

Alador's eyes were wide with surprise. He had not considered that perhaps the dominant dragon nature of the beast would outweigh the Lerdenian man that Keensight had spent so much time portraying. He scrambled and slid down the left side of the mound as the dragon rounded to the right.

"I was curious what you found worth saving in your pile beside slips and medure." He stated breathlessly. He did not take his eyes off the muzzle of the dragon. He had almost not gotten a shield around himself the first time.

"It is none of your business," growled the dragon. He nudged the pile with concern, trying to push slips upward as if he knew where each one went.

"I am sorry. Please, I meant no disrespect or harm." Alador put both his hands out pleading with the dragon.

Keensight moved up onto his pile protectively, and Alador carefully swung around as he moved to keep the dragon fully in front of him. The dragon nudged where the wooden chest was then swung a fully angered gaze to the mage. Flickers of smoke smoldered from the dragon's mouth showing how great his anger truly was.

"Thief!" he snarled.

"I took nothing, I swear." Alador was beginning to fear he would not get through to the side of Keensight that had acted as father and mentor.

"You touched my chest. If you had no intent to steal, you would have no need to dig it loose." Keensight hissed; smoke billowed from both nostrils as the dragon raised his head a bit higher.

Alador stood stunned. How did he answer that? He swallowed hard as he thought because he had indeed touched that chest with the intention of finding the key. Alador kept his hands free to work a shield if he had to. He was sweating in the heavy robes now after the heat he had endured.

"I was just curious," Alador feebly defended.

Keensight slid forward on his pile for a short distance. He stretched his neck out and began to sniff Alador. Alador held his ground, but his heart was thumping wildly in his chest. The dragon's head came up and his mouth opened for a moment as if he were about to unleash the fire burning wildly within in him. Alador raised a shield reflexively. The dragon snapped his mouth shut and stared at the mage for a long moment.

"You presume where you should not." Keensight raised his head satisfied. "I may have nurtured you, but that does not give you the right to touch my hoard." Keensight returned to fixing his pile that was clearly out of sorts now. "You are enough dragon to know that it is not right. It is known that dragons do not enter other dragons' caves without permission," the dragon huffed.

Alador breathed out the breath that had remained caught in his chest. When he let the shield go, he realized that he was trembling and even his hands were sweating. He slowly began to remove his cloak as he was drenched with sweat within his robes. The cave was no longer cold after the scorching onslaught. Keensight was right, he had not searched his memories though they came flaring through his mind now. He should have known about the possessiveness and of the spells that dragons cast to protect their hoard.

The dragon snorted his displeasure. "You made me melt some of it." Keensight nudges a melted pile of metal down the side of his hoard.

Alador looked up in surprise. Had Keensight just whined? If he had, the mage did not intend to point it out. Alador carefully moved to the throne and laid his cloak on it. He noted that some of the gilding was scorched with heat.

He waited, ready for the dragon's anger to surge again. Alador was not sure how many more shields he could hold if the dragon decided to destroy him, geas or no geas. As he waited, he realized that he had told Rena to bring Amaum here. He should warn the dragon before they arrived, given his own disastrous reception.

He took a deep breath and blew it out before starting. "So, umm, how did you know I was here?" It was a stupid question and Alador realized it the moment that it left his mouth.

The dragon lifted its head from the careful resorting of his pile and fixed a disbelieving glare on Alador. "You do not think a dragon leaves his hoard unguarded?"

"To be honest, I had not thought about it," Alador admitted. "I did not see a guard?"

"If you saw it, it would not be much of a guard." The dragon huffed as he continued to set his pile right.

"A spell then?" he asked, braving a move a little closer.

"To tell you that would let you successfully rob me blind," the dragon snarled, looking down at the mortal before him. "What were you doing here, anyway? I doubt you came just to snoop through my hoard."

"Ah, yes that." Alador shifted uneasily.

Keensight did not miss his hesitant tone. "By the gods, what else have you done?" He looked about the cavern with concern.

"Well, with winter in full season at the lake and nowhere else to speak in comfort that we both knew, I sent Rena to fetch Amaum so I could speak with him." Alador cleared his throat.

"I see." The dragon's tone was edged with resurging anger as he clearly suspected where Amaum was to meet Alador. "And where is this meeting to occur?"

"Here," Alador stated with a boldness he was no longer feeling. He readied a shield as the dragon drew up as fully as he was able in the cavern.

"You invited…" sputtered the dragon. Smoke was billowing out Keensight's nostrils, and the dragon's chest was heaving. "Here…" He apparently could not even form speech.

The sudden lack of communication was Alador's first warning. The heaving chest was the second, so when the dragon's fire raged outward, the shield was already in place. This time the fire was not directly aimed at the mage, but Alador was thankful for the shield from flame and heat nonetheless.

The dragon surged off the pile, the top of his muzzle hit Alador sending him flying backwards. "You have no right to use my cave as your own!" he bellowed moving forward.

Alador hit the ground and rolled up, his training in the guard serving him well. "Henrick, LISTEN TO ME!" He had to get through to the man he knew for the dragon was clearly beyond reason.

"Blood always wins out they say. You are just like your father. I should have eaten you as soon as possible after finding out you existed." The dragon paced around Alador, clearly thinking of doing just that.

"Father… Please?" he called, making one last attempt.

The dragon had reared up over Alador, but Keensight paused when he heard the words. He hovered over the mage, huffing with indignation and outrage. "I should eat you," he repeated. The great head lowered. "You had no right," Keensight muttered again. He turned and crawled back onto the hoard.

Alador was trembling with real fear. Here was the bestial side of the dragons that he had known about, but had not personally encountered. He bent over placing his hands on his knees just breathing in and trying to steady himself. He looked up, Keensight had gone back to nuzzling various pieces of treasure in the mound into its proper place.

He knew that this was a mistake he would not repeat. However, the damage done now was what concerned him most. Knowing that his use of the word father had reached the dragon when apologies had not, he pulled himself up to try again.

"Father, I truly apologize. There is much that I still have to learn." He stepped forward, his hands out beseeching the dragon.

"Do the Daezun go into one another's houses, pawing through each other's stuff?" The dragon huffed his question as he continued working. He did not deign to honour Alador with a glance.

Alador frowned. He had not looked at it like that. "No, no they do not."

The dragon picked up a melted goblet and carefully moved it to the bottom of the pile before asking, "Then what made you think that it was okay to riffle through a dragon's home?"

"I did not think…" he began.

Keensight rounded on him with his great head, the neck stretching forth to almost reach Alador. "YOU NEVER THINK!"

That stung a bit and Alador found himself becoming a bit ruffled himself. "That is not true," he hotly defended.

"It is mostly true." The dragon snapped his mouth shut and returned to fixing the treasured mound.

Alador wanted to deny that, but he knew that the dragon would just pull up past errors. "What do you want me to do about Amaum?"

"If the fledgling is smart, he will not come," snarled Keensight.

"I assured them it was safe." Alador licked his lips worriedly. "Please do not hurt them. Continue to take your anger out on me if you wish, but they have only done what I asked of them."

"Oh, you and I are not done boy. I assure you of that," hissed the beast.

Alador did not even want to know what that meant. Right now his concern was for Rena and Amaum. He stared at the dragon for a long moment. "Please father. Do not hurt Rena." His voice held an edge of protective panic. "She did not want to come, I insisted it was safe."

"You had no right." The dragon repeated.

Alador wiped his free hand over his face. "You have made this clear, and it will not happen again. I swear it." He moved forward. "Father, please. I do not want Rena harmed," he insisted more boldly.

The dragon stopped what he was doing and slowly turned his head to look at Alador. There was a strange scrutiny from the dragon. "You have asked me thrice to spare Rena. You have asked for Amaum only once." The dragon slowly turned around on his pile. "Do they know I am Henrick?"

"They do not seem to." Alador answered quickly. He had not realized he had focused his concern clearly on Rena. He did not want to answer more questions there.

The dragon stared at him for a long, uncomfortable minute, then finally answered. "You may meet with them on the ledge. Make it clear that I am at home. They will know better than to enter without invitation."

Alador's relief was audible. "Thank you, father." He was sure to continue that use of word as it seemed the only thing that had kept Keensight from swallowing him as he had originally threatened.

He picked up his cloak and turned to head for the entrance of the cave. He had made it across the open space to the tunnel when the dragon called after him.

"Alador, did you mate with Rena?" The question was gruff and still held the edge of previous anger.

Alador stopped in his tracks. His back stiffened at the question that he had hoped to avoid. He turned slowly to look at the great dragon who was staring at him. He called back loudly.

"I am a man, and she is a dragon. I doubt the mechanics are possible." He was careful not to lie to the dragon.

"Did you mate on the winds of magic?" The dragon pressed.

Alador could not lie to him. He wanted to. The lie lay on his lips ready to spill over, but he could not do it. His eyes dropped as he fought for words that would explain.

"It was not intentional," he murmured. "She was helping with the spell and it just sort of happened." His words sounded hollow even to him. Rena had asked him to stop, but he had not known why she was concerned and the storm had been almost complete.

Keensight shook his head sadly. "You have started something you may not be able to finish. Go… Speak to the pair. I will sit here and decide if I should still eat you."

Alador had a serious feeling that Keensight was not jesting. He hurried down the tunnel toward the ledge.

He had to wait for some time. Alador had to remind himself that he had traveled by magic and Rena was flying. In addition, she had warned him that she would have to find Amaum. It was cold on the ledge, but given the reception he had just received he did not want to complain.

Finally, he saw the two younger dragons slowly circling. It took sometime before Amaum landed on the very edge and clearly with slight hesitation. "Are you sure this is safe?" He sniffed the air. Rena landed as Alador answered.

"It is. Keensight is aware of your visit and has decided to let us speak alone." He moved forward stiffly, the blow by the dragon's head had left him sore.

"You are hurt!" Rena exclaimed. She hurried forward and sniffed at his robes. "What happened? You smell of dragon's breath."

"Let us just say that Keensight and I had a slight disagreement," he offered. He watched Rena puff up with outrage and look to the cavern.

To divert her anger, he swiftly added. "Rena, he is not in a good mood and I don't think we should tarry too long here. I am fine." He put a hand on her neck, bringing her attention back to him. Amaum just watched the two of them.

Alador turned back to her brother. "Amaum, I want to ask you to do something for me that I think you will enjoy." Alador was intent on getting the two of them on their way. "There is a ship that I am going to be sending back and forth to and from the Daezun. I need it to have fair weather. However, this is the fun part. If it is attacked, I need you to sink whatever ship fires upon it."

"Can I keep whatever is aboard?" Amaum perked up at the word attack.

"Yes, I do not care what is on the attacking ship. I just need this one ship to go back and forth quickly and safely." Alador stated. "It will be flying a flag of blue with a silver dragon embellished on it. Will you do this for me?" He looked up at the dragon hopefully. He had no right to command them, so their cooperation was not guaranteed.

"I will see your ship safe, if for no other reason but to honor my sire." Amaum's toothy grin was a bit alarming after Keensight's attack. "The sinking of others is a bonus I will enjoy. I can only hope your ship comes under attack."

"The ship has already left Silverport. It will sail around the south to the lowest Daezun port. You will find it somewhere en route." Alador promised him. "I really appreciate your help with this as I have other tasks to see to." He closed his eyes with the relief that he felt, and to shutter away the pain throbbing throughout his bruised body.

"Is that all that you want?" Amaum looked toward the cave, obviously hearing something that Alador could not.

Knowing now how grievously he had erred, Alador nodded. "It is important that this happen, so it is no little thing I ask of you. It will take your constant scrutiny as it moves back and forth. You will have probably have a day each time it is in port for hunting or other needs you have."

Amaum laughed. "Yes, other needs. We both have been seeing to those, yes?" Amaum nudged him gently, then turned and launched himself into the air. Rena and Alador watched the dragon climb into the sky and disappear on the horizon.

Alador looked at Rena with alarm. "Does he know?"

Rena shook her head. "He just assumes that all males are like himself."

"Keensight knows," Alador bluntly stated.

"Why would you tell him?" Rena squeaked, her features holding genuine alarm.

Alador shook his head. "I didn't. He just seemed to know. That ... dragon always just seems … to know things." He had almost slipped and called him Henrick.

"I hope he does not tell my dame." Rena moved to him and touched his cheek gently with her muzzle.

Alador realized that Pruatra was likely to disapprove the most, and he swallowed his concern. "So do I, Rena, probably more than you. At least you can fly." He smiled at her though the concern was real. "I should go speak to my brother then get back to Silverport."

"I want to spend time with you," Rena shook her wings as she spoke. "You should spend time with your heartmate." She reminded him. There was a gentle nuzzle. "We can dance on power again if you wish."

"Soon, Rena. Let me get everything in motion and I promise that you and I will have a very long talk about what all this means." His gaze was firm.

"Maybe I do not want to have that talk after all," she rumbled. She dove off the ledge and snapped her wings open. He watched her climb into the clouds and out of sight.

Chapter Thirty-Three

Alador had not gone back into the dragon's cave that day. He had decided to give Keensight all the room that he needed to set his pile to rights. However, the bestial protection of the chest by the great dragon had made him very curious. It was a curiosity that he did not intend to satisfy. He had come too close to losing friend, mentor, and surrogate father.

He spent the ensuing weeks learning everything he could about the bloodmines. His studies had to be fitted around his uncle's wishes, carrying out Luthian's instructions, visits with Rena, practicing sword with the guard, and trips back to Smallbrook. He smiled whenever he thought of Rena. They had enjoyed long conversations. She had often helped with the storms, and more than once they had danced on the wings of power. He was getting better at melding their power to his purpose and their pleasure.

He stood at the window of the library watching the small birds play along the balcony. In two nights, the moon would be full. In two nights, he would attempt to set the largest part of the geas to rest. The dragon, Renamaum, had imprinted the need to save the fledglings and hatchlings so deeply that he had found himself increasingly anxious as the time to assault the bloodmines grew closer.

He wandered back to the desk and went over the plan one more time. The desk was bare: he had not dared to commit anything to paper so was forced to mull it over in his own mind. This plan could go wrong in so many ways. There was a knock at the door; he looked up to see Radney.

"Lord Alador, there is a woman to see you. Her card says *Lady Morana, High Priestess of Dethara*." Radney looked at Alador, obviously impressed.

Speaking of ways the plan could go wrong, Alador felt his heart skip a beat and he swallowed hard. "I suppose it is too late to tell the lady I am not at home?"

"Much too late," the lady answered as she swept into the room. She looked at Radney. "Do be a sweet man and fetch me some warm cider and something to eat. I fear that I am quite taxed after that journey."

Alador nodded his assent to the servant. He moved to the woman who now stood in the center of his library. "May I take your cloak, milady?" His offer was out of politeness, he did not want her in his home any longer than she had to be. However, she had just ordered food so he might as well attempt to be civil.

She smiled and turned her back to him. He carefully took the item without touching her.

"I am surprised to see you here, my Lady." Alador frowned. He laid the cloak across a chair. "Shall we sit by the fire?"

"I would like that." She settled into a chair to one side of it.

Alador could not miss the obvious sensuality the woman oozed, nor the obvious fact that her clothes were hardly appropriate for the cool thaw of early spring. "Now, what could possibly bring you to my door?"

Morana pouted; her lush lips were also hard to miss. "Must we get down to business so peremptorily? Surely the situation warrants a little conversation first." Morana leaned back in the deep chair, her hands clasping the ends of the rounded arms.

"I find when a lady comes to bargain dressed as you are, I am usually bested." He was trying to affect the same easy humor as his father. It sounded false even to his own ears.

"Yes, well I imagine your uncle sends you all kinds of tempting leavings." Her eyes hardened although she smiled.

Alador sat down across from her. "Is that what you are, tempting leavings?" He let his eyes rove over her; there was no way he was letting this woman's lips touch his again. Whether priestess or Goddess, she was dangerous.

"I should be insulted." Morana huffed with indignation.

Alador chuckled. "Yet you are not." He leaned forward, resting his arms on his legs as he looked over. "Why are you here Morana?" He was more direct this time. The sooner they got to the heart of the matter, the sooner she was out of his house.

"I have come to arrange your bonding," she stated quite bluntly. She crossed her ankles and the split in her dress opened, showing a shapely length of thigh.

Alador blinked at her in confusion before he managed to find words. "My **bonding**?" He coughed into his hand to try to hide his shock and dismay.

"Yes, I have, residing in my temple, a priestess who is also a princess from across the sea. A bonding with one of the ruling houses of Lerdenia would cement trade and a peaceful voice in the lands beyond our oceans." She spoke casually as if she were speaking about the weather or the harvest. "She is not from our island so does not have the predisposition of prejudice against the Daezun that you will find in these elite quarters."

"I assure you, Lady Morana, I am quite capable of finding my own bond mate," he managed to answer calmly. He made himself sit slowly upright.

"Oh, I am quite sure you can. However, I am offering you a royal princess of a large land," she pointed out.

Radney opened the door at that moment to wheel in the cart. Alador stood, grateful for the interruption and hurried to the cart to guide his servant in hastily putting together a small plate of titbits. Once the man had served Morana both plate and cider, Alador nodded to the door. "Thank you, Radney. Please make sure no one interrupts us," he commanded.

"No one at all?" Radney asked.

"Absolutely no one." Alador insisted. He moved to his chair and sat back down with a drink to fortify himself against this conversation. He had availed himself of the few moments of respite to construct a careful answer, but did not speak until Radney had left, closing the door gently behind him.

"While I am honored you would think me a fitting hand for a princess, I am but a bastard and know my place." Alador toasted her with his glass and took a drink.

"Pssshhht, half the occupants of this tier are bastards if one looks close enough. You bear your father's name; that is what matters." She sipped her own drink in a very dainty manner as if too great a sip would break the cup.

"I am flattered you think it an appropriate match, but I am really not looking to bond right now." Alador tried again to dissuade her from her cause. He found his eyes straying to her lips as she pulled her cup away.

Morana laid her small cup aside, popped a sweetmeat into her mouth, and turned her full attention on Alador. "I am not looking for you to bond right now either." She held out an envelope. "I am throwing a ball at the house of a friend - Lord Tenzin. I would like you to attend and meet the young lady for yourself. If you are not pleased by the end of the ball, well then you may bow out and I will cross you off the list of those I am considering." She fluttered her lashes as she smiled at him.

Alador forced his eyes away and took the envelope. "Well, I suppose that seems fair enough." He had no intention of attending any ball that this woman held, but if it would get her out of his home, he would pacify her.

"Wonderful." She picked up her cup and resumed drinking as if she had no intentions of leaving now that she had stated her business.

Unable to quell his distaste or curiosity, he forced himself to remain calm. "I do have one question."

She set her cup on the saucer. "Yes, Lord Guldalian."

Alador unconsciously winced at the stressing of his family name. "Why should I attend a ball organized by the woman who tried to kill me?"

Lady Morana looked perplexed. She set her cup down on the table. This time she leaned forward exposing a large expanse of breast to his gaze. "It was not personal," she said. "Removing the ruling Council would allow new blood to lead our fair country."

She rose and moved over to him. Like a fly caught in a spider's web, he could do nothing but watch her slow approach. Alador found himself trapped between her body and his chair as she straddled his knees. Her dress split to allow her such a movement exposing her smooth white thighs.

"I assure you, removing such a fine mage as yourself would have bothered me." He caught her hands as she went to put them on his chest. "It was simply an opportunity that would rarely come again."

Alador rose forcing her backwards while still holding her hands. "Do not attempt to use your wiles on me, Priestess. I know who and what you are. If you think for a moment that I did not take trying to kill me personally, you are either deluded or just plain crazy." He looked her over. "While I might go with insane, I suspect it's more likely that you simply lie when the truth would suit you better." He gently pushed her away.

Her perfect ruby lips set into a small pout. "What is it with you Guldalian men that you constantly rebuff my favor?"

"Would you like the list?" Alador could not help himself. His anger was building and he knew he dare not strike this woman in any of her manifestations. Dethara had shown her pleasure with her priestess, and her death or injury would attract even more of the Goddess' attention. "I think our business here is done."

"I do have one other message for you from my beloved Goddess." She spoke as she watched him cross to where he had laid out her cloak.

Alador held it out for her. "I doubt that any message is going to be pleasing, so out with it and then you can be on your way." Morana turned to force him to lay the cloak on her shoulders and he winced when her fingers touched his while taking it from him. Her long silken hair smelled of lavender and fruit. The scent was pleasing and he shook his head and stepped back.

"I will be honest; I do not know the meaning of it. She indicated that I was not to worry about it, that you would know." She turned to face him after she fastened the clasp of her cloak.

"Well, what is it then?" he growled.

"She said that if you continue along the path you now travel, you will regret the choice with every fiber of your being." Morana licked her lips. "She went on to say that some pains in life cannot be healed."

Alador felt his heart turn over in his chest, and the lump in his throat was palpable. "I will take her words to heart," he said. It was vague, but given his plans in two days, it drove fear through him. Did Dethara know exactly what he was about?

He escorted her out of his library and down the hall to the great door. He had a firm hand in her back. Considering her quick step, she was being forced to move faster than she desired and it was not fast enough for him.

"I do hope you will not let the matter of your test prejudice your opinion of the princess?" She was pouting, but he did not care. She put a hand on his arm when he opened the door with his other hand.

"I make no promises, Lady Morana. You say it was not personal, but I can tell you that when someone tries to kill you, it IS personal." He rolled his eyes at her and indicated the open door. "I hope your ball is successful."

She licked her luscious lips and stared up at him with those large, lined eyes. "Please Alador, please say you will come." She searched his face worriedly. "I do fear something terrible will happen to you if you do not."

The only horrid thing he could think of at the moment was falling into this woman's web of lies and deceit. "I will consider it, but I make no promises, Milady. Good day."

She seemed satisfied with that and finally left. He shut the door and leaned his forehead against it. The last few weeks he had grown quite comfortable. His studies, his time with Rena and family had brought him moments of peace and happiness.

Because he was getting his way, Luthian had been a pleasant host and guide. They had not ever spoken of his test again, and his uncle seemed to be intentionally doing things to keep Alador, at the very least, content.

In addition to his main activities, he occasionally spent his evenings with either Sordith or General Levielle. Sordith was knowledgeable on many subjects not taught in the guard. He made sure Alador knew the main events of Lerdenian history taught to most Lerdenian small ones at a young age. They discussed trade within and beyond the Great Isle.

General Levielle concentrated on strategy and history from a more military point of view. He enjoyed these discussions best because they were usually over a game of King's Men. Levielle had given him information on the likely strengths of encampments such as the one protecting the main bloodmine. They had discussed the siege of Silverport during the Great War and why it had failed. He felt a bit guilty, but at the same time, he was fairly certain Levielle had an inkling of the reasons for Alador's many questions. He may have been conjecturing, but the general had never pressed or questioned the mage about his motives.

During his time with Rena, he had learned a spell that enabled him to see the places she had been. She would visualize a place, then he would use the amulet to join her there. They would start the day in frigid cold and end it on some small warm island. He loved those times. She taught him dragon history, spells that might be of use, and most of all she talked to him as an equal. There were no designs on his life, no demands for his time; just simple conversation. They had talked about everything from the gods to the little animals that formed the reefs off one island that they had visited. Only with Rena did he find himself completely relaxed.

Alador pushed off the door. "Radney!" he shouted. The servant appeared before Alador had hardly turned around. "With me." He strode to the library. "I don't ever want that woman in this manor again unless I have given you orders to the contrary. Am I clear?" He did not look back because he could hear the man stumbling behind him.

"Yes Lord Alador," Radney stated, his tone indicating worry.

"I am out, dead, absent, I do not care. She does not come in," he snarled.

"Understood."

"Good!" Alador picked up the invitation and eyed it with repulsion. He broke it open and his heart sank even further if that were possible. The night of Lady Morana's ball was the same night that he was supposed to be assaulting the mine. "Get my cloak, I am going out." He tossed the invitation on his desk. He had to make a counter move and quickly. Every notable person in the city was going to be at that ball.

Chapter Thirty-Four

Sordith watched in amusement while his half-brother, paced back and forth in front of his desk. With each passing day, he reminded Sordith more and more of their father, or at least the man they called father. He still had not gotten his head around the fact that Henrick was really a dragon in disguise. He had not even known that was possible. Alador's last words brought him out of his musing.

"I don't know where Keensight stands. The few times that I have gone to see my family he has been absent." He stopped pacing and turned to Sordith. "Do you think going through his hoard could have lost his support?" The words were more muttered as if speaking to himself rather than to the Trench Lord.

"Wait, I missed something." Sordith's eyes grew rather large as he stared at Alador. "You went through his hoard?"

"Bells and bats, Sordith, were you even listening to me at all?" Alador plopped down in the chair that had been provided for him, sinking into it with a heavy sigh.

"I fear you lost me for a bit when you got to fancy balls and such. I fail to see what you are all worked up about?" Sordith got up and poured them a drink. "So this priestess throws a ball intent on cajoling you into a proper bonding. May not be such a bad idea. We could get chained the same day." He walked over and handed a silver mug to Alador. The amused grin on Sordith's face did little to mollify his brother.

Alador took the mug gratefully and resumed his brotherly rant. "Okay, first of all, I am not marrying any woman who has served in that temple. I might find a snake in my bed rather than a woman." He took a sip. "Lastly, it is not **who** is throwing the ball, it is ***when***." Alador took a gulp while glaring at Sordith over the edge of his mug. I can't believe you stopped listening."

Sordith chuckled and returned to his seat. "Well, you must admit; you have acquired Henrick's skill at prattling on." Sordith set his mug down and leaned forward, his eyes gleaming with greed. "So how big a hoard is it?"

"Hoard...what?" Alador frowned. "Oh… Keensight's." He sat for a moment. "It would fill the Council hall. I would say he has been collecting it for a while."

"Then my answer is 'yes'." Sordith knew he had completely twisted the conversation, but he rather liked to watch his little brother struggle to keep up.

"YES?' Your answer to WHICH question?" Alador frowned at Sordith. "Can we talk in a straight line please?"

"I was. I cannot help it if you can't keep up." Sordith chuckled. "Yes, I believe that you could lose a dragon's support by mucking through its treasure mound. It would be like rifling through a lady's collection of lacy underwear. There are some things you just don't do." Sordith picked back up the mug. "Well, unless you intended to steal from him."

Alador stood up again and began to pace. "I have to go to him I guess. I need to know. Without the dragons' support, the plan will fail and people will die uselessly." He leaned on Sordith's desk. "How do I approach him, Sordith?"

"Why don't you ask him yourself?" Sordith pointed to the door.

Sordith watched Alador spin to see where Henrick was leaning in the door frame, much as Sordith himself often did. His arms were crossed. His jet black hair was loose today and he had a feral look about him even in this form.

"About time you came to realize that you need dragons… that you need me." Henrick pushed off the frame and walked into the room. "Sordith…"

"I know: you need food." Sordith was already moving to the bell pull. "Wine is there on the table." At least Henrick's constant desire for food now made more sense.

Alador had fallen silent and remained so while Sordith ordered food to be brought into his office. Henrick moved to the drink table and filled a mug of his own. Alador stood like a fish, mouth opening as if to speak, then shutting again, a silent gasp for words instead of water. Sordith found it fairly amusing.

Finally, Alador found his words. Sordith returned with a chair from the side of the room and set it next to the one Alador had been occupying.

"Henrick… father… I have come to you so many times to apologize." Alador began.

Sordith watched Henrick sit gracefully. The man's robes were a deep red, trimmed in black. He went around the desk and settled into his own chair, watching the two men closely. It was clear that Henrick was still rather miffed at Alador.

"I did not wish to hear your apology." Henrick looked over at Alador then looked at Sordith. "How would you feel if someone pawed their way through your weapons collection?"

"I would be right pissed off." Sordith admitted. That was an understatement. He would likely skin anyone who dared to paw their way through it.

"Traitor," Alador murmured. Sordith toasted him, eliciting a bigger frown from his brother.

Henrick looked at Alador. "However, you have swung in the wind long enough. Your apology is now accepted." He waved his mug at Alador before taking a long sip.

The large exhale of relief that escaped the young mage seemed to ease his bottled tension. "Thank you," Alador said.

Henrick toasted Alador silently. "Now, what is amiss? I could sense something was wrong even as I approached the door."

"Morana," both men replied simultaneously.

Henrick's eyes narrowed. "All right, what has the witch done now?" Henrick took a further sip as Alador began to explain.

"She has decided to marry me off to some princess. But that is not the worst part." Alador rubbed a hand over his face.

"I would hope, as my son, that that would be the best part," quipped Henrick.

Sordith laughed. "My thoughts exactly."

Alador glanced angrily at Sordith. "She has set her ball for the night of our attack. Now, do we move the attack?" He glanced between them.

"Good question. My question is… can we turn this to our advantage?" Henrick tapped the mug with his forefinger.

Sordith slowly grinned. "Ooh, I have a wicked idea." He waited till he had both men's attention. "We throw our own party the same night. A far more sordid affair. I can provide the women. You can invite as many of the Blackguard as you need and some extras. Between myself and the High Master, we can keep everyone entertained, and you all can slip off in pairs." Sordith grinned even larger. “With enough alcohol, women, and good music we can provide a cover for your absence and save you from this princess you seem afraid of meeting.”

Alador rolled his eyes. “I am not afraid to meet her. I just have my sights set elsewhere right now. Well, that and the identity of the person wanting to introduce me. First she tries to kill me, tells me it was not personal, then she wants to marry me off. I swear her brain is addled."

Henrick chimed in with a murmur: “…but the idea has merit.” He looked up excitedly when an older woman wheeled in a loaded cart and jumped to his feet. “Ah my good woman, you are truly a treasure,” he said. He moved to her and grabbed her hand, sweeping it up to his lips.

Sordith looked on in amazement as his usually stolid housekeeper flushed like a young maiden and hurried from the room. The fact she had arrived so quickly indicated she had already been laying food out on a cart. Owen must have given her a warning that Henrick had arrived.

“She won’t wash that hand for a bit, I will wager,” Sordith mused. He smiled and took a sip from his mug.

“With the way you two have women swooning about you, you would think I would have better luck,” grumbled Alador.

“Yes, well some of us have learned where the ice is thin, boy,” Henrick said with a mouth full of food. His words were barely understandable.

“Yes, I suppose you are right.” Alador admitted. The younger mage joined his father at the cart. “So, you two want me to throw my own party?” he asked. “I really do not know the first thing about party-throwing - other than you have to send out invitations.”

Henrick swallowed the meat from the piece of fowl he had been gnawing on. “Did you keep my staff?”

"Yes, they were loyal and I wanted people I could trust, not spies of Luthian." Alador nodded. He picked at some pieces of tree fruit.

"Just tell Radney you want to hold a low-tier affair. He will know exactly how to set up the manor and what to order." Henrick waved the bone at him. "Fine servant that Radney. I had half a mind to take him with me. Of course, he mightn't have liked the quarters."

"What, a small treasure pile of my own to sleep upon, sir?" Sordith grinned wide, doing his best impression of a servant. "I would serve you to your heart's content." He really wanted to see a dragon's treasure mound. It must be a wondrous sight.

"Not if I eat you first," growled Henrick. "Besides, I was meaning the quarters in Smallbrook." Henrick tossed his cleaned bone at Alador's head. "How many people are you blabbing to?"

Alador caught it and laid it on the cart. "Sordith is the only one I have told of your duality or your treasure trove." He shook his head. "I have even kept it from Rena."

"Ah yes, Rena." Henrick eyed Alador carefully. "How are matters there?"

Alador smiled, thinking fondly of the dragon. "We are fast friends."

"Just friends, yes?" Henrick pressed.

Alador looked away from Henrick when he answered. "Just friends."

Sordith watched the two of them carefully. There was something here that he was missing. "Isn't Rena one of the dragons helping you?" If he were right, then Alador's response was odd. He looked like a young lad with a crush.

"Yes." Henrick and Alador answered. An uneasy silence settled around the three of them. Henrick returned to munching, and Alador was suddenly interested in the hem of his mage robe.

Sordith realized that this was a nut for later cracking and moved the conversation along. "Speaking of dragons, I thought you would want to know. There are tales on the docks of a great blue dragon that guards the merchant ship. No one has seen a pirate since the last one was sunk in a dancing arc of lightning that ignited the strange gas the dragon breathed over it."

"I am glad to hear that goes as planned." Alador flashed Sordith a look of relief.

Henrick nodded. "That dragon is going to be bored when this is over."

"Speaking of boring, let us plan this party. It will put a nice twist on things," Sordith offered.

"You just want the women and wine." Alador accused.

The Trench Lord put a hand over his heart. "I am a changed man. Just one woman for me now." He smiled at the thought of Keelee. She always seemed to know when Alador was about and put herself far from his path. While he was not a jealous man, his brother had bedded her first, and Alador was turning into a striking figure as he matured. He preferred keeping the two of them apart.

"Right." Alador shook his head with a grin. He picked up a piece of pie and took it back to his chair to eat there. "That is like saying Henrick will settle down again with just one mate."

"Seriously, I have all the woman I need." Sordith defended.

"Back to the party," Henrick interrupted. "Have the High Master bring a few of the instructors at the caverns. It will give some legitimacy to your party. If Luthian suspects, we can assure him that many people saw you that night. I am sure you have some beautiful woman that you can be caught in bed with, should he decide to descend upon you."

Alador frowned and his fork paused halfway to his mouth. "How long do you think it will take him to know about it?"

Henrick looked Alador in the eyes as he answered in low tones. "That depends on how long it takes us to lay them all low. Each minute means there is a greater chance that someone will get away with an account of what occurred, or will be able to send a message by magical means."

Alador nodded slowly at the summation. "I will get home then and begin those preparations." Alador began stuffing the last of the pie into his mouth.

"I will speak with Reynel. Just leave me a list of the Blackguard you need off-duty for the attack." Sordith offered.

Henrick was absently stuffing his pockets with food. "I will get the dragons together, and we will descend at the first sign of fire on those ballistae."

Alador nodded. "We will be making that our first priority." He swallowed his forkful. "If everything is to go according to plan, I need every ballista aflame first. Do not move in till most are on fire," he said firmly.

Henrick smiled. "Giving orders now?" He put a hand up before Alador could respond. "Pruatra will be there early. She is going to ensure that the men on guard duty have a very thick fog to deal with after she gets done drenching them in a vicious rainstorm."

Sordith laughed. "Sounds like my kind of evil." He kicked his feet up onto his desk. "Too bad I have to stay home and mind the defences. I suspect this is something I would very much enjoy being a part of."

"I need someone I can trust to vouch for my presence in our worst scene scenario." Alador pointed out.

Sordith shook his head. "Luthian's wrath is not your worst scene scenario."

"Then what is?" Alador frowned.

Sordith eyed his brother then his impostor father for a long moment before answering. "Not coming back at all." His low tones were matter-of-fact, but they held an edge of concern.

"Right," Alador answered and by the look on his face, Sordith was fairly certain that Alador had not considered that possibility.

Chapter Thirty-Five

Everything was set for the party and yet Alador paced through the dining room with great anxiety. Radney had taken care of it all, just as Henrick had predicted. The amount of food and drinks that had been laid out along the wall would have fed a village for a couple of days. The tables had been moved to allow for a small area to dance and mingle. Musicians were now setting up and the first guests would be arriving at any moment. Sordith had not arrived yet, and Alador found himself needing his brother's calm demeanor about now.

He had dressed for the first part of the evening in a simple blue tunic and pants. Though the outfit was simplistic in style, he had ensured it was of the finest materials. His hair was tied at the base of his neck, except for the white streak which he had left loose. It was a reminder to others of the power he was capable of pulling: a mark of status in his position as a fifth tier mage.

When a knock came at the door, Alador took a deep breath and headed down the hall. Radney would open it, but he was hoping Sordith would get here first. Sure enough, Radney was taking Keelee's cloak. Their eyes met and she flushed as Alador could not help staring at her.

She was the most breath-taking beauty that he had ever seen. The emerald eyes were lined in kohl, making them stand out more than usual. Her dress was a deep green, bringing those eyes out further. Her hair was loose except for the strands that would have crossed her face; these were braided until they met the hair at the back of her head, which then fell in waves with the rest to her waist.

Several women were coming through the door behind the couple. Each was dressed in a similar fashion as Keelee: a low cut flowing fabric despite the cool spring weather. All the dresses were in a different color obviously chosen to match their eyes and features. Keelee's dress stood out because of the decorative stones where the material met just below her largely exposed breasts. A punch in the arm brought him out of his stunned observations

"Quit ogling my woman," Sordith said. His voice held humor instead of outrage which relieved Alador. "They do look amazing, don't they? Keelee spent all day making sure they did not clash with one another."

Alador could barely hear him over the din of women who were laughing and talking. "I think you found every beautiful woman in the city," he murmured.

"Yes, well I do have quite a few at hand willing to show a bit of appreciation for a chance to step out of the trenches." Sordith indicated the women. Alador was saddened by the truth in what Sordith had said, but he could not fix everything for everyone. He turned his attention to the rest of the women, striving to keep his eyes off Keelee.

"Right this way Ladies. Let me show you the lay-out." He showed them all the library open for their use - and the locations of the privy closets before leading them into the dining room. They showed appropriate appreciation as they marvelled at the manor. Alador could not help smiling with pride.

The next hour was spent in welcoming people to his home. Radney had helped him with the invitations, and had been quick to point out who might rather be at

Alador's party than at Morana's ball. Alador had added an invitation to General Levielle as an afterthought. The man was married, so it was unlikely that he would make an appearance; but if he did, it would help confirm the legitimacy of the social gathering. Alador had almost thought twice about it. Levielle had a way of discerning things that he had no business knowing.

Those invited from the Blackguard were the last to arrive. High Master Reynel Bariton led in a large group which was just as joyous and talkative as the first group of ladies with Sordith had been. In addition to those that Nemara had gathered, a number of men had been invited to pair off with the women that Sordith brought. Radney had been sure to point out that an equal number of men needed to be invited to match the women for dancing and other ... activities. Most of his classmates had swapped their leathers for more casual clothing. They'd done their best to dress up from what they had available. Blackguard rarely had the opportunity to attend a party like this.

The last to enter had been Nemara. Again, Alador found himself speechless. He had seen her in casual clothing, armor and, well, with nothing. He had never seen her fix herself up for anything special. She looked as beautiful as any of the women that Sordith had escorted. Nemara had braided sections of her hair and let it fall in amongst the loose locks. The red strands gleamed with streaks of golden highlights. The most shocking thing was to find her in a dress. The brown gown had trimmings of golden ribbons and clung to every curve as she moved towards him.

She ran her hands self-consciously over the fine material as she looked up at him. "Do I look a fright?"

she asked worriedly. Her eyes widened in possible horror at his fixed gaze.

He shook his head and took up her hand. "You look… amazing Nemara." His honest words were low just for her ears, then for the sake of those looking he pulled her to him and kissed her. He could hear her nervous giggle as they pulled apart, the calls and teasing behind them expected and necessary for their plan.

He smoothed a piece of hair from her face. "I am serious. I have never seen you look lovelier." His words were tender and intended to reassure her.

"Thank you," she murmured, then tucked her hand into the crook of his arm. She spoke with genuine happiness for all those about her. "So where is the food and the drink? We have a party to attend." This brought cheers from her fellow guardsmen.

Alador led them into the dining room. The room was full of laughter, the chatter of relaxed conversation and the soft chords of music. Sordith stood up and called for silence.

"I would have us all salute our host for what is sure to be quite a party." He held up his glass and downed its contents.

Alador flushed slightly as everyone echoed the salutation. It amazed him that he was standing here in his own manor, holding a party with his own slips, and surrounded by people who accepted him completely as he was. It was very different from where he had been when he first found the cursed bloodstone. He toasted them back with a smile. It would be a much happier occasion if he did not intend to slip away to murder fellow guardsmen in order to free the dragons.

Sordith called for the musicians to play something a bit livelier. Alador escorted Nemara over to him. Nemara and Sordith seemed to work well together and Alador did not miss the look Sordith gave her as they began conspiring. Alador shook away the momentary flash of jealousy.

The two were pairing the men and women who needed to be with Alador so that they could slip away as if to tryst. Alador had ensured that Radney had opened up and aired the many bedrooms. All of those going with Alador would meet in his own room at the midnight hour. Thankfully, that horrid bed had been taken apart and sold off. He would have been horrified to have others think he was so ostentatious.

Alador left them to their task and continued to mill around. Sordith had attached a young blonde to him who was thankfully not the giggling or chattering sort. He learned her name was Chastity, an ironic name given her profession as a bed servant. She moved with him through the party and made appropriate comments here and there. So far, everything was going wonderfully.

As he was moving about, he happened to glance up towards the doorway of the large room. There, in the opening, was General Levielle and his wife. Alador's glass paused halfway to his lips. While he had invited him, he had been fairly sure the man would not attend. Carefully threading his companion through the crowded room, he approached the man and offered him his hand.

"I am so pleased the two of you could make it." Alador's greeting was genuine, he offered his hand. There were a few other invited couples throughout the throng, and so far there had been no offense taken by having members of a lower tier in attendance. General Levielle grasped his arm firmly in greeting before returning his hand to the back of the woman beside him.

General Levielle's eyes moved from the colorful throng to Alador. "I see this will not be a particularly refined affair?" His casual question held an edge to it.

"I do not believe in refined affairs, sir. I believe people should laugh, talk and dance to their hearts' content without being concerned about who might be watching." Alador reached for the lady's hand at Levielle's side. "And who is this beautiful woman? -surely not your wife, for I am quite sure such a lovely lady would never settle for a hard time with such a formidable husband."

The lady was wearing a dress that spoke of wealth and status. It held gems much as Keelee's did, and the pink was a vibrant color designed to bring a perceived flush to a lady's cheeks. His words had the desired effect. The older woman laughed good-naturedly. "You know my husband well, I see. I am Nakyra."

"An attractive name for a very attractive woman." Alador kissed her hand, glancing over her knuckles as he had seen both Sordith and Henrick do a thousand times. As he stood, he slowly let go of her hand. She was indeed a striking woman. The tinge of age had silvered her hair, but her face still held the genuine life of her younger self. Her eyes were more like citrines, and her hair was black except for the shoots of silver.

He glanced at Levielle who was frowning at him. "Come now, sir. I meant no offense. You are truly a taskmaster in the classroom, and I imagine more so on the battlefield. One cannot help but assume that you would be the same at home." He smiled at the General.

"I see what you mean, Levielle." Nakyra said with a grin. "He is quick to speak, and he does obviously know you." She glanced at Alador with a conspiratorial wink. "I assure you he can be quite gruff at home as well."

"Careful Nakyra, I can tell tales about what goes on at home as well." Levielle seemed to relax a bit observing his wife's own acceptance of their company.

Alador winked back. "Let us get you both a plate and drink. There are seats along the sides if you wish to eat. I am sure there are others here that you know. Among others, General, the High Master is here."

Levielle looked about. "As is the Trench Lord."

Alador looked over at Sordith to see him laughing with a small group, mug in hand as usual. He looked back to Levielle when he continued with a softly murmured question.

"Odd mixture of people you have managed to gather tonight." Levielle looked pointedly about them. "Special occasion?"

Alador led the three over to the tables. Chastity was being quiet, seemingly somewhat intimidated by the presence of the other couple. "I like to think of it as the anti-ball party."

"Ah, Lady Morana's ball. Yes. We were not invited, but I am surprised that you were not." Levielle eyed him curiously.

"Oh, I was; but I prefer the company here to the pompous crowd that turns up for any stiff ball my Uncle and Lady Morana decide to hold." He looked around the room then back to the man honestly. "I will have a lot more fun here, I assure you."

Levielle seemed to accept this. Alador pressed a drink into his hand. "Please, stay as long as you like and if it gets, well, too rowdy later… I will not be offended if you sneak away." He indicated some of the guardsmen whom Levielle would recognize. "It is not often that my classmates get to attend such an affair so I am expecting it will get quite… loud." He grinned at the man.

Nakyra looked around. "I think I will be able to judge when it might be proper for a married couple to slip away to their own quarters, or ones closer by." She tucked her hand around Levielle's arm as she accepted a drink from Alador with the other.

"You should have introduced us sooner, sir." Alador smiled from Nakyra to Levielle.

Levielle shook his head. "A man knows which adversaries to keep apart - lest they gang up on him in a battle of wits. She is sharp enough and does not need your help."

They all laughed and Alador spent some time just getting to know the man's wife. Like her husband, Nakyra had a quick mind and a sharper tongue. It was truly a pleasure to get to know her. Chastity even managed to add a titbit here and there. It made it a pleasant interlude in the proceedings.

At some point, Nemara replaced Chastity. He had not seen it happen. Alador had looked away and when he looked back, Nemara was at his side. He introduced her to Nakyra. Once the formalities were out of the way, Nemara looked at the couple.

"I hope you will not mind, General Levielle, but I have been waiting to dance with Alador all evening. He has been so busy playing host that he is neglecting me." She placed her lips into a small, pretty pout. As if on cue, the musicians struck up a slower song.

"Of course, Nemara. It was not our intent to monopolize our host. Besides," Levielle admitted, "I have yet to dance with my wife." The two couples took to the floor. Nemara and Alador slowly drifted away from them so that they could speak.

"It is time for us to slip away," she murmured into his ear. She nodded towards the door where two guardsmen as close as lovers were slipping out of the room.

"Time has moved swiftly." Alador admitted. "I need to hold one of these when I don't need to leave." He was having a surprisingly good time. He looked around for Sordith who was surrounded by various guests. There was some sort of avid discussion going on that obviously held an edge of seriousness.

"Yes, I would like it if we could stay," Nemara admitted. "But there is work to do and plans are too far advanced to stop now."

Alador nodded. "I did not intend to stop." As they danced closer to the door, Nemara stopped them and leaned up and kissed him slowly. Alador was caught off guard for a moment by the sensuality of the kiss.

"Let's find somewhere private for a while." She spoke her words just loudly enough that a couple near them could hear.

"I would love that." Alador answered, more than eager to play his part. Since he had found the stone, everything had been moving to this point. He placed an arm around her shoulders and led her from the room. Nestled close together, he was surprised to see how many other couples had paired off. Sordith's women were performing their roles perfectly, based on the grunts coming from beneath his stairs. Alador shook his head and led the way up to his own master suite.

They both slipped inside to find ten other guardsmen in the midst of checking gear, tightening armor and such. Alador, like the others, used magic to switch. He grabbed his weapons from the closet. No one spoke as they readied themselves. The tension in the room was palpable. The sound of his sword sliding home into its sheath was echoed by others.

Nemara nodded to him, and Alador swallowed hard. He was leading these people into a mission that could mean their deaths. It would be the first time he had truly moved in a leader's role, and he was nervous.

"For those of you that don't know, I am Alador," he said.

"We all know who you are, Guldalian," one said with a dark tone.

Alador eyes focused on the man. "Is there a problem with who I am?" His tone was harsh. "Because if there is, maybe you should bow out now."

"I am not passing up a chance to give some pay back to elitist Lerdenian snobs. I also believe in freeing the dragons." The man looked Alador over. "Whether you are a man truly worth following remains to be proven."

"Fair enough." Alador admitted. "You are?"

"Ben," came the short reply.

"Well Ben, here is the plan." Alador knelt down and formed magic into a glittering representation of the mine using the images he had been given by Renamaum. "We will arrive here." He indicated the cliff. "We will break into teams of two. These here…" - he indicated the glowing ballistae - "…are all pointed at the dragons. They have kept the free dragons at bay by murdering the captive ones whenever attacks are mounted. The free dragons have held off, knowing that any assault brings about the deaths of their kin."

"How we going to get there?" one of the women asked. "Seems like a long flight by lexital at night."

"I am going to use a travel spell to take us all." Alador watched their eyes widen.

"You can do that, take us all at once?" Ben asked.

"I can," Alador stated firmly.

Ben knelt down beside Alador. "Well, now you have my attention."

Alador grinned. "As I was saying, we will break into teams of two and our first goal will be to take out these ballistae. We will have to kill any guard we come across." He looked around the gathered circle. "If you have a problem with that, you need to say so now."

They all shook their heads and Nemara spoke up. "If they are helping to hold the dragons captive, they deserve their fate."

Alador nodded. "There is one on the inside who may be working with us. How many of you remember Jon, the death mage?"

Several around the circle indicated that they knew who Jon was. That would make things a bit easier, thought Alador. "If you come across him, don't kill him unless he attacks you first. I would hate to lose our one potential inside man."

He stood and went to the closet. There he pulled out the specially made tabards. He began to hand them out. They first appeared identical to the tabards they all wore on duty, signifying the Blackguard. "These will allow you to get close in the fog and wet weather to the men guarding the ballistae. You will seem to be one of them."

Alador separated two pieces of cloth on the back portion of the tabard. "They have a third panel in the back. Once you have secured your ballista, pull the back cloth over your head." He demonstrated showing how it would change the tabard to blue with a silver dragon. "This is how the dragons will know if you are friend or foe. Be sure you change the tabard; it is your only protection against the flight of dragons."

"Nemara mentioned there would be dragons helping us. I… I was a bit reluctant to believe her. Are we really getting help from dragons?" Another man asked.

"Very angry ones, so be sure to stay out of their path. They won't care about accidentally inflaming one of us if we are in the way while they're freeing their fledglings," Alador cautioned.

He pulled the amulet from his chest piece, holding it both to cast the spell and to gain a little reassurance from it. "Okay, gather around me. For this to work, each of you has to be touching me. When we get there, I might need a minute to gather myself - it will take more power to move us all."

One by one, they put their hands on him. Nemara stood before him. Her hair was now pulled tightly back, and the lady from downstairs seemed to have disappeared behind the ferocity of her expression. "Let's go kill some bastards," she hissed.

Chapter Thirty-Six

The world re-formed as the spell delivered them to the cliff top, just as Alador had envisioned. The air was moist and cold. Fog swirled around them so thickly that Alador could barely make out the enclosure below them. He stood in quiet awe for a long moment, as did all the others. None of his companions had ever used a travel spell, let alone heard of one that could bring a whole group. They stood close to him, wide-eyed, gaining their own bearings.

Alador was not in awe of the fact that he had found the spell and power to bring them all here. He had come to expect the sudden insights brought by spells and knowledge that had not previously been his. For him, it was the wonder of finally standing above the mines. He had seen this place in various dreams and memories from a dragon's eyes. To stand here of his own accord, his geas fully laid before him after all this time, was a little overwhelming.

He moved to the edge and the others clustered about him. Fully focused now, he scanned the valley and the skies. He could not see the dragons, but there was no doubt in his mind that they were here. He could sense Rena close by, and he could feel the power in the wind.

Alador pointed down below them, when he spoke his voice low so that it did not carry on the stillness of the night. "We will drop down from here. It is a natural wall to the grounds below. It is not patrolled as they know dragons cannot drop straight down without a great deal of noise."

"I think the distance is longer than our ropes, Lord Guldalian," Ben whispered.

Alador flinched at the use of title. "Alador, please. I am not my uncle or my father." He looked about. The man was right, it was too far for their ropes. "You will have to use a featherfall spell."

He realized by their blank stares that the spell was one of Renamaum's memories. Alador swiftly gave them the words. He had everyone memorize them and then cast the spell. He had each jump off a near rock to make sure it had worked properly. It took about fifteen minutes, but the people Nemara had chosen were strong with magic and intelligent.

"All right. I will go first. Say the spell and step off. You should fall slowly to the ground below. Once we're all down, we'll split up from there. Remember, once your ballista is aflame, don't forget to change your tabard." Alador took a deep breath and drew his sword. The fog was thick, but there was no guarantee that they would not still be spotted floating to the ground.

"Everyone ready?" He looked around at the team, then at Nemara. They all nodded, and Nemara readied her bow with a nod of her own.

Knowing there was no more time to waste, he whispered the words of the featherfall spell then stepped off the edge. It was a bit disconcerting at first as there was still a sense of falling. However, his slow descent allowed him to keep his eyes open for anyone close by. He could smell the scent of animal waste, the strong whiffs of sulphur, and the fires of the guards. There were two towers on the far side by the entrance to the mine, but he could not see them in the fog.

He hit the ground lightly and moved out of the way, crouching down along the rock face, waiting for each of the group to land. Fortunately, no one misspoke the spell and each landed as lightly as he had. They split into two teams: six went one way and Nemara, he and four others went to the right. Once the first set of guards were neutralized, the plan was for the team of four to move on to the next target. Once they were spread about the compound, they would then set fire to the ballistae simultaneously.

There were diffused lights coming from locations around the compound. In the thick fog, they looked like beckoning swamp lights. Alador and Nemara called a halt as they reached the cave. They would have to cross in front of it to get to their first ballista.

Pressed against the rock wall, he listened for any sounds of footfalls or voices. It was quiet at this late hour. Guards out at the ballistae could be heard now and then, but there were no sounds from the entrance of the cave. He motioned for Nemara to be ready. She and one other pulled back their arrows in preparation. Once this was done, Alador darted across. There was no alarm or sound from within the cave. So far everything was going according to the plan.

Once safely across, he motioned the others to move. One by one they also darted to the other side of him. Alador's heart was pounding so loudly that he was certain that those with him had to be able to hear it. They were approaching the point where the rock wall gave way to the wooden poles of the stockade. This would be the location of the first ballista. As they crawled forward, the light of the fire for the men at this location became more than a flickering fairy light.

Just as Alador had been about to give the signal to move in, there was a muffled cry that was cut off across the compound. The dragons chained in the center shifted and a few of them let out guttural cries. Alador and his team froze. He hoped that the cry had been one of the mine guards falling. He also hoped that the dragons' irritation in the center would cover any additional movements of his own people.

"What has got them all stirred up?" snarled a male voice nearby.

"Who knows? Stupid beasts get riled up at the darndest things. Two days ago, you would have thought they had all seen their mother flying over. All there was in the air was a large eagle." The woman's voice sounded unhappy. "Not bound to be able to tell what's got them in a snit in this fog and I do not intend to go look. If one got a bit loose, you wouldn't know it before they bit your head off."

"This fog is the thickest I have ever seen," the male stated. "The only consolation is the dragons that are loose can't see any better than we can."

"That we know of…" The woman's voice held slight humor, and Alador could tell she was enjoying her partner's discomfort.

"Gee… thanks." The man moved a bit closer to Alador's position while peering out towards the middle of the space. Alador could only just make out his shape. He motioned for Nemara to be ready, he pulled his dagger. When the man turned his back, Alador moved. His hand went over the man's mouth and his knife slid swiftly across his throat. The guard made a gurgling sound and sagged.

"Pate?" The woman moved forward and as soon as her outline was clear against the dimmed firelight, Nemara let her arrow fly, catching the woman in the throat. She fell to her knees, clawing at the arrow. A second arrow landed in her chest before she could manage to make more noise. Her only sounds were the ones that signified she was drowning in her own blood.

The dragons became even more irritated and a couple began howling. Alador realized suddenly what had them agitated: it had to be the smell of blood, the scent must have been strong on the air. He cursed softly: it was unlikely that they would catch anyone else off guard. The dragons' cries and groans were sure to make their guards more alert.

A light suddenly cut through the fog from one of the towers. Swiftly they pulled their two guards behind the ballista and Alador motioned to Nemara to stand still. It was doubtful in the night and fog that any tower guard was going to be able to make out more than shapes. Two blackguards at this guard point was what they would expect to see. Sometimes, you could fool people more by being what they expected then by trying to hide.

He watched the light curiously. It was too bright to be a lightstone and too white to be fire. It was focused into a beam that swept through the ranks of chained dragons on the main grounds. Even in the fog, the light seemed to allow the men in the tower to see, for even here from the ground he was able to make out the shape and general color of the dragons when the light swept over them. Later, he would have to find out what made such a light.

As the light swept to the far side of the enclosure, Alador beckoned the other four forward. They had two more ballistae to see to on this side of the enclosure. While Alador stood watch, Nemara swiftly doused the large crossbow-like contraption with oil. She then carefully damaged the pullback in case the fire was doused somehow. Their goal was to make sure the device could not be used.

He picked up a flaming stick from the guard post fire and waited, listening closely. He felt lucky so far. The plan seemed to be working – aside from the agitation of the dragons, which he hadn't anticipated. It might actually be assisting them, as the attention in the compound seemed to be focused on what had the dragons riled up.

Far to his right, he heard a scream of alarm and the sound of swords clashing. He swiftly threw the flaming brand onto the ballista, watching it go up. The three across from him lit up right after his, as did one of those to his right. The last one did not, alarms began to ring.

"Nemara, switch your tabard," he called swiftly. He also pulled the middle piece of cloth from his back over his head. No longer were they showing the colors of the Blackguard. They were now flagged so that the dragons could clearly see them and differentiate friend from foe.

"We have company," Nemara hissed. He glanced at the cavern entrance, men and women began to flow from it. She unleashed an arrow, dropping one as she moved forward out of the light of the now fully enflamed ballista.

The fog around them began swiftly to lift and Alador heard the first call of an adult dragon. He moved forward with his sword. There were more coming out of the cave than he had expected. The dragons were going to have to move quickly.

A guard spotted Alador and rushed at him. Nemara dropped a second with her bow and then Alador was fully engaged. He brought his sword up and parried the blow, which narrowly slid by his face. The two circled one another warily. He heard Nemara's bow snap again and a grunt from someone falling nearby.

Alador came in low, and his blow was met soundly as swords clashed in an age-old cacophony. It echoed about him as others of his compatriots were engaged. He swiped twice missing both times and found his opponent's blade at his middle. Alador jumped back barely missing being impaled. He came in again first with a blow to the head and back around with one intent to the man's left side. Both blows were again met soundly. His momentum carried him forward and he did not see how but somehow as the man passed him, the blade caught Alador in the midriff. His leather dulled most of the slicing cut as they moved beyond one another, but it still stung as first blood was drawn. Alador cursed softly.

As their swords clashed first left than right, Alador realized that this man was better with a sword than he was. He swung and his sword found nothing but air. He had to hop backwards to prevent a hard slice to his left leg. They came back together, swords crossed before their faces. He did not know the man, but he could see the determination to kill in his eyes.

They pushed off one another and circled. Alador did not have time for this. The only reason he was not fighting more than one adversary was that Nemara was dropping those that might interfere.

Alador put one hand behind his back as he met the other man's blade twice more, barely able to deflect it one-handed. He pulled lightning into his hand and when he felt the power pulsing, he spun around as hard as he could with both hands on the hilt of his sword. As he did so, he let the spell loose to flow up the blade. When their blades met, the lightning flared onto the other man's sword, dancing down to the hilt. He dropped it in surprise, even as Alador's back swing came around. Alador's sword caught him between helm and shoulder, biting deep into his neck.

Alador pulled his sword free staggering back. He glanced around just in time to see Keensight baring down on those that had flooded out of the cave. He dove for Nemara, shielding her against the rock wall next to the cave opening, flame lashed out along the ground towards the opening. Alador barely got his water shield up in time to protect the two of them. When he looked up, there were no guards standing at the cave entrance. He looked up into the sky to see it full of dragons.

“Nemara, we have to get that last ballista down.” Even as he spoke, a large arrow lanced up into the sky barely missing a green dragon’s wing. “Stick to the wall. Some of those dragons may not care who is friend or foe.”

“Right behind you.” The two of them began to make their way around the enclosure, bent low and as close to the stockade wall as possible.

When they got to the second ballista that had been lit up, they found one of their party against the wooden wall, holding her side. Alador paused. She was alive and alert. “You okay?”

“Yes, took a blow to the side. It hurts, but I think the bleeding is slowing,” the woman moaned out.

Alador looked down at the size of the pool of blood and the blood still oozing between her fingers. He did not have the heart to tell her that the slowing was due to the amount on the ground. “Rest.” He pulled her sword over and put it in her other hand. “Keep this close.” She was not likely to live and he could not spare Nemara to see to the woman. He met Nemara’s eyes and saw the truth in them.

“Go!” The woman nodded. “I will be fine. I will just wait here till it is over.”

"Press this to the wound.” Nemara pulled a paste from her pouch and handed it to the woman. "It will help ease the pain and slow the bleeding.” She pressed it into the woman's hands. “May the gods be with you,” Nemara whispered.

Alador led the way to the third ballista. He saw four bodies on the ground as they approached. A fifth woman was winding back the ballista for another shot. Alador motioned for Nemara, he turned his back to her to ensure they were not surprised. Nemara drew back carefully and dropped the woman just as she was sighting the weapon. She tapped Alador, and they both hurried forward. Alador sheathed his sword and looked around for the oil they had brought. He found some in one of the packs of the men who had joined them. He doused the weapon with oil until an arrow lanced through his right shoulder spinning him around. Alador crawled swiftly to the other side of the ballista, winded by the force of the blow.

"Light it, Nemara!" He called out. He pushed the arrow through. Tears of pain stung his eyes, but he managed to get it most of the way.

Nemara set the weapon on fire then grabbed Alador's hand and helped him move tight up against the wall. She scanned the walls to see where the arrow had come from. Alador watched as she feathered another arrow and drew it back carefully. He said nothing till she let the arrow fly and watched a man drop off the wall about one hundred feet from them. The curved wall held advantages for both friend and foe.

Nemara dropped her bow and moved around him. "I am going to pull it the rest of the way. You can't cast with this embedded as it is." She broke off the fletching.

Alador nodded and gritted his teeth, preparing himself. When she yanked, he could not contain the yell of pain. Nemara ripped the Blackguard portion of the tabard. She swiftly pulled a leaf from a pouch on her belt and pressed it into the wound, then shoved the portion of tabard against it as well, using his armor to hold it in place. The pain eased somewhat where the leaf was pressed tightly to him.

"Come on. We have work to do." She pulled him up with a playful grin. They both scooped up their weapons while scanning the compound. Dragons were everywhere. Adults were landing in the enclosure and ripping loose the chains of the fledglings. The remaining guards on the walls were the target of every dragon in the air.

"We have to get into the cave." Alador shouted over the crackling of flames and the roars of dragons on the ground and in the air. The two of them headed around the outskirts again towards the opening in the rock wall. They were almost there when Alador saw one of their own against the palisade, a dragon moving in on him. It was Ben; he had not switched his tabard.

"Go ahead and start to clear the inside with the others, I will get Ben." He raced across the yard waving one hand at the brown dragon. It looked up to see his tabard and took a step back. "BEN! Show your tabard," he yelled.

Ben frantically ripped the tabard over his head showing the blue dragon. He tossed his sword to the side to do so. Seeing his tabard, the dragon gave an indignant huff and flew off towards another bowman on the wall. Alador got to him and scooped up his sword, handing it to him.

"You okay?"

"Yeah," Ben panted out. "Thanks."

"No problem, let's go. There are bound to be a few still inside." Alador drew his sword once more and the two hurried toward the opening in the cave wall.

Just before he was about to enter the cave, he heard a shout of his name then a large blow to his back. He hit the ground hard, sliding forward a few feet. Alador labored for breath as the blow had knocked the wind from him. He could not see anything but blue scale. He realized that it was Rena when the most horrible heart wrenching scream filled his ears. The lance of its volume and the heart wrenching wail coursed through him. He tried to move, but the claws against his back had him pinned firmly to the ground. The dragon's wings were wrapped so tightly about him that everything was obscured.

Pain coursed through him, and he felt as if his skin were on fire. It took a moment before he realized that it was not his pain. "Rena!" he screamed.

Chapter Thirty-Seven

Panic surged through Alador, pinned as he was. He knew something terrible had just happened, but not what. He struggled and could feel her talons through his leathers pinning him to the ground. She had pulled them enough that they did not penetrate his skin, but he could feel their sharp points.

"Rena, let me up!" he screamed from beneath her.

Rena managed to lift one wing and shift her weight enough to allow Alador to wiggle free from beneath her. Just as he managed to scoot loose, Amaum landed next to Rena as well. The sight that met his eyes sent pain then rage shooting through him. Even in the faint light he could see the acid bubbling along the dragon's back. Sections of her wings were hissing in the pale light as the acid ate its way towards bone. He looked around quickly for what could have done such a thing and spotted them spiralling around the vale; three black dragons in a tight formation.

"Oh gods Rena! What can I do?" He moved to her head and put a hand on either side.

"I need a gold dragon," she moaned.

Alador looked to Amaum who shook his great head. They did not have a gold dragon in their midst. "Hang on Rena, we will find something."

He looked up to see that the black dragons were setting up for another run. "Amaum, warn the others."

He was sure they had seen the three, but he did not want anyone else caught off guard.

Amaum let out a great roar and some strange sounds as Alador turned to Nemara who had come back to the entrance. “Guard her,” he snapped. His tone left no room for argument. Nemara gave a single nod and moved to Rena’s head.

He swung around to see the three black dragons swinging around at the far end of the valley. “Take the left or right, the large one in the center is mine!” growled Alador. Amaum took off into the air calling the other dragons as he did.

Alador strode forward into the center of the compound. A large avenue between where the dragons had been chained led to the cave and to where Rena lay. He moved forward, dragons swooped in, pulling the left and right dragons off and a fight began in mid-air. While the black dragons were outnumbered, their breath weapon of acid was deadly to any wing caught in its wake.

Alador had eyes only for the one in the center. He did not know which had caught Rena, but he had been their target and the one in the middle would be in charge. The dragon did not veer from its course straight at Alador, despite the battle raging to either side of it. Alador noted that Keensight moved to his left and a little behind him. Alador suspected that if he did not kill the dragon, Keensight and Pruatra would. He caught sight of Pruatra, and sure enough she was positioning herself to his right.

His eyes flashed back to the black dragon now making its run. It dropped low into the valley and came straight at him. Alador came to rest in the center of the compound pulling power from every pool of water he could sense. He held his hands together, letting the power build…

The black dragon gave a final thrust of its wings to approach the compound. It was as large as Keensight. Its hide was so black and glossy that the scales glimmered in the various flickering fires about them. Each wing had three points with talon hooks. Its true talons were outstretched and glimmered with some form of metal on each end.

Alador waited, just as he had so long ago with Keensight. The dragon would use its breath weapon as the acid was far more effective than any direct contact. It jumped forward in his vision as he focused. Acid dripped from its fangs, the great mouth opened to draw the breath it needed to expel its breath weapon…

Alador let his ball of lightning fly when the mouth was half open. He needed to catch it just before it began to breathe. The dragon was committed to its strafing run. Acid began to spew from its mouth about thirty feet from Alador; he back pedalled as the bright ball of light hit the back of the dragon's mouth.

The dragon was knocked back by the force of the magic that hit it. It floundered, wings beating madly in an instinctive attempt at survival. Lightning rocketed through its head, out of its mouth and danced along its wings. Keensight and Pruatra were already on the move, each sweeping in with their own weapons. Fire laced the floundering dragon from one side; steam hit it from the other. Its own acid was gasping out in sputtering, upward waves. Fortunately, it had been knocked far enough back by the three-pronged attack that none of the remaining chained dragons were hit.

Alador did not intend to concede the killing of the beast to the two elder dragons. He hit it again with two smaller balls of lightning, one catching it in its right wing. It was too much for the wings and the dragon fell, belly-up. It landed on the palisades of the stockade; a sharpened pole lanced through one wing and another through its chest. One wing was still blazing from the onslaught of Keensight's fire. The other two black dragons were faltering under the onslaught of multiple dragons in the skies.

Once sure that it was not getting up, Alador turned and ran back towards Rena. He could see a strange glow surrounding her and Nemara, who was kneeling near the dragon's head. It faded as he approached, sliding to his knees as he came to a stop before her.

"Rena. He is dead. I killed him." He was babbling. "Why did you do that? Why did you dive over me like that?" He surveyed the damage to the young dragon. He could see ribs and bubbled meat where the acid had eaten in. He knew that without a strong healer, which they did not have, Rena was not going to live. Tears filled his eyes as the realization that there was no hope sank in.

Rena opened her eye that looked up at Alador. "I told you that I would die for you," she wheezed out. Her chest gave a heaving sigh as she labored to breathe.

Keensight and Pruatra landed nearby and moved to either side of the ailing dragon. Alador looked up at them pleading. "There must be some dragon magic, something you can do?" Tears fell down his cheeks as the realization that he was losing her set in.

Keensight shook his great head as Pruatra began making a strange keening noise. It sounded like sobs on some strange mortal level. "There is too much damage, son. She has chosen this path. There is nothing we can do." Keensight placed a wing over the grieving mother, nuzzling Pruatra gently.

Alador scooted forward, laying Rena's great head in his lap. "What use is magic if it cannot undo this?" He put his face against Rena's.

The young dragon gave him a weak smile. "Don't mourn, heartmate. I will wait for you where the dragons rest." Rena gave a strange cough and blood began to trickle from her mouth.

"NO!" Alador stroked her head. "I just found happiness. You cannot take it away now."

"I am… glad... we had our… time together." Rena's chest heaved.

"Don't talk." Alador stroked her muzzle and laid a gentle kiss on her nose.

Rena lifted her head. "There is so much I still wanted to know," she began. She coughed again and blood spewed over Alador.

Alador did not care about the blood. He rubbed between her eyes, something that he had learned she loved. "Shhh, it can wait," he said.

"I never got to find out why mortals kiss," she lamented and gave a great cough. Blood spattered the ground from her mouth and began to ooze out her muzzle.

"You have to hold on. We will go to the Pool of the Gods as you suggested," he promised. "Just stay with me."

Rena did not answer him though he thought she smiled sadly. She gave a great heave of her chest; her great eye shut.

"Nooooo!" He buried his face into her muzzle.

Keensight and Pruatra began the dragons' song of death. It was picked up by every adult dragon in the vale. Amaum landed close to his mother and began to sing too. Alador just rocked Rena's head as he grieved.

"I am so sorry, Rena. I loved you." He cried against her muzzle. "I didn't tell you, I loved you." Even as the words left his mouth, he knew it was true.

"She knew that, Alador," Nemara murmured softly. She was still kneeling beside him.

The dragons and Nemara let him be while the dragons sang. Nemara slipped away with the four remaining comrades to clear the inside of the cavern. Alador realized he understood the words. The dragons sang to all the gods, asking them to accept this child's soul and give it rest in the eternal land of sun and magic. It was a beautiful song and he sang the last few words himself, lifting his head to try to sing them. It was more a whispered plea than a song when it left his lips

Keensight let him sit there rocking Rena's head for a few more minutes before he interrupted Alador. "It is not done, mage. You must get the eggs and hatchlings from within. It is likely men are there to put them down if they have not already with this delay."

"Bugger the geas," he snarled, stroking Rena's now peaceful head.

"It must be finished, boy." Keensight's voice took a harsher edge. "Otherwise, Rena will have died for nothing?"

"She did die for nothing," Alador snapped. "It is a terrible waste."

Keensight nudged him hard with his nose and gave an exasperated huff. "She died protecting you. You, the mortal she loved and believed in. I will not let you desecrate that sacrifice." Keensight's face was inches from Alador's. The dragon's breath reeked of death and sulphur. "Finish it!"

Alador sat stunned for a further moment. Keensight was right: she had died so that he might finish what they had all started. He reached out, digging beneath her wing until he found his sword. Alador had lost it when she had shoved him into the dirt.

He stood shakily, looking about them. "I don't want Luthian's men to find her." He looked from Keensight to Pruatra. "Is there anything you can do?"

"Yes," Pruatra growled. Alador could feel the pain in her voice. "Amaum and I will see that she is properly laid to rest."

Alador gave a nod then turned on his heel to head into the caverns. He set his jaw and moved forward carefully. He shoved his more tender emotions aside, letting anger replace his deep grief.

Being stabbed earlier in the year at the stable lord's abode had been a harsh lesson. He checked each recess before he passed it. Shed tears left drying trails in the blood on his face. He did not bother to dash them away as he moved step by step into the recesses of the cavern.

He caught up with Nemara in the main hall. She put a comforting hand on his arm, giving it a squeeze before she spoke. "We have cleared the halls. We didn't get here in time. The commander was making a report of the assault into a scrying bowl."

"Tell me you did not get close to that bowl." Alador looked at her worriedly.

"No. I knew what it was, I shot it off the desk after I shot him. He is still alive if you wish to speak to him?" Nemara looked rather proud of herself.

"Well done," He considered for a moment then turned to the others. "Ben, go put the commander out of his misery." Alador commanded.

Ben did not question Alador's order. He gave a nod and hurried off to do as he was bid. Alador looked around at their numbers, realizing that the losses had extended beyond the dragons. He took a deep breath. "Any sign of Jon?"

"Yes, commander," one of the remaining women answered. "We found him in a strange room filled with eggs and small dragons. He won't leave them. Said you needed to come talk to him."

Alador did not like the sound of that. If Jon had decided to work with his plan, he should have been willing to escort the dragons out. He ran a hand across his face, smearing the blood and dirt there.

"All right. Let us go talk to our dear death mage." His command was soft and deadly. He knew at that moment that if Jon had sided against them that he would kill him. He would kill each and every person whose conduct had led to Rena's death.

Alador suddenly remembered Dethara's warning, delivered by Lady Morana.

'If you continue on the path you now travel, then you will regret it with every fiber of your being.'

Morana had gone on to say that 'some pains in life cannot be healed.' He stopped for a moment as the words rang in his ears and drove deeply into the very center of his being. His sudden movement brought the rest of the party to a halt, weapons up.

Morana had known. She had warned him, and she had been right. His eyes narrowed as the words settled into his heart. He was going to kill her too.

Chapter Thirty-Eight

Sword in hand, Alador approached the end of the hall cautiously, in touch with the well of magic within him. He stepped around the corner and looked about quickly. He was standing on a ledge above a pit. Jon sat on a wall at the far side of it. Clustered about him were dragons of various sizes and around Jon's neck was a black fledgling. It sat on his shoulder like an imperious cat, its tail wrapped around the death mage's neck. The smell from the nest below made Alador's eyes water. The smell of urine and sulfur was overwhelming.

"Hello Alador." The greeting was so flat that Alador could not tell if the mage were glad to see him or not.

Alador gave a brief nod. "Jon," he acknowledged. He heard the others slowly join him on the ledge. The tension in the air was instantly thick and the dragons became agitated. They moved around Jon nervously as if he were their mother and would protect them.

"If you have got this far, I assume you were successful." Jon's monotone had not changed in the time they had been separated.

"Yes, the elder dragons are freeing the chained dragons and leading them to safety even as we speak." Alador's tone did not show any relief. The anger driving him at the moment was all that was holding him together.

"Yet, you are not happy, old friend." Jon looked him over. "The losses were great then?"

"Too great," Alador snapped. "Why are we chatting like this if we are old friends? You obviously did not join the battle." Alador did not want to play games right now.

"I stayed to protect the young ones. The orders were to kill them if the stockade was overrun. I was not inclined to allow that to happen." Jon admitted. Yet despite his words, he did not move.

"Then let me send these out to find their parents," Alador suggested slowly.

"You will need some meat to get them to leave." Jon nodded towards the far wall. "You will find it in the box to your left. Let the others lead them out so that you and I can talk."

Alador nodded to Nemara who let her bow relax and went to the box. She handed meat to the others. Ben joined them just in time to be handed a large slab of it. Alador looked to his right. There was a tall gate at the end of a sloping ramp. "So open that and show them the meat?"

"Yes, though they are a greedy lot: so once you have their attention, I suggest that you run." Jon grinned. "Very fast."

Nemara hesitated. "I am not getting eaten by one of your dragons," Her tone was emphatic. She looked at Alador.

"First, they are not mine," Alador pointed out. "Secondly, once out the entrance dive to the left, but toss the meat forward. From there, the dragons should take over."

"What if one of us doesn't get there fast enough," Ben asked, calling over to Jon.

"If it looks like you are going to be overrun, toss it forward." Jon suggested. "It will be the meat they're after, not you."

Nemara took a deep breath and moved to the large door. She threw back the bolt which brought every little dragon head up. It was rather an amazing sight. There were all sorts of colors except for black. The only black dragon that Alador saw was the one around Jon's neck.

Nemara dangled the meat out and the eager little hatchlings began to run forward. "Oh, no," Nemara exclaimed and turned to run. She did not have to worry about tripping over any of her comrades: Ben and the others had already taken off. She sprinted away as fast as she could. Alador stood by, sword lowered as the little dragons began to run by after her. It was like watching a nest of birds with their mouths open; well, except that each of these birds ranged from the size of a large dog to the size of a lexital.

Alador went down the ramp as soon as the last little dragon ran by him. He stepped carefully into the nest as there were feces everywhere. "How do you stand it in here?" He was nearly gagging and his eyes stung.

Jon shrugged. He still had not moved from where he sat. "You get used to it over time."

"I don't think I could get used to this," Alador admitted. He made his way over to Jon, passing a keg of water in which there was a blue egg. A small fire was burning beneath it to keep it warm.

"How many eggs?" Alador asked, carefully looking around.

"Five unhatched," Jon answered in his matter-of-fact monotone. "Now that the others are away, we must speak." Jon looked at Alador evenly. "I cannot return with you, nor can I stay here. There will be questions in either case that have no safe answer."

Alador considered his words. Jon was right. If he returned, he would have abandoned his post. If he stayed, there would be questions about how he alone had managed to survive, who had carried out the attack and every minute detail of what had happened.

"What do you suggest?" Alador had finally made it close enough to Jon to be able to lower his voice.

"I will flee to the South and seek refuge in Dethara's temple." Jon stroked the little black dragon's head absently.

Alador's eyes narrowed. "Why would you even want to go there?" His voice was cold and hard.

"She is the Goddess of my sphere." The death mage's answer was even and without emotion.

"Jon, since you left that woman, the high priestess had tried to kill me. I have met Dethara personally in the sea, and I can tell you she did not make a favourable impression. To go to her is to ally yourself with my ***enemy!***" Alador spat out that last word. His hand tightened on his pommel at the mere thought.

"All the more reason for me to go," Jon stated. "You will have a man on the inside."

"But Jon, how can you serve that...? How can you serve this Goddess with a clear heart?" Alador shook his head clearly in distress at the thought.

"You mistake the Goddess for her priestess. Despite her devotion to Dethara, Lady Morana is still a mortal woman...," Jon began to explain.

"Who I AM going to kill," Alador interrupted furiously. "I am going to ensure before I am done that she no longer serves anyone." Alador paused. "I do not mistake the two. Dethara tried to kill me and a lot of other people during my tier test."

"Well, there you go: your plans for Morana will further my own designs." Jon nodded, clearly pleased. There was a hint of a smile that seemed more like a grimace on the stoic mage's face. Wisely, he chose not to focus on Alador's revelation about Dethara's attempt at mass murder.

"What do you mean?" Alador's eyes narrowed.

"I plan to become the High Priest. I will flee south, bringing her this small but valuable treasure." He stroked the dragon. "Having 'saved' her from certain death at the hands of guards following the commander's orders to destroy all fledglings, I will earn Dethara's favor and be rewarded with high office in Morana's service."

"That … dragon is not leaving here alive," Alador snarled.

"It is." Jon's tone became deadly. "You will not touch it."

"Jon, those beasts killed my best friend." Alador took a step forward. The hand on the hilt of his sword gripped so tightly that his fingers were white. "Nothing deserves to die like that. You know that Morana or her replacement will have this one trained the same."

"And black dragons deserve to be burned alive, or steamed?" Jon pointed out. "Every dragon's breath-weapon is deadly. It is a baby; it has done nothing to merit its execution."

"It will grow to serve her whims just as the three that attacked my force did." Alador shook his head. "It dies."

"And the black dragons that attacked your force - they lived?" Jon asked, his tone again even and monotone.

Alador frowned. "Well, no." He did not like where Jon was going. He remembered that arguing with Jon was like hitting your head against a brick wall.

Jon finally got up from his seat and shook out his robes. "Then they got what they deserved for attacking their own kin. This dragon will grow to serve myself and Dethara, not Morana or anyone like her."

"Jon..." Alador shook his head. "The temple has become an enemy of the people it was set up to serve. You are asking me to let you go become a part of that with the intention of taking over as its High Priest. How can I let you do that?"

"You really have no choice. You can try to kill me and you will die…" - Jon shrugged - "…or you can trust in our friendship and allow me to follow this path. You base your fears on your experiences to date, which do not reflect Dethara's true purpose."

"Dethara seeks death." Alador snapped.

"See, that's where you are wrong: she ***mitigates*** death. She doesn't need to seek it out, as it's inevitable for us all." Jon leaned over to tap Alador in the temple. "Use your head, my friend. There must be a gatekeeper in order for the souls of the dead to move on where they should. She guards the nine doors to Paradise, the regions beyond for each of the gods." He shook his head. "The priests of her temples and shrines ease the suffering of those approaching death."

"Nine? There are only eight gods." Alador pointed out. "What is the ninth door for?"

Jon pulled the little dragon around to his chest as if to emphasize his answer. "It leads to the resting place of the dragons. As envoys of magic for the gods, they have a shared space that all the gods can visit."

Alador remembered his visions of drinking from the pool and the facing of all the gods as Renamaum. This must be the land that Jon spoke about. He swallowed a huge lump in his throat. The place that Rena had said she would wait for him.

"You will still be on my side? You will warn me of danger from Morana or her like?" Alador was giving it serious thought. Sordith had told him that he had been unable to get a man into the temple. This would be his inside man. Could he trust Jon though? Could he trust any servant of Dethara?

"I will not serve another; but as long as our goals are not in conflict then I will be your eyes and ears." Jon's cryptic answer did not entirely assuage his concerns.

"And if our goals ever conflict?" he pressed.

Jon put out one hand in a position of openness, while the other held the dragon. "I will be honest and tell you that I cannot answer your question or do as you wish because to do so would undermine my own objectives." Jon tipped his head. Is that not a role of a friend? - to assist when one can and to be honest when one cannot?"

Alador slowly let go of the pommel of his sword. His fingers were stiff from the previous tightness of his grip and the consequent lack of blood to them. "You won't be able to leave here straight away," he pointed out. "The dragons will be outside the cavern for a while." It was as close to an agreement as he could manage in the circumstances. He eyed the little black dragon with such hatred that it looked at him and hissed its own displeasure.

"Shhh little one. It is okay. He is just upset." Jon's tenderness came as a surprise, given his usual lack of emotion. Once the hatchling was soothed, he looked over at Alador. "I will stay as long as I dare. Someone will come investigating when there are no further reports on the situation."

Alador nodded. "I will tell you honestly that while I do need a man inside that temple, I am afraid of losing my friend to the madness within it." He searched Jon's face with genuine concern.

"Then a wiser mind would be better seated. All will be well, Alador. You are my only friend. I do not intend to discard that friendship as if it didn't matter to me," Jon admitted. "But if you ask me if I care, I will deny it," he added, as if that momentary sharing of emotion had been too much for him.

The others entered. Ben looked a little worse for wear. "Everyone okay?" Alador called up to the five peering down at them.

Nemara chuckled as Ben cursed. "Ben didn't run fast enough. When he threw the meat forward, the leading dragon knocked him over in its rush to get it and then the rest ran right over him." The others laughed at the memory of Ben being run over by a flock of fledgling dragons.

"It is not funny," Ben protested. "I could have been killed."

"You are fine. After all, how many can claim to have been stepped on by a dragon and lived." Nemara answered him with a laugh. "Your red dragon spoke ..." Nemara sounded in awe. "A dragon spoke to me; it was amazing."

Alador looked up to the ledge, and a slight smile tipped his lips. He remembered the first time Keensight had spoken to him. "You become accustomed to it after a while."

"I hope not." She grinned down at him. "He wants to know if there are eggs."

"Yes, five. Each of you come and get one. Careful where you step, there is... shite everywhere." Alador looked back at Jon.

"What you ask goes against what I feel to be right." Alador murmured almost in a whisper. "I still fear losing you once you are on the inside."

"So are you going to try and kill me now?" Jon grinned at him. "That might be a laugh - though sad as well, of course."

Alador shook his head in frustration. "No. You kept the fledglings and eggs safe. You raised no spell or hand to any that came to free them. What kind of a friend would I be stopping you from pursuing your own path?"

"Good. Will you hold Nightmare while I help our comrades with the eggs?"

Alador eyed the fledgling. "Can't you just…put it down?" He had no desire to hold that spawn of evil.

"It is a baby, Alador. All babies are innocent." Jon held the fledgling out. "Besides, it will be good to impress your scent on it as someone who is not a threat. It might just save your life one day."

Slowly Alador put his hands out. The dragon hissed in concern, but Jon soothed it as he handed it over.

"Rub it between the eyes; they seem to like that." Jon said as Alador carefully took the small helpless creature.

Jon's words brought a sting of tears to Alador's eyes. Rena had loved this too. He did as he was told, and soon the dragon was nestling up against his chest and curling its long whip like tail around Alador's arm. Was Jon right? Were they innocent as hatchlings? Could a black dragon be anything else but evil?

Jon led the others to the eggs, and one by one they were carried out. When the last egg was ferried out carefully by Ben, Jon returned to Alador. He stood watching Alador and the young dragon for a long moment. Alador was lost in petting it between the eyes and enjoying the soft coos of pleasure from the little beast.

"See, I told you. It has yet to learn about right or wrong. It knows only the things that babies know: who is kind, who feeds it, who gives it comfort." Jon reached out and gently took the dragon from Alador. "To kill at someone's command… that comes with training."

"Will you teach it to kill?" Alador's voice broke. He looked at Jon with eyes full of pain and concern.

"I may have to so as to keep my place close to Morana. Let us hope an opening to remove her from power comes before the dragon is old enough to be trained to do such things." Jon caressed it. "It is bonded to me, so the training of it will be entrusted to me. I will ensure it knows the difference between defense of its lair and killing at whim."

"Do they speak? Can they talk like the other flights?" Alador was now quite curious, having held it. It had responded just as any other small animal would.

"They can. They are literal and loyal beasts. Once their affection is won, they will defend friends and family to the death." Jon sighed. "A character strength if properly focused, but a flaw in the wrong, manipulative hands."

Alador sobered at that thought. "Make sure it is your friend, Jon. Please, I beg you to not let it believe Morana is a friend."

"I will do what I can," Jon promised. "Now, you had best be off before you are discovered."

"You'll be all right?" Alador looked about them.

"I will wait for a while for the other dragons to get clear, then move up to a secret place off the main hall, where Lucian's reinforcements will not find me. Then in a couple days, I will slip away at night." Jon laid it out with that same casually stoic manner.

"Take care, my friend." Alador offered his arm which Jon clasped. They stood that way for a moment, then Alador let go and turned on his heel and walked away. He did not look back. He was uncertain if he was making the right choice and did not want to second-guess it. When he reached the entrance to the cavern, the others were waiting for him.

"Where's Jon?" Nemara looked behind Alador and back to him.

"He has another mission he needs to see about. He will not be returning with us." Alador said. "As far as we are concerned, he died tonight with the rest. Understood?"

The five of them nodded wearily. "Good," Alador stated. "Gather round. We need to get back before Luthian has had time to check who is innocently where they ought to be and who is not."

They gathered around him, placing hands on him. Seconds later they were all back in his bedchamber. The whole event had taken just a couple of hours. Daylight glimmered in the East...

Alador sat on the floor, put his head against his knees and wrapped it in his arms. It was done, but what was lost was greater to him than what had been gained.

Nemara took the lead. With one hand on Alador's shoulder she began commanding the others. "Everyone cast a clean spell and change back into your party clothes. Master Bariton will be waiting for you downstairs."

One of the women looked sadly at Nemara. "What of those that didn't make it back?"

"The High Master has a plan in place to cover that eventuality. Just return to the barracks with him and keep your mouths shut."

"What about you, Nemara?" Ben asked.

"I will be staying the night with my lover." She emphasized the last word.

Alador did not react to Nemara's statement. He was exhausted and overwrought. He felt the throb of his wounds and the true depth of the loss of Rena. He was content to let her take the lead.

"I know we all lost friends tonight. Try to remember they died for a great cause - saving all those dragons," Nemara said. She let go of Alador and escorted them to the door.

Once she had shooed the others out, she turned to Alador. She cast a clean spell over him, then helped him out of his armor. "I need to put poultices on these," she muttered, gazing at his wounds.

Alador sat numbly and let her do as she wished. She was a nature mage with basic healing skills. Once she had dressed his wounds, she formed a nightshirt over him. Alador let her guide him to the bed and dozed while she saw to her own needs. She had apparently used his bathing room as she was damp and naked when she crawled into the bed beside him.

"What are you doing?" he asked, half awake. The depth of his grief was keeping sleep just out of reach, despite his exhaustion.

"Keeping up appearances," she answered quietly. "Don't worry. I am also too tired and overwhelmed by the night's events to jump on you in the hope of carnal pleasure." Her words, though meant to tease, held an edge of sadness to them.

"I'm sorry," Alador murmured.

"I could use a warm hug, and I think you need one as well," she said. She moved to press her back against him.

Alador realized she was right and pulled her close. He buried his face against her damp hair to hide the silent tears that had begun to flow. After some time, he finally fell into an exhausted sleep.

Chapter Thirty-Nine

Luthian sat back in his leather chair; his fingers drummed both arms of the chair. He mulled over what he knew. He had read the reports from the aides in charge of the night watch over the scrying bowls. He was perplexed and concerned by the information provided - not because of its content, but because it was incomplete: as if the communication had been interrupted. The only reason he could think of why the commander - or his next in command - would not have completed the report was if the bloodmine had fallen.

Bloodmining had started long before he was appointed High Minister. However, since he had become High Minister, the practice had been refined. With the help of Lady Morana, the stealing of eggs had become easier. Dragon nests were invariably hard to find and well defended. Using the black dragon as scouts, they had been able to raid nests with greater success and fewer losses. The only price that Morana had demanded was the hatchlings of black eggs. The temple then imprinted and trained the black dragons.

To have the oldest bloodmine fall on his watch was going to cause him a great deal of trouble with the Council. Luthian leaned forward and read the report again. The commander had reported that a sudden storm had manifested out of a clear night. The storm had abated, but only to leave an obscuring fog so thick that the watch posts were unable to see one another. It bore the hallmark of a skilled storm mage or a very intelligent blue dragon. He did not believe that dragons were all that intelligent, so most likely it had been the former.

Under the cover of this fog, an attack had been mounted on the mine. The commander spoke of sword-wielding mages wearing blue tabards working with dragons to assault the compound. That was where the report ended. There was no further information concerning losses, numbers involved, damage inflicted or anything else that Luthian would certainly have expected by now.

Dragons had attacked before, but the compound had always managed to repel them. Mages working with dragons was unheard of because of the breaking of the pact hundreds of years ago. Dragons had worked with the Daezun in past wars, but never with mages. Mages carrying swords were also uncommon. It suggested men of his own Blackguard, and this he could not fathom.

Luthian tossed down the report. He rubbed his weary eyes and sighed heavily with annoyance. He was going to have to assess the damage. His mind was racing; he sat back again. There was a myriad of explanations that he could give the Council, but he could not be sure which path would most limit the damage. He rose from his chair decisively. He would go alone to the mine: to minimize rumor and speculation.

He strode through the High Minister's magnificent manor to his own personal laboratory. Having armed himself with various spell components as well as the snake dagger and a normal boot dagger, swiftly he formed robes more appropriate for cold weather. He chose a simple gray cloak to blend in as much as possible. If the dragons were still around, he did not need to present them with a bright red target.

The travel spell was always a little taxing, so before casting it he ate from a nearby table kept stocked for his use. He also stuffed some more food into his belt pouch – he had no way of knowing how much energy he would have to expend before returning. He stepped into his casting circle in the center of his lab and spoke the words to take him to the mine.

The world swirled out of view, the feeling always disconcerting. When it came to a sudden nauseating stop, the command room of the mine surrounded him. He stood for a moment allowing his body to adjust to the sudden change of environment, his eyes blinking rapidly. He pulled some jerky from his belt and began to gnaw on it, looking about. The space for mages to arrive in was always kept clear, but not this time: a chair had been upended and kicked near where he had just manifested.

The scrying bowl was not on the table, and the smell of death hung heavily in the room. He moved forward and around the table. There on the floor was the body of the commander. He had an arrow in the chest and his throat had been slit. The scrying bowl lay shattered on the floor nearby, explaining the sudden interruption of the communication he had reviewed.

He shoved the last of the jerky into his mouth then moved to the commander's body. He broke the fletching of the arrow off. Sometimes, one could trace an archer by the fletching of their arrows. He fingered the flight feathers. The craftsmanship was excellent but the fletching quite common.

He put the fletching in his belt pouch. There was no evidence to be seen within the room beyond the arrow. Whatever had happened in here had been swift and decisive. He saw no sign of struggle or conflict. The commander had been taken by surprise.

He strode from the room and headed for the hatchery. If orders had been followed, the hatchlings and fledglings too small for bloodletting would have been destroyed. Cautiously he peered around the corner into the hatchery. Discerning no movement, he moved forward. The room reeked of feces and urine. He formed a ball of light and sent it floating down into the pit.

There were no eggs, no fledglings. He glanced to his right and saw that the door to the pit had been left open. Whoever had assaulted the mine had freed the hatchlings and taken the eggs. He had been about to send a ball of fire to cleanse the hatchery when he sensed movement to his right and below him.

"Who is there? Show yourself!" Luthian demanded. He formed a ball of fire reflexively unsure if a fledgling had remained behind or if any of the assault force remained. Luthian moved to put the wall behind him, glancing swiftly at the hall. He was more than prepared for a trap.

"I have a fondness for life. I do hope you will hold your spell." A man in black robes stepped into the aura of the ball of light. He had a black hatchling in his arms. "I have heard burning to death is quite unpleasant." The man's words were even and respectful but held no fear.

"Who are you?" Luthian was more than prepared to kill him and the dragon rather than risk his own safety.

"My name is Jon. I was assigned to the hatchery. We were overrun so swiftly that there was not time to cleanse it." Jon looked down at the creature in his arms. "I took the black hatchling and hid within the recesses of this room." The man's hands were stroking the black beast within his arms, trying to keep it calm.

"I see." Luthian eyed him over slowly. "If they came to get the eggs, how did you remain hidden?"

"I cast an illusion spell. They were moving so swiftly that they were too busy to discern it." Jon's factual answer held no emotion.

"How many?" Luthian demanded.

"I saw at least ten." Jon met Luthian's eyes calmly.

"Could you identify anyone?" Luthian was looking about the hatchery.

"It was dark, and I knew none of the faces I saw." Jon took a cautious step forward. "I can tell you that they wore blue tabards marked with a silver dragon."

"A silver dragon you say?" Luthian's eyes narrowed. His mind swiftly raced over the fact. Where had he seen that combination before?

"Yes, it shimmered in the light of their torches." Jon answered. "If the danger is passed, Lord Guldalian, I would like to leave this pit. The stench is unbearable."

"Yes, approach." Luthian released the ball of fire that writhed within his hand. The heat of it had finally become unbearable.

Jon moved cautiously through the pit and up the ramp. Luthian watched him warily every step. This man claimed to survive by means of deceptive magic. Luthian had learned to trust nothing at face value. Once Jon was close enough to see within the glimmer of the lightstone, he resumed his questioning.

"There were three black eggs at the last report. What of the other two?" He eyed the small fledgling with distaste. He had no liking for dragons.

"This one ate the other two before we realized they had even hatched." Jon stroked the creature as if it were his child, comforting its distressed hissing.

"A killer, then." Luthian muttered to himself. He eyed the creature with interest. "It will need to be delivered to Dethara's temple."

"I had planned to do so, Lord Guldalian. I was just waiting to be sure the danger had passed." Jon frowned. "I felt certain that they would not release this one as they did the others."

"You realize that hatchlings do not survive transit by means of a travel spell." Luthian pointed out. It was odd. Though they were creatures of magic, they had yet to devise a means of transportation to the temple by magic. The little creatures did not survive the reformation at the target location.

"Yes, my Lord. I had planned to head south by foot until I reached Halfbrook – it's a village nearby. From there, I can arrange transport by lexital." Jon's even words betrayed no distress.

"You have done well, Jon. I will be certain that the High Master is made aware of your service. Let us go and see if the way is clear outside. I have found no sign or sound of an enemy within the cavern." Luthian turned on his heel, expecting the younger mage to follow.

Jon followed two paces behind the High Minister, taking care to make sure he was downwind. Luthian appreciated the man's respect and insight. Despite his reasonable certainty that no one else was about, he moved with caution.

"Lord Guldalian, may I ask a question?" Jon's voice struck him as strangely monotonous.

Questions and answers were distracting at this point, and Luthian's eyes constantly swept the area for danger. "Yes, you may."

"Do others besides those assigned here and sworn to the secrecy, know that the dragons are intelligent?"

Luthian could feel the man's piercing eyes on his back as they approached the cave entrance. "What makes you so certain that the beasts of legend are anything more than a fishwife's tale? You have learned here that even from birth they are killers." Luthian paused and turned to face the man. The young fledgling hissed as their eyes met. He so hated the dirty beasts. They were nothing more than large killing ravens that stole anything that glittered and was not nailed down. Sometimes, he mused, they even took what was nailed down.

"Well, they speak for one thing. They are quick to pick up words from the guards around them. More than once, I am certain we have caught them plotting. We rearrange the bloodmine regularly so they are never next to one another for too long." Jon's hand covered the eyes of the fledgling which seemed to settle it.

"Nothing more than mimicry, I can assure you," Luthian answered with a dismissive wave of his hand. "They may have a basic knowledge that sets them apart from the other beasts of the land, but if they were so intelligent then why have their older kin or flight mates not rescued them long ago?" Luthian's piercing lavender eyes moved from the dragon to the man. He noted with pleasure the puzzled look on the mage's face.

"I have no answer to that," Jon admitted. The death mage looked down at the creature, curled as it was around his arm. Even Luthian had to admit it seemed to be a loving little thing in response to this Jon fellow.

"Because there isn't one." Luthian turned and moved to the edge of the opening. In the early rays of dawn, the scene before him held a surreal, ominous feel. The red of the sunrise cast an eerie gloom through the wisps of fog snaking along the ground and through the air. The mountains above them towered over the small valley like leaning vultures, waiting to scoop up the leavings of death below them. Across the compound was the huge carcass of a black dragon, impaled on the palisade with its back to the ground.

Luthian eyed the ground before him outside the cave. There were the marks of scuffling one would expect during a battle. There was blood here and there on the ground. Nearby was a large pool of it: as if someone had bled out. What was missing were the bodies. He could see the dragonfire scorched into the ground, and even the outline of a body where the ground beneath showed no sign of fire.

He moved to the left as he left the cave. What he saw next brought to him to a puzzled stop. There, across a path of acid-bathed ground, was a large clear patch - as if something had been there. It was too large to have been a man. Had a dragon been in the path of the rain of acid?

Why were there no bodies, no carcasses except for the one black dragon impaled upon the far palisade? "Guardsman, have you ever heard of dragons carrying off their dead?" He looked back to Jon, eyeing the death mage evenly.

"I have not; though to be honest, the only tales of dragons in battle I have heard are from the histories of the great wars." Jon moved to the edge of the acid-bathed ground. "Are we at the start of another?"

"I sincerely hope not," the older mage answered coldly. Luthian knelt down, having spotted something on the ground within the strangely-shaped, unscathed space. "It cost the entire isle greatly. All races were bathed in the blood of their own." He picked up a scrap of blue cloth. There was intricate silver stitching on it. He had seen that stitching before. He had admired it in a cloak that his nephew had worn. His eyes narrowed thoughtfully. He slid the piece of the cloth into his belt pouch then rose.

Had his nephew turned against him through subversion? It would account for much of what he saw here, and what he had gathered from the rudely interrupted report: a strong storm mage, the blue tabard with a silver dragon, the appearance of an assault force out of nowhere... Luthian tapped his lip thoughtfully looking about him. That did not account for the presence of dragons. They had obviously fought here. No mortal had held any sway with dragons for as long as he could remember.

Luthian moved forward, taking in the damage with quiet assessment. His accustomed eye for detail picked up the way the ballistae had been damaged by fire. The fire had not started from natural causes, nor from dragon's breath. Oil had been used, the smoking of it evident on the unburned wood and in the nostrils. Whoever had been here, had known to take out the ballistae first. The dragons would have needed them out of the battle. He touched the blackened wood, sniffing the oily residue that came off on his fingers. The scent confirmed his suspicions: it was a fire accelerant.

He made his way to the dragon, examining it first from below. His softly spoken draconic words raised him from the ground till he hovered over the fallen dragon. The dragon had taken at least three major hits.

The first had been with a fierce blow of lightning. The head showed signs of the zigzag lines burned into its scales, all of them originating from the mouth. A mage or dragon had landed the strike when the black behemoth had opened its mouth.

He eyed the wings. One had been burnt with fire, and some of the scorching moved over earlier damage from the lightning bolt. A second or third blow then, he mused. He looked over the second wing. It also held signs of having been cooked, but not with fire. He looked closer: perhaps steam, for the flesh looked more boiled than cooked. He could not tell if the damage had been caused by three powerful mages, dragons, or by some combination. He lowered himself to the ground where the guardsman waited.

"I must return to Silverport. Get yourself to safety and keep that beast hidden. I will expect to hear you have delivered it safely to the temple." Luthian's orders were swift and decisive. He began drawing a circle around himself in blue shimmering powder. Once he had completed the simple magical enclosure, he tossed Jon a small pouch who caught it deftly. "That will help you on your way." The man saluted, turned on his heel and headed for the main gate.

Luthian spoke the casting words and closed his eyes against the swirling images of color that rose up. There was always a sense of falling and though he had cast this spell many times, his stomach had never come to tolerate it. He bit back the bile as the sensation ended as quickly as it had occurred. Slowly he opened his eyes, pulling out a piece of jerky even as he did so. He was relieved to see his office once more. He tore off a piece while getting into his stride. He was going calling, before his nephew had time to cook up an alibi.

Chapter Forty

Luthian did not knock, he strode into his nephew's home. Strangely, the door was unlocked. He made his way straight to the library, familiar with the layout of the house, having visited Henrick many times. He threw the door open and his eyes widened in surprise.

The room was in complete disarray. There were glasses - some partly filled and others empty - around the room. Articles of clothing that the wearers must surely have noticed they were missing were scattered about, and plates of half eaten food were abandoned all over the place. There had obviously been quite a few people here last evening.

A servant was cleaning up. He came to a halt with a tray full of plates and glasses, staring wide-eyed at the High Minister. Luthian pulled off his gloves and tucked them into his belt. "Where is my nephew?" he bit out tersely.

"He has not yet risen from his bed, Milord. I would not disturb him as he has company." The servant wilted at the look Luthian gave him for suggesting that he not disturb his master. The tray in the man's hands trembled so violently that the glasses clinked against one another.

Radney chose that moment to put in a timely appearance. "Lord Guldalian. We were not expecting company so early this morning. May I get you a spot of tea while I notify the master that you have come calling?" Radney's tone was smooth and even.

"Was my nephew here last night, all night?" Luthian demanded. He gave the servant his most menacing frown. Strangely, the man did not show the slightest sign of discomfort. "Oh yes, my Lord. He held a grand affair last evening for those not wishing to attend - or those not invited to - Lady Morana's ball." Radney grinned. "I assure you it was the most lurid affair and quite outdid any of his father's gatherings. Why, even the Trench Lord was here."

Luthian's eyes narrowed. Much of what he had seen and found at the mine had hinted at his nephew's involvement. "I see. And you are sure he was here the whole time?" Luthian drew a little fire to his hand to emphasize his desire to be told the truth.

The servant swallowed hard, and his eyes widened. "I took the last meal to his rooms personally, and I can assure you they were fully… occupied sir. He had more than one companion in his rooms the entire evening. It is true, my Lord. I swear it by the gods."

Luthian slowing closed his hand, quenching the small ball of flame that it held and bringing a look of relief to the servant's face. "That is pleasing to hear." Luthian switched to affable uncle with a nod and a smile. "I think I will surprise him with an early morning greeting." Luthian turned on his heel and headed for the master suite. He knew this manor well. He strode up the stairs with the servant close to his heels.

"Lord Guldalian, Master Alador does not like to be disturbed before he first calls." Radney was clearly flustered by the High Minister's stated intention and in a bit of a panic.

"I do not care what my nephew likes or does not like." Luthian paused to turn and look down at the servant. It was clear the man had had little sleep that night. "You had better hope that he is in there." He was satisfied with Radney's slight look of confusion. "Why wouldn't he be in there?" that look said.

Luthian threw open the door. The first thing he saw was Sordith sitting up, releasing a blade. He swiftly drew power to himself, holding out his hand to stop the offending knife. It stopped just an inch from his hands and dropped harmlessly to the floor.

"Really, Lord Sordith, attempts on my life count as treason you know," he said sarcastically. He took in the room. The Trench Lord was in Alador's large bed and two alarmed young women had sat up with him. One of them was the wench, Keelee, who had disappeared on him weeks ago. Luthian growled slightly seeing her in Sordith's arms, but he said nothing more as he examined the room further. There were clothes everywhere. There was a mound on the bed to Sordith's left. Surprisingly, two additional women were now sitting up from the foot of the bed. In addition, the room stank with the musk of unwashed bodies and sex.

Sordith shrugged casually and pulled the two women back against him as he scooted back against the pillows. "Shouldn't go flying into rooms without knocking," he pointed out. "Alador, you have company." Sordith drawled out.

A voice grumbled out from beneath the blankets, "Tell whoever it is to come back later; my head hurts."

A red head came out of the mound on that side of the bed. She was rubbing her eyes as she sat up. The blanket fell away to expose her breasts. Luthian took in the fact that she was a half-breed with a more Lerdenian look. As he assessed her, he had to admit that if Alador were really in that bed, he had taste in his bed companions. She was a fine specimen, even if she was a half breed. After a moment, he realized that she was the same woman he had caught Alador with when the boy had not been allowed to attend Luthian on his half day.

"Alador, your uncle's here." The redhead shook the mound of blankets with appropriate concern, pulling the covers up over her breasts.

"Bugger! It is too early in the morning for people to come calling," Alador complained as he peeked his head out, squinting against the morning light coming in through the windows. His eyes widened when he saw it was indeed his uncle.

Luthian's eyes roved over his nephew's face. The boy was pale and red eyed, as one would be if one had partied till all hours of the night. The room suggested a great deal of alcohol had been consumed along the way. Had Alador really been here the whole time?

He looked to Sordith with a pointed glance. "Has my nephew been here all night?" His tone was brusque and demanding.

"Let me ask the ladies, as I was fully occupied at times and could not have cared less where your nephew was." Sordith looked at the women at the foot of the bed then to the redhead pressed against Alador. "Has the lord of the manor been here all night?"

The women, including the redhead, all giggled and blushed at Sordith's question. "Oh he was here all right." The blonde at the foot of the bed, who was totally unclothed and clearly comfortable to be so, had spoken up. "With three of us at once, at one point." She eyed him with evident admiration. "I don't remember anyone complaining."

Alador groaned and pulled the covers over his head. "Uncle, can this wait till later?"

"No, it cannot. I will wait in your antechamber while you bid your guests farewell and then you will attend me. Do not make me wait, boy." Luthian still felt that something was not quite right. He stormed across the bed chamber and through the door that led to the small office off it. He looked about for any anomalies. There was no sign of disturbance in this room; the obvious party had not overflowed into it.

He moved to the fireplace, bringing it to life with a flick of his wrist. The wood took hold with a roaring hiss in response to the small use of magic. Luthian was now puzzled. The hints of his nephew's involvement in the attack on the mine were strong, and yet the evidence that he had been here all night was compelling. He stood staring into the blaze, considering what he knew while he waited. His thoughts flowed over the facts, comforted by the fire which crackled and popped.

It took more time than Luthian would have liked for his nephew to step in through the door. He turned to watch the boy. Alador was clothed in a simple blue dressing gown tied at the waist with matching material. The boy had taken no time to set his hair to rights, and his face remained pale. His eyes betrayed the lack of sleep. Alador stumbled, bleary eyed, toward the table where a small assortment of drinks set awaiting his pleasure. Luthian said nothing as the mage poured two glasses and moved to him. He took the offered glass, watching Alador closely.

"Now Uncle, what is this about?" Alador drained half the glass, wincing slightly at the burn.

"The bloodmines were assaulted last night. I have reason to believe you were directly involved." Luthian's accusation hung between them.

Alador's glass stilled on the way from his lips. "Me?! You know I was here last evening." His sore-headed reply did nothing to assuage his uncle's suspicions.

Luthian's tone was just as low and measured. "So it would seem." He took a drink from the glass in his hand.

"Yet we both know that things are not always what they seem?"

"There were many people who saw me here last evening till I retired to my own chamber with plenty of extremely pleasant female company." Alador sat down in a chair by the fire and looked up at his uncle without concern. "And as you just heard, a very good time was had by all." He grinned at his uncle and toasted him.

Either the boy was very good, or he was innocent. Luthian wanted to believe the latter, but he had learned long ago not to underestimate those around him. He pulled the blue scrap out of his belt pouch and handed it to Alador.

"Recognize this?" He stood over the boy in an attempt to be intimidating.

Alador took it and casually fingered it. "It is much like the stuff one of my cloaks is made of," he admitted with a shrug.

"Yes, odd that the same design that is on your cloak was on the tabards worn by those who assaulted the mine." Luthian pointed out, almost too casually.

"Perhaps someone is trying to implicate me," Alador handed it back up.

"Perhaps." Luthian acknowledged as he set his glass down. "Let me make one thing clear, Alador." Luthian leaned down with his hands on both sides of Alador's chair. Their faces were very close. Alador did not flinch as Luthian would have liked, but he did drop his gaze in deference to him. "If I find out you had anything to do with the destruction of the bloodmine, you will wish for death many times over before I am done with you."

Alador brought his gaze up slowly to meet Luthian's. Luthian noted a moment of coldness in them. There it was, the sign that the boy was not always as affable as he pretended to be. Luthian knew at that moment that there was more to his nephew than had so far met his eye. The boy had learned to play the game, and the High Minister suspected that on occasions he was excelling at it. Was this party more evidence of the young mage's rapid climb towards the power Luthian held?

"Then I have nothing to fear." The young mage's tone was as serious as Luthian's had been.

"Oh lad, you are mistaken." Luthian said. He rose and straightened his robes. "You have much to fear." Luthian took a step back. He needed to plot a new course: one that would still unite the isle under his domination but also control this powerful tool that he had created. The boy lived because of Luthian's carefully manipulations of Daezun circles, and he was not going to let him forget it any time soon.

Luthian turned towards the second door out of the office. "I will expect to see you at the High Minister's dinner tonight. All the heads of the cities will be attending. It is time you learned to distinguish our friends from our enemies. Those who do not support our cause will have to be removed." Luthian looked back at Alador and wagged a finger at him. "Do not fail me. My patience is thin and my suspicions still high." He frowned, considering. "I think you and I will be spending a lot more time together from now on." He stepped through the door, shutting it behind him. Better to keep the boy in plain sight, he thought, he strode out of Alador's manor and turned for home.

Alador let out a sigh of tension as his uncle closed the door. He poured another glass and headed back into his bedroom. Sordith, Keelee and Nemara were all that remained. He handed the glass to Sordith who grinned happily to see the drink. Alador moved to a window and stared blankly out it. The silence began to weigh heavy in the room.

"Well?" Nemara was the first to speak.

Alador held up his hand for them to wait then shielded the room before he answered. "He suspects, but has no proof. He had a fragment of tabard, but no way to tie it to me." He took a drink to still his pounding head. His mind was filled with Rena's last breaths and words. He had to force himself to interact with the others.

Finally, the weary, heartbroken mage looked about the room. "I don't remember you all coming in here?" He looked at Sordith in confusion. At least now his brother had on a pair of pants.

"Lad, you could sleep through the resurrection of the dead at the last trumpet. The girls and I made sure the room was looking as it needed to for our ruse to work. You didn't even moan at the noise we were making." Sordith chuckled. "I would have laid a bet the girls could have had their wicked way with you and you wouldn't even have noticed."

Alador flushed at the implied goings-on around him as he slept. He looked at Nemara. "You knew about all that?"

Nemara grinned. "No worries, I never left your side. You were clinging on to me so tightly that I dared not move; but I can tell you that the Trench Lord certainly lives up to his reputation," she teased lightly.

Alador shook his head, not wishing to hear such things. He took a drink, trying to force the events of the night far from his mind. His hand with the glass was shaking now that he could relax.

"I can sense that all did not go exactly as you had hoped." Sordith stepped up to Alador putting a concerned hand on his brother's arm.

"We lost half of those we took with us. I don't know how many dragons were lost, but one I cared for very much died saving my life. On the positive side, the dragons were liberated and the eggs retrieved along with hatched young. So you could say we were successful." Alador stared into the amber liquid in his glass.

"Is that not a good thing, then?" Sordith searched his brother's face with concern.

"The cost was high." Alador looked straight into his brother's eyes. "Much too high." He drained his glass.

Epilogue

The last few months had fallen into a routine that was busy but tolerable. The monotony of it all was extreme but left him time to grieve. Each day he met with his uncle who had taken him on as a sort of aide.

He learned how to take reports from the scrying bowls. He learned how to follow the finances of the entire country and how the taxes were applied. Whenever he thought he could escape having completed his tasks for the day, his uncle would lay another in front of him. He was rarely out of Luthian's sight other than from late evenings until early mornings.

He rarely had time for his friends, especially those that remained in the Blackguard. The only way he could see them was when Luthian gave him permission to attend a specific class or weapons training. He had managed to carve out some time a couple of days a week for sword practice and keeping up his archery skills.

If his uncle attended a social engagement, Alador would be commanded to attend as well. He was learning a great deal about leadership, and for that he was grateful. In a manner of speaking, he was glad to be busy, as it kept his thoughts from straying constantly to Rena and the sense of loss he felt. Though it still hurt when small things reminded him of her, the pain was slowly ebbing.

Strangely, Nemara had been gone as well, ever since the morning after the assault. She had left no word of where she was. The High Master could not or would not tell him. He insisted that he did not know and that the woman had abandoned her commission. Alador knew she would not do this and though he had reached out to the other surviving members of the assault party, no one had seen or heard from her.

He had finally given up hope. There was just no trace of her anywhere. It had only added to the pain of losing Rena: two of his closest friends gone in what seemed a single moment. He felt truly alone. It had helped him dive headlong into the tasks his uncle constantly provided him with. If one was busy, there was little time for painful memories.

Henrick had let him know that the rescued fledglings that were not able to fly had been escorted to his own valley to live out their lives in safety. Few knew the way into the mountain hold, and a procession of dragons on foot could be just as dangerous as a flight by air - even more so because of their hatred for almost all human beings, especially those wearing the tabards of the Blackguard.

The fledglings and eggs had been matched with parents as best as they could, and the others were adopted by dragons who had lost young to the mines. It would seem that all was as it should be, but Alador could feel the pressure of the geas. It was not done. There was more he must do, and the pressure was building with time.

He did not know what it would do to him if he could not complete whatever it was that had been pressed upon him. Henrick had once spoken with him about it being a larger task. He did not want it to be larger than it had already proved to be. The geas had taken so much from him, and he suspected that he had much more to lose before it was done. Would killing Luthian bring an end to it? He could only hope.

He shook that thought away. He needed to focus on more pleasant things as tonight was the night of the mating circle in Smallbrook. Alador had promised that he would be there. He had claimed an illness of the lungs and been convincingly miserable and feeble about getting anything done. Finally, his uncle sent him home rather than risk falling foul of whatever malady had inflicted his nephew.

Alador had taken other fleeting opportunities to sneak home and talk with his family, Mesiande, and even Henrick. Mesiande had cooled in the face of his shared grief. Tonight would be the fulfillment of a desire he had cherished since before he had found the stone; Mesi would finally be his.

He was apprehensive. In some way, he felt he was betraying something between him and Rena. But ... Rena... Rena had died. He reminded himself that they could never have been a truly bonded pair, given the fundamental differences between dragons and human beings. Yet, he still could not quite let her go in his heart and mind. That night on the mountain had done something to them both. He ran a hand over his face as if to wipe away those memories.

He was hoping that this night with Mesiande would finally cleanse him of his grief and remind him of his great love for the Daezun middlin. Well, she was not really a middlin now, he mused. He pulled on the boots that he'd laid out ready. He had found a spell in his great grandfather's spell book that would allow him to take the appearance of another for a few hours. It would be enough to get through the dancing part of the ceremony, and to find privacy for the two of them within the tent.

Mesiande would have built her own nest. Some new to the circle closed off their nest with many curtains of blankets and sheets, so it would not be unusual for Mesiande to do this. Dorien was going to a nearby village circle, and had planned to sneak off so that Alador could take his place. Mesiande knew that Alador would be masquerading as his brother. As long as the spell held, all would be well.

Yet, here he sat in his rooms in Silverport. The sun was fading and yet he had not quite been able to bring himself to leave for Smallbrook. He felt as if there were something that he was missing, but try as he might, he had been unable to place his finger on it. Finally, he activated the talisman around his neck.

When he stepped from the coal room, the house was already empty. The women often prepared throughout the day, and Alador was now late for the meeting of the men. It would be his first circle, but he knew the gist of what was expected. The two brothers had decided it was best his mother know nothing of either of their actions for the evening.

He entered Dorien's room and found the clothes laid out for him. He removed his own clothing as Dorien's form would be larger. Carefully, he intoned the spell, dropping the components as needed. Pain immediately assaulted him. He clutched his abdomen. Pain radiated through his body as muscles enlarged, his torso stretched, and even his eyes felt as if they were being wrenched from the sockets. When it was finally over, he lay panting on the floor. Sweat was pooled about him, he forced himself up. The pain was ebbing, but it had taken a toll.

He cast a clean spell, not willing to go to Mesiande in such a state, then pulled on the clothes that Dorien had left for him, headed out of the house and hurried to the ale house where the adult men gathered. There was a drink that supposedly made a man fertile and increased his energy for the night of dancing and mating ahead. He had never taken it before, and was not quite sure how it would work; but he did know he could use the energy after that painful transformation.

When he stepped into the ale house, many of the village men hailed him. The room was filled with smiles. Everyone was looking forward to the night ahead. A mug was pressed into his hand and he endured a good deal of additional back-smacking and geniality while he downed it without a thought. If it were ale, it would steady his nerves and if it were the mating drink, well even better.

He forced a smile at the warmth of Dorien's welcome. It was something he had never had when he lived in Smallbrook. It felt very strange to be so completely accepted, and it gnawed at him that he never had been in his own form.

He had not prepared himself for the strength of the drink. Within minutes, the room seemed to be a blur of happy bodies. He could not remember ever feeling so good - outside of dancing with Rena. Then the drums started up. As if called by the gods themselves, the men veered towards the sound. It was intoxicating. Alador could feel every drum beat in his blood. His heart seemed to pound in rhythm with it, and he felt as if he could soar on the sky at that moment.

Somehow the circle formed amongst the blur and haze of ancestral throbbing beats. From the moment he saw Mesiande, he had eyes only for her. Her hair was down in loose waves. Her body was covered only by a sheer robe of linen that did little to hide the firm contours of her body beneath. He reached for her as she danced closer.

Through the haze and pulsing rhythms, she danced out of reach. Other women had reached for him, seeing Dorien and not Alador. He somehow managed to evade their clutch and dance his way back into position. Mesiande teased him unmercifully, passing him by two more times. She would toss her loose hair over her shoulder rather than choose him. Her mischievous eyes made it clear that he was her choice, and yet she made no move to claim him.

During the course of the dance, a fire was growing within him: a need so compelling that he cried out with the strength of it. The desire to have her became desperate. Just when he might have given in and let another claim him, he felt a hand on his arm. Looking down in confusion, he followed the arm up and found Mesiande's beautiful brown eyes. The surge of need coursed through him, and he grabbed her close kissing her with a feral hunger.

With pounding beats and writhing bodies all about them, he let Mesiande pull loose from his kiss and lead him into the tent. Once they were hidden behind the curtain, he reversed the spell, not wanting her to kiss his brother. He wanted her to want him and only him, and was relieved to find that returning to his own form wasn't painful at all. Maybe it was because that was the way his body really wanted to be, or maybe the Daezun love potion had dulled all his other senses.

She moved closer and kissed him as she once had by the pool so long ago. He gently laid her down on the nest that she had created, his longing coursing through his blood, his voice and his loins. Though his desire was almost bestial, driven by the sounds of mating around them, he restrained the desire to just take her. Remembering the elder's lessons so long ago, he made sure her desire was as great as his own. Finally, the two surrendered to the passion denied them for so long by the fate of one bloodstone.

Alador returned home in the early hours of the morning when he realized that people were beginning to move about. He had held Mesiande close for as long as he could, and felt at peace for the first time since the assault on the bloodmine. The consummation of his long-standing relationship with her had done a great deal to ease his pain. Her kisses would sustain him through the drudgery his uncle seemed to take pleasure in piling upon him.

He kissed her gently before leaving her, moving hair from her sleeping face while carefully untangling himself. He located the medallion where it had been tossed aside with Dorien's clothes and materialized stark naked in his office off his bedroom suite. He headed wearily for his own bed: the night had been long, and he had lost count of how many times they had both found release in the peaks of pleasure promised by the ritual.

When he opened the door, he saw a figure on the bed. It was dark and he could not fully make it out. Cautiously he moved closer, and then stopped and stared in amazement. What was Nemara doing turning up out of nowhere and sitting on his bed?

"Nemara?" He rushed forward, his own fatigue and nakedness forgotten. "Where have you been?" She had her arms wrapped around something large and swathed in.

"I had to do something for Rena." Though her words were weary, there was an edge of pride to them. She looked as if she had not slept or eaten in weeks. There were large circles under her eyes, and her face was somewhat gaunt.

"For Rena?" Alador knelt before the beleaguered woman. "I don't understand."

Nemara unwrapped the item in her lap. There lay the most beautiful egg he had ever seen. It was the size of a large melon and a deep rich blue that got lighter towards the end of the scales that covered it. The edges were trimmed in shining silver. "It is my… her egg," she whispered, stroking the egg lovingly.

"Her egg?" Alador heart wrenched. All his work to remove his grief was undone in that single moment. "She never mentioned a mate." They had been close; surely she would have mentioned an egg.

"She was going to tell you after the assault on the bloodmine," Nemara whispered. "She told me while you were fighting that black dragon. It isn't just her egg; it's yours as well." She looked up at Alador with a strange look in her eye. "From the night on the mountain."

"How…" Alador started, staring at the egg, his eyes widening in disbelief at Nemara's words. "Oh… my… SHITE!!"

Preview from Completing the Geas (Title May Change) Book 5

Jon looked up on hearing the soft footsteps. He had known she was coming. Nightmare had bristled first at sounds that Jon could not hear. It had given him time to prepare himself for what he must do next. He would take no pleasure in it and yet he knew it was the only way he could accomplish his own ends.

"I have come to check on your progress, Prelate." Lady Morana's dress today was reserved. When in the temple, she often wore simple black robes. They still fitted in a way that made you very aware that she was a beautiful woman.

Jon simply nodded. "He is growing quickly and is very smart." The black dragon was now the size of a full flight lexital and able to understand Jon. It puffed itself up with pride, and ruffled its wings, showing off for the High Priestess.

Morana nodded. "How are his hunting skills coming along?" Morana moved to Nightmare and held out her hand. The dragon slowly lowered his head until the top of his muzzle was against her hand.

Jon frowned when she touched Nightmare. The dragon was too young to understand the woman's motives. He had to allow this light bonding between them or risk losing his position. "I no longer have to feed him. He gets only treats for training." He moved next to the High Priestess.

"He is really beautiful," she ran her hand up between the dragon's eyes, bringing a rumble from the black's chest.

"You are well matched." Jon's voice held a tremor of admiration. It was not a lie fortunately. The High Priestess's raven-black hair shone every bit as much as Nightmare's polished scales. Her lined eyes seemed large like the dragon's, as well.

Morana smiled and looked over at Jon. "I have to wonder if your admiration is more for the dragon than the woman."

"Cannot a man admire both?" Jon answered. "May I be frank, Lady Morana?" He dared to reach up to stroke the side of the dragon's head, putting him very close to the woman.

"You may." She turned slightly to face him.

Jon took a breath to prepare himself. "You are not admired as much as you could and should be. Why do you dance to the strings of the leaders of the Great Isle when you could lead it all? You are smart, beautiful, and so talented in magic." Jon dropped his hand from the dragon and dared to take the priestess' hand in his own. "You are the chosen of our Goddess. You should be revered and loved." He watched her eyes closely, seeing the pupils dilate as he hoped.

Morana did not pull her hand away. She looked at the mage curiously. "What would you do differently, Praetor?"

Jon smiled and put a tender hand to her face, moving some hair back from her eyes. When she did not admonish him, he leaned forward and kissed her with all the tenderness he could muster. When she returned the kiss, he smiled within. Some people were so predictable.

Author's Note

It is always a pleasure to interact with my fans. You can ask me questions and follow me at these locations.

Facebook: https://www.facebook.com/dragonsgeas/

Twitter: @balanceguide

Blog: http://dragonsgeas.blogspot.com/

I am an independent Author. This means I do all my own formatting, uploading and publicity. There is no big company paving the way to the New York Bestseller List. I need your help. If you liked this book, please tell others about my series. Most importantly, even if you just fill in the stars and say good book, please leave a review on Amazon and/or Goodreads. That more than anything will help free me to write more frequently and put work out faster. Even if you didn't like all of it, I can take the bad with the good. Thank you so much in advance.

Cheryl Matthynssens

73714332R00283

Made in the USA
San Bernardino, CA
09 April 2018